THE MONUMENT

THE MONUMENT

Erich Loest

Translated from the German by
Ian Mitchell

Secker & Warburg
London

Originally published in German as *Völkerschlachtdenkmal*
Copyright © 1984 by Hoffman und Campe Verlag, Hamburg

First published in England 1987 by
Martin Secker & Warburg Limited
54 Poland Street, London W1V 3DF

English translation copyright © 1987
Martin Secker & Warburg Limited

British Library Cataloguing in Publication Data
Loest, Erich
The monument.
I. Title   II.   Völkerschlachtdenkmal.*English*
833'.914   [F]   PT2672.029

ISBN 0 436 25673 8

Set in 10½ on 12pt Linotron Ehrhardt
by Hewer Text Composition Services, Edinburgh
and printed in Great Britain by
Billing and Sons Ltd, Worcester

CONTENTS

CHAPTER 1

Your particulars, Herr Linden?

So I'm not under arrest, or are you just saying that to pacify me? Well, can I go home, then? That smile – years ago they would have said there's perfidy in it. You say you want to discover *all* the reasons behind my forced entry into the Monument. But I've been through all that already, in that harsh institution in the city centre; you want to hear all the *background* details – well, all right, then. I don't for a moment deny that I wanted to blow up the Monument to the Battle of the Nations.

One thing I'm grateful for – you didn't have me led across the yard in handcuffs. Those last three days, it was different. Not really necessary in the case of an old man like me. Particulars? Name: Carl Friedrich Fürchtegott Voiciech Felix Alfred Linden. If you want to know how to write Voiciech, I'll spell it for you. The first two Christian names go together. Born 20 October 1913; the Monument to the Battle of the Nations had been officially opened two days before.

Address: Number 12, Weissestrasse. Whenever I looked down from the Monument, I could see our roof. Born in Stötteritz, hardly ever been out of Leipzig. Profession: master demolition expert. Last employed as gate-keeper. Demolition expert, that always raises a few eyebrows. When you're sitting in a pub, sorry, when one is sitting, well anyway, any time I've said, over a beer, 'I'm a demolition expert,' then everything would go quiet. Some would think I was pulling their leg. Then I'd perform my famous trick with the beer-mats, fourteen of them built into a pyramid, I can still do it sometimes. You can only do that if you have nerves in your fingers as fine as cobwebs. I could have been a safebreaker, too.

Demolition expert: marvellous job, that. Without blasting, you can't build – no stone. You need space – we can clear it. You can destroy things with blasting, but don't go thinking it's the blasters who are chiefly responsible for knocking the world about.

In my identity papers it says: Alfred Johannes. I've gradually dropped the Johannes, a pointless notion of my parents. The other Christian names have added themselves from time to time, Carl Friedrich was the first. In the cemetery in Otterwisch I came upon a tombstone for Carl Friedrich Lindner, killed on 20 October 1813, a hundred years to the day before I was born. Linden or Lindner, they're pretty well one and the same.

Hold on, I'm none too keen on sudden supplementary questions. Nobody had to show me the tunnel under the Monument, I've known about it since the end of the war. The SS dug it, it led out into the open, past an air-raid shelter with a system of passages and chambers. We began digging that in the spring of 1940. It was forty years before there was the slightest sign of subsidence – and even then it was nothing to make a fuss about. We pushed the first tunnel in from the Russenstrasse, what's now Leninstrasse. Coming on for eighty thousand cubic metres of earth had been excavated before building started on the Monument, a million cubic metres had been needed for the ramparts. For ten years on end, Leipzig's garbage-men tipped out their loads there. We found odd bits of that here and there: chunks of brickwork, pale-coloured lumps of stucco, layers of rusting, crumbling iron. After we had gone in thirty metres we put in electric lights, forty metres in we laid rails for the skips to run on.

The first aid-raid alerts were little more than a joke. I belonged to the 'Voluntary Defence Unit, Battle of the Nations Monument Section', complete with armband. Most of the time I was on look-out on the parapet above the entrance, with, below me, the stone

Archangel Michael, his arms spread out over the city. He stares out towards the north-west, that's where the bombers had to come from. 'God with us' is carved into the stone there in Art-Nouveau lettering. A mobile anti-aircraft battery stood in the Wahren marshalling yards, and from there sheaves of searchlight beams would scratch across the sky, sometimes they'd latch on to a tiny speck. I'd look up behind me; if it was a clear night, I could make out the warriors with their swords point-down between their feet, and I'd think: if one of them was to cut a swathe across the sky with his sword, I wouldn't fancy being an airman up there in one of those planes.

For many Leipzig folk, the Monument to the Battle of the Nations just happens to be there, they take it for granted; if they have visitors from other parts, they take them up there, but half-heartedly. It was different for me, though. My father quarried the stones for it in Beucha, Voiciech worked on the building of it right up to the topmost platform. Sometimes I look up at a joint and think: Voiciech trowelled the mortar in there. Voiciech helped to build Leipzig, the Crystal Palace and the western suburbs and, of course, the Monument. Before the First World War there were more hotels, restaurants, cafés, pubs and snack-bars inside the Ring than there are today in the whole county. You just *cannot* imagine how Leipzig looked in those days. Not even someone who knew it at first hand can!

The underground air-raid shelter: after a year's work we had dug right in from the southernmost corner, starting from the edge of the cemetery. We had to be careful not to go too close to the main support-pillars, for fear of the weight causing a cave-in. And we kept our distance, too, from the point where the tunnels met. From that junction we dug upwards to make a ventilation shaft, and we came out in the meadow south of the Monument. So now there was always a fresh little Saxon breeze wafting through the tunnels. We, the 'Voluntary Defence Unit, Battle of the Nations Monument Section', along with our families, had our own reserved niche with a sign on the door: 'Shelter Management. Keep Out.' It was almost cosy in there. And as warm as in a cow's backside.

Then, in April 1945, the Waffen-SS did scratch their way through the foundations. If it hadn't been for their passageway I wouldn't have tangled with the men in the yellow overalls. It was that passage that I . . .

I thought I was supposed to tell you about the shelter. But if you want to make notes on other stages of my life, then fine: I went to the elementary school on the Weisseplatz, the old building is still standing, nothing much has changed. It was Easter 1920 that my mother took me there, before she went to do people's laundry, and she kept saying to me, 'Now you mind out, Freddie, and be good, Freddie, there's my good boy now, Freddie, right? And mind you don't get lost on the way home.'

By Easter 1928 my schooldays were behind me. I was best of them all at arithmetic. My father worked at the quarry in Beucha, he had a word with his boss, and that's where I began as an apprentice. I started off on the drill, and a year later I was on to explosives and detonators, and when I set off my first big bang I felt a shiver going up my arms. I'll never forget that detonation, the roar swelling through the ground and the air, great lumps of stone breaking away from the face as if cut out by a knife. I'll still be able, in my dying hour, to taste the stone-dust – from that first moment, not from the thousands of other times that followed. In that second, I knew that I could never become anything other than someone who worked with dynamite and Donarite and mercury fulminate – not a destroyer, though, and I want to insist on that. I have never once destroyed anything, least of all the University Church. So it's supposed just to have flown away, like an angel, ascended heavenward, is that it?

I rose to master craftsman just before the war. I was at the military training area at Zeithain a few times, learning how to defuse bombs and shells, British and French ones, too. Of course, I thought, they'll call me up at the first opportunity, but I was graded R.O. Funny, the abbreviation just rolls off my tongue, but what did it stand for – 'reserved occupation'?

No, no, it's not my fault that you're making such slow progress with your questioning. Every answer calls up history, and stories. I just have to mention Christian names – Carl Friedrich – and that immediately conjures up a whole life. You say that so casually, that I've simply made up these names. I like visiting graveyards. I try to figure out for myself who that is, lying there, what he was like. In the cemetery behind the Monument to the Battle of the Nations there will soon be more people lying buried than there are living in the city. If I hadn't ended up as a keeper at the Monument, I'd have liked to be keeper of the cemetery records.

Carl Friedrich Lindner, died 20 October 1813. I deciphered that on a stone behind the church at Otterwisch. Only twenty-three he was, infantryman in a reserve Saxon regiment of the line, before that, just a country lad. The stone was grey and weathered. Basalt with

4

xenocrysts, from the quarries at Klinga. His father was a farmer – not exactly hard up.

Call it fantasy, if you like. I know all about Carl Friedrich, after a hundred years his life has merged into mine. I would rather we agreed to differ over this point. At seventy, young man, you see things differently.

No, no sugar, thanks. We Saxons have always supported the wrong side – take my Carl Friedrich Lindner for example. It has always amazed me that we Saxons are perpetually looking at history from the Prussian angle. Austrians, Russians and Prussians defeated Napoleon at Leipzig – and what did the Saxons do? As usual, something stupid.

I didn't become a soldier until the spring of 1813, that is, after the terrible debacle in Russia. I always slip into the first person whenever I talk about Carl Friedrich for any length of time. Then I can see him more clearly. We had a farm, with six horses and good arable land, and a bit of woodland, too. Two of our horses had met a wretched end in Russia. Five lads from the village had gone off to the war, nothing more was heard from them. There are times when most lads want to be soldiers, and there are others when war has become such an integral part of life that it drums into everyone the fear of killing and being killed. In our village, raw young Frenchmen with quick eyes and tongues had been billeted, along with Dutchmen with broad, red hands, and rogues from Naples. They had all declared open season on chickens and girls alike, and then had departed, leaving scabies behind them. In Russia they had perished to a man, shot and beaten to death, picked clean by looters and left for dead, they had starved in captivity or, along with the entire field-hospital and a hundred, two hundred sick and wounded comrades, had been reduced to ashes; that way the victors were quickest rid of them. Nobody can imagine nowadays what a torture scabies can be.

Carl Friedrich Lindner had them on his hands and arms and, worst of all, on his belly. He rubbed pig-fat on them, in his sleep he scratched himself raw and bleeding. One morning he was ordered to report to Riesa, and later transferred to Zeithain. Carl Friedrich Lindner – I could write a bit and count in dozens and scores, knew how to walk behind a plough and shear sheep. Now I learned how to stand to attention and lunge with fixed bayonet, learned to clean my uniform and equipment and was trained in guard duty, learned how to present arms and to shout password and response. The Saxon army was under the command of Lieutenant-General Baron von

5

Thielmann. In and around the fortress of Torgau, Thielmann re-mustered his scattered battalions and topped them up, with me among others. He sent off to the King, safe in Bohemia, secret reports about going over to the side of the Russians and Prussians: but the King hesitated, for the Prussians had declared their intention to depose him.

I was on watch on the inner ring when Thielmann celebrated his birthday, saw candles flickering behind open windows, watched baskets with bottles of wine being carried past. Uproar broke out, and a little later I heard from the orderlies that Thielmann had shouted that the Saxons, too, would soon share the good fortune of being able to fight against the common enemy, within the ranks of the noble allies, to whose health he drained his glass. At this, another general had leapt to his feet and refused as an officer and a gentleman to meddle in politics, his oath bound him to the King and that was an end of it.

This miserable war: a soldier got half a pound of bread and a bowl of wretched soup a day, there was hardly even enough meat for the officers. This gut-gnawing hunger! We advanced towards the Elbe and down from the hills towards Dresden. A doctor carried out amputations in the open air; the light was best there. Feet and legs, hands and arms lay in a heap, the blood seeping away into the dirt. The war was wedging itself into deadlock, lurching back and forth until, from all sides, armies were marching into Saxony, Austrians from the south and Russians and Prussians from the north and the east.

Poor old Thielmann! He kept Torgau Frenchless for his king, but the King, for his part, threatened from two sides with compulsory redundancy, wrote to inform him that he felt moved, at the request of the Emperor of France, to put the fortress of Torgau and its garrison under the command of General Reynier. So Thielmann finally did desert to the Red Army – I mean to the Russians. In the propaganda business, we Saxons are pretty inept: we could have built up Thielmann long ago into a resistance hero, like the poet Körner or the people in the National Committee for Free Germany. Was it treason or not? That's always a matter of timing.

Where do you hail from, Doctor? From Fürstenwalde – a peripheral Berliner, then. Studied in Berlin, been in Leipzig for five years – I don't want it to sound like a reproach, but in fact you haven't a clue about Saxon history. We Saxons have ourselves very much played our past down.

6

I marched and scratched, searched for straw and a few grains of corn in wet ears; I stole rotting feed from the nosebag of a Württemberg Dragoon's horse. It's nonsense to believe that every soldier constantly and fervently desires victory for his own flag. Of course very few, on the other hand, wish triumph upon the opposing side, for that would put their own necks at risk. All I yearned for was a corner to sleep in and a soothing ointment. The wind swept wetly over trampled fields. We were approaching Machern, and I wept with cold and because I couldn't pluck up the courage to run away and have myself hidden in bush and bog by my own folk. At that time there were three thousand Saxons camped in a field that slopes away gently eastwards from Holzhausen – from it the view stretches as far as the Kohlenberg and the heights of Ammelshain, a long way off. The field was criss-crossed by trenches; I prayed that enemy cavalry would be deterred by them. A terrible word ran through our ranks: Cossacks! Cossaaacks! Just as a hundred and thirty years later: Tanks! Taaanks! We fixed bayonets and trembled at the thought of having to stab them into a cavalryman's legs or the breast of a horse. After a while, the first ones sat down on the ground, the officers yelled and beat them back on their feet. The north-west wind rose to a hurricane that lifted roofs and uprooted trees, the rain fell in streams on the starving soldiers, whose bed was the wet earth. Starving – nobody uses the word in its double sense any more, and yet it's so handy; it means both dying of hunger and dying of cold. From all the surrounding villages trees, fences, doors and floorboards were scavenged together for the campfires, which belched smoke into the rain.

The elements subsided, and then the thunder of cannon rumbled up from the south – that's where the slaughter was beginning. I squatted on the ground and scratched. A blow across the back of my neck startled me to my feet again. We had to present our cartridges for inspection, the paper in many of them had gone soft. From the town came the pealing of bells. Napoleon ordered them to be rung, for he believed victory was already his. While this was going on, the King of Saxony was peering out from the highest tower, his old eyes were dim, he had young sharp-eyed adjutants explain to him the significance of the various puffs of powder-smoke here and there. Near me, nineteen Saxon cannon were drawn up, the last my army had left. I hoped they would blow apart any possible Cossack attack. Towards evening, we advanced a hundred paces, the officers shouted that we were to spend the night there. So we lay down on the ground; anyone who had a greatcoat wrapped himself up in it. In no history of the battle will you find a description of that night, although there's plenty about the marathon forced march of our conquerors, who set out from my native village of Machern at three in the morning in order to encircle us, the left flank, at the very start of the battle.

The officers had dinned into us what a square was, and what a column, we had practised re-forming out of one into the other without a single one of us getting out of line. They had rammed it home that we were to hold our heads erect when the bullets were whistling around, to stand shoulder to shoulder when a cannonball cut a swathe through the bodies next to us. If anyone had to pee, he had to take care not to soak the backside of the man in front. I remember how a comrade next to me in the square squatted and crapped while I held his rifle for him. With his boot, he scraped earth over the little mound, there were curses, there was laughter, too. In square formation, we were almost secure against enemy cavalry, and our officers knew that none of us could break out. The square was regarded as the natural habitat of the foot-soldier.

We were ordered to our feet at first light. Beyond the trenches and the rows of trees, on the hill above Beucha, sprinklings of marching columns materialised, with flags at their head, fast-moving dots, cavalry, perhaps Cossacks. In films of such battles – perhaps you've seen a few – whole divisions have taken part. If a film were to be made about the Battle of the Nations, we Saxons wouldn't even be in it. From today's perspective, we're a scrap of litter, a remnant on the wrong side, an embarrassment, the scabies of history.

Carts loaded with brandy barrels rolled up, each of us sluiced a mug of it down into an empty stomach, at once our spirits changed, rose: a few bellowed, now they'd show these damned Prussians! Constantly, Saxons had fought against Prussians, and always the boast was that the Saxons had put up a gallant fight, but in the end they had lost, all the same. Now we would win at last; the brandy kindled rage and stupid bravado. Soldiers who had been unable to get to their feet in the morning because they were in fever were lifted onto carts and jolted off towards the town – who knows whether they died on the way or were thrown onto the roadside because some officer considered it more essential to transport munitions to the front than sick men to the rear.

No defiant intoxication rose in me. Instead, I just prayed: dear God, let me live to see evening and the end of this battle, which might yet rumble on for days and weeks, as long as soldiers can march and be beaten into squares, let me come through, even if I have to scratch scabies for the rest of my days, let me go home to our farm, and never again will I . . . I was looking for something I could promise to renounce for the future. Sucking eggs in secret. Stealing sheaves from neighbours' fields. Making amorous advances to the goat. I trudged along behind the man in front, stumbled towards a village surrounded by fortifications, cannon staring out from between baskets filled with sand. Mölkau.

Of course, I've been to Mölkau in the footsteps of my Carl Friedrich. To the east, as indeed on all other sides, Leipzig peters out gradually or begins imperceptibly. I've cycled around and looked for the hearts of the old villages. Where streets now wind round ponds, round little old churches, in those days farmsteads stood cheek by jowl, and there muskets lay in ranks across the tops of clay walls, ready to loose off a salvo. Today, the railway line to Karl-Marx-Stadt cuts straight through. Forty years after the battle, the spades levelling the trenches were still crunching through skulls and hip-bones. One ditch, full of stagnant water, cuts through here, the East Rietzschke. There the Saxons allowed themselves the luxury of a short respite, detached themselves from their close formations and mingled with the sixteen-year-olds that Napoleon had had thrust into uniforms and sent marching off to the land of the Teutons. These were beardless youths, this was their first battle, and for many their last. Their corporals cut up fallen horses and handed the boys sinewy lumps of flesh which were then skewered on ramrods, blackened over fires of broken wagons and rafters and kitchen tables, and gulped down half raw. Carl Friedrich Lindner came within a hairsbreadth of getting hold of a pound of horse's haunch, but the cry of 'Cossaaacks!' shrilled out and drove the Saxons into position, shoulder to shoulder and bayonets thrust forward at the ready.

It's a terrible thing to lose a battle, never mind a war. For once, I don't mean that from the point of view of the front-line soldier, the cannon-fodder, the poor bloody infantry, but from the historian's. 'The nation rises, the storm breaks loose' – this is still something they celebrate a hundred years after, and so you can read everywhere how the Prussian Bülow Corps, side by side with the cavalry of the Russian Corps, stormed Wintzingerrode. Who, though, commanded the three thousand trembling, scabious Saxons between Mölkau and Stünz? None of the last remaining Saxon generals was keen to change sides empty-handed, the fifth hour of the afternoon had struck when one of them gave the command 'Shoulder arms! Forward march!' with the intention of leading his troops over to the former enemy. When they had gone a hundred metres, another ordered, 'Halt! Order arms!' The first declared the other to be under arrest, the second announced the first had been relieved of his command, the formations advanced and retreated till they began to crumble at the edges. Already the French were shooting at the waverers, the vacillators, English incendiary batteries were giving the fugitives covering fire, then, right and left of Carl Friedrich, the company disintegrated, his neighbours began to run, he took to his heels along with them. The dissolving throng leapt over to the eastern bank of the East Rietzschke, some trampled their rifles into the fields and threw away their cartridges as they ran, others unbuckled their knapsacks so as to be able to run more freely. They later took the worst beatings, because they had the least booty on them, and many a man expired because he didn't have a coat to wrap himself in. A gap opened up in the conquerors' front line and the Saxons poured into it, with every step their terror rose and then ebbed away again, a few raised a mud-caked musket to prove they were attacking, then threw it away to show that they wanted to surrender. A thousand paces away, a wall of living horse-flesh was building up.

A very different battle from the one in the history books, you might say. Napoleon doesn't come into my version, nor the suicide charge on Probstheida by the Guards under Murat, nor, for that matter, the storming of the Grimma Gate and the flight of the French westwards across the Elster till the last bridge blew up round their ears, nor is there any mention of how the Polish hero, Poniatowski, drowned: the demise of the Saxon battalions had nothing to do with all that. It wasn't heroic, it had no bearing on the outcome of the battle, it was rational and it was pitiful.

The Saxons stumbling in their haste away from the front hoped that the enemy's battle-lust would be sucked in by the maws of the nineteen cannon and that they themselves would be paid little heed by the Prussian cavalry, for whom great odds meant great honour, but then the Saxon gunners swung their cannon round, hearts that beat for the Confederation of the Rhine yielded in an instant to Germanic consciousness. They had no desire to leave the field of conflict on the losing side yet again, but instead, while they still could, as liberators of the Fatherland from the Corsican monster.

10

For a few fleeting instants, Carl Friedrich would dearly have loved to be among the nimble gunners, for they held on to their baggage, with their crust of bread and their bits and bobs in their packs; they could use their horses for food and their own ammunition-wagons for firewood. They didn't end up as the meanest dregs, but instead, in the nick of time, threw in their lot with history's victors.

Finally, the fugitives found themselves confronted with Russian dragoons, there were twelve of them facing a hundred milling Saxons who so dearly wanted to be taken prisoner. The Saxons didn't put their hands up, it wasn't till the First World War that that became the common practice of those in mortal terror, when Germans, French or British stumbled out of shattered bolt-holes. The SS-men, when they crawled out of the bunkers under the Monument to the Battle of the Nations, hoisted their hands highest of all, because facing them were American index-fingers, loosely crooked round the triggers of sub-machine guns, ready to combat trickery or wreak revenge, and not at all averse to 'a misunderstanding'. The Saxons around Carl Friedrich gave ample proof of their desire for peace by the fact that their hands no longer held musket or sabre, but rather, at best, packs belonging to those who had taken to the undergrowth, dead men's knapsacks, or the rolled-up greatcoat from the saddle of a dead cavalryman. They plodded along, without fanfares or drum-rolls, their downcast eyes fixed on cart-tracks, corpses and wounded. A few of them were yelled at by Silesian ammunition-wagon drivers to get their arses over here and give a hand to heave a wagon through a patch of mud, they took hold of a spoke and chorused: All together! Heave! And as they did so, the thought sneaked into their minds that perhaps they no longer needed an act of mercy, but here they were, already on the road to victory, in pursuit of Napoleon. The uniforms were so multi-coloured nobody could identify all the colours, all the badges, all the sashes. Forwards, heeeeave ho! In the midst of the Silesian baggage-train the Cossacks were no longer a threat. So, forwards, or, as the case may be, backwards.

Behind a hedge lay a wounded man, his legs shattered. A captain, from the Uckermark, he was; his batman was kneeling by him and I squatted down at his side. I told him about our barn in Machern, with warm straw in it, and about the healing arts of my grandmother; and if our rooms hadn't been looted, then the Prussian officer, sir, could get well in a bed, under a duvet, and I'd make the stove sweltering hot, sir. I adorned our room with copper basins, linen and a sheepskin, on which my lord the officer could lay his damaged feet. The batman asked me all sorts of questions, I reassured him again and again in my dialect, 'I've scarpered! Skedaddled!' By which I meant to convey – though how was he to understand? – that I had deserted.

It had all been swept from my mind, everything that had been shouted into it by officers and sergeants: Now we'll show these Prussians! Revenge for Kesselsdorf! Loyalty to Napoleon, the greatest commander of all time! Loyalty is our honour, when all others prove disloyal, we shall stand fast . . . Sorry, that's what the SS sang. What I mean is, it took me no time at all to realise what had happened to me; I shouted to a convoy driver with a swarthy, peasant face to come over here, I asked the batman: does your master have any money? He fumbled in his master's breast pocket and fished out a gold coin. Together, the three of us hoisted the captain onto the cart. In my joy and exhaustion I had forgotten my scabies. And in the excitement, I unfortunately slipped the gold coin into my own pocket.

We didn't get to Machern. At the River Mulde, everyone trying to go east was stopped by a cordon, and although I clung on to the cart with the Prussian and protested that it had been his orders, before he had passed out, to take him to Machern to a warm house where there were people skilled in medicine, I was dragged off into a paddock where other Saxons, Frenchmen, Württembergers and Hessians were camped out on the wet grass.

Oh, if only I had stayed with my unit, in a cluster of Saxons. For a general had whatever was left of the scuttling mass of Saxons lined up in formation and took them over to the Russian reserve army, he even managed to fix it so that the nineteen Saxon cannon could stop firing on their former comrades of the Confederation of the Rhine. Ceasefire, internment. Oh, if only I had had the chance to stoop and snatch up a musket, perhaps I might have been there, a few days later, taking part in the siege of the French at Torgau. And then I, too, would have marched to the Rhine and into France under the new old Saxon General Thielmann, who had returned from the 'National Committee for Free Germany', sorry, from the Russian side, and now basked in the confidence of this new ally.

While all that was going on, though, the columns of prisoners were being driven southwards through wind and rain. Along the way, we came upon the corpses of thousands of fallen Frenchmen. They had all been stripped by their conquerors. The naked corpses lay on their backs with their faces towards the east; the vultures who had robbed them – being Russians or Austrians they were of course good Christians – had put three little piles of earth on the chest of each of them and so had given them at least a symbolic burial. The worms, foxes and crows could take care of the rest.

If you're going off duty for the day now, Doctor, I'll be brief. Simply to say, the next day, on 20 October 1813, Carl Friedrich Lindner was beaten to death by Pomeranian Hussars in a field near Otterwisch. When they searched him for booty, they found a Prussian Thaler in his pocket and punished him on the grounds of the shameful suspicion that *he* had been looting.

So, Doctor, you're dissatisfied with the results of this interrogation, are you? Too disjointed, and I didn't respond to your supplementary questions. The gentlemen in that strict establishment in the city centre, who questioned me during the few days before I came here, raised the same objection. Well, what do you expect? I'm an old man full of memories, let me spin them out. The interrogators in the city centre kept telling me, with some relish: we've plenty of time! I wish you felt the same.

CHAPTER 2

Where did you get this skull?

I can't understand why you keep trying to convince me that this *isn't* a prison. You offer me coffee and you'd rather not hear the word interrogation: this is a *conversation*, you say – but what about the bars on all the windows? And if I were to say: I'll just go for a stroll in town till lunchtime – there you go again, you just laugh.

I didn't have too bad a night's sleep. Every night, I lie awake for two, maybe three hours, that's normal at my age. There's so much to reflect on. You want to know how I slipped in under the Monument. By way of a tomb – I can show you the way in. In April 1945 a troop of Waffen-SS sneaked out into the open that way. These fellows were dressed in pall-bearers' frock coats, too small for them all round. What's more, they were carting corpses along with them – that was another time when these were pretty easy to come by. A fair number of them fooled the Americans that way.

Sure, any kind of building can be blown up. The better you know the edifice, the smaller the charge you need. Decades ago I had already given thought to how you would go about doing away with the Monument to the Battle of the Nations, that's part and parcel of my profession. Now you, Doctor, can you share a person's company without quietly thinking to yourself, he could be suffering from this or that disease?

The ground under the Monument is ideal, a four-metre deep layer of gravel on top of a seven-metre thick clay base; the table of pressed concrete on top of that is two metres thick. The Monument is supported by four main buttresses and sixty-one intermediate and secondary ones. The main support-pillars are twenty-six metres high, taller than the nave of almost any church. Voiciech was involved in the work on them. If you were to shove one of the main pillars out of line – I'd have to do a drawing for you, but I'm not sure I really want to. It would take an expert to demolish that, and of course there would be an enormous pile of rubble left. Who'd shift that? No, the Monument will still be standing when everything in Leipzig has fallen apart, the vaulted canopy of the main station will have rusted away, already the lift-cables in the university skyscraper have broken, its air-conditioning has boiled over, Reudnitz has fallen to bits just like Gohlis, in Grünau there's warm water stagnating in every cellar. When Leipzig has crumbled and rotted, the Monument to the Battle of the Nations will still stand solid, towering up to the skies. Like one of the Pyramids of Ancient Egypt.

Well now, yesterday's evening meal was anything but sumptuous, but at my age you don't need much anyway. Two slices of bread and margarine with smoked sausage and curd cheese – I wouldn't have eaten any more than that at home, either. But you'll have to tell the nurses not to force medicines on me. Not even a so-called sedative. I'll not take anything, and the sooner the nurses accept that, the better for us all. The fact that you prescribed this medicine makes no difference at all in my book. Instead, you should see to it that *Neues Deutschland* and the *Leipziger Volkszeitung* find their way to my table, since both of these newspapers would have us believe that here in the GDR everything is in the best of order, every man, woman and child from Cape Arkona in the north right down to the Fichtelberg is perfectly happy! So who needs pills!

The Monument. Or my Christian names. I've read every word that was ever written about the Monument. My library . . . oh, you know it; house-search, I might have known. All I ask is that everything is kept together. One day I'll donate my collection to the

Leipzig Museum of Local History. The skull, the five hundred-odd postcards . . .

On the very top shelf you'll have found several little books and a manuscript. The author of these was Fürchtegott von Lindenau, tenant of a manor in the Altenburg area. A history of the Monument, if such a thing existed, would give him no more than a passing mention, but in fact, without him, many an idea wouldn't have got off the ground.

Hardly was the Battle over, and Carl Friedrich's tombstone paid for by his parents, when already there was talk of erecting a memorial. In my library you will find a slim volume, dated 1912 and published by the Wandervogel youth movement under the title, *Leipziger Land.* It recommends walking tours, among them one across the southern battlefield. The writer questions whether the allied monarchs did in fact stand at the spot marked by a square stone block, and asks why they shouldn't have set up their observation point higher up, on the other side of what is today the F95 trunk-road. There, too, according to him, there had been a monument for many years; the guide-book gives it as standing in the garden of the Monarchs' Hill Inn, where, in a wooden hut, skulls found on the battlefield were kept as a reminder of the gruesome slaughter. To heighten the reader's wanderlust, the work also recommends a range of homœopathic delights, various 'Thalysia'-brand snug-fitting boots and sandals with plaited-thong uppers, 'Thalysia' lightweight ventilated underwear, invigorating delicacies in handy-size packs, as well as porous braces. But back to the skulls.

In the memoirs of a contemporary I once read: 'Since the Angel of Death could find nothing more on the field on which to work his way, he came on the wings of the chill night into the sighing city and mercilessly mowed down its starving ranks.' The stench of corpses wafted all the way over to the towns of Grimma and Wurzen. Blacksmiths for miles around had laid in stocks, which would last them for years, of scrap-iron in the form of sabres, cannon-balls, musket-barrels and wrecked wagons. Private looters had competed with the uniformed men officially detailed to clear the battlefield, lads, whose stomachs were strong enough to withstand rummaging among corpses, became the possessors of truly amazing collections of coins and medals. Buyers came from as far as Mecklenburg and Bohemia, provinces that had not been so richly blessed with the debris of this war. The battle petered out in a vast open-air flea-market.

16

Every spring, at ploughing time, the earth surrendered up mouldering bones. Among the first to be disturbed by this mystic ballast was Fürchtegott von Lindenau. You're familiar with the fuss over the Unknown Soldier, whom the French dredged up out of a mass grave at Verdun and brought to Paris; bleached skulls exercised a similar fascination on Lindenau. You can't tell from looking at a skull whether it belonged to a Russian, Swede, Tuscan or Basque, nor, apart from the rare cases where it has been holed by a bullet or cloven by a sabre, can you identify whether its former bearer was struck head-on in mid-charge or in the back in full flight, whether he was crazed with fear or with bloodlust, whether he had succumbed to gangrene or typhoid. One skull looks like any other. So, von Lindenau suggested that the skulls should be gathered together and piled up in a pyramid surmounted by a cross. To be on the safe side, he wanted to put a building round the whole thing.

The estate on which he lived has long since been gobbled up by the brown-coal excavators. When the area was being cleared, I demolished the manor-house and a pavilion in the garden, and blasted out the stumps of oaks and beeches. Sandstone sculptures from the park were preserved. I find it touching how, in these forests that have the sentence of death hanging over them, the conservationists stand guard to the very end over lily of the valley, cowslip, greater feathered mouldiwort and spotted twaddlebell and threaten legal action against anyone digging them up. And a year later the bulldozer devours the rare little bloom along with the massed armies of weeds.

While we were drilling our first bore-holes, books, furniture and paintings were still being carried out of the little castle. A portrait of Lindenau stood propped against the wheel of a lorry; I got the feeling he was staring at me, pleading, imploring. He lived through the energy-crisis post-1830; the forests had been so depleted that the day when every last chimney would go cold seemed imminent. However, open-cast mining began, and mankind rescued itself once again. I picked up one or two books, leafed through them, and so it was that I came across the document in which Lindenau had set down his ideas on a repository for skulls; it was an easy matter to slip the little book into my jacket pocket. The next day I rescued all the manuscripts and later I studied his slender collected works.

The period after the Battle was, for many, a time lacking in any recognisable meaning. As a power, the Saxon state had ceased to exist, the King had been led away into captivity, a Russian colonel was in command over the city. After him, Prussian commissars governed it and the very name of Saxony came within a hairsbreadth of being erased altogether by the Congress of Vienna. In the end, two-fifths of Saxon territory was annexed to Prussia, the black eagle was hoisted at customs barriers on three sides of Leipzig, and the city itself was virtually cut off from all its previous sources of timber supplies.

Where would man be without his capacity for forgetting? Lindenau developed that faculty in exemplary manner. The Corsican as the Anti-Christ incarnate – an early Hitler. Lindenau was careful not to recall that Napoleon had been draped with garlands in the Fairs City itself, while he swathed the Saxon Royal House in mourning-crêpe – the valiant old king, now he was languishing in exile in arch-Prussian Schwedt! But had not young men from the best Leipzig families secretly rushed to the patriots' flag very early in the proceedings? 'Thou, sword at my left side, what bodes thy gleam so bright?' The poet Körner, Saxons could cry in raptures, he was one of us! Körner as a resistance fighter. One united Germany it had to be! exulted Arndt, and Lindenau took up his cry. He was there on the first anniversary of the Battle, when students paraded to the spot where the allied monarchs were alleged to have fallen to their knees to give thanks for the victory; he had brought a cart-load of skulls, and with them he garnished the plinth from which fiery speeches were delivered. There were no calls for de-Napoleonification commissions, which would have branded many a burgher of Leipzig as a fellow-traveller. A whole tribe had to turn a collective blind eye. At some time or other, there is strife in every family, and then the password is: let bygones be bygones. One of them is in the nick, or he's kicked over the traces – you can't go on making a song and dance about it for ever. The stew has to be cooked and the laundry has to be done, the kids have to be put to bed, and then together you settle down in front of the TV to watch a whodunnit. Without this capacity, we Saxons would have been an extinct species long ago.

I found the manuscript of Lindenau's speech in the attic of the little castle, which I was reducing to manageable lumps. No, I didn't blow it up – only someone who doesn't know the first thing about demolition would use that expression. Proper demolition has something gentle about it. The merest rumble, no more, and a house sinks, a chimney leans and buckles. I folded up that little castle as a housewife folds a bedsheet.

Let's have no post-mortems on past mistakes! Lindenau had done some trading in remounts, young, fresh horses for the service of the

18

Confederation of the Rhine. Down in the Vogtland he had had trimmings and edgings stitched for Westphalian uniforms and had run sweat-shops around Altenburg, where French army trousers and coats were renovated. Later he boasted that the girls there had also sewn together pitch-black coats for the Lützow Volunteers, in secret, under cover – no one was so imprudent as to try to contradict him. 'And if you ask the Comrades in Black, That's Lützow's wild and daring charge' – the Lützow Volunteers wore skull-and-crossbones insignia; anybody kitted out like that makes dying easier for himself. Skulls all around Leipzig, wherever you set foot. 'Ill-fated times' was one of Lindenau's favourite expressions. And he wore it threadbare in the course of his speech on 18 October 1814, when he vociferously proclaimed his proposal for the pyramid of skulls. In doing so he was able to quote from an article in which the publisher, Brockhaus, urged the erection of a lasting memorial on the bloodsoaked battlefield of Leipzig. Arndt's demand was adopted by Lindenau, too: it wasn't to be some inconspicuous monument that would fade into the landscape, it was to stand out proudly, out there where so much blood had flowed, visible from every highway, a colossus, a pyramid, a cathedral like the one in Cologne.

You're quite right to ask, Doctor, why yesterday I slipped from the third person into the first in my narrative about Carl Friedrich Lindner but today, in talking about Lindenau, have remained firmly in the third. Only rarely do I have the feeling of actually having been this man in a previous existence. The fact that his lifetime overlapped that of the poor soldier Lindner is of only the slightest significance. It is conceivable that two men who lived simultaneously might later be jointly reincarnated in a third; it's a question of empathy, of affinity.

Fürchtegott von Lindenau was an obsessive collector. He was a familiar figure in all the villages which, little by little, rose again from the battlefield. He had a light carriage, drawn by a pair of horses, and in it he drove through the deepest mud, forded streams, cut through copses and forests. Instead of a hamper, he had strapped on to it a wooden chest, in which he salvaged skull after skull, which the earth had yielded up to the plough or the farmers had laid aside for him. Youngsters used to stop him with raised hand; for some small change they would direct him to gruesome resting-places by the roadside or in claypits. Fürchtegott would dig, uncover and extract. Ten thousand skulls was his target; nobody knows how close he got to it. He corresponded with doctors, apothecaries and soap-boilers on the

19

subject of effective methods of conserving bones; he didn't get very far with that. To many, his activities were distinctly spooky, but no one thought to make fun of him.

In an anteroom in the little pavilion I found a part of the legendary collection. There was a room at the back, with no means of access. I drilled into the brick wall, broke lumps out of it and recoiled as a dozen brain-pans fell with a clatter at my feet. My assistants enlarged the hole with pickaxes, and we pulled out one skull after another. We in the demolition trade know the procedure when we come across human remains. The cemeteries department has to be informed, rough and ready lads then cart the bones away in zinc containers, to deposit them in ground set aside for that purpose. There are hardened schnapps and vodka drinkers among their ranks, skeletons coated with skin and sinews themselves, and alongside them, bloated beer-swillers with wobbling bellies. They aren't squeamish when it comes to turning dental gold into ready cash; it's not just to medical students that good, sound skulls are sold off on the quiet.

I sent my assistants off to other work and searched for a skull whose jawbone was intact and still attached. The strong set of teeth indicated that in this case a young man had met his death, a twenty-year-old peasant lad, raised on rough bread, raw carrots and salt meat, from the Ukraine or from Normandy, who knows. With my spade I carried the skull to one side and hid it in a clump of goldenrod. A mass of egg-yolk-yellow blooms, beautiful to behold – my hatred of goldenrod developed later. Today it sprouts two or three times more vigorously than in the past, well above head-high, eating its way into the city, it thrives luxuriantly on the banks of the hot mud-streams of the Pleisse and the Elster, and I wonder whether you've noticed that it's now beginning to take over the roof of the central railway station. Perhaps the goldenrod will outlive everything else in Leipzig, other than the Monument to the Battle of the Nations: golden yellow carpets over the rubble, a jungle shrouding all the ruins, the boiling sewers running through it, the air permeated with sulphurous fumes, the horizon framed by domes whose existence you, in your loyalty to the state, deny.

I took one skull away with me, boiled it clean in a bucket, painted it with wax and set it on top of the cupboard that holds my collection. Marianne, my wife, couldn't bring herself to dust the skull at first, then she got used to it. For a while, I tried running my hands over it to make out who its owner had been. It belonged to *my* Unknown Soldier. For me, the important thing was that I didn't know his country of origin or what side he had fought on. That's a contrast to the famous soldier in Paris, who was, of course, quite definitely a Frenchman, and not some Boche, some swine, some Hun.

Lindenau steadfastly beat the big drum for the idea of a monument. His rival was Baron von Seckendorff, a landowner from near Querfurt. Letters to the newspapers regularly supported the suggestion that the first priority should be to take care of the victims and orphans of the war. The playwright, Kotzebue, wanted to have a granite column that had lain in the Odenwald since Roman times set up in Leipzig; he failed in this, because doubt was cast on the authenticity of the monstrosity. A memorial column was proposed, supporting 'a male figure in the prime of life, clad in a lion's skin'. Somebody else wanted to have an oak cast in iron – but enough of that.

The nobility had every reason to pass over the Napoleonic years in silence; if it had been in their power, they would simply have erased them from history. Lindenau's aim represented a completely new Saxon consciousness: we shall live on, and build a memorial, here was the battle, and ours was the victory!

Now and then the polarity of patriotic feeling has to be reversed – you must be old enough to remember when you, as a good citizen of the GDR, no longer yearned for the reunification of Germany. From that day on, a genuine patriot hereabouts no longer loved Heligoland or the Moselle. Journalists have recorded the night when the broadcasting stations of the GDR let the national anthem ring out with the words 'Germany, our united Fatherland' for the last time. Thenceforth it withered away into a national signature-tune. The Saxons of those times had their cross to bear. Napoleon had built them up against arrogant Prussia, Saxony was all of a sudden a kingdom, allied to the genius, the most powerful ruler in the world. The cheering crowds cried 'Vive l'Empereur!' whenever they caught sight of him, even at a distance. In May 1813, Saxony was practically disenFrenchised, in the safety of the university cocky voices were raised against the Corsican, and in the city the Lützow Volunteers recruited openly and uninhibitedly. When an irate Napoleon drew near, three city fathers hastened to meet him and kow-towed a bit, and after that the citizens of Leipzig once more supplied him with bread and equipment. On 17 June 1813 – a hundred and forty years before a more famous commotion – some Leipzigers attacked a few sentries and tried to get hold of weapons; they didn't get very far with that. The rabble-rousers were sentenced to imprisonment or hard labour; according to the ordinance, they were all 'contemptible persons from the suburbs'. Today, the term used would be 'criminal elements'. There is the story of the Leipzig merchant who often travelled to his country house near Weissenfels. Each time they came to the border he is supposed to have said to his children, 'Have a real good spit, we're coming into bloody Prussia now!'

When Lindenau threw himself into his skull-cult he was a young man with thinning curly hair. You have to picture him as slim, rather delicate and pale, his voice was quiet, his eye shaded by fluttering lid. He had a fear of authority, even of the Duke's tax officials or customs men at the borders. Before his mother, an overbearing woman, he never dared utter a self-assertive word. Cousins tormented him; one of them, whom he loved, was still beating him when he was twenty years old. The dead of the battlefield, on the other hand, lay mute, he could walk over them and just let his imagination run: here lay five hundred, here a thousand, five thousand. He would linger where peasants had pointed out mass graves to him and imagine, under his feet, all these stomachs, ribs, guts, lungs, dissolving into the earth. But the skulls would remain.

For some years, Lindenau's friends maintained the custom of foregathering in private houses to commemorate the Battle, but then their initiative fizzled out in the face of Metternich's systematic persecution. Inquisitions stamped out every flame and glimmer that had been kindled by liberalism. Lindenau improved his sheep flocks with the acquisition of an English ram, and himself married and sired some daughters and a son. Looking out over the barren autumn fields, he would pensively declaim Kleist's choruses from 'The Children of Mother Germania':

> Your rape in battle put aside,
> Few are there now who it recall.
> Towards higher treasures than the earth's
> The sinew swells, the blood takes flame!
>
> And let us now a pyramid
> In heaven's pastures build,
> And cover it with crowning-stone –
> Or take it for our monument!

A few things there that sound a bit overblown today. 'The sinew swells' – doesn't that rather call to mind a nagging tendonitis? And

22

'the blood takes flame' sounds ridiculous: all it makes me think of is a frying-pan, with a blood sausage starting to burn in it. Lindenau could flatter himself that he had drowned out any stirrings in Saxon hearts and minds of inclinations towards the Confederation of the Rhine in the sheer clamour of fanfares *à la* Körner, and now he was aiming at perpetuating that effect. On the seventh anniversary he rode to Leipzig, to celebrate in secret with some patriotic friends and fellow-thinkers. Prince Schwarzenberg, the former commanding officer of the allied forces, had died in Leipzig and was lying in state; he was to be laid to rest in the field of his triumph. Off into the night they set, hats pulled low over their eyes, torches flickered as they defied the law to gather around the orator, Karl von Haase. Ever since the yoke of foreign domination had been broken, he said, since the sins of servitude and hypocrisy had been washed clean with streams of blood, they had been compelled, for seven years now, to fetch from the well the water to extinguish the sacred flames, and now all was once again cold and dark. Every state, every province, every individual had become self-centred and obsessed with the problem of how to eke out this wretched life, this life stripped of all adornment; love of the Fatherland was once again denounced as infatuation, the yearning for freedom was, at best, written off as folly, generally condemned as Jacobinism and demagogy. The ideals of a German empire and a German nation had reverted to the status of curios and fairy-tales.

Owls screeched and the patriots gathered their coat-tails around them; it might have been a scene from a painting by Moritz von Schwindt. Not for a moment were those assembled free of the fear of spies.

Was this meeting the reason someone grassed on him? A week later he was summoned to Altenburg Castle, three gentlemen sat behind a large table, one of them introduced himself as the assistant head of a government department answerable to the police force, the others uttered not a word. Fürchtegott had to listen to a harangue about subversive activities that they were on to, and that they were therefore obliged to spell out an admonition, not to say a warning: what purpose was being served by all this exaggerated harking back to that certain battle? Could not a memorial be open to dangerous misinterpretation? Why this cult of skulls? Think how readily inexperienced youth could be led astray by dangerous thinking – so let's have an end of this collecting nonsense. This was after all the Grand Duchy of Altenburg, Herr von Lindenau was, they hoped and assumed, a loyal subject, so what concern of his were Saxon royal, far less so-called German, affairs?

I'm sorry to have to say it, but Fürchtegott capitulated. He walled up all the assembled skulls, hid his writings in a chest. Too bad about his great project.

I'm as close to the early Lindenau as I am to myself; later on, though, featureless decades trickle by. The tree of freedom had been felled, nobody wanted to know about a monument – did Lindenau still drive out across the battlefield? Certainly, rousing public opinion was a lost cause, and anyone who nevertheless made the attempt paid for it in prison. The Leipzigers, for their part, did once put up barricades between the Café Français and Hanisch's flower-shop – sorry, where the Grimmaische Strasse opens out on to the Augustusplatz, which was in those days a run-down, puddle-dotted open space. In a campaign for the abolition of censorship, the rioters set some Trade Fair stalls alight with the aim of attracting reinforcements from the surrounding villages, but in vain. Leipzig's bookseller, Blum, paid the supreme sacrifice for it in far-off Vienna. Snuffed-out like Robert Blum – in my youth, that was an expression we used when we wanted to say of somebody: he's completely had it. A grey age.

The Trade Fair brought in money and fresh ideas. Down with the customs barriers, away with petty nationalisms and on towards a great Germany, even if it had to be at the cost of Prussian supremacy! This all aroused the suspicions of the government in Dresden, and so they were not best pleased there when the choice of venue for a German Gymnastic Festival fell on Leipzig. Merchants, bankers and lawyers got themselves elected to the committees, even the Vice-Chancellor of the University was a member of the main Festival Organising Committee. To the south of what was then the city boundary and north of Connewitz Cross, from where today the Leading Party of the Working Class runs the district, a banqueting hall was built, with seating for seven thousand. The aisles between the tables had to be wide, for crinolines were in fashion. In front of this festival hall were gymnastic and dance arenas, with two grandstands accommodating five thousand spectators along their edges.

Fürchtegott had himself driven by landau from his little estate to Borna, and from there he went on by train. His coachman had heaved his two suitcases up into the luggage rack, and at Leipzig's Bavarian Station gymnasts from Coburg assisted the old gentleman.

24

Leipzig *was* Germany; the place was resplendent with flowers and garlands, a fire-brigade band blared, schoolchildren acted as guides to take visitors to their lodgings – Fürchtegott's shoulders went back, he looked around in delight and, in a voice quaking with emotion, said: 'This is what we fought for, forty years ago!'

His walking-stick clicking on the pavement, he strode through the Nürnberger Strasse to St John's Church. All around was a great hurly-burly, for, in addition to the city's eighty-thousand population, a further sixteen thousand had gathered from all parts. With loud 'Huzza!' and 'Gut Heil!', gymnasts from Bavaria and Silesia, Hamburg and the Rhine, hailed one another. Black-red-gold flags fluttered, symbolising the message: out of the darkness, through bloody battle and into golden liberty. Only twenty years before, anyone showing these colours would have landed in jail. Gymnastics was an expression of political stance, attitude and purpose. Fürchtegott von Lindenau was a gymnast through and through.

He put up at an inn in the Wintergartenstrasse. The suitcase with his night things he allowed the chambermaid to unpack, the other, still locked, she had to hoist up onto the wardrobe. For lunch, he ordered Leipzig larks. These weren't some kind of fancy pastries, they were real birds, stuffed and roasted, and you ate them with sauerkraut. They were caught in their tens of thousands out in the fields, and it never occurred to anyone that they might be committing a crime against nature by doing so. Larks were a delicacy, as was Leipziger Allerlei, that dish made from tender young vegetables, asparagus and morels, garnished with small dumplings and bound with prawn sauce, which has little in common with the mixed veg. that masquerades under the same name today. Lindenau ate with a light heart and a healthy appetite.

He had made previous application by letter for an appointment at the city hall; the building, on the Market Square, was decorated from top to bottom. His attempt to gain admission to the office of the Mayor, Bürgermeister Georgi, was thwarted by the information that the latter was at that very moment on his way to the clubhouse of the Rifle Society, where flags and standards were to be raised. A friendly secretary, with the rosette of the Gymnastic Festival in his buttonhole, imparted this news. At a stall on the market Fürchtegott bought a similar emblem made from linen and paper, with fluttering ribbons hanging from it. 'Frisch, fromm, fröhlich und frei' – true to the motto of the gymnastic movement, he did indeed feel hale and hearty, God-fearing and free. He couldn't find Herr Georgi in the clubhouse, nor in the big festival marquee. All around, grizzled old-timers were falling into each other's embrace, veterans of the good old days. A number of former sutler-women, and the first-aid nurse who had treated the wounded Körner after the skirmish at Kitzen, were being honoured. At the Café Français a triumphal arch graced the entrance, a double eagle spread its brocaded pinions. In shop-windows keepsakes were on display, weapons and proclamations, portraits and drawings. There was no lack of curios either, like, for example, a dried-up bread-roll from the great days.

Fürchtegott followed a cheering crowd over to the squares on the south side. Meat was being roasted and boiled in the open, he found a seat between a Swabian and a Franconian and stood them a fair few glasses. Many a customer took off his coat and tried his hand at the high-jump, whoever cleared the rope was greeted with cries of 'Hurrah!' Choruses were bellowed out, with throats loosening up as fast as muscles. There was no call here for stop-watches or measuring-tapes, the victors' brows were crowned with oak-wreaths, a handshake and that was that. How Lindenau regretted having left his case at the inn, with the result that he was not in a position to reveal its contents now, at this festive hour! In the case were twelve skulls from the Battle of the Nations.

Now I must turn my attention to the tipple of my native city, good old 'Gose', a sharp-tasting, top-fermented beer, refreshing and good for the digestion. Twice a year it was brewed, filled into bulbous bottles and drunk from long-stemmed glasses. There were pubs specialising in Gose all over the city, the Caution-to-the-Winds in Mencke Strasse, the Gose Castle in Plagwitz, the Golden Saw in Dresdner Strasse, and, famed through the city, the Gose Tavern on Eutritzsch Market. I drank Gose right up till the fifties of this twentieth century; you had to be careful, otherwise, on the morning after, you had the feeling you had two skulls, and the larger of them was on the inside. Then it was 'rationalised' out of existence. The brewing equipment was worn out, it was too wasteful to maintain stocks of special bottles and glasses, so away with it! I only hope that whoever ultimately proposed the closure of the Gose breweries wasn't awarded an innovator's bonus for his efforts. Bottles and glasses were systematically reduced to smithereens, streams of Sternburg Light and Silver Pilsener would in future flow from all the beer-taps. It's only old men that look back. If only someone in power had put his oar in at the time, then everything would have turned out differently. If Ulbricht had been a Gose-fan –

but of course he was far too ascetic for that. Fröhlich, the Party District Secretary, was a Bautzen man, so no hope in that direction either. Gose, the taste of local tradition, the favourite of the proletariat, as far back as old Liebknecht – there would have been no shortage of arguments in its favour. Gose is gone for ever. The River Pleisse will boil over, goldenrod and acacia will . . . yes, all right, all right, I'll stop.

Lindenau, normally a man of moderation, drank Gose in Cajeri's, Lehmann's Garden, in the Good Spring on Brühl, where the free-thinking Professor Rossmässler and master wood-turner Bebel were regulars, and in the Blue Pike in Nikolai Strasse, where the lanky beanpole of a tailor, who had sat as model for the Döllnitz Brewery's advertisement of 'The Octogenarian Gose-Drinker', boozed bliss-fully in a corner. In the Dovecote in the Preussengasse, Lindenau ordered a bottle, on him, for Harpie-Jeannie, a wizened old wife, while all around him sat gymnasts, among them one from Allenstein and one from Basle; they sipped at the unfamiliar brew and pronounced it highly palatable. Then he shouted, in his own thick Saxon accent, into the hotch-potch of German dialects: 'Tomorrow I'm going to hand over to the Mayor a dozen skulls from the Battle of the Nations!' A man from Zwickau raised his glass to him, the others hadn't understood a word. Lindenau drained his glass and staggered off in the direction of his hotel.

Next day it was near noon when he woke. He had missed a whole lot of patriotically significant events: wagon-loads of oak-branches had been brought in, and everyone stuck a twig in his hat-band. Starting from the Augustusplatz, the gymnasts had marched through the city centre, at their head guests from Amsterdam, Basle, Kronstadt, London, Pisa and even Melbourne, followed by the German provinces with Schleswig-Holstein in the van, since it still languished under the Danish yoke. Last of all came the Saxons; the various Leipzig Battlefield Clubs and Associations alone had mustered 2,350 members. While all this was going on, Fürchtegott von Lindenau was ordering camomile tea.

But he did arrive in time to join the procession on its way to the Marienstrasse; this time he had one of the twelve skulls in his bag. The foundation stone was to be laid for a monument, a pile of cannon-balls found on the battlefield. Lindenau elbowed his way through the crowd, right up to the barrier-ropes. There stood the friendly secretary he had met the day before in the city hall – today, of course, we'd call him Personal Consultant to the Lord Mayor. He

27

had brought one of the skulls from the Battle of the Nations with him, Lindenau told him excitedly, and wouldn't that be a marvellous adornment for the monument if it could crown the summit of the cannon-balls? Interesting, opined the secretary, but unfortunately this was not the appropriate moment to introduce this new factor into the calculations, the Lord Mayor was just about to make his speech – protocol, you understand? Fürchtegott tried again, got into a tangle, his head was none too clear yet, his tongue was furry. 'Whose skull is it?' asked the secretary. 'I mean, from which army?' That it might be a French skull never entered the secretary's head, but – especially at this time when unity, concord, was paramount – might not one German race feel discriminated against if the skull of a brother from another tribe were to be put on display and thus given preference? The secretary passed the bag, into which, duty bound to be fair to all sides, he had cast a pained but none the less suitably dignified glance, back to Fürchtegott. A quick fanfare, the Lord Mayor stepped forward to the lectern, while in Fürchtegott that great emptiness opened up which is familiar to anyone who has dragged himself up out of the depths of a crushing hangover and back into clarity of thought. The greatest project of his life had failed.

Three years later, the Saxons once again stood in the midst of turmoil, they fought at the side of the Austrians against Prussia, and lost as usual. The Franco-German war changed everything. In that one, the only occasion in two centuries, we Saxons fought on the victorious side. Fifteen hundred soldiers of the Leipzig Garrison died; that was regarded as paying their toll in blood. The victory was celebrated in great style, the city hall was decorated with a hundred flags and a banner bearing the legend: 'Lipsia kneels in homage to Germania.' Thirty-five thousand gas-lanterns and three thousand oil-lamps illuminated the city hall. That was when that idiotic expression originated: 'In Leipty/Leipty-one.' It's still trotted out when people want to say: You know, back then, I'm not really sure exactly when. That's the sort of thing that many a time helps us Saxons to pull through. Somehow our history was always a case of 'Leipty/Leipty-one.'

In the years after that, Germany was well stocked up with monuments to Kaiser Wilhelm and Bismarck, so the calls for a pile to commemorate the Battle of the Nations sounded more muted. Lindenau never put his skulls on offer again. He died at a ripe old age.

Knocking-off time? All right by me, Doctor.

28

CHAPTER 3

Surely not single-handed, though?

I really must protest! You assured me you wouldn't treat me as a prisoner, but as a patient. A patient under security conditions, as you put it. This is my fourth day here now, and I was in the building in the city centre for three days before that, and still I'm being denied newspapers, radio and television. All my life I've taken a close interest in current events. There might have been, for all I know, a report in yesterday's paper about the signing of some far-reaching trade agreement. As the official GDR news agency, ADN, learned from sources in Leipzig, the construction of a dozen atomic power . . .

Talking a lot of nonsense, am I? Normally you take down every word I say, but when I get down to the heart of the matter, to the nucleus, you fend me off. Nucleus — that's another word that will no doubt incur your displeasure.

Did I have an accomplice? I'll prove to you that I didn't need one. At seventy I feel more sprightly than many a sixty-year-old. Exercise in the fresh air, hard physical work, that's what I put it down to, and then I was a wrestler for many years. We sportsmen have always upheld the idea of a monument. In fact, during the preliminaries to the dedication ceremony, gymnasts were doing their stuff on the parallel and horizontal bars, led by Rudolf Witzgall, Gymnastics Supervisor to the 12th German Gymnastics Festival in August 1913. There's still a street in Stötteritz named after him. He lies in the Southern Cemetery side by side with the Honorary Regional Representatives Melhorn and Hennig, and Goldstein, the Regional Gymnastics Supervisor – they were all in the national team.

I couldn't imagine a more sublimely solemn spot in the cemetery. Those who made their arrangements for the afterlife here didn't begrudge visitors space to walk about on flagstones and lawns. Forty square metres' resting-place for one family – I ask you, compare that with today's traffic-jam conditions, with urns jostling each other for space! Oaks and beeches frame the sky, and, behind the roof they form, the mass of the Monument looms darkly. There could be no worthier place imaginable for Court Privy Councillor Clemens Thieme, creator of the Monument, born 1861, deceased on that sorry 11th of the 11th, 1945, when nobody felt much like celebrating the start of Carnival, and when I was still salvaging tins of blood-sausage and sardines, woollen blankets and soggy cigarettes from the escape tunnel of the SS, just close by. If it ever came to a resurrection, the great man would immediately have the Monument right before his very eyes. Rabbits and squirrels scurry about. If it weren't already out of the question, I'd reserve my plot for a last resting-place here.

Next to the graves of the master-gymnasts lies the family vault of the von Pussenkomms, one of whom fell at the Somme in 1916, with the rank of captain, and under that it reads: 'The last bearer of the family name.' May I, just by the way, remind you that you gave me no answer at all when I asked you for newspapers? Apart from the fact that the press, radio and television in the GDR exercise the most soothing effect, I really *must* keep up to date with what's going on in the world. Perhaps, right out of the blue, new evidence will prove me right? Maybe I'll read that the neighbouring suburbs of Stötteritz and Marienbrunn are being evacuated and the Southern Cemetery has to be closed – would that not prove that I wasn't hallucinating when, under the Monument, I saw the men in yellow ... Fine, you'll have a word with your superiors.

I had to clean soil and grass off a metal ring in the slab in front of the von Pussenkomm family stone – this would be a week ago now – before I could pull the covering of the vault to one side. I found the SS-men's escape tunnel intact, droplets of water glistening on the beams. For about twenty metres in, it was shored up with short-barrelled Carbine 98s, of which there was an abundance lying around at the end of the war. As I moved forwards on hands and knees, I held my torch between my teeth. I recognised one niche; tins of dripping and beef had been piled up in there. And Scho-Ka-Kola – a chocolate confection whose name has become a historical by-word. At the first main pillar there was a bend in the passageway, I looked up and saw the initials VM: Voiciech Machulski had immortalised himself in the pressed concrete. Under them lay my five ack-ack shells. I can tell you, my mouth went dry. The shells lay there wrapped up like papooses. I unpicked the knots in the string and undid the wrappings; the leaf-patterning on the tarpaulin was still discernible, it was well known that the Waffen-SS used a particular design. The grease broke open with a crackle, under it the metal lay shiny and dry, the detonators were in perfect condition. I caressed the shells, lifted one and carried it to the foot of the buttress I intended to blow up. That was when I came across the unexpected door and stepped into the brightly lit room. And at that moment the men in the yellow overalls rushed me.

Whenever I touch on this point, you dismiss it with an indignant wave: there were no men there, you say, there is no brightly lit room, there are no control panels. You insist, on the contrary, that I was discovered in the von Pussenkomm family vault by women sweeping up leaves in the cemetery, and as they struggled to pull me out of it they found a shell among the coffins and shouted for help. A pack of lies from a bunch of self-important limelight-cases, that's all that is. I'm supposed to have reeked of cheap drink – Do me a favour! But now here's my trump-card: if all that were true, would you keep me here and grill me every day from dawn to dusk? I'm quite prepared to give you a description of the men in the Monument. Without exception they were all under thirty, at least two of them were bearded. They rushed forwards, startled, but without a sound, obviously on rubber soles. They had instruments like thermometers sticking out of their breast-pockets. I'm not sure if they all wore shapeless gloves, or only some of them. They looked and talked like highly educated specialists. I can't recall recognising any particular regional accents. If you like, yes, let's have tea, it doesn't always have to be coffee.

So what's behind my other forenames? The fourth one I took from Voiciech Machulski, who came from deepest Upper Silesia, the son of agricultural workers who owned a croft and a patch of land, on rare occasions a pig, but mostly just a few hens and geese and a dozen children – never more than four at any one time, though, for the mortality rate was high. The local teacher, who taught four classes in the one room, spotted Voiciech's gift for grasping things quickly, and, since the teacher's own son was pretty dull, he used to invite Voiciech over to his house in the afternoons; Voiciech was to act as a motivator. In this way, Voiciech learned a lot more than would otherwise have been possible, he was soon writing almost flawless German in a clear, upright hand, read a widely circulated progressive journal, *The Arbour*, a year's issues at a time, and developed all sorts of insights into geometry and physics. When he was twelve, he built a water-mill that was meant to drive a chaff-cutter and in fact broke two of his fingers. At thirteen, he astounded folk with plans for catching cumulus clouds in enormous canvas bags, harnessing gondolas to these and travelling around the world in them. Unfortunately, the problem of how to hoist the canvas bags up to cloud-level remained unresolved. When he was fourteen, he moved west with some older friends. They worked for farmers in Silesia and market-gardeners in the Lausitz, and in 1892 Voiciech found his way to Leipzig. He was sixteen by this time. A haulier in Stötteritz took him on as a stable lad. When he groomed the horses' backs, he had to stand on a box; as a finishing touch, he would comb a V and an M into their coat. He slept on straw in a lean-to at the back of the feed-store; that was neither humiliating nor anything out of the ordinary. His boss found him able and hard-working and helped him to acquire papers in which his name was entered as Viktor Machul.

Voiciech carted wood, stone, bricks. He lived through the time when Leipzig was taking on the shape which predominates today, in spite of the recently emerged concrete suburbs. He delivered building materials to the inner western suburbs: Kolonnadenstrasse, Nikischplatz, Apel's Garden. The bombs destroyed three-fifths of all the houses there, the rest are now in the process of falling apart. Nowadays the west end looks like a small forest of acacia, relieved only by crumbling roads and shabby houses. He brought in granite slabs for the pavements, he learned how to lift and lay them without any technology other than pieces of timber and a crowbar, and it became second nature to him to apply the physical laws of leverage, which had been no more than matters of vague theory away back home beyond the dark forests. Aaall together! Heeeave! The proletarian VM built pavements and houses for the bourgeoisie, five storeys high with bay-windows and gables, he carried bricks up scaffolding ladders, and was paid piece-rates for it; his arms and thighs grew iron-hard, his heart expanded like a modern-day sportsman's, but for him the end-product was always *a house*, and not some meaningless statistic and a useless medal. And everywhere he scratched his VM into the plaster. Number 17 in the Kolonnadenstrasse still stands today, with its wrought-iron door, the handle in the form of a knight in armour, and so solidly made that, in ninety years, it has been neither stolen nor broken off.

14 Kolonnadenstrasse: here was Heinrich Bauer's factory, which furnished castles, churches and hotels; there you could have your drawing-room done out in mahogany, cherrywood or birch. Heinrich Bauer designed and installed all the woodwork in the Fürstenhof (the Hotel International today), a master craftsman who slogged his way to the top. All right, all right, I'm not going to fall into raptures for these days, which you, with your tongue in your cheek, call the good old ones. 'Willy Schubert, Fresh- and Saltwater Fish,' the sign can still just be made out, the windows below it are blind with dirt and the shop has degenerated into a storage shed. Of course there was a pub, in the building on the corner, the Alexander Nook, and opposite, a café. The pub was gutted by fire, the café has gone to the dogs. Ah, Doctor, what a life that was, cramped, urban, and productive right down to the cellars and backyards. 11 Alexanderstrasse, with the coat of arms above the door and the VM on the cellar steps. 'Clean – quick – value for money' can still be dimly deciphered, nobody knows now what service was being advertised.

Voiciech heaved granite slabs from his truck, laid them on the bed of gravel, and then the good burghers in their patent-leather shoes could walk, and their good ladies push their prams, on them. Once across the Ring, and they were in the city centre. The slabs lay so level, with such narrow seams, that the children were hard put to it to wedge their tops between them until the first stroke of the whip landed. Today, the slabs lie cracked and broken, their base washed away. No one is doing anything to stem the decay, and that's another reason why I took my flak-shells out of their wrappings. Just like the inner west end, so also are Stötteritz, Plagwitz and the Waldstrassen quarter falling into disrepair, and the streets leading south from Connewitz Cross. Goldenrod and acacia will triumph. Both are plants native to the Steppes.

By birth, Voiciech was Polish, by nationality, a citizen of the German Reich; three villages farther away, and the Tsar would have called him up to serve under the Russian flag. It's important to me to be able to count a Slav among my ancestors. Members of that wave of guest-workers have enriched our blood, pepped up our temperament, they played a lively part in the building of towns and factories, and without them the course of these years would have been a lot tougher, a lot drearier.

On the rise above Stötteritz, in the Reitzenhainer Strasse, there stood a tall, unusually bushy, poplar. Around its foot, dry grass, trampled hard, and ice-age rocks overgrown with a jungle of bramble-bushes. It was a trysting-place for lads and lasses from Stötteritz and Thonberg. Voiciech liked to sit among them, serving-maids, factory-girls, carters like himself, bakers' apprentices, market hands. They sang folk-songs and soldiers' songs, even soppy ditties: 'A king of Rome, Napoleon's son, he was much too wee, an emperor to be.' From the rise, they used to watch the gas-lamps going on in the city. Voiciech basted Saxon words into his vocabulary. 'Euja,' for example, which means something along the lines of 'of course'.

He was flaxen-haired, his eyes were a pale cornflower-blue narrow and mischievous, his ears, tiny like a seal's, lay close to his round skull. He wore his hair cut short at the back and in a brush at the front. He'd walk girls home, sometimes this one, sometimes that, and cuddle them on the doorstep. When he went off to the army, he hadn't yet slept with a girl; those were different times. The poplar: the trams on route F went round it on both sides. Later it was felled; old age had weakened it. Even after that, adolescents would still arrange to meet 'at th' lopped popple.' Today, the most northerly arc of the embankment round the Monument passes through the spot. At the kiosk there you can buy beer, or frankfurters and schnapps. Shabby, hardened drinkers take up their regular stance here and remain glued to it from morn till night; sometimes they use a window-ledge to play Klammergass, a favourite card-game in Leipzig pubs, a bit like pontoon. There's no singing there any more. At most, you may hear a drunken bawl of 'Sing, my Sax'n, sing!'

Voiciech wrote home at Christmas and Easter. He never went back there again. It would have been too far and too expensive, and anyway he didn't get such a thing as a holiday. Once, there was one of his younger brothers, standing on his doorstep, quite unheralded, ready to stay or to move on, it all depended. This brother dossed

34

down on the floor for a week, bummed around, stole a jacket and two shirts from a washing-line, apples and carrots from a market stall. Voiciech refused to help him look for work. His brother pushed off to Belgium and France. Later, the story was that they had fought on opposite sides at Verdun.

Did Voiciech go willingly to join the army? That question was – for us today, surprisingly – of little consequence. Whether a haulage contractor or a corporal gave him a bollocking was a matter of complete indifference to him. A uniform was almost always sturdier and warmer than working clothes, not to mention having something to put on your feet. He enlisted with the engineers battalion of the 107th in Gohlis, and from the third day on he was combing his VM into horses' coats as before. He was trained to use a carbine and wasn't a bad shot, and the simulated close combat, using long cudgels for bayonets, was fun. He drove loads of sleepers and boards out to the Bienitz, where he practised throwing bridges across the Elster and the Luppe. From time to time, he and his mates would spend afternoons lying in the firing-line, cradling their carbines, having a quiet snooze for half an hour as they waited for the imaginary enemy to come at them. There was little time and less money for pub-crawling, which was nothing new anyway. Sapper Viktor Machul seldom counted off the days till his release, he wasn't one of those who cut centimetre notches along a stick. Two-thirds of his fellow-sappers came from Leipzig, the others from surrounding villages and towns. All the officers were Saxons, they were convinced that Saxon soldiers were the best in the Reich and looked down their noses at Prussians, Hessians and Bavarians – only metaphorically, of course, for they never laid eyes on any of them. The last war lay so far back in the past that nobody could remember it properly. Wars happened, of course, but in China, or somewhere like that, but not in Europe, oh no. Army life was a kind of toughening-up process, 'orrible little men were licked into shape. Officers were generally regarded as superfluous, and a few of them felt that way themselves. Even by the end of his service, Voiciech hadn't managed to get his lance-corporal's stripe, but that had never been his ambition anyway. Once, when he was stuck up in front of the rest, as a kind of leadership test, he pretended to stammer and slip back into the Polish of his childhood, and he was immediately shoved back into the ranks. Lying on his straw mattress, he devised a long-trajectory hand-grenade launcher; it was based on the principles of leverage and made of rods and beams nailed together. Three men had to jump simultaneously onto the short end. He kept his invention to himself. And got his honourable discharge.

Voiciech was still growing at twenty, even at twenty-two. There he stood, there I stood – I can remember it more clearly this way – there I stood, then, Voiciech Machulski, dressed in polished boots, a clean pair of trousers in good-quality cloth, a jacket bought second-hand and a baggy, floppy cap, as, on 18 October 1889, the symbolic first sod was cut for the Monument. The day had started dull; as the procession reached the top of the rise, the sun broke through. I had previously been directed, by gentlemen in frock-coats, to my proper place, and now stood alongside my bonny middleweight chestnuts with VM curried into their coats, stroking their muzzles and talking soothingly to them. Gentlemen in their Sunday best, with sashes and medals, marched up bearing flags, flags of Gymnastic or Choral Societies, old soldiers' associations and student societies, and especially of the League of German Patriots, which had been the principal advocates of the case for a monument. I had brought a spade, it was passed along a line of hands, a band played a flourish, a gentleman raised his head and his voice: 'With God's help, for Kaiser and Reich, for King and Fatherland – let work commence!' That was Clemens Thieme. He stabbed a clod of turf loose and threw it in the general direction of my cart. Then he waved his hat, cheering rang out, a mixture of 'Long live . . .' and 'Hurrah!' Other gentlemen made a grab for the spade and pecked at the ground, everybody wanted to be the second, the fifth, the tenth. One, in a fit of clumsy enthusiasm, threw earth up in the air so that it descended again on frock-coated shoulders. 'To work! To work!' the cry was repeated. 'Long live the Fatherland!' The band played: 'Out rings the call like thunder-roll!' The gentlemen threw their top-hats heavenward. 'To the Rhine, the Rhine, the German Rhine,' they sang, 'the river's guardians we will be.' In those days, nothing could happen without that river sloshing along in accompaniment. 'A Rhenish girl from the Rhenish Rhine, that's a heaven on earth of mine.'

The patriots dispersed. With snatches of heroic song still floating in the air, I climbed onto the box-seat, my chestnuts started off and I ambled towards town along the Reitzenhainer Strasse in a procession of coaches in which burghers were making their way back, heading, most of them, towards the banquet, towards perch, saddle of venison and hock. Shortly before, two of them had stood in front of the house at 17 Kolonnaden Strasse, heads back, pointing up at

36

where I was balancing my way across ladders and planks with a hod full of bricks – the owner and his architect. Now I was clearing their rubble away, not taking it very far, though, for in Stötteritz foundations had to be filled in, so I was killing two birds with one stone.

In the evenings, I would sit in my social-democratic Workers' Savings and Education Co-operative clubrooms. A new member would be enrolled, wage-cuts in spinning-mills reported, never a word was uttered about the monument, and I certainly didn't feel any urge to give a talk on the subject! It was quite clear to us all that the whole monument-craze was to be regarded strictly as an example of bourgeois frippery. I allowed myself two beers, I wanted to treat my girl-friend, Erna, to a liqueur; with a mixture of pride and modesty, she declined. I had difficulty in following the thread of discussion; sphinx-like riddles on subjects such as the fair distribution of wealth, expropriation, the cottage-industry system, latent association. A Herr Sax wanted to provide the workers with gas-lighting, hot-water central heating, bathrooms, day nurseries for their children, schools, prayer halls and libraries, not to mention wine- and beer-bars, and I thought, what wonderful ideas, only to hear that Comrade Engels had rejected all that as creeping bourgeoisie. The problem had to be tackled from a different angle – but which? I could heave granite slabs for ten hours on end, but one hour's listening had my eyelids drooping. *Pschakreff*! – Bugger it!

That year I married Erna, we moved into the Alexanderstrasse, through the courtyard to the back, third floor, kitchen, living-room, bedroom, water-tap in the hall, water-closet on the landing. I joined the firm of Stoye in the Kreuzstrasse, structural and civil engineers with the very latest machinery, powered by electric motors. Shoulder to shoulder with expert bricklayers, I slogged away at the wall, sweated, lagged behind, laid bricks, spread mortar, caught up again, cursed and swore in Polish. But I was stronger than all of them. Of course I was exploited. I don't need you to tell me that.

It was three years later I came to work on the Monument. I helped put up the outside walls of the Crystal Palace, the biggest pleasure-palace in all Germany, with a circus, a theatre, gardens with a bandstand, ball-room, eight bowling-alleys, a wine-restaurant, a Viennese café, cake shop and beer-bars. Can you guess how many people it could hold at one time? You'd never get near it. One single entertainment complex for *fifteen thousand* people – just count up for yourself whether all the present-day pubs and the like in the city put together could hold as many! The Crystal Palace burned down in 1943, and the following spring I demolished the ruins.

Yes, back to Voiciech: I was earning over twenty Marks a week, for a ten-hour day, six days a week. Wherever I was working, I went there and back on foot, no worker could afford the tram-fare. I was involved in the building of Hübel & Denck's, Barthel's Court Bookbinders, by appointment to the Royal Houses of Bavaria and Rumania, Blüthner's piano works and Nauck's the furriers on the Brühl. And everywhere I scratched my initials into wood, stone or concrete. Then one day I stood in the office of Rudolf Wolle, handing over my papers. Wolle was a small, wiry man, whom I never saw dressed in anything but his mason's overalls, neither on the site nor behind a desk piled with paperwork. He may well have been stinking rich even then, but he had never forgotten his origins. Did I know anything about panelling, he asked, or about electric hoists? One week, on probation!

I used to leave the house just before four, the bakers' boys were already about, with their baskets of crisp morning rolls on their shoulders and little lanterns at their belts, filling the bags hanging from the door-handles of the middle-class houses. The milk-carts were trotting in from the villages, newspapers were being delivered, columns of street-sweepers wheeled their barrows along. Light carts ran a race out to the south: the butchers' lads, dashing to the slaughterhouse. A jostling crush behind the covered market on the Panorama. The fleets of trams didn't start clanging out of their sheds until later, for the office-workers and the tradespeople. In the *Reclam's Universal Encyclopaedia* of those days you can read that endless streams of folk made daily pilgrimage to the east and west ends of the city, where a forest of giant chimneys darkened the dawning sky with their swirling pall, so that the morning sun had a hard struggle to make its presence known. Thousands upon thousands of them, both sexes, all ages, were swallowed up by the yawning factory gates, so that, by dint of hard labour, they might help to carry the victory slogan out into the world: 'Glory to Germany's, and Leipzig's, Industry!' Nice, don't you think?

Nowadays, next to every house in the process of construction, there stands an electric cement-mixer; we mixed by hand. The gravel was swung over on a cable railway, we tipped it out, added best Saxon-Bohemian-Portland cement, then water, and took up our extra-broad shovels, working from the outside in, cutting figures-of-eight through it, shunting and lifting and turning the concrete until it was thick and creamy as a good cake-dough. Our foreman stood at the chute, down into the hole he let the concrete pour, that immaculately kneaded porridge, in which every single pebble lay evenly in its grey mantle. Roughly a hundred cubic metres every day. The foundation stone for the Gymnastic Festival of 1863 was delivered and set in place where today the Archangel Michael stands. We cast the buttresses, a metre at a time, making the next level ten centimetres narrower, supporting the next mould on the jutting edge, so that we managed without scaffolding. There was no reinforcement of any kind in the pillars, which, of course, is something worth knowing for anyone wanting to blow them up.

The world, Germany, Leipzig and Voiciech Machulski celebrated the dawn of a new century. The League of Patriots treated its workers to a brawn-dinner with free beer and five glasses of schnapps per man, Clemens Thieme did the speechifying. In my Savings and Education Co-operative, too, I was told that the new century was to be incomparably better than the old. Friedrich Engels had written in 1892 that, in the event of war, capitalism would collapse within two or three years, ten at the most, and make way for socialism. If anyone impatiently asked when it was all going to start, he was pacified by the chairman of the discussion: in dealing with a historical occurrence of such great moment, you couldn't commit yourself to a prediction of the precise day and hour. In the meantime, they said, the pace of capitalist momentum had shifted its focus from England to Germany, and so it was no longer possible to predict *scientifically* whether the revolution *was bound* to to break out in England first; Belgium, too, even the United States, were now possible candidates. So, Comrades, a little revolutionary patience, please!

In my collection you will find postcards: cherubs with trumpets against a starry-sky background, Germania with torch and sword, the sun in all its radiant glory, artisans at the anvil, hammering out the figures '1900' – it was to be the most brilliant century in the history of mankind, packed with outstanding technological achievements, the century of the aeroplane, the automobile, the electric lamp, and of the name of Germany on the world's lips. Only eccentrics talked of a century of peace.

Erna used to bring my lunch to the site. She'd make bean-soup with chervil, barley broth with celery and parsley, potatoes in vinegar with stewed onions. She carried the pot in a basket, wrapped up in newspaper and a woollen underskirt. She'd wait till I had eaten my fill and then quickly spoon up the rest, not, she'd insist, because she was at all hungry, but just so that nothing went to waste. As we ate, we would perhaps be leaning against the head of a statue we were assembling; it was supposed to represent the 'Self-sacrificing Rich'. The head was as tall as Erna, its ear forty centimetres long, its nose thirty-five, and the middle finger a hundred and ten. A boy, seven metres tall, was to lie in his father's lap – Erna shook her head, half disbelieving, half admiring: 'What that must be costing!' The cost was quoted in all the papers, and in my Education Club sums had been bandied about: fifty thousand, a hundred thousand, two hundred thousand Marks a year were being collected and poured into the building. 'They're collecting in the schools, too,' said Erna. 'Penny by penny.'

'Well they're getting nothing from us.' Our attitude was clear-cut: we couldn't prevent the building of the monument, indeed we earned our living building it, but one day soon, come the proletarian revolution, we'd take it over. We might possibly leave it as a capitalist ruin, or we might complete it as a memorial to fallen revolutionaries – 'The Self-sacrificing Rich Man' would then be the 'Father of a Sacrifice for the Revolution'. That the League of Patriots might succeed in completing the monument in the spirit they intended was for me unthinkable: there was no chance of capitalism holding out till 1913.

Erna brought me baked white-fish with potatoes, lamb soup with green beans or spiced purée of lung – not *once* did I ever eat the same thing twice within a fortnight. In her bag she always took home scraps of timber, ends of planks and offcuts from scaffolding beams; in the evenings my rucksack was seldom empty. I helped to build the column for the mask of Fate in the crypt and the outer layers of the base. Wolle gave me the job of operating his electric crane; tons of stone hovered in the air at my command. What would become of Wolle after the proletarian revolution? I reckoned he might later make a useful master-craftsman in socialist industry.

Once the chain on the crane broke, a granite block smashed down on the square edges of the pillars, burst and landed in pieces. We builders told the suppliers in Beucha, quite casually: there you are, our concrete won that one. We were faced with a pretty tricky and complicated dilemma: here we were, convinced social democrats, one a Pole, piling up a bourgeois-reactionary monument, and we were taking a pride in its first-class German quality.

I'd really like to take a walk through the Monument with you. Not while the official guides are going about their business, but very early on a summer's morning, when it's cool and quiet, with sunlight slanting through the east window. The figures in there are more than simply gigantic things weighing umpteen tons; there's more to them than that. I'd like to take you up the steps, up from the ornamental lake. The statue of Michael, the eagles, the horses' heads, the inscription above them, 'Gott mit uns,' the parapet, and then, all the way round, no matter what side you look up from, the sentinels with their swords and bearded faces – just don't let anybody try to tell you that that's ugly, pompous, megalomaniac. That's a piece of German history standing there.

But back to Voiciech again: archaeologists in some distant future age will find, if they take the Monument apart stage by stage, my commentaries deep in its heart. On one of the buttresses, at crypt level, I scratched into the creamy concrete: '1900, Boxer Rebellion in China. Yellow brothers, not all Germans are Huns!' Ten metres higher up, under the west window: '1903, Bantu and Bushmen, the workers of Germany will restore your liberty!'

In the newspapers Erna used to keep my lunch warm, I read that Karl Liebknecht had appeared for the defence in a trial in Königsberg: social democrats had smuggled pamphlets into Russia, in which they accused Tsarism of barbarous acts, and they were convicted – in *Germany* – for membership of illegal clandestine organisations, high treason against Russia and *lèse-majesté* against the Tsar. And here was I, Voiciech Machulski, Viktor Machul, helping to build this monument that was intended as a glorification of the alliance with the Tsar, I, a member of the Social Democratic Party! I stuck the paper with Liebknecht's speech into a tin can and moulded it in under the east stairway up to the entrance. When the workers in Russia rose, I etched 'Socialists arise, and close ranks!' into the supports of the main chamber under the dome. Gradually, the deadlines set by Engels for the revolution came and went, even allowing for the most generous interpretation of his prognostication. When the arch for the round north window was being set in place, I helped to insert into the stonework the symbols of Piety and the Power of the People. Between two granite blocks I jammed a piece of paper with the inscription: 'Wilhelm, not a single shot for Morocco!' Above the north fanlights I wrote into the mortar: 'In Spain and Sweden the thrones are tottering. Here too!'

You find that all very naïve, do you? That has the arrogant ring of a later generation's unhistorical hindsight. Pre-First World War social democracy without faith in *imminent* victory is simply inconceivable. Every phase of history has its prophets and its believers, and without both of these there would be nothing left but cynicism.

In 1908, the pile was already fifty-three metres high. Sightseers swarmed around its foundations, and their entrance money made a fair contribution towards building costs. That winter and spring it was very stormy up at our level. On the inside of the upper dome, I helped to construct three-dimensional figures of horsemen. We laid out moulds of iron mesh, poured in the plaster, set the riders up in a ring, and concreted them on to the face. To this day, not so much as one single horse's hoof has broken off, and that's really something, when you take into account the forces that are inevitably at work in such a massive construction. In behind one of the horsemen on the fourth circle from the bottom, I stuck an SPD electioneering pamphlet. That was 1907, the party suffered heavy losses at the polls. Two years later, the Right split over the question of estate duties, and this brought down the Chancellor. We social democrats stood by, unmoved.

At the evening instructional meetings run by my party, I heard how we had to strengthen the trades unions, to win seats in the Reichstag, to provide political education for young people. The events in Russia had shown, so we were told, that nothing could be more damaging than an over-precipitate uprising. Here and there, groups were supposed to have been infiltrated into Leipzig, led by Russian and Polish émigrés who preached insurrection, aimed at stirring up anarchism – all organised social democrats were to steer well clear of them. The enemy was lurking not only on the right!

In a back room in a pub on the Bayerischer Platz, I got to know a little group who sat and licked their wounds over tea and vodka. One of them had escaped from exile in Siberia, another had just been released from prison in Warsaw. The Polish of my childhood days came in handy, but suspicion remained: was this a spy worming his way in? They argued bitterly about revolution and reform, and by now I no longer lacked the proper vocabulary as I had done in my earliest days in Leipzig. Bernstein and Kautsky were no longer Double-Dutch to me. Bearded men wept for rage at the fact that the Tsar, conducted by the Kaiser and protected by hundreds of police, should have been allowed to set foot on German soil. 'And you stand by and let that happen!' they yelled at me. 'That bloodhound, and you make no attempt to kill him?'

A fiery Polish couple drew me over to their table: Maria and

Tadeusz. She was a student, he a printer by trade, now they were scraping a living as unskilled labourers. Social and national questions, their struggle against Tsar, industrialist, landowner; their allies, if they had any, a priest here and there, and against that, what were we Germans, with the strongest Social Democratic Party in the world and, in Bebel, the most eloquent and skilled parliamentarian, what were we doing for ourselves and for Poland? I think if I had let slip where I sweated out my working day, they would have chased me from their table in an instant.

After endless cups of tea, they lost interest in me. Maria kissed me and said: 'Venn you make rrrevolution, leedle one, you can come back to us!'

CHAPTER 4

Your social background, Herr Linden?

Very kind of you, really, to allow us to stroll as we chat today. Stretch the old bones a bit. I've always loved these early autumn days. The air is still, with the haze breaking up the light and softening the edges of the shadows. Were there always as many weeds growing in the grounds of the clinic? They're head-high over by the fence there. And nobody about – what are they all doing? Ah, now you're laughing.

You're right, there's been little or no mention so far of my father, Felix. Voiciech and he first met on that 13 May 1912; Felix was one of the group representing the firm in Beucha who cut the granite for the Monument. In their freshly washed lightweight overalls, the two of them slid the last block into its crown. Voiciech held the mortar and the trowel at the ready for Clemens Thieme to point the joints. Over there, on our right – the Monument in the morning light. Of course there are visitors already up there, just dots. Guards in yellow overalls, maybe?

The folk in the building trade called the huge flat block roofing the Monument the crowning terrace; they had laid it on top of the upper dome in five layers, three and a half metres thick in all. Often, in my capacity as keeper, I let as many as a hundred visitors up there at a time. Voiciech and his colleagues fitted together its hundred and twenty rectangular blocks, the heaviest of them weighing ten tons. Sometimes he'd clamber across to the outside edge of the scaffolding and look out over the city. He was the highest Leipziger of all, then.

Ah, this weather! An Indian summer. Over there, where the hospital now stands, that was part of the battlefield. Napoleon was still holding this line on 18 October. Open fields for miles around. Now the Monument soars high above the trees in the cemetery and the tower of the chapel. Beautiful, isn't it? I'm grateful to you for this stroll.

But back to May 1912: the date of the ceremony had been set to coincide with Thieme's birthday. Site-foreman Günther, who had been on the job from the start, thumped the wedges away from the keystone, my father pushed from one side, Voiciech from the other. 'Master, our work is done!' cried Günther. A hardy old custom. Now Thieme was by no manner of means a master-craftsman, but a member of the Royal Saxon Cabinet. Without Thieme, though, there would have been no Monument: when funds ran short, he put his private fortune up as a surety. When the Monument Lottery was getting nowhere, he took over the management of it. Thieme cried: 'With God for King and Fatherland, for Kaiser and Reich!' Of course, that riled Voiciech, but he refrained from spoiling the mood of the ceremony by bawling out something like, say, 'Down with all royal riff-raff!'

During the meal given by the League of German Patriots, Voiciech and my father were sat next to each other. Voiciech muttered, 'Madness, madness!' And after a while, 'Dey *mus*' be off deir heads!'

'Who?' asked my father.

Voiciech pointed towards the top table. There sat Thieme with the other officials of the League, next to them the owners of the companies who had made money off the project, Hempel the stonemason from Connewitz, Brüggemann, who had put up the lightning-conductors, Sievers, the head of the carpenters' guild, who had supplied the doors, Leonardo di Pol, who had laid the floors, Rurack the ornamental blacksmith, and so on. The Patriots'

League had laid on clear soup with calves' milk, roast venison with Cumberland sauce, and a cask of beer that the merchant, Katzenstein, broached. 'There was a time,' Dr Spitzner was speaking, 'when this building project served as a solemn exhortation to us for the distant future. Now that we have inserted the final stone into this symbol of a nation's gratitude, a shadow over the splendour of our national honour has been dissipated.' At this, they all leapt to their feet, drew their glasses to their hearts and chorused a triple 'Hip-hip-hurrah!' Voiciech's lips made only the merest suggestion of a movement. For my father, though, it was a great moment. Year after year he had cut blocks of stone for the Monument, the first one and now the last, and there it now stood, a part of him. He could have recited by heart, twenty-six thousand five hundred pieces of granite-work! Near and far, there would never again be a pile to match it. From here on, it was downhill all the way.

They didn't squabble right away, my father and Voiciech. They ate and drank and listened to speeches. The construction work, they heard, had reached this stage without a serious accident, and for that they owed thanks to God and the exemplary safety precautions. Katzenstein the beer-provider twirled the points of his moustache, which boasted a span of forty-six centimetres, a measurement regularly checked and verified. 'A toast to our young Kaiser!', he shouted. Voiciech's memories of the language of his homeland were strong enough for him to suspect Katzenstein for an immigrant from the east. He asked around discreetly and learned that Katzenstein was a furrier and came from Lodz. 'In far-off Sedan' – Katzenstein started to sing, my father joined in. Then Voiciech began to make a stink: 'You been in the army? You'll laugh on the other side of your face if it all starts up again. After all, I bet our enemies would be jealous we got such a fine he-man as you. They're sure to want to steal you!'

'You're crazy!'

'And what are you in the army, then?'

My father had done his service with the sappers, too, dispersed and concentrated charges, neither held any secrets for him, nor any terrors. Drawings of French and Belgian forts had been shown to him with ground plan and cross-sections, he had learned how you could reduce a steep face to a rolling landslide with explosives, how you climbed onto the roof of a fort and wiped out its occupants with a few hand-grenades down their air-shafts. 'I'm an NCO,' answered father Felix. 'Next time we'll knock the hell out o' the French, same as last! Cheers, mate!'

Afterwards, Voiciech and my father stood stiff-legged out in the street, and in a firm voice the sergeant reassured the private that the stronger the Reich, the more likely were its enemies to keep their hands to themselves. 'You a socialist? An' you're helpin' to build the Monument? But you're not a real German, are you?'

'Nah, but I can play at wars for Germany, can't I?'

My father's gesture, in reaching out a hand towards Voiciech's shoulder, wasn't intended to be hearty, but neither was there any aggressive intent, he simply wanted to add emphasis to his words, no more than that; here was an NCO talking to a private, a genuine German to one still working at it, a Leipziger to an incomer. But that's not the way Voiciech understood it at all, and he fiercely knocked the hand away. 'Hey,' said Father, 'steady on, steady on!' Voiciech cursed in a mixture of Polish and German, and finished with a warning in careful Saxon: 'A friendly piece of advice – keep your paws off!' And my father shoved his great quarryman-goalkeeper's mitts in his pockets.

A week later, Voiciech finished his work at the Monument, he wasn't required for fitting out the interior. He went a few hundred metres farther on down the road, where the International Construction Industry Exhibition was beginning to take shape. He helped to mould the foundations for the Hall for Concrete-Work. Next to it rose the Pavilion of Interior Design, the Monument to the Iron Industry and the Architecture and Building Materials Pavilion. To the west of the Monument, the Marienbrunn Garden City was growing up as a model for a healthy living environment. It's still there today. A year later, four million visitors passed through the exhibition, by which time Wolle the building contractor had already sent his dependable workers off to the northern outskirts of Leipzig, and there Voiciech laid the apron in front of the new airship hangar. This hangar was 202 metres long, 67 metres wide and 35 metres high – in present-day Leipzig there isn't a roofed enclosure that's anything like a match for it. When it was opened – by the King, of course – two airships floated over from Potsdam, the *Saxony* and the *Viktoria Luise*, and at the helm of the *Saxony* stood old Count Zeppelin himself. Almost every day – well, when the weather was fine, that goes without saying – an airship droned over the city. There was room in the hangar for two at a time, side by side, and Graf Zeppelin described it as the most modern in the world. Whenever an airship approached, everybody stared skywards, children waved, dogs howled and traffic came to a standstill. Once, when a military airship was sucked up by a gust of wind over Mockau, Voiciech had to grab his horses' heads to stop them shying. Four soldiers of the mooring crew clung on to the ropes in an excess of dutiful zeal. One was hauled into the gondola by an NCO, another hung on to the cables until the airship landed, two lost their nerve and plummeted a hundred and fifty metres. Their names were Friesenhausen and Polster. Ah, yes, when I get started on a story!

Wouldn't have imagined the grounds of the clinic were as big as this. The blocks of the new housing estate in Lössnig – a mindless wall, like a penitentiary. And over there, to the left of the winding tower, what do you see? One of these twelve domes that ring Leipzig. Hardly a kilometre away, it's almost as if you could reach out and touch it. I might have known you'd start an argument with me even now. A slag-heap? Don't make me laugh! All right, let's turn back.

It's all very well for you to complain that I didn't answer any of your questions on the way back. No wonder: I point out the dome to you, and you tell me there isn't one there. Now, I don't want to turn the tables on you and insist that *I*'m the one who should be wearing the white coat . . . Fine, all right. But just don't get worked up if, after such a put-down, I'm not immediately ready and eager to tell you about my father. The coffee will do me good.

Felix Linden played in goal for VfB Leipzig. During our walk earlier on, we could see the roof of Lokomotive's grandstand, that's where the VfB, the 'club for active games', used to play, the first German National Champions. Maybe one of these days I'll be able to hear from my cell the fans braying their defiant 'Two, four, six, eight . . . !' If I say that Leipzig's best times were before the First World War, then that applies to football, too: VfB were champions of Germany three times. First of all they played in Lindenau, where they had rented dressing-room 1. Number 2 served Britannia 1899, which, at the outbreak of war, changed its name, with true patriotic consciousness, to Leipzig FC, the Leipziger Fussballverein 1899. A few other clubs from those days: there was Olympia, with their own stadium in Gohlis, the United, or Eintracht 1904, and the 'friends of sport' 1900, in Connewitz, Fortuna 1902 in Paunsdorf, the 'Valiants', Wacker, and Lipsia 1893, Leipzig's oldest established football club, in Eutritzsch. Felix was Leipzig's first ever goalkeeper to dare to punch the ball clear. The idea of wearing gloves would

48

never have occurred to him, his knuckles were iron-hard. He never gave me a hiding; that was mother's job, and, anyway, 'One single clout, an' my kid would ha' been a cripple.'

My father seldom attended the club's social evenings in the Thüringer Hof, but he never missed training. There were two goalkeepers, equally good; the other, Dr Ernst Raydt, was a barrister at the County and District Court, his office was in the Barfussgässchen – Barefoot Lane. He dived more elegantly than my father, and ventured farther out of his goal, but in a goalmouth mêlée, Father was braver. One kept goal like an academic, the other like a prole from the quarry.

For the Cup Final against the German Football Club of Prague on 31 May 1903, in Hamburg, Dr Raydt was preferred to Father because of his doctorate and because he advised the club in legal matters without charging a fee. Anyway, Father's employer was being difficult; orders were piling up, and here was somebody wanting Saturday and Monday off? Football? So what was football anyway? Was the world going crazy?

Felix Linden had kept goal in an earlier round, when VfB Leipzig beat Altona 93 by six goals to three. In Hamburg, Dr Raydt floated about the penalty area with obvious relish, only twice did the ball beat his dive, but his team-mates hit the target seven times. When the Champions returned home, there was none of this nonsense of them being met by a brass band, no speech by the Mayor, no triumphal procession through the streets of the city. The team from Prague travelled with them in the same train and were entertained to schnitzel and asparagus in the Thüringer Hof; my father had just gone on shift.

Of course, Felix Linden did gymnastics, too, he exercised with dumb-bells, putted the shot and did all the exercises in the gym. Judging by all my mother's photos and raptures, he was a good-looking man, respected in his trade, and earned a reasonable wage. In his capacity as a goalkeeper – his boss gradually came round to allowing him to work a shift early or to make it up later – he travelled more widely than most labourers of his day: he kept goal in Liegnitz, Stettin, Göttingen, Hanau and Karlsbad.

In the spring of 1913, his Klara, with head bowed shyly over her plate, whispered, 'Felix, maybe there'll be three of us for Christmas.' He picked her up and carried her three times round the table.

And what was Voiciech Machulski doing? He grumbled, he sulked. Leipzig was getting richer, swankier with each passing day, its main railway station was the biggest in Europe, the German National Library was growing, this was being inaugurated, that was being unveiled, the other was being founded, the bourgeoisie even seemed to have come to terms with social democracy, as it would with some irritating bout of athlete's foot. Old Bebel, sapped of his strength and not a little disillusioned, had been laid in his coffin far from his homeland, and there was less and less talk of revolution in party meetings. But the contributions to party funds still rolled in merrily.

I, too, Voiciech Machulski, had imagined many things quite differently. Red flags would have fluttered on top of the Monument at the inauguration ceremony, and I would have had the warriors' helmets re-chiselled into workers' caps, their swords into shovels. Not 'God with us', but 'Brothers, hand in hand in common cause' should have graced the front. Sometimes I would mutter darkly to Erna: 'We'll have to blow the lot up!' Then she'd be more generous with the melted fat she poured over the potatoes and make some braised beef-olives rolled in cabbage, my favourite dish. 'If we had children,' Erna would say, blaming herself. She reckoned that if I had kids to look after, I wouldn't come up with such wild ideas.

I didn't stick any job for long. I'd insist on stopping work on the dot, and on Sunday bonuses, I stood up for others more than for myself, and then on many a Friday I'd hear they wouldn't be needing me the following Monday. I greased axles on the trams, was a furnace-man in a gasworks, a driver for a circus. One great demonstrative deed, but what? I barrowed feed into the cages, barrowed dung out. Every day, every hour almost, I saw more masts, banners and flags going up in the city. One significant action – princes by the drove would be coming to the unveiling of the Monument to the Battle of the Nations, the Kaiser, ambassadors from Russia and Austria and all the crowned heads of Germany, they would all stream into the big chamber under the cupola – suddenly the idea came to me, not of them parading in but fleeing out, in terror, head over heels down the steps, perhaps jumping in panic into the ornamental lake, losing their helmets and sashes, tearing off their medal-bedizened coats, Grand Dukes and Crown Princes and Field-Marshals, the Kaiser in their midst, a laughing-stock in the eyes of the whole world, if only . . .

I wandered over from the stables for the zebra and the horses to the bears, the tigers and the lions, looked into drowsy eyes and tried to picture the way they would flash to life if, instead of a keeper, a horde of royalty with flags and helmet-plumes strutted before them; if, instead of iron bars, all that was between them was empty Monument air.

There was no time to lose. The night before the ceremony, I was going to manoeuvre a pack of lions into a trailer, ferry them out and decant them into the Monument; by the time it was opened next morning, lions would be rampaging around the crypt, lolling on the laps of the stone giants, jumping up to the arched windows, tails lashing.

With the very idea itself came the fear of it. I, a labourer, alone and unaided, acting on no orders or instructions, was putting a spoke in the wheel of history. It wasn't fear of punishment in the event of being caught that tormented me: I'd be put in a German prison, where discipline and order ruled, not hauled off to Siberia with a bullet in my leg and the lash on my back. I could see myself standing before the judge, thundering out a speech, saw the nobility tumbling down the steps, with the lions snapping at their heels, the whole patriotic commotion ending in a morass of ridicule. Simba, the biggest and strongest of our lions, stared me in the eye, unmoved.

There were ten days to go till the opening ceremony. I busied myself every morning in the predators' cages, chatted to their keepers and watched carefully all their movements as they opened and closed doors and assembled the cat-walk. If I was to get the lions to the Monument at the dead of night, it had to be done without a racket, I couldn't drive through the streets with a frenzied horde in the cage-wagon, and even in the Monument itself the lions would have to be quiet at first. It just couldn't be done without help.

I suddenly thought of Maria and Tadeusz, the pair of Polish activists. I inquired in the pub where I had first met them, and was told the émigrés had moved on – where, nobody knew. For three whole evenings I combed one pub after another, peering into bearded faces, at ascetic lips, under wild shocks of hair, behind steel-rimmed spectacles. Landlords with tattooed arms, filling batteries of beer-glasses, listened impassively, suspiciously: a spy? In a pub on the corner of Kochstrasse I finally ran them to earth; Tadeusz was bending, eyes screwed up, over a billiard table, Maria, prodding the air with a self-opinionated finger, sat in deep debate among a tight knot of people. Tadeusz unhurriedly completed his game and the three of us huddled at an empty table, heads close together; I dangled the bait right away: 'I've come up with something!'

51

It was exactly to the taste of both of them. 'Dis deed vill carry avay de masses!' breathed Maria. Tadeusz asked at once: 'Bot do you know anytink about lions?' How was the Monument guarded? How many would be needed to take out the guards? Tadeusz went off into the details, Maria into the overall strategy: the monarchs as hostages, and the promise squeezed out of them to disband their armies and scrap their fleets! Tadeusz came to a decision: 'You make reconnoitre of Monument guards. Is now ten o'clock, tomorrow four o'clock is firrrst rrreporrrt!' Maria lashed down her headscarf even more tightly.

I had summoned up demons; even if I had wanted to exorcise them now, it would have been impossible. Whenever there had been a struggle for freedom in Germany, there had been no lack of Polish hired heroes. Next evening, Maria, Tadeusz and a half-dozen of their friends were sitting at the circus ringside watching Simba jumping through the hoop and his harem squatting on their haunches, begging. Afterwards, behind a wagon, two of the conspirators admitted that that was the first time in their lives they had seen a real lion and that they had imagined them to be much yellower. Maria reported having seen not a living soul around the colossus, only the moon reflecting peacefully in the lake. In sinister tones, Tadeusz said, 'Anyone want pull out, is still time!' No one backed out.

I couldn't sleep at nights. Erna cooked swedes in smoked bacon-fat, I let them go cold on my plate. On my way to and from work I had to cross the city centre. The old city hall was decked to the roof with spruce-twigs. The central carriageway through the Augustusplatz was lined with rows of Ionic columns resting on golden tripods, and in the evenings flames came out of the tops; the gas-pipes fuelling them were wound round with greenery. The street in front of the new city hall was hedged with artificial cypresses, golden fruit shimmering among their branches. The Gewandhaus was barely recognisable behind all the foliage. I wandered through those streets, a renegade. If most of the passers-by had known what operation I had set in motion, they would have lynched me on the spot.

Tadeusz allotted the various tasks and responsibilities. In the definitive version of the plan, all that was left for me to do was to help build the barred cat-walk and herd the lions into the wagons, drive a wagon to the Monument, and there help again to assemble the cat-walks. Tadeusz kept himself centre-stage, while Maria was to

52

cover our retreat, obliterate our tracks, you might say, to put out the light behind us.

So there I stood now, Voiciech Machulski, Viktor Machul, born beyond the black forests, arrived in Leipzig still no more than a child, reservist in the Royal Saxon army, up to my neck in a plot which, if Maria was to be believed, was about to unleash world revolution. Who was first to burst into the Bastille? Who was first over the gates of the Winter Palace? Perhaps, one day, it would be there in black and white in all the history books: the idea for the lion-attack on Europe's assembled monarchs came from Voiciech Machulski. I inspected myself in the mirror, the round head with the seal's ears, the straw-blond beard, the liquid blue eyes. I had just turned thirty, *Pschakreff*!

Erna fussed around me, asked, 'What's bothering you?' I confessed everything, she wouldn't believe it. 'Viktor, pet, you thinking up something like that? Did you maybe read about it somewhere?'

'No, it's my own idea, really it is.'

She sniffled. 'And there was I, thinking you had another woman.'

The night was dark and still – ah, nonsense, there were no dark, still nights; illuminations were being tested out on window-sills all over the place, licensing hours had been extended, every hotel was full to overflowing, the spanking new Central Station was still a main attraction for many Leipzig folk; they strolled along the concourse as on a boulevard. 'Get your lovely 'ot sausages 'ere!' yelled the men with the shiny trays slung round their necks. The ladies of Goldfinch Lane were booked out.

After the evening show I remained behind to stand guard over the cages. I put out most of the lights, sat down on a box in the lion-house, waited. My knees twitched as if from electric shocks. Punctual to the minute, Tadeusz came through the doorway, wearing a black coat, black scarf, black cap and black gloves, and as deadly earnest as the avenging angel in person. He half-raised a hand in a kind of blessing, and this was at the same time the signal to start. Behind him, his helpers slipped in and, without a word, set about assembling the cat-walk. Simba shook his beautiful mane. The twitching in my limbs had gone, action absorbed every thought and dispelled all fears. In less time than it took even in a gala performance, we screwed together all the arched bars, I prodded one of the lionesses with a pole, she rose with a yawn and ambled off. Another followed her, a third, the fourth, the first cage-wagon could be closed now and already I was harnessing my horses between the

53

shafts. At that moment, Maria rushed through the curtain and gasped, 'Bloody gymnasts at Monument!'

Tadeusz raised his hand again as a signal to stop, we swarmed round Maria and heard that gymnasts with flags and bands had assembled out there, torches blazing and belching smoke, some kind of preliminary celebration was under way.

'There was nothing about that in the papers!' I put in my miserable tuppence-worth. Tadeusz looked around, brooding. 'Vill myself make rrreconnaissance, vit' Voiciech!'

We took the tram out to the Monument, and there we saw the whole fine mess: gymnasts in front of the Monument, gymnasts around the lake, on the staircases, gymnasts *en masse*, marching in a circle along the crown of the embankment, singing, 'Gymnasts, into the fray, into th' arena make your way!' I stared at the teeming white swarm and then glanced at my watch: time was slipping away. Inside and out, the Monument was flooded with glaring light, there would not be a moment's peace here this night. 'Call it off, do we?' I asked. Then I spied a tall man, waving the flag of the VfB Leipzig, Felix Linden, quarryman and goalkeeper. We went back to the circus by the next tram and shooed the lions back into their cages. I sat down again on my feed-box.

It was the restless night before the inauguration, the crowned heads were in town, which was of course full of police, of both the instantly recognisable and the secret varieties. Next day, Leipzigers and their visitors were up betimes, as were Felix Linden and many gymnasts, but not Voiciech Machulski, who, after completing his guard-duty in the lion-house, pushed off home to Alexanderstrasse and pulled the blankets over his head so as to shut out the sounds of bands and music-corps fanfaring, drumming, tootling the citizenry of Leipzig into the proper patriotic frame of mind. Felix Linden was among the runners of the last stage of the enormous relays that raced into Leipzig from all points of the compass. Graf Zeppelin had sent the first man on his way from the shores of Lake Constance, from Strasbourg over six thousand runners carried the baton along the twelve-hundred-kilometre route. One relay trotted in from Waterloo, others from farthest Upper Silesia and from Tauroggen on the Baltic. Forty thousand German men had done the great cross-country marathon in nine races, not counting the many minor runs off the beaten track organised by schools and clubs. All Germany was going at the trot. By comparison, today's jogging mania is pretty small beer.

Felix Linden was a member of the team on Route IV, on the last stage north from Borna. He wore a white shirt with a black belt, and the VfB badge on the chest, white shorts reaching down over his knees, and long black cotton socks. He was able to take his time, for a marshal had called to him that the relay was five minutes ahead of schedule, so he jogged comfortably along his three hundred metres, paying no heed to the shouts of the schoolchildren urging him to get a move on. Far off in the haze stood the Monument, while on the right, copses hid the little estate and modest castle of Fürchtegott von Lindenau, which I hadn't yet demolished. The briquette-works poured out their smoke, and the fields stretched away bare into the distance. On top of the rise, where today the Espenhain works pollute the air and the water, a horse-drawn wagon, decorated with greenery, collected up the runners who had already completed their stint and brought them citywards. As they rode along, they sang: 'The God who made the iron grow, he wahanted no slaves.'

In due course, as a result of organisation that would have done credit to a military general staff, the last nine runners in this nationwide rally converged simultaneously on the Monument, and there the Kaiser and the King of Saxony received the batons from them; an adjutant laid them in a box – no detail had been overlooked.

In my archives you will find the *Illustrierte Zeitung* of 23 October 1913. It's packed with reports, drawings and prints of the official opening ceremony. The leading article is a paean to German yearnings for a unified Reich, an ideal stretching in one continuous blood-red thread from Walther von der Vogelweide through the Battle of Leipzig to Königgrätz and Versailles, from the bloodbath in the Teutoburg Forest to Sedan.

It's difficult for me to describe these pictures to you, take a look at them for yourself. Teeming crowds with flags and sashes, the crowned heads, with Thieme in the middle, striding down the flight of steps, the pavilion of honour, under whose canopy Thieme delivered his address; this whole scene has been captured by Special Artist W. Gause from Vienna. Similarly, the decor in the Goethe Strasse outside the Royal Palace, the dedication of the Russian Church by Grand Prince Cyril, the celebration at the Schwarzenberg Memorial in the park at Meusdorf, attended by the Heir Apparent to the Austrian Throne, Archduke Franz Ferdinand, the condemned man of Sarajevo. In the foyer of the Gewandhaus, after the royal banquet, Prince William of Sweden presented the gentlemen of his entourage to the Kaiser, and this scene was preserved for eternity by Commissioned Artist F. Schwormstädt of Munich. Based on water-colours by local artists, reproductions of the festive illuminations were produced in yellow and red prints, a highly creditable performance by the graphics industry. Germany was great, all seemed well with the world. All Leipzig was out and about, Felix Linden always in the thick of it, his wife rather less so, because of her now heavily swollen womb. Buying baking powder? Then always ask for Backin, to be sure you get the genuine Dr Oetker Baking Powder. The name Backin is a registered trade mark and may not be . . . I'm sorry, I slipped into the adverts in the *Illustrierte Zeitung* just then.

What was Voiciech doing? Sulking. The capitalist system just refused to collapse, indeed, on the contrary, it was building one factory and one symbolic pile after another. In the bowels of the Central Station, the site already stood prepared for the construction of an underground platform, from which trains would pull out for the Bavarian Station, on the other side of the city centre; work was to begin in two, perhaps three, years. I don't have to remind you that that underground railway was never built, and never will be.

Voiciech slept through most of 18 October, woke in the afternoon, when, naturally, inevitably, some group of Patriots, gymnasts or student duelling fraternity was marching past, singing. In his mind's eye, he saw himself, Maria and Tadeusz and thousands of the proletariat marching on the city centre, from Lindenau and Plagwitz and across the bridges, throwing up barricades, and workers advancing from the north, south and east, engineers, leather-workers, the women from the textile-works, miners from the Borna coalfield, the best printers and bookbinders in the world, while at the railway station not so much as a signal moved: Germany's aristocracy was caught in a trap! He could have wept for sheer frustration.

That evening, the circus gave its last performance, and after it Voiciech did another turn as night-watchman at the cages; sullenly he carved his VM into a wooden post. The lion, it occurred to Voiciech, was the emblem of Leipzig, it would have been marvellous if the lions had occupied the Monument, even if the proletarians wouldn't. Or, for that matter, the monstrosity as an outsize lion-cage, why not in fact as a zoo, with monkeys clambering all over the outside, till the whole thing was smothered in shit?

Almost midnight, and there stood Tadeusz in the doorway, dressed in black like Mephistopheles. 'Vot about lions?' he asked, as he theatrically threw open his cycling-cape.

'They're being loaded up tomorrow, going off the day after.'

'You vit' us next night? Monument is empty!'

'Whew,' admitted Voiciech, 'you're a cool customer!'

On 19 October the visitors to the celebrations were leaving town, and Voiciech helped to transport the big top and the ring, the camels and mules, horses and lions to the goods station. Now and again he caught a glimpse of Maria and Tadeusz at the railing. In the early evening, on his way home, he met columns of street-sweepers, clearing up the remains of the triumph, greenery and paper-chains, special editions of the newspapers with pictures of the Kaiser, and leaflets advertising the Royal Saxon Regional Lottery. For one last time, the illuminations were on, the remains of the candles were, you might say, being tested to destruction. Hostelries were closing early, landlords and staff could hardly keep their eyes open, and the takings were in and counted. An ideal night for the lions to take over the Monument. As he chewed his blood-sausage sandwich, Voiciech considered this new variation: the lions would be liberating the Monument.

Once again the people of Leipzig were out and about as the pylons on the Augustusplatz spewed their tails of fire, and then the gas-tap was finally turned off. The stearine nightlights, only later to be known as Hindenburg-lights, guttered and died on the window-ledges of the university, the Opera House and the Café Français. Voiciech turned into Blücherstrasse and, behind an advertising pillar, he came upon his Polish comrades. Fog surged round the gas-lamps, as befits any conspiracy worthy of the name.

It all seemed much more straightforward than two nights ago: the lions were already ensconced in their cage-wagon, and only it and the one containing the cat-walk had to be manoeuvred out of the station yard. Unfortunately, they would have to tie up and gag the watchman. You can't have a revolution without some violence. I, Voiciech Machulski, was imbued with that calm that overcomes you when you have already cut off your own retreat, out of the conviction that to do otherwise you'd be a coward and a knave. Maria and Tadeusz were the driving-force, fair enough, but without my local knowledge and expertise, they'd have been up the creek. I smiled smugly to myself: you revolutionaries just can't manage without *some* help from the workers, can you!

The fog was thickening. I pulled the carthorses out of their horse-box and they snorted as the smell of the lions hit their nostrils. Deftly, I fingered my VM into the hair on their necks, and brushed it away again, the way you obliterate fingerprints nowadays. Working by touch rather than sight, I harnessed them up, released the brake, a quiet 'Hah!' and the wagon carrying the beasts eased gently away. Far away, over on the passenger platforms, a homeward-bound male-voice choir was meanwhile working its word-perfect way through every last verse of 'At the well out by the gate.'

In the meantime, Tadeusz and his associates had hauled the wagon with the cat-walk out of a shed and hitched horses to it. Tadeusz swung himself up onto the box-seat and raised his whip. My wagon jolted over railway tracks and I looked warily to right and left for fear of being run down by a locomotive. Maria flitted past, hissing something at me, probably a curse on all adversaries, or the reassurance that victory would be ours. A gas-lamp cast a dull light on a metal hoarding extolling the qualities of SUN briquettes.

Fifty metres on, and Tadeusz, the idiot, rammed his wagon into the side of mine. A crash of splintering wood, roaring, whinnying, my chestnuts reared up, and then I saw – and my blood ran cold – a shadow flitting away under them, a scurrying, a rushing, striding paws, and finally a tail-tuft like a disappearing dot: a lion was loose, making a terrified dart for freedom, and then Simba, too, roared, he let out the call of the wild, that thunderous bellow from oxygen-swollen lungs, the king of the beasts was leaving no one in any possible doubt that he was now rising up from his life of slavery. He swept down a ramp, took a defiant, rearing swipe at a street-lamp, gave one final roar and then the darkness swallowed him up.

I had drawn up my legs and wrapped my arms around myself, making myself as small as possible; totally inconspicuous, I squatted up on the box-seat, as if trying to show everyone, and especially every lion, just look how harmless I am! I had even dropped my whip, my only weapon, however inadequate. The horses just stood there, trembling, their heads back, their eyes starting in terror. Seconds passed, my heart hammering through every one of them. I was quaking. I didn't pray, or weep, or curse. Running away was out of the question, I was incapable of defending myself or reacting in any way at all. I just sat there and had a real good quake.

Just as well that it was Tadeusz, the great revolutionary himself, who had buggered everything up. Maria tore me out of my catalepsy and down from my driving-seat, dragging me behind the end coalshed. 'All eight lions gone!' she gasped, snorted, sobbed.

'Bloody shitty bloody driver, you!'

Tadeusz was almost the commanding officer again, when he announced: 'Meession accomplished, comrades! All to bed, immediate! Death to bourgeoisie!' Before I went home, I put the horses back in their stall. By going home the long way, through the Waldstrasse estate, I gave the bloodbath of the following hours a wide berth. During that time, the lions advanced, along the flank of the railway sidings, down Blücherstrasse. Two leapt on the backs of horses, one dived through the windows of an omnibus, one charged into the foyer of the Hotel Blücher and sent the terrified guests scurrying to their rooms. On top of the bar, in a welter of shattered glasses, it made itself comfortable, its swishing tail scything pickled eggs, mustard and meat-balls onto the tiled floor. From the kitchen, a waiter raised the alarm to incredulous policemen.

Thirteen men from the 8th District police station set out at dead of night on a lion-hunt. They roused the circus-folk from their beds, and these lured two lionesses back into the cages with great difficulty and fresh horsemeat cutlets. The other lions, with Simba at the head, went simply berserk. The citizens of Leipzig were sleeping off their black-white-and-red patriotic skinful, so no one came to any harm. Torches smouldered, bloodcurdling calls of the hunters and the terrified hunted creatures rang through the night. Shots cracked out. The next morning, thirteen policemen, eleven of them in spiked helmets, had their photographs taken with their catch: they had bagged six lions, Simba last of all.

Our revolutionary exploit ended up as a bit of a curiosity, the Leipzigers noted it with some relish and amusement in special editions of their newspapers and in their periodicals. The background details remained shrouded in mystery. Tadeusz and Maria fell out over the wording of a declaration by means of which, with fanfares of publicity, they would have conceitedly claimed responsibility. Above all, they could not agree on a name for their group: 'The Battle of the Nations Goes On!', or 'Red October', 'Avengers of the People' or 'Sword of the Left'. And so the possible dawn of a possible revolution trickled away down the drain of memory as a grotesque farce that turned out well in the end. The owner of the Hotel Blücher, not short of business acumen, renamed his establishment The Lion. And if it hasn't yet fallen down, then that's its name to this day.

A week later, Voiciech reported to the barracks in Gohlis for two months' reserve training – it was purely routine, nobody wanted seriously to believe that war-games could turn into a shooting war. There had been peace for so long, the veterans of that last one, way back when, were now as old as the hills. It seemed to Voiciech as if there had almost always been peace up till then. And since then, there's been constant war, hasn't there?

CHAPTER 5

Did you have any childhood traumas?

On the morning of 20 October 1913 Klara Magdalena Linden, or Klärchen, as she was known, was, along with a neighbour, pulling a handcart up Gletscherstein Strasse. Felix had impressed upon her that she wasn't to lift anything, or carry anything, and was to lie down for an hour or so after lunch, for nobody could be more pregnant than Klärchen was. The midwife had carried out a reconnaissance, and was unstinting in her exclamations of praise and admiration: the child was lying just splendidly.

Up near the 'lopped popple', the women found what they were looking for, brushwood; it had been used for the patriotic decorations and then thrown in a heap. They regarded it as unclaimed property and loaded it up, thinking that not only might it come in handy for strewing on the graves of their own dear departed, it might also be offered for sale at the cemetery gates or on some street corner. They might, of course, be poaching on the preserves of the cemetery gardeners, who maychance – that was their word – could call the police? But half a Mark for a barrow-load wasn't to be sneezed at. So what about it?

What does 'maychance' mean? It's a rich local word that means something like 'possibly', it's made up of 'maybe' and 'by chance', run together. Well, anyway, on that October morning, as I was saying: the Monument stood in all its glory in the cold light. The wind had driven the clouds away to the east and swept all the leaves and bits of paper off the paths. Ducks dropped in to settle on the lake, not yet accustomed to being fed here; the might and dignity of the surroundings did nothing to encourage such familiarities. As usual, there was no shortage of visitors, a grammar-school teacher from Glaucha stood by the temples to the dead, at the north end of the lake, and drew the attention of his pupils to their bold configuration; completely innovative it was, he said, gigantic, in the best sense of the word, the expression of inspired architectural thought. 'See for yourselves,' he declared, while my mother gathered up spruce-twig bargains, 'not a single Gothic ogive, no Romanesque curves, no Classical frieze, no conventional columns, and yet how great must have been the temptation to indulge in the usual stylistic borrowings! Where is genuine originality still to be found? Make careful note of these names, for I shall question you on them in an oral test in class: Bruno Schmitz for the design, Clemens Thieme who translated it into reality. Lehmann, repeat!' Klara heard this with only half an ear, for she was listening within herself, where the gentle stretching was giving way to violent spasms, then she dropped her twigs and, through the involuntary rush of all the breath from her body, said, 'Hertha, listen, that was . . . I've just had a contraction, oh God, oh dear God!' And her neighbour: 'Right, out with half of the twigs, then you sit yourself on the rest, like a nice soft bed, and I'll wheel you home'.

Awkwardly, Klara Linden took her seat, with knees spread, which was no problem under ankle-length skirts. Her neighbour unhurriedly wobbled her barrow down towards Stötteritz, sympathetic glances met the mother-to-be lying there, a little pale, but in no noticeable distress. 'This is it,' she thought, and for a full quarter of an hour she thought nothing else than 'This is it!' It caused her no fear, but joy, albeit a rather tired joy. At her front door, she was hoisted out by eight willing hands, four arms half-supported, half-shoved her up the stairs, someone was on the spot to rush off for the midwife, someone to heat the stove and borrow pans for hot

62

water. Somebody had beef-tea on the stove, known even in humblest Saxon circles as *bullyong*, and they fed the labouring mother a cup of this bouillon, spoonful by spoonful. A whole tenement was getting itself ready for a birth to happen, an event that roused curiosity, sympathy and even the odd lecherous speculation. The midwife set to work, praised Frau Linden for her co-operation, comforted her after a cry of pain, wiped sweat, pressed, massaged, helped coffee down her throat – let's be quite specific, real *ground* coffee – and then, shortly after noon, something slid into her trained hands, slippery, with a wrinkled bum and an old man's face, squawking at once; the midwife held it up and pronounced the answer to what was now the most vital question: 'A boy!'

A butter-soft, child's-play delivery, then, nothing to burden my little soul, or, in more fashionable terms, induce neuroses. No existential Angst or traumas of a marriage on the rocks, for example, were transmitted by my mother to her offspring, I had slipped easily from the gill-stage into the lung-stage without mental scars from fears of impending war, no forceps birth had instilled in me a terror of torture, I was fifty-one centimetres long and weighed a few grams over six pounds, and that was considered a good starting-weight. When father Felix came home, Klara smiled at him and said again, 'A boy.' My father sniffed as he gently laid his great paws on my mother's cheeks, then he drew back the blanket over the laundry basket in which I lay, eyes screwed up, little hands still trembling from the excitement of having ventured the great leap from the sea of fluid in the womb onto dry land. And the second thing my mother said was, 'Well, there he is then, our Freddie.' Four weeks later, I was baptised, without a hitch, Alfred Johannes.

As an infant, I lacked for nothing. My mother suckled me till I was sated, I suffered no more from nappy-rash than any other child. On Sundays, my parents together pushed a high-wheeled pram through the cemetery and round the Monument, through the little wood at Stötteritz, too, where I saw my first snow; the year 1914 had by then already begun.

Felix quarried stone in Beucha, what else. North of Leipzig, work had started on building a hospital complex, lavishly laid out in open country, with possibilities for further expansion, and named after St George. In the spring, my father was called up for reservist training: four weeks, they'd soon pass, especially with week-end leave. He and his fellows stormed through ditches and over obstacles on the Bienitz Heath, blasted out paths and piled up sandbags and erected steel defence shields between them, the latest development in military technology. On the march back to camp, Felix could make out on the southern horizon the silhouette of the Monument, and he knew: a thumb-breadth to the left of that, and there were Klara and Freddie. The soldiers sang as they marched, 'Gently sank the sun in the heavens, a blackbird, I heard it sihinging, in the far distance rihinging . . .', a song rich in descants and so-called flourishes. The second verse began, 'Sleep well, sleep well, my little darling.' Felix sang that with something akin to fervour.

He handed in his uniform at the quartermaster's, and his boss welcomed him back with a raise. Klara hummed and hawed, he gently raised her chin, but still she avoided his gaze, but finally plucked up the courage to tell him, 'It's clicked again, love.'

At that, Felix scratched the back of his head, this came as a surprise and no mistake. Well, so what, others had ten or twelve children and they weren't starving, and anyway, maybe it wasn't such a bad thing to have two in quick succession? Two birds with the one stone, if you like? 'But after this one, we take care!' By this time, he was playing in the VfB veterans' team.

In these July days, I'd lie on a rug on the meadow behind the Monument, not a stitch on, above me the clouds and the figures of warriors, and I'd point up at them and chuckle. Summer clouds and bearded sentries, dandelions and daisies, the last summer of an era, as everybody knows today, with the benefit of hindsight. My father climbed up the embankment and laid his hand on the lowest blocks. He peered at the joints: you couldn't find cleaner work anywhere. Some bloke with a Polish name had wanted to have the whole pile down at the topping-out ceremony – daft. My father climbed up on a ledge, looked down, on the carriages in the Preussen Strasse, and up, straight into the downcast eyes of the stone guardians.

That dry, sun-bright summer! In the shadow of the Monument, an international exhibition of books and graphics was opened by the King of Saxony, another world exhibition in my city, for Leipzig was number one in these trades. Many countries had put up pavilions. The Russian one was a replica of the Kremlin, in garish red and yellow, and above it the double eagle strutted in splendour.

I don't have to explain here how war gnawed its way forward from the shots fired at Sarajevo. Felix Linden trusted his Kaiser and his King to sort everything out. Not so Voiciech Machulski. Wherever he went he engaged in heated debate, and pushed forward to read every placard. War, war – and no revolution? On one of the first evenings in August, Comrade Machul reported to the city bureau of his party and asked for orders, only to be told to calm himself and go home, they were waiting for instructions from headquarters.

On the stairs, just next to the lavatory door, a man was squatting on the window-sill, his cap pulled low over his eyes. 'Tadeusz, it's you!' said a startled Voiciech. 'What are you doing here?' He drew him into the kitchen and was given, in a few terse words and quick gestures, to understand that Tadeusz was on the run. He had campaigned against Tsarism at a time when Russia was Germany's ally and the Tsar himself had been regarded as the Kaiser's beloved cousin, so the authorities hereabouts had looked askance upon him. Now all the papers, including the social democrat ones, were proclaiming the Tsarist monster as the arch-enemy, ready to lash out at Germany. Yet this didn't automatically confer on Tadeusz the status of a friend, he was now regarded as an inimical foreigner; perhaps he was even a spy? Were not convoys of gold being transported at speed and dead of night clear across the Reich from France to Russia, or maybe it was the other way round. Hadn't French aircraft been sighted over Nuremberg? 'Hell, Tadeusz,' moaned Voiciech dully, 'and where've you hidden Maria?'

She had found refuge with friends in the eastern outskirts, Tadeusz wanted to fetch her out of there as soon as he had found somewhere for them to lie low. And then they'd be off and away to Sweden, or Switzerland.

Erna came back from her shopping, and seemed only slightly startled when she heard who the guest was. 'Aha, the chauffeur to the lions!' She cooked potatoes and cabbage with caraway, dripping and Liebig's meat extract, thickened up with flour. 'That'll put hair on your chest,' was Voiciech's commendation as he tucked in. Among all the ideas they chewed over and spat out that evening was the one that Maria and Tadeusz should mingle with the staff of the Russian stand at the World Exhibition, take advantage of the immunity they undoubtedly enjoyed and make their exit via a neutral country. But supposing they were interned along with them? Or the Tsarist secret service picked up their trail? A distinct non-starter, that, they decided. Or they might ask the priest at the Russian Church to hide them?

Tadeusz spent the night on the sofa in the kitchen, swathed in the aroma of cabbage. In the morning, Voiciech and Tadeusz set off for the exhibition grounds: perhaps the solution to the problem would present itself on the spot? A crowd had gathered at the Russian pavilion, fists were being shaken, curses being spat out. The doors were locked, so seething patriots dragged a ladder over, clambered up and dismembered the double eagle with axes. Tadeusz and Voiciech slipped away to take stock of the situation on a bench in front of the Monument to the Battle of the Nations. Over the ticket-office hung a notice: 'Closed for technical reasons.' Voiciech looked up to the figures of the warriors, he felt a certain fellowship with them, they weren't rejoicing, 'On to victory over France!' and waving their swords in the air, they didn't want to give perfidious Albion a bloody nose, they weren't swearing Nibelungen-like loyalty to anyone. For them, there had been enough dead for once and for all. The furies of war on either side of St Michael snorted as they had always done.

'There's still the priest,' murmured Voiciech. The church doors, too, were locked. Workmen were busy boarding over the inscription detailing how many Austrians, Prussians, Swedes and of course Russians had fallen in the great battle. Within the walls of the New St John's Cemetery, the two held their last round of discussions. At the grave of the wounded French who then died in Leipzig hospitals in 1870/71 they took their leave, and each walked off towards a different future. A few days later, the postman brought call-up papers for Viktor Machul. Of Maria and Tadeusz, nothing has been heard since.

Voiciech's squad commander was sergeant Felix Linden. The old familiarity between workmates was gone, through clenched teeth Voiciech addressed my father with 'Yes, sergeant, no, sergeant.' A week after their enlistment, they stood on the sweat-soaked Bienitz Heath, the Monument to the Battle of the Nations lowered unmistakable behind all the towers and spires. 'Is it goin' to be pulled down now, sarge?' asked Voiciech, all innocence. 'I mean, it *was* put up because of the Russians bein' comrades in arms, wasn't it?'

'Machine-gun fire from the left!' was my father's quick-witted reply. 'Flat on your face!'

The railway carriages they climbed into had just come back from the Belgian border and were chalked with slogans: 'Paris, in four weeks!' and 'Russian caviar, French champagne, German fists – what a feast!' To the Rhine, to the Rhine, to the German Rhine they rolled, and cast expert eyes over the Cathedral in Cologne. At that moment, they were quarryman and bricklayer again, not NCO and private, and used the familiar 'du' to each other in their conversation as they inspected the joints. The whole thing, in their judgement,

66

was confectioner's work, mere icing-sugar; it'll give constant trouble, and the stone! Just look at that, they'll need to replace their whole cathedral every hundred years. Man! compare that with our granite! They climbed up as high as they could go, and had to admit this thing was a bit higher all right. They would have liked to work out in tons and cubic metres which construction was the more massive, but they didn't have the exact figures for the Cologne one. Voiciech peered up into the cumulus – how long ago was it that he wanted to wrap them in canvas and suspend gondolas from them? To sail, to drift peacefully in them across German countryside to Leipzig, to pull the ripcord over flat fields . . . A dream, one that brought tears to the eyes.

In a quiet sector of the front in the Vosges they laid tracks for a field railway, constructed dug-outs, barbed-wire entanglements, and again Voiciech curried his initials into the hair of long-suffering horses. When letters from home came through the forces' postal service, they read them out to each other, and shared scrupulously fairly what Klärchen or Erna had sent, cigars, tea, gingerbread. Voiciech drove into the hinterland for feed for the horses and for ammunition, and there was always something that 'fell off his cart': a tin of sausage-meat, a loaf, a bag of apples. Together, they celebrated the birth of my little sister Hildrun in February 1915. And my second birthday saw their glasses raised together. That 20 October 1915 was a mild, windless day, both in the Vosges and at the Monument to the Battle of the Nations. My mother wheeled Hildrun and me along crunching gravel paths and pointed upwards: 'Pappy made all these stones, Freddie!' Pappy – I had an indistinct vision of a bitter-smelling moustache; Father had recently been home on leave. Those were the days when my mother often recited a child's poem to me:

> On the town-hall's little tower,
> There sits a little worm
> With a little flower.
> Up comes a little storm,
> And blows the little worm
> With his little flower
> Off the town-hall's little tower.

In the long evenings in the dug-out, my father, like others among his comrades, had taken up carving. No pipe-racks, key-racks and other bric-à-brac taxed his skills, but figures and gadgets, the kind you found in quarries, men with hammers, chisels and stone-saws. My father once set out to carve a football goalkeeper, on one leg as he parried with both fists; he had got well on with it, when the arms broke off. But one thing, out of limewood, was a success – a coat of arms of the three-times German football champions, VfB Leipzig. He hung it up on the wall of the dug-out. And that's where it was left, forgotten during an alert. The Saxon battalion moved farther south and was attached to a Württemberg division which, high up in the Vosges, was to consolidate a mountain salient, the Lingekopf, into a fortress. To be 'temporarily attached' was considered a bad bargain, you were there to pull the chestnuts out of the fire for somebody; the glory and the medals were harvested by the others. Nothing had changed since the Battle of the Nations. Forest hid the mountain from sight, the work progressed unhindered; trenches were blasted out of the rock, niches for storing ammunition and weapons hacked out, and machine-gun positions cast in concrete. On the summit, a bunker was roofed over with six layers of railway rails (Voiciech was in charge of concreting them in) then rubble was spread on top of the lot and rolled flat. 'Fort Lingekopf' was the flashy inscription at the entrance; you can still read it today. Anyone applying just a little imagination will find, to one side of it, the inevitable VM, weathered and overgrown with moss.

The Lingekopf rises almost a thousand metres high, often shrouded in mist and cloud. The French would soon launch a determined attack, that was the general feeling. The officers didn't have to keep driving on the sappers to blast out more and more communication trenches, observation posts and machine-gun nests, to throw up walls and concrete blocks and construct deeper and thicker wire-entanglements. Opposite them lay the *chasseurs alpins*, the French élite. The Württembergers hung a sign on the barbed wire: 'The Lingekopf will be the grave of the French chasseurs!'

On the western ledge of the hilltop, where it falls steeply away into a ravine, Voiciech walled in the last machine-gun nest, arched a dome over it, stamped out a clay mould and cast in it twelve warrior-figures, swords pointing between their feet, heads bowed, each about thirty centimetres tall. He fixed the figures on the outside of the cupola and laid a rectangular slab on top of it, the crown-stone. When he had finished, he drew Felix Linden through the zig-zag of trenches to have a look at it. He stared in astonishment: 'My God, man, our Monument!' Then he read in the concrete under the arched window that was the embrasure:

Here will die:
10,000 Germans
10,000 French

'You're crazy,' the NCO grunted, 'get rid of that at once!'
'Don't you believe I'll be right?'
'If an officer reads that, there'll be hell to pay.'

The next day, a hail of machine-gun fire and shrapnel from the French chipped, carved and frayed away the inscription as the *chasseurs alpins* scrambled up, fired, threw grenades, screamed, killed, bled, died. Voiciech defended himself from inside his Monument until the cooling-jacket on his machine-gun was shot away; he did it out of sweat-drenching fear, not out of blood-lust or hatred. The Germans were pushed back to the very edge of the Lingekopf, the tricolour was raised over the fort, then a heavy barrage cut a swathe through the ranks of the *chasseurs*; most of them had just turned twenty. It was the same as in Murat's cavalry charge a hundred and two years before, when the cream of French soldiery had come within a hairsbreadth of a breakthrough, now Württembergers and Saxons went over to the counter-attack; on that other occasion, they had gone over to the other side in mid-battle, but now . . .

Yes, fine, Doctor, fine. Of course we can have a break for you to read through a report. While you're doing that, perhaps I might have a look at the newspaper . . . I'm afraid I'm going to keep on bringing that up, in spite of your dismissive wave. By the way, that young man who brought you the report just now, I know him from that grim house in the city centre where I spent the first days of my arrest: an employee of that institution that doesn't like to hear its name mentioned. I beg your pardon, of course I'll leave you to read in peace.

Quite. On one point at least we're in agreement: the existence of a flak-shell is not in dispute, 88mm. Anyone else would be only too glad to have nothing to do with such a compromising firecracker, but I, on the contrary . . .

At home? No. There is nothing at all in my home that has anything to do with blasting. *One* flak-shell was found at the Monument, so, from there it's only a short step to the men in yellow . . .

Oh, you have a list of confiscated articles. Nazi literature – I really have all sorts of things in my possession, you know. When Günther Prien's boat was sunk – the famous U-boat commander came from the Waldstrasse suburb here – when he was received by Lord Mayor Freitag, when his former school-mates at the Friedrich Nietzsche School formed a guard of honour for him, when Frau Prien was decorated with the Cross of Honour of German Motherhood – yes, I've kept some photos. Hitler's fiftieth birthday, the city was decorated then, just like for the dedication of the Monument to the Battle of the Nations, crowds streamed onto the open areas near the Elster Bridge, fireworks in the evening – and would you look at that, there are the postcards with the special postmark for the unveiling of the monument to Richard Wagner in March 1934, a philatelic rarity, because the memorial was, as everybody well knows, never built. This list is no doubt correct, I'll sign, no bother.

Well, back to Voiciech Machulski and Felix Linden: the battle raged on at the Lingekopf, again the Germans pushed forward from the eastern edge to the western one – fifty, sixty metres. By now the skeleton of every last tree had been scythed down, every lump of stone churned up over and over again, the trenches caved in. Two thousand Frenchmen hung on the wire, or had been crushed flat in the dug-outs. Under cover of darkness and the mist, groups were detailed to creep across the moon-landscape and pour phenol all over the corpses to stop them rotting; in vain. Swarms of flies descended on them. It was sheer hell. During a break in firing, the Saxon sappers were withdrawn. Down on the Rhine plain near Colmar, they rested up in a hutted camp, where they ate, slept and did running repairs on their uniforms and equipment. Whenever Erna got a letter from Viktor, or Klärchen one from Felix, she would joyfully set off half across the city to visit the other, faces would light up, heads bow over the kitchen table: thank heaven, our menfolk are well! Hugs, tears. I sat on my mother's lap, tried to grab the paper, was given my little piece of wood, my toy duck:

> On the town-hall's little tower,
> There sits a little worm.

I was thriving, though milk and butter were in short supply, and were getting still harder to come by. My mother washed for gentry, as they used to say; breakfast and lunch were part of her wages. While she was out, I stayed with neighbours, played in the yard with other

70

children; later Mother took me with her to folk who had a garden, where I sat under lines of washing and breathed in its fragrance along with that of blossoming trees or ripening fruit. Many a child was a lot worse off.

In the rest-camp at Colmar, my father took up his knife again. Voiciech did him a drawing of one of the horsemen that rode along in a circle inside the dome of the Monument. My father carved a rider at peace, heading homeward after the battle, killing no more, pillaging no more, ready to hand in his shield to the quartermaster, to lie down beside his wife, to eat his fill. No doubt he had scabies. These horsemen high up in the Monument are sick and tired of war, but that naturally hadn't been appreciated either during the building or at the opening. When my father came home on leave, he brought horse and rider with him and presented me with them, but took them back immediately and put them on top of the sideboard, for it would have been a shame if they got broken in my games. If I was sitting on his lap, he would put them carefully into my hand, I'd stroke the wood and say, 'Horsey, horsey.' My father played 'ride a cock horse' with me and I squealed with delight when he pretended I was falling off into the ditch. A father, playing with his boy on his leave from the front line – naturally, in his laughter there was pain, too, and the desire not to let the pain and the fear show through.

When he was going off to the front line again, he carried me all the way to the station platform. When my mother started to cry, I cried along with her and shouted, 'Horsey, horsey!' By that I meant my father, I had forgotten he was called 'Pappy.' He rejoined his unit just as it was moving off, now with its full complement of men and equipment again. The battalion was rolling towards Metz and farther on westwards, and then an evil name came up: Verdun! The fortress of Douaumont had been captured, though strangely enough, taking the village of the same name was proving a much tougher nut to crack; that task was to fall to Saxons.

Snow was falling as the battalion was led up to the front through the Gorges of the Orne. Shells crumped at regular intervals, officers with local knowledge drove the sappers on: keep going, faster! The men were loaded down with rifles, trenching tools, planks, crates of rations, between them they carried rolls of barbed wire and water canisters, they were festooned with sacks full of hand-grenades and tinned food. Their helmets – the first German tin-helmets – slipped down over their eyes, they hadn't a free hand to push them back. Under the breaking dawn, they fell panting into a position that was no more than shell-craters and fox-holes which they were then to link up to form trenches. They sweated and shivered, dug their way through frozen clods of earth into the mud. Around midday, the first wounded were brought to the rear. The following day, for four solid hours, German shells howled overhead on their way to the village of Douaumont, even one of Krupp's 42cm heavies joined in. When the companies scrambled over the sides of their holes, my Saxons trudged forward too, scurrying through mud and the remains of barbed-wire entanglements, stepping on corpses and slipping into holes full of water. This was nothing like the incisive, dashing thrusts on the flat training-grounds of the Bienitz back home. Three hundred metres on, and the attack disintegrated under fire from the flanks. That brought back memories of the Lingekopf: there, they themselves had mown down the French *chasseurs alpins*, Voiciech from the embrasure of his cute little Monument.

Voiciech didn't lift his head, Felix peered forwards: white flares over the village. Did that mean it had been captured? But they were actually green flares, paling in the noonday brightness, and so the generals misinterpreted them and ordered the simultaneous attack on the Thiaumont fortifications, and in so doing they precipitated the catastrophe. Now there was no more fire being directed on the village, the French rose from their trenches, leaned on the parapets and opened up a session of target practice on the Saxons moving off laterally. A blizzard preserved them from total annihilation. The ensuing night could not have been more punishing. In all haste, a half caved-in road-ditch was scratched out to accommodate an assault formation for the next day. It was like on the fields east of Leipzig before the last day of the Battle of the Nations. Voiciech Machulski, Sapper Viktor Machul, went through torment, as had Carl Friedrich Lindner. He was soaked through and hungry, had hardly the strength left to grip his shovel, but he dug all the same, and gained for himself a hand's breadth of a hollow for chest and belly, but not for his legs, which stuck out in the open on the cold earth of France. No assault formation turned up to relieve them at first light, but French observers in the captive balloons over the Meuse spotted the sprinklings of freshly dug soil and directed the fire onto these; the products of Schneider-Creuzot were every bit a match for those of Krupp, and they straddled the road-ditch, covered it with random-fire and blanket-fire and various other specialities from the gunner's repertoire. 'We should've engraved the numbers of dead Frenchmen while we were at it!' Voiciech shouted through the roar to my father, who only half-heard the words, and understood their meaning not at all. Voiciech was trying to convey that the Monument to the Battle of the Nations commemorated only the dead of the victorious side, not those of the poor mercenaries of the Confederation of the Rhine, far less the French, and not at all those most miserable of the lot, the butchered Saxons. While the earth under Voiciech quaked, while he shivered with cold and terror, it flashed through his mind that he wouldn't have had to be lying here if the French had taken part as well, with flags and military bands, in the festivities surrounding the dedication of the Monument to the Battle of the Nations, if the President of the French Republic had paraded down the steps alongside the German Kaiser and the King of Saxony and the Russian and Austrian Princes. 'We should've invited the French!' yelled Voiciech through the explosion, and then he felt a blow on his legs, heat seared him like a bite from a lion, and he thought: then we wouldn't have needed to set the lions loose.

Felix Linden bound five packs of field-dressings round Voiciech's legs, three on the right one, two on the left. A chunk of shrapnel, scything sideways, had torn open the calves and shattered both tibia and fibula. Voiciech was half-swooning as my father carried him to the rear. Dodging among shell-holes and shot-up trenches, corpses and explosions, Felix Linden lost his way, slid into a gully and found himself face to face with a gap in a wall, one of the shattered entrances to the Douaumont fortress. Other soldiers relieved him of his wounded burden, which was then passed on down the line, laid on a stretcher, carried along congested passageways, and so Voiciech landed on an operating table, his boots were cut off his feet, two doctors took one look at the broth of blood, bone-splinters and tatters of muscle, nodded to each other, and lopped the right leg off above the knee. Amputation was their speciality; day in, day out, they hardly did anything else.

Sergeant Linden had only a few short minutes, in which he was allowed to drink a mug of tea, spoon up a pot-lidful of lentil soup and smoke a cigarette, before a lieutenant dispatched him back out again.

Voiciech Machulski came out of the anaesthetic, boards above his head, in the yellowish light of dim oil-lamps. Carl Friedrich Lindner would have croaked out on the bare fields of Otterwisch anyway, without a coat under his back, without a knapsack under his head, a prisoner of the Prussians. Anyone that was already pegging out didn't have to be fed and watered, it was a straightforward piece of arithmetic. He would have succumbed to weakness or typhoid, if they hadn't beaten him to death out of hand. But I, Voiciech Machulski, on the other hand, I was lying warm in the fug, feeling pressure on my legs, but no pain as such. I tried out my arms, raising them under the blanket, felt my nose, my mouth, counted off my fingers on my lips, they were all still there. Sinking back, I ran my hand over the wall: concrete. Strange; so this was the crypt of the Monument to the Battle of the Nations, rigged up as a field hospital, I was home, safe. Erna would come and visit me, and so, for sure, would my friend, Felix, and I'd tell him, 'Now the Monument has a purpose, after all.' I could make out the impressions of the seams between the moulding boards on the concrete wall and tried to work out whether I was lying deep down below, near one of the main buttresses into which I had sealed a memento, a proclamation of victory in the elections in 1910, a postcard bearing portraits of leading party comrades. The mud of the battlefield was still sticking to my hand; with it I painted my initials on the wall. I dozed off, came to again to the sound of voices calling, 'Come on, mate, don't you want something to eat? A drink?' For a while I thought visitors were pouring through the Monument, and the guide was doing his commentary: Before us you see the statue of the Spirit of Sacrifice, it weighs, measures, the hand alone, the length of the toes. My toes were cosy and warm, outside on the ramparts and by the lake it had been bitter cold, but I had crept into the Monument, it was warm in the Hall of Fame, and up aloft the horsemen were riding home from the battle. I felt a cup at my lips, one of the horsemen had climbed down and was supporting my head. The crypt was packed with horsemen, their horses were cropping outside on the embankments. The riders sat on benches round the sides, slept where they sat, chatted quietly. Names were called out. Here! called the horsemen, here! Very good, lieutenant, yes sir! Frenchmen in blue coats came in. Through the embrasure on the Lingekopf I had shot at Frenchmen, and hit them, they had avenged themselves from Douaumont village, we were quits. I would have liked to explain to them that it would all have been different if they had helped with the building of the Monument: Russian and Austrian and French and Württemberg masons side by side, not just Saxons, who had built the Monument for all the others – all, that is, except the Saxons. It was a magnificent idea, but I was too tired to put it into words. Two Frenchmen picked up the stretcher and carried me along passage-ways, overhead I saw cables, light-bulbs, water dripped from the stones. I couldn't tell what part of the Monument we were in, I couldn't remember a corridor as long as this. They carried me out into the open, up an embankment, they were in a hurry, gasping, running for their life, and for mine, and, all due credit to them, when a shell whistled over, they put down the stretcher before they hurled themselves into the mud.

I beg your pardon? No, no more coffee, thanks. When the French prisoners handed over their burden at a first-aid dug-out a few kilometres to the rear, Sapper Viktor Machul was dead. Whether he died of cold or loss of blood, whether he was hit by another splinter, was never investigated. His identity disc was broken in two and one half was sent home with his pay-book through official channels. In a mass grave, Viktor Machul was – I'm looking for the right word – laid to rest, buried, interred, these all sound high-flown; he certainly wasn't dumped in a shallow grave. He was laid in line, next to other corpses, a sprinkling of lime on top, right, next layer, keep it moving. The procedure hadn't changed since the Battle of the Nations, only in those days lime was in shorter supply than at Verdun.

CHAPTER 6

Was your father a Nazi?

I am puzzled. Might I be permitted to ask for an explanation? Yesterday evening – what did the nurse bring in? A little blob of curd cheese, a mini-slice of smoked sausage and a knob of butter, not to mention that so-called tea? Far from it! Grilled sausages, presumably from Halberstadt, anyway, quite delicious, and potato salad to go with them, even my wife could not have mixed it better, a nice little wedge of cheese, two tomatoes; and this morning, a pot of real coffee, two rolls, a boiled egg, jam, salami – have I been transferred to a higher category?

Your argument that you have nothing to do with the management of the clinic and so cannot provide me with an answer to that question seems to me, with all due respect, to hold little water. I have seen the men in the yellow overalls, I heard their call for help, and I could imagine that, as a Category One state prisoner, I would receive the very best of provisions. Those in authority will want to be on the best of terms with me – isn't there a certain logic in that? Now you need *both* hands to dismiss that idea! No thanks, no more coffee just yet. Not so soon after the last lot.

You say you only want to know what I can really recall; I'm to exclude anything that might have filtered into my memory from tales told by my parents – you must know yourself how difficult it is to make such a distinction. I can still remember how our kitchen looked, in fact it didn't change at all, right up until well into the thirties. The tap over the sink, next to it a small metal jug, we called it 'the dipper', the cupboard with the glass doors on the top half, the enamelled container bearing the legend: 'Give us this day our daily bread.' My little sister, Hildrun, under the table, my mother and Auntie Erna weeping; Auntie Erna is wearing a black dress, the two women put their arms round each other, the grief of the one seems as profound as that of the other. Someone had *fallen*, well, I often fell, too, and I knew that it could hurt. By the end, Hildrun had joined in the bawling. I played with the cow, sheep and horse my Pappy had carved. He was far away, that I knew; there, he sat in a house called Dug-Out, and carved for me goats and men pushing tipper-wagons. Mother no longer took in washing for gentlefolk, but was now working in a printer's; sometimes she was away all day and sometimes nights, a neighbour looked after us or we went to Auntie Erna's. A picture with a black border stood on the chest of drawers there: Uncle Viktor, who had fallen. Gradually the significance of this word took shape in my mind, it had some connection with cemetery and Monument to the Battle of the Nations.

My mother worked as a paper-feeder in Spamer's printing works, Germany's biggest graphics firm. Great names had emanated from Leipzig: Brockhaus' Encyclopaedias, Meyer's *Lexikon*, Baedecker's Guides, Reclam's little paperbacks, the Insel series. They were all there pre-1914 – what has come along since then? My mother earned twenty-eight pfennigs an hour, later it went up to thirty-two-and-a-half. Once she worked on laying an appeal under the presses: the artist, Max Klinger, had produced a work of importance that the Viennese wanted to buy; donations were being sought to keep it in Leipzig where it would be handed over to the city museum. Mother printed a catalogue for an exhibition of Klinger's works and she brought home a reject copy that had gone off the straight. A man was running along a path towards me, to right and left stood skeletal trees at the edge of the fields, the man was running for all he was worth – I could tell that from the hunch of his shoulders. Other men were chasing him, they were still maybe fifty metres behind, and I wondered whether they would catch up with the fugitive, whether he had stolen something, but perhaps they simply wanted to give him a beating or to kill him out of sheer badness. That picture was called 'Persecution'. I stared at it for hours on end; all my heart went out to that man out in front. At night I would dream that he burst into our kitchen, gasping, it was my father, and he said, 'I didn't fall'.

When I was five, boys from our street took me to a gravel-pit. There were ditches and holes full of water, shrubs grew wild on the slopes, we could build hiding-places out of boards and sheets of metal. We seldom went to the Monument itself, everything was too neat and orderly there. But in winter we used to toboggan on our runners down the embankments, and sometimes even between the cab-drivers' wheels! What were 'runners'? Short, manoeuvrable sledges made out of a metal frame and, across it, a board big enough for one or, at the most, two skinny kids' backsides.

I grew up into the hunger of wartime. Bread and dripping – I got stomach cramps at the very thought of it. On Sunday, Mother and I would pull the handcart out to the fields round Mölkau and Liebertwolkwitsz, where we scrabbled for potatoes and turnips. With older boys I'd pinch ears of wheat and apples; Mother accepted them without asking questions. When I was five, everyone in our house beamed with happiness, for the war was over, Father would be coming home. I waited expectantly for any number of carved cows and horses.

On a misty winter evening he came in, carrying no weapons, but still recognisable as a sergeant. He put his knapsack down in a corner, took his Klärchen in his arms. They held each other tight and stood for minutes on end without saying a word or moving a muscle. After a while, I went up and pushed my head between their stomachs. We didn't talk, didn't sob; it was only when Hildrun had come and clung to our legs that we let go of one another. I helped to unpack the knapsack; half an army loaf, a knitted jacket, footcloths and a bundle of letters from my mother.

When Mother took me to school for my first day, there could be no question of my getting the traditional big cone full of sweets. Father hacked out a lot fewer animals than I had hoped for; most of the time he just lay on the kitchen sofa and slept. Mother said Pappy hadn't had anything like enough sleep in the trenches and now he was catching up on it. Later Mother often talked about a fantastic special effort she had been involved in at Spamer's. In a lightning operation, a 460-page book had been type-set, printed and bound all in the space of thirty-six hours. One Saturday night, work began on all the type-setting machines simultaneously, all through the night proofs were corrected, matrices were cast, in the morning the printers took over and on the Sunday afternoon the binders, and on the Monday morning, ten o'clock, the first five hundred copies lay on the tables in front of the National Assembly in Weimar. What had been printed was the Treaty of Versailles. We really don't have to get into an argument about the fact that no Leipzig firm today could match such a performance, not even with their improved machinery.

Felix Linden had come back a confused and disturbed man. The old order was no more; for it to have survived, we would have had to win the war. There was no King, no Kaiser, no Hindenburg any more, there was no possibility of a 1914–18 appendix to the Victory Memorial of 1870/71. Lying on the sofa, Felix read the Versailles Treaty – my mother had brought a copy home – from cover to cover. For days after that he uttered not a single word.

In the quarry, too, there had been many changes. A works committee wanted to push a few measures through, mere trivia; it went about it clumsily and achieved nothing. Orders were scarce, the workforce was halved, quartered, my father was kept on. The works committee protested; faced with empty order-books, they could come up with nothing better than that. After the lost war, Leipzig's economy had a hard struggle to get back on its feet, there were no public-works contracts. There was no more talk of the arena in front of the Monument to the Battle of the Nations, nor of the magnificent boulevard that was to link it with the Bayerischer Platz. The National Library stood alone and forlorn among allotments. A few wagon-loads of paving-stones were sometimes the total turnover for a month.

My father went back to the VfB Leipzig and played in goal for the third team. At training sessions, I'd run after the balls that his team-mates shot past, retrieve them and lay them at his feet. He would dearly have loved to see me become a good footballer, but my reflexes weren't quick enough. I had to think first about what my legs were to do with the ball, and of course by then it had been taken off me. The VfB won the Central Germany Provincial League three times, their arch-rivals, the Spielvereinigung, took the title twice. In the national finals, however, our teams were defeated by the best clubs in Germany, Nuremberg, the Hamburg Sportverein or Munich 1860. I knew all the players, yelled and threw my arms in the air when a goal was scored. Then I'd go home to plum-cake or potato pancakes or fruit-loaf Stollen, according to the time of year. Hildrun was too small to join in my games, and anyway she was a girl.

Father took only one magazine; it was published by the Reich War Graves Commission and the pictures were full of black crosses. Reading this magazine, and paying for it, was, he said, his duty to his dead comrades, and to Viktor above all. He tried to carve figures of soldiers, charging, marching; they were too good for toys. My mother set them up on a shelf, above which hung souvenir pennants exchanged with football clubs he had helped defeat or who had fired a netful of goals past him. There were no new additions to the collection coming in now. On the way home from the football ground, Father would often take me round by the Monument, and at those moments he would have even less to say than usual. I kept asking, 'Pappy, when we goin' up there?' and Father would answer that I was too small for that.

The ascent of the Monument was his present to me on my tenth birthday. We went up Schönbach Strasse, turned off at the 'lopped popple' just in front of the ornamental lake, and suddenly I had the urge to run, for sheer joy, but Father said, 'No running here!' I had to hold on to his hand while we bought our tickets and then climbed the steps beside the Archangel Michael; they were high for my little legs and I couldn't reach the banister. Outside the entrance, Father lifted me onto the parapet. There, below me, lay the lake, seeming to taper towards its far end. I let out a cry of surprise: trees and roofs, chimneys, church spires, domes, wind driving clouds that frayed into blackish-grey and rust-red and bluish rags, a cooling-tower spewing vapour high over a gas-works; I had never seen so much of my city all at once, and the vastness of it made me giddy. I wriggled and tried to free myself from Father's hands as he lifted me down again, I could have stood there gazing for an eternity. A passage-way led between enormous stone blocks up to a doorway, every stone was taller than I was. I had heard many a time that Father had cut them, and in my fantasies I had added the picture of him carrying each and every one of them here on his back and piling them up. And now everything was here at once, laid out before my eyes, the giants towering above me, the great height of the dome, the horsemen away up there. All the sounds merged into a hovering, lingering resonance, my whispers were sucked up into it and became part of it, perhaps preserved in it for ever. I hadn't heard much about God, our Saxon brand of Christianity was pretty tenuous, religious education lessons in school, well, they held little interest for me, and no more than two or three times had Mother ever taken me with her to church. If anyone had told me at that moment that this was where God lived, I would have believed it on the spot. I bent my head back until it hurt, until I felt dizzy and the horsemen began to circle, as if on a Christmas carousel; they were riding home. Today, as an old man, I know of no more beautiful words in the language than 'going home'. A woman was giving a lecture; I hardly took in her words, but her sing-song lapped over me. It's an acknowledged fact that the acoustics in the Monument hold sounds for a full fifteen seconds. 'The figuuure faaacing youuu symboliiises the sufferiiingsss of the dyyyinnng warriooors.' The horsemen rode in a circle and I turned to follow them, turned faster and faster till I had abruptly to bow my head into a shimmering, whirling darkness. 'Stop fooling about, Freddie,' Father said gently. We went on up, till we were on a level with the horsemen and I was told that they were virtually lifesize. I had long since stopped counting the steps, I hadn't learned to count up that far, I trudged on up, my hand on the stone wall, my father behind me. 'Can you still manage all right, Freddie?' Behind slit-windows, light streamed, clouds floated, and I felt as if I was up among them. I would have liked to go out there, but I climbed higher; I'd be nothing but a tiny dot right at the top, just like the tiny dots I had often seen up there. According to Father, we were climbing up and round inside the leg of one of the sentries; I would readily have believed things even more fantastic than that. And then, daylight again, outside, a big, black bird swept past. On a little interior balcony, Father lifted me up again and there were all the horsemen riding along beneath me now. I shrank back and then immediately wanted to go still higher, as high as it was possible to go. When I stepped out into the open, the wind rushed into my lungs, I ran forward to the stone wall that was taller than myself, looked for a step up, ran to Father's legs and clung on tightly for sheer happiness. 'Pappy, Pappy!' I cried, and loved my father as never before. Back I ran to the stone wall and felt myself being lifted up; now I stood higher than everyone else, held firmly round the hips, and I looked downwards and outwards and, timidly, sideways. I felt a little dizzy, but that went away when I remembered my father's grip. Beneath me, the city, as far as the eye could see, the city, with endless towers and roofs and chimney-stacks, and the realisation struck me all at once and I gave voice to it: 'I can see the whole world!' Many years later, an artist painted that scene: a lad running ahead of his friends up a rubble-tip and throwing his arms wide and shouting these words. That's the way someone feels who is lifted up out of our plain and who has never known what mountains and valleys are. I was flying with the clouds, and all I had to do was spread my arms and I'd swoop down among the crows that rose, just at that moment, from the trees in the cemetery. No danger, though, for, after all, Father was holding on to me, so I could yell and enjoy the sensation of flying, and the wind drove into me, stopping my breath and making me gulp and giving me that dizzy feeling that was perhaps the greatest joy of that whole joyous day. Holding Father's hand, I walked right the way round the parapet, until I had seen *everything*, the dark heights of the Kolm and the Hohburg Mountains, the waterworks at the foot of the Monument, Stötteritz, over there the roof of my school, the Russian Church, the National Library, St Thomas' Church, St Nicholas' and St Paul's, the double rump of the Central Station, the Albert Hall, the needle-like spire above the Congress Hall, Leipzig West with its chimney-stacks, the crowding tree-tops over the Southern Cemetery, the chapel looking like an imperial palace, and then, with a yell of triumph, I jumped into my father's arms and now I really was flying and I clung to his shoulders and kissed him and babbled for joy, so that when he sat me on the stone blocks I practically collapsed with exhaustion. 'Freddie,' said Father, 'the Monument is exactly ten years old, and yet there's to be no anniversary celebration. No flags, no bands. It's as if we're supposed to be ashamed of it.'

For weeks after, I floated in my dreams over the ornamental lake, all I had to do to hold myself aloft was head into the wind the right way and spread out my nightshirt. The world was vast and limitless, I now knew what I wanted to be – either a pilot or an attendant at the Monument, or, best of all, both. I wanted to be my father and to have quarried the stone and I wanted to be a horseman, returning home from the Battle. One thing I wanted never to be, whenever I thought of the Monument – which I did every day – and that was a soldier. Not Carl Friedrich Lindner, even if I had had any notion of his existence at that time, not Voiciech Machulski at Verdun, nor Felix Linden during the mustard-gas attack at the Somme. We never played wars at the Monument, only in the sand-pits behind it. And that wasn't just on account of the women who swept up the leaves or cleared the snow and would have chased us away.

A few years had elapsed since the war's end when old front-line soldiers started preparing for a reunion; they wanted to commemorate their deeds and their dead. The man who came to call on my father had been a lieutenant. 'Lift our heads high again,' I heard at the kitchen table, 'great days mustn't be forgotten,' and then, 'Youth needs a sign, a torch!' Mother shifted her gaze from the erstwhile Lieutenant to her Felix, and the words 'undefeated in the field' didn't strike such a chord in her as to wipe out memories of four years of fear. 'It's only a parade at the Monument,' Father sensed she was worried and tried to placate her. 'Soon be over.' I made my cows advance against the sheep, the cows broke through and I hoped that the Lieutenant, retd., would see it as German tanks overrunning French lines. 'Brrrm! Brrruumm!' I added the sound effects, but all I got was a warning from Mother, 'Freddie, behave!' The Kyffhäuser League would be there, with flag-parties from all over the Reich, the conqueror of Fort Douaumont, Captain Brandls, had given assur ances of his intention to attend, and Generals Ludendorff and Mackensen could be counted on to send telegrams. The former officer suggested that the proper dress for the occasion should be 'military- casual', with boots, a windcheater, on no account a hat. My father was, he said, a fine figure of a man, and just right for the front rank.

Naturally, I was there as my father made his way up to the Monument in his light-coloured sports jacket and summery baggy cap. At the assembly point he looked around for a familiar face, when a man with a waxed moustache approached him and asked, 'Don't we know each other?' After some to-ing and fro-ing, it transpired that they hadn't met under fire but at the topping-out ceremony of the Monument, to the accompaniment not of artillery fire but of roast venison and Cumberland sauce and beer. 'I broached the barrel!' exclaimed Katzenstein. In his lapel he was wearing a miniature replica of the two Iron Crosses; now he was back among the coypu and the mink in his furrier's on the Brühl. 'Those were the days,' the two said as if with one voice, and that made them laugh. They looked up at the Monument and Father said, 'The other fellow that pushed the topping-out stone into place with me, he fell at Verdun.' At that, Katzenstein the merchant wanted to shake my father's hand in condolence, but the latter was still gazing up at the Monument. My father was trying to remember exactly: was it Katzenstein who shouted out the toast that day, 'To our young Kaiser'?

All the boys from our street were swarming around; someone had thrust little black-white-and-red flags into our hands. We stood to attention as commands rang out, as if they were aimed at us, too, and we stared, wide-eyed, as the men, Felix Linden among them, formed into a line and snapped their heads back, as a ripple ran along the line of feet with all the men simultaneously bringing the left one smartly alongside the right, as a military band marched up, real soldiers with drums and trumpets, and I experienced an uneasy feeling at this sight of my father marching along with other men, as if he was being led away. They took up position in front of the Archangel Michael, I heard a pensioned-off general making a speech and understood little of it, then they all shouted 'Hurrah!', for the conqueror of Fort Douaumont had stepped forward, and I was glad that Auntie Erna wasn't here.

The soldiers and civilians marched down past the gasworks and almost to Connewitz Cross, where they dispersed among a throng of children. I was immediately at my father's side, making a grab for his hand. I assumed he would now be coming home with me, but he said that an old comrades' dinner had been laid on, and I was to give his love to Mum.

Unfortunately of course, of course unfortunately, I wasn't there when four hundred old soldiers and ex-officers sat down to their roast and their beer, when they sang their songs and when the various conquerors of Fort Douaumont began to squabble among themselves. By then I had trotted back to Stötteritz with my pals, we had thrown away our little flags. Felix Linden sat surrounded by men from his company, pictures of their children were handed round. Where do you work? Have you heard anything of so-and-so or what's-his-name? Then Captain von Brandis stepped up to the lectern, the famous bearer of the *Pour le Mérite*, and showed slides, Frenchmen with their hands raised in surrender, the usual stuff. He described his company's attack on Douaumont Fortress and spared nothing in the way of onomatopoeic underlinings: 'Ratatatat! Bangbangbang! Brrrrwhooshwhooosh!' He reported on the fiery eagerness of his infantrymen who hadn't been satisfied merely with the prescribed targets for the attack and dramatised the Fortress as a bullet-spewing concrete pile, as an armour-plated monster surrounded by trenches metres deep, invincible, yet vanquished. Somebody from the back rows shouted, 'You weren't even there!' The speaker seemed not to hear this. 'When I reported to my regiment that Douaumont had fallen, the good news flashed like lightning back to the Fatherland! Never did the hymn to the bravery of the German soldier ring out more clearly, more purely than in that hour!' And so on. The troublemaker raised his voice again: 'There

84

was hardly anybody left in the fort! Lieutenant Radtke was the first to go in!' At this the former Lieutenant, who had invited my father, got to his feet and pleaded that the unblemished reputation of front-line soldiers should not be sullied by dragging it through the mud of petty squabbling! 'Radtke took the fort!' rang out the reply, 'Brandis only got there the following day!' The speaker conceded that it might possibly have been the case that some non-commissioned officer or some private soldier or other could indeed have infiltrated the fort by way of some shattered side entrance – who could have been sure, or would claim to have been sure of that, in the heat of battle? The hymn of praise for the German front-line soldier, who had taken his courage in both hands, indeed the honour of all those who died . . .

And another heckler: 'Lies, all lies!'

'Red rabble-rouser!' shouted somebody else, 'Whose pocket are you in, you traitor?' Then, suddenly, the story was that it was Warrant-Officer Kunze, a farmer from Thuringia, who had been first in, had taken French officers prisoner and stupidly let them escape again and, finally, having lost all sense of duty, had thrown himself greedily upon white bread and pâté. 'Ratatatat!' yelled the captain once more. He wanted to describe the subsequent break-out from the fort, but it was by now impossible to drown out the group discussions. 'Viktor didn't die for this,' said Felix Linden and left the meeting. In the foyer stood Katzenstein, silent, smoking a cigarette; he searched for some expression of common ground. What front did you serve on? he could have asked, or, did you come through unscathed? They were no longer poor bloody infantry, though; they were upper-class and proletariat, the one couldn't say to the other, you must come and visit us some time. Katzenstein didn't like to inquire: not unemployed, are you? And Felix Linden couldn't very well express the hope that the other's books had balanced last year.

Felix Linden slunk home. 'It was awful,' he said to Klärchen, and went to bed. The explanation of why it had been awful didn't emerge until three days later. He never so much as mentioned his speechlessness in the face of Katzenstein.

There was many a week now when Father sat around without work, the building trade wasn't really picking up, even though a few more Trade Fair pavilions were adding the finishing touches to the city centre. The Market Square was being dug up from end to end, the first cobblestone was torn out the day after the Spring Trade Fair closed, and, by the start of the Autumn Fair, the underground hall was ready, occupied by exhibitors and admired by visitors. The radial village in Lössnig, the Bauhaus-style Kroch housing-estate – it wasn't much compared to pre-war times.

Easter 1928, and I left school. Next day, I was trotting along behind the foreman-blaster, carrying the things that were in future to go to make up a fair part of my life: drill and cartridges, detonators and fuses. It was obvious to me right from the start: I could never have become anything else. I was just as happy in the quarry as in the technical college, our training in mathematics and geology was the equal of any. Early each morning I sat with Father in the train, and in the afternoons we travelled together back into the city. Out of my first pay-packet I bought myself a bicycle, a Brennabor, fourth-hand; the road through Mölkau was more direct than the railway loop, and I was there just as quickly by bike. In the summer of 1929, I was working on my own for the first time. I marked out the boring-points, drilled, packed, laid fuses and lit them. I took cover at Father's side, watched his face earnestly, and together we listened for every nuance in the detonation. A wall broke loose from the rock-face, well anyway, a slice. It was a routine piece of blasting, an everyday job, but to me it seemed as if the whole earth must have been blasted open to its core. I knew as a matter of course how many grams of Donarite I had laid, and how many tons of stone that would yield. So why shouldn't this moment fill me with wonder? I felt exactly as I had done six years before, when I had stood for the first time on top of the Monument and had screamed, 'I can see the whole world!' Now my hands were shaking and my eyelids twitching, my father gave a congratulatory snort and the foreman said, 'When I was a lad, an apprentice put up a round of drinks after doing his first blast.' That I did, in the station bar; the foreman and my father naturally each followed it up with another round.

A good footballer was something I hadn't become, nor would I ever. But maybe a cyclist, a wrestler – I contributed my share to the whistling and bawling at the professional wrestling matches at the Crystal Palace. Whenever the gladiators plodded in at the start, looking as if they could hardly walk for sheer bursting strength, flexing their muscles, waving to the crowd on all sides, there was always the same march playing, and at the velodrome there was always the Sport Palace's characteristic waltz – strange how football, to this day, has managed to get by without some kind of signature tune.

I wrestled for a club in Leipzig's east end, and we travelled to matches in Taucha, Wurzen and Eilenburg, to villages that nobody would have suspected of being able to put a full team together. We wrestled in the Central Hall in Gaschwitz, and then in the evening there was a dance. During Carnival season, we'd put on demonstration bouts for a hot meal and two Marks. I worked as a waiter in a beer-garden in Abtnaudorf, humping beer, coffee and portions of cake and whipped cream out to customers under the chestnut trees.

When the time came for me to sit my examinations, I experienced not so much as the slightest suggestion of stage-fright, and passed with flying colours. I delivered the *coup de grâce* to a disused factory chimney, and the way that it just folded up, as if it had been felled by a quick one-two karate-chop, was magnificent to behold. The following Sunday, still on a high, I strolled out to Probstheida, to see the VfB, and that was when the thought first came to me: where would you have to lay the charges if you wanted to bring down the Monument? I rehearsed the job in my mind, until I recoiled, as if I had been planning a murder.

We blasted out tree-stumps, the foundations of old barns, of a bridge, so that the mechanical diggers wouldn't break their teeth on them. Down in the excavations, metal screamed on stone, chains rattled, buckets clattered. The sirens in the brickworks proclaimed changes of shift to the surrounding villages, a rhythm that governed everything except the cattle in their stalls. We worked close by the farmers; where the digger was now scooping out, grain had stood a month previously. On the way home, my rucksack was always full: briquettes, kindling, potatoes, a few beetroot, whatever came to hand.

At this time, Father was mostly out of work. Mother was on short time, Hildrun had failed to get an apprenticeship and was doing some domestic work for a baker. Suddenly, I was the principal breadwinner in our family.

One day, Felix Linden appeared in brown breeches and started binding puttees round his calves. There he sat in the kitchen, knees pressed together as if he had to sit to attention, the same way you stood to attention. He had been given the breeches as a present; a Sturmführer had promised him that, if he turned up regularly on parade, the whole uniform would be put together in due course.

Was my father a Nazi? Felix Linden became an SA-man in the

summer of 1932, he was approaching fifty then, a giant of a man, and probably at the height of his physical powers. Most of the Storm Troopers were fellows around twenty, he towered over them and it annoyed him when they played the fool. He held no rank of command, but one snort from him and they would fall quiet for a while. A propaganda boss soon had his eye on him, he wanted to set up a formation of *real men*, family men were what he was looking for, ex-front-line soldiers, he wanted to be able to set them up as an example: look here, *that*'s the SA, too! And so Felix Linden was creamed off from the rough and ready and it wasn't long before he was standing with other Storm Troopers, collecting-box in hand, at the corner of Hainstrasse and Brühl, with instructions to accost the better dressed, hold out the collecting-box and bark: 'For campaign funds!' This they did during shopping hours, small change and even Mark pieces rattled in their tins, they shouted louder, 'For campaign funds!' One man came towards Felix Linden, wearing an overcoat with a fine fur collar, Felix held out his collecting-tin and said, 'For cam . . .', and then, although the man's moustache no longer boasted the same wing-span as in the Kaiser's day, he recognised in him the former member of the former League of German Patriots, the bearer of two Iron Crosses, the ex-lieutenant, the furrier Katzenstein, once emigrated from Poland, and now, in fact, a Jew. Felix withdrew his tin.

In his SA Sturm, Felix Linden soon became one of the troop that took the name 'The German Oaks'. Whenever the 'German Oaks' marched past the platform at a propaganda meeting, a murmur would run through the crowd and all brawling would cease. Felix Linden rose to the rank of *Rottenführer*, the equivalent of lance-corporal. There was some talk of providing this troop with quarters in an empty factory, to station them in barracks, as it were; when Klärchen heard of that, she said, 'Now that's going beyond a joke, if you ask me!' It never actually came to that.

These were times when I hadn't a care in the world, despite the international economic crisis and the Nazis puffing themselves up. I was active in sports, without going overboard, girls played an agreeable part in my life, without being all that important; I didn't get involved in any undying love-affair, none of them wanted to corner me in marriage, none got pregnant by me. In my profession, I saw prospects for promotion: the war had left a lot of gaps, a few foremen were nearing retirement age, I wouldn't have too long to wait. In America, a canal fifty kilometres long had been blasted out of the prairies at one fell swoop; that roused me to greater excitement than any emergency decree did. Then love did hit me – like a ton of bricks. Marianne served behind the counter in a dairy and wore her hair in a dark fringe down to her eyebrows. I felt neither pleasure when Hitler came to power, nor fear, for nobody in my circle of acquaintances was arrested. For days and weeks on end, Felix Linden, the German Oak, was seldom out of uniform. Klärchen made fun of her ramrod warrior, but in moderation, and was quite content to accept the packets of flour and barley he brought home after being on duty. Meanwhile, I was reading about revolutionary new blasting techniques in the copper-mines of Rhodesia and the gold-mines of South Africa. If I had been abruptly shaken out of my sleep, I could have reeled off pat the terms 'deflagration', 'explosion' and 'detonation' and their precise definitions, I could have rattled off the formula for dynamite, ecrasite, cellulose trinitrate, Oxliquit, gelignite, ammonium nitrate-based gelatinous explosive, and their respective velocities of detonation, I was an assistant blaster with all my heart and soul. Looking back today, I can only shake my head at such blindness.

For a while, my father worked as a navvy on the construction of a canal to the west of the city, then his old firm took him on again. When conscription was announced and the first draft was called up, fate treated me kindly: younger lads than I reported to barracks with their cardboard boxes; in celebration, I treated Marianne and myself to the first bottle of champagne in our lives. We rented a small flat not far from my parents. Hildrun went off, a half-hearted volunteer, to help on the land in East Prussia, and the Labour Service soon took her on as a group-leader. Her letters were full of blood-and-soil words like 'Landvolk', 'Brauchtum' and 'Ostwind' – terms which meant one thing in ordinary language, but in this context were intended to convey something quite different.

From time to time, we were hired out on contract work. Land was to be cleared near the lock on the Elster to accommodate a spacious memorial to that revered son of the city, Richard Wagner. The Palm Gardens, with their pavilions and grottoes, were to make way for it. Put your backs into it, lads, came the order, go at it, the Führer wants this memorial, the Führer has promised to attend the unveiling, even, for that matter: if we don't get this memorial precinct laid out in double-quick time, the Führer will never come near here at all.

We polished off all sorts of romantic, extravagantly adorned and ornamented masonry, dear to the heart of many a Leipziger. Some days ago I insisted that I had never demolished anything I was later to regret; I have to take that back now. We came up against a deal of ill-feeling on the part of the locals, for the Palm Gardens were not only a gem among collections of rare plants, but also the annual meeting place, on the occasion of the autumn fun-fair, the 'Tauchsche', for all young people in the city. The five- to fourteen-year-olds dressed up as trappers and Indians, stuck cardboard knives and wooden tomahawks in their belts and streamed in their gangs and tribes to the Palm Gardens, where stalls had been set up, selling candy-floss and toy pistols; the most sought-after of these were the sort that could take a strip of a hundred caps. The whole place reverberated to the war-cries of countless Winnetous and Old Shatterhands, hills were stormed and lost, the trappers defeated the Indians and *vice versa*. Come evening, and the hordes would make their way home, tired and ecstatic, the feathers of their head-dresses drooping, many a one with a torn jacket and a few bruises. The 'Tauchsche' was always a great day out, and now here we were, demolishing the happy hunting grounds, the battleground for the great last stand. Youngsters hung gloomily about the boundary fencing, their ringleaders wanted to know what was going on here, then, and were chased away: Go on, clear off! Have you ever heard of the 'Leipzig gangs' of those days? Boys and girls between fourteen and twenty-one, they were, the boys wore brightly coloured ski-shirts, leather trousers with braces and belts studded with rivets. All apprentices and young workers. There was the Greyhound Trap gang in Kleinzschocher, the Reeperbahn in Lindenau, the Lily-Whites from the Lilienplatz in Reudnitz – all forgotten nowadays. They used to take on the Hitler Youth, even gave their leaders a good hiding. They would go off on outings, lads and lasses together, and play their guitars and sing romantic, generally silly, songs. They were rebels – I can quite understand why nobody talks about them now or praises them for having been anti-Nazi. They would be just as determined to live according to their own lights today, too. They were none too chuffed at what we were doing! Naturally, during blasting operations, the place was cordoned off by the police. Disappointment and rage in many faces.

There's one more thing to be said about the 'Tauchsche': it died at the same time as Gose was rationalised out of existence, the mid-fifties. The argument was that it didn't fit into the image of the era of the new socialist departure. And of course Karl May had been consigned to the dung-heap too. The 'Tauchsche' remains as dead as Gose.

In quick succession, my children, Joachim and Erika, came into the world. Hildrun in East Prussia, by now the wife of an estate manager, had three children. So that made five grandchildren for Klärchen and Felix; all their photographs were set out on the kitchen dresser. Grandfather Felix took his grandson to the Monument, as he had taken me, Joachim lay in the grass and looked up to the stone sentries as I had done in the summer of 1914. Anyone that could distinguish an Opel Olympia from a Horch 170V also knew what that was, droning overhead, a Junkers 52 perhaps, or a Messerschmitt 109 or a Dornier 18. Erika was a name very much in vogue because of a popular song with the message that out there on the heath there blooms a little flower, and its name was – two, three, four – Erika! I'm trying to remember whether we put out flags on special occasions. Yes, we did. Of course, I was in the Arbeitsfront – that trips easily off the tongue, it's the way everybody talks, when they want to kid themselves about those days.

Mother Klärchen and Father Felix were only too happy to look after our children. My mother gave up work and spent many days caring for our two, and again she was able to trot out her little piece: 'On the town-hall's little tower.' Marianne was a bright and cheerful woman, and there was always a happy atmosphere in her shop, even when the manufacture of whipped cream was banned.

One evening, Felix was called out on alert. One SA-man ran to the next, who went to the next again, it had been worked out exactly what was to happen if any one of them wasn't to be found at home. 9pm, at the Johanna Park, was the message, in the Tauchnitzstrasse, in civvies, unobtrusive! Not a word, secret operation! 'What's it all about?' asked Klärchen; he shrugged.

As Felix Linden walked along the Tauchnitzstrasse, he saw one or two out of his Sturm, wearing coats, caps, hats, those were the days when even working men wore hats, too. Many of them had heard on the radio that a Jew had shot down a German Embassy official in Paris – revenge! they foamed, the Jews will pay for this! When Jew-blood spurts at the knife-blade's point! This Storm Troop was supposed to form the 'spontaneous' background, they filled a whole side-street, and from the 'German Oaks' there rang out shouts, bursts of applause, too, as flames leapt up behind window-panes. From his superiors he heard that this was only the beginning of the night's proceedings, soon they'd be moving on, to the Brühl, the fur would literally fly tonight. At that, he detached himself from the loose formation and pushed forwards, there he took his chance to dodge into a doorway and disappear through a backyard. The glow of the blazing synagogue fell fiery-red on a wall, behind it was a garden, with the strength of his fists and the weight of his body, Felix Linden smashed down a fence, panted through the park, across a bridge over the Elster, barged his way through crowds swarming towards the city centre and arrived at the villa of the furrier, Katzenstein, before the time scheduled by the National Socialists' local leadership for the spontaneous combustion of the people's anger at that particular spot. He didn't take his thumb off the doorbell until lights had gone on in the windows and a head, the head of a woman with tousled hair, had appeared between the curtains. When he was finally convinced he could make out Katzenstein's face above him, he shouted, 'I've come from the League of German Patriots!'

That was an absolutely daft thing to say; the League having faded into oblivion long since, but the name itself was a cry from times past, redolent of something that rose from buried depths, that conjured up comradeship, a world that was still unscathed, intact. To shout the word 'German' at the Jew Katzenstein of all people was downright absurd.

'You've got to get away at once,' said Father, once Katzenstein had opened the door. Felix Linden wasted no time on reminders, of either the topping-out ceremony at the Monument or the reunion of the victors of Douaumont. 'They'll be here any minute.' He said: they'll be here, without explaining who 'they' were, clearer terms were beyond him, he couldn't bring himself to formulate a warning against the Fascists, the murdering arsonists. 'Quick, get away, through the garden!' Felix Linden went back out on to the street, across to the other side, where he watched lights going on and off in rapid succession all through the house. The proletarian had warned the upper-class businessman, the Storm Trooper the non-Aryan, the 'German Oak' the so-called Eastern Jew. My father made his way back towards the inner city, his boots crunching on broken glass, he dodged out of the way of speeding lorries, crossed the Market and the Augustusplatz. A tram was heading for Stötteritz, he jumped onto the rear platform, and as he stood there he felt welling up in him the urge to stretch out his hands and plead: They don't stink of petrol, I've no ashes on my coat, I'm a worker, I'm coming off shift and I'm going home, minding my own business!

On the next few occasions he avoided reporting in for SA duty, later he reported sick. My father a Nazi? I don't want to make him out to be better than he was.

CHAPTER 7

When did your father die? And how?

Today, you find me in a nasty frame of mind. I had a disturbed night – one dream after another. I was assailed by relics of the past. Perhaps old Carl Friedrich was tossing and turning inside me, unable as he must be to find any rest out there in Otterwisch. I've been brooding over the possibility that, in me, there might be some throwback to a Royal Saxon gunnery sergeant, that maybe an ancestor of mine had acted prematurely when, on the final day of the Battle of the Nations, a mine under the Elster Bridge was detonated in panic, and hundreds of bodies were blown to pieces; afterwards, torn-off arms lay in gardens, guts hung from plum-trees. I feel absolutely shattered.

Or Voiciech. Might he not have survived Verdun and then dug tunnels under the British lines at the Somme and blown holes in their positions? Whenever a section of their trenches had crumbled, assault troops swarmed in over the top, but there was always that one

94

machine-gun left, which never seemed to jam, but cut down the attack from its flank. In the middle of the night, I imagined Voiciech, during the celebrations in the autumn of 1913, driving a wagon-load of shells up to the Monument to the Battle of the Nations; the lions had metamorphosed into ammunition for Big Bertha. I have to admit it, if anything had gone wrong with these ageing flak-shells under the Monument, if I had been buried by the falling masonry – let me put it another way: my own death had been included in my calculations. You can be as careful as you like, but obsolete explosives can be the very devil.

Ah, yes, the Leipzig lions: there was another lion with an opportunity to make history, Caesar, the great-great-great-grandson of old Simba, with whom Tadeusz aimed to scare off the assembled nobility. Caesar – I thought of him last night – was ten months old when the sycophantic manager of the zoo, egged on by the even more obsequious Lord Mayor, made a present of him to Göring. That suited Fatso down to the ground; with the lion on a lead, he strode down the steps of his country seat as if he himself were a Caesar, a Nero. I saw him in that pose on the front cover of the *Berliner Illustrierte*, and later on I thought, suppose Caesar had bitten his master in his fat backside, and he had then caught rabies and snuffed it! That tale would then have been related in every commemorative brochure that the zoo publishes on the occasion of any jubilee: Leipzig even produced a class-conscious lion, a lion true to the spirit of Liebknecht! As things are, of course, that act of fawning subservience is passed over in silence.

Believe me, I have no fear of death. 'Many die too late, and a few die too soon,' insisted that atrabilious old nihilist, Nietzsche, who was born not far from Leipzig. It would be quite fair to turn that round: many die too soon and only a few too late. Of my ancestors, only Fürchtegott didn't die before his time. Perhaps my father perished just at the right moment? Nietzsche's cry was: 'I show you the death that consummates, which will be as a spur and a solemn pledge to the living.' Echoes of Körner there, of 'Comrades in Black' and 'The Glory of the Deeds of the Dead' and 'The Flag is Mightier than Death.' I didn't wish for death and would have done everything to give it the slip. I wouldn't have been a dedicated expert blaster if I hadn't wanted to watch, at a safe distance from flying rocks, the dome of the Monument bursting outwards, the platform at its apex crashing to the ground and the horsemen rushing in a headlong race with the twelve guardians to follow it. Billowing dust, the ground rumbling, shaking, job completed.

I took my examination for my master craftsman's diploma in the spring of 1939. In the theory part, the examining board had to interrupt me repeatedly, because I kept on coming up with some new titbit of the trade. A month later, I reported once again to Zeithain for training with a very specific purpose: defence of the home front against unexploded bombs; in an emergency I was to be called up into the fire-fighting services. On my return, I drank with Marianne the second bottle of champagne in our life together. In the shadow of the clouds of war, strange as it may sound today, I led a peaceful life at first, was happily married and took an active interest in Joachim and Erika's every activity. Rearmament, the construction of the Siegfried Line, the Sudeten Crisis – then the war was upon us, acclaimed by no one, my firm registered me as 'reserved occupation', and six months later I was enlisted as a fire-fighter. Many's the drop of milk that was 'left over' in Marianne's shop, while Hildrun sent food-parcels of flour, dripping and sausage from East Prussia.

Where should I take up the story again? Late autumn, 1943, perhaps? In those days I was usually on duty at my fire-station in the afternoons. In the forenoons I often tinkered about in our air-raid shelter; shoring-up boards would have come loose, puddles formed at the entrance, or maybe the place just needed tidying out.

One morning, some SS-men appeared on the scene, all obviously chosen for their height, not Waffen-SS, but black-clad, genuine *Schutzstaffel*, a rare occurrence in those days. They wore ankle-length greatcoats and carried sub-machine guns, they had thin mouths that looked as if they weren't really designed for talking with, not for harmless friendly conversation and certainly not for kissing, but at the outside for the barking of commands like 'Halt!' or 'Flat on your face!', but mostly for silence; silent and loyal they were, every last one of them. The first thing the Boys in Black did was to chase away a pack of Ukrainian girls; tearing open their padded jackets as they ran, these leaf-sweepers disappeared through gaps in the cemetery fence, clumping along in their gumboots, stumbling in their terrified haste, as if they had come face to face with the devil himself. Then pairs of SS men took up position at all the approaches to the Monument, strollers turned on their heel even before the sentries raised a forbidding hand. They were there, they stood there, and everyone knew, right away, from now on this was no place for them.

It was some time before they found their way down to where I was. I was raking sand into a puddle and watching them out of the corner of my eye. Two self-propelled gun-carriages with four-barrelled anti-aircraft guns pulled up at the ornamental lake, traffic was diverted from the Preussen Strasse, SS guard-dogs took care of that. Then the Führer arrived.

I use that expression, even though it sounds totally inappropriate nowadays. In my mind were the words, 'Here comes the Führer,' and not 'Hitler' or some disparaging term. He wore a field-grey coat and a high-peaked cap; when he had got out of his Mercedes, he put his hands together just like a football player lining up in the wall at a free-kick, and, standing there with his hands over his balls, looked up to the Monument. At that, his entourage turned to stone, for the Führer wasn't just looking, he was measuring the Monument with an architect's eye; after all, he would have become an architect, we all knew that in those days, if Providence had not singled him out to become the Führer of the Great German Reich. A tall man in a uniform I couldn't identify emerged from behind him, gesticulating as he explained details of the Monument, using both hands to carve its outline in the air. Speer? Was the fat one beside him Robert Ley? The three of them climbed up the embankment, loosely surrounded by SS-men who swept the bare tree-tops and every mole-hill with hawk-eyed suspicion. The whole affair went off in almost complete silence, so that I couldn't help feeling, now there should be an explosion of military music, after all, it was the done thing, whenever the Führer appeared, for the Badenweiler March to cut loose, taraa! taraa! taraa! The Führer – it would have sent a tingle down anyone's spine, whether of fear or admiration, and even feelings of joy would not be unmingled with fright and alarm – there strode the mightiest man in Germany (and, still, in half of Europe), straight across the lawns and up to the Monument from the rear; later, I read that of course it was a self-evident safety precaution for him to keep changing his plans, and in this way he foiled many a would-be assassin. Anyone who might have known that the Führer was due to visit the Monument would naturally have assumed that he would approach it from the front and walk up the open staircase, and that's where the bomb would have been planted, but the foxy dictator sneaked up from behind, probably two hours ahead of or behind schedule. A swarm of people followed him, among them younger men carrying folders and files. All sorts of speculations flashed across my mind: was the Monument to be modified according to directions from the Führer? The man I took to be Speer was standing in front of the arched window on the south side, obviously fulfilling the functions of a guide, again the Führer stared upwards, his head tilted right back, his hands protecting his testicles. My angle of vision was exactly as befitted a member of the rank and file, a *Volksgenosse*: I was looking up at him from below, so that he seemed taller, outlined against the sky. Never before had any of the powerful of this world taken the Monument from the rear, and I thought, the old fox, that's why his enemies find him such a handful, he always thinks of some way of baffling or bluffing them. And I made a mental note: you must keep this picture in your mind – Hitler in his high-peaked cap, gone was the double chin, instead his throat was taut, as he gazed upwards to the guardians, and in fact Hitler never looked up, he always looked down from the heights of a dais. Everything was always beneath him, with the exception, perhaps, of a German airship, but then the last Zeppelin had already been destroyed by fire. At that moment, two SS-men from his retinue swung abruptly off course and ran down towards me, rifles at the ready, and from between the lips of one of them came a barked 'That man! Just what d'you think you're doing here?'

'Voluntary Civil Guard, Monument!' I reported, military-style, or as near as I could get to it, 'Bunker-warden Linden!', and presented arms with my shovel.

'Get inside, sharpish!' I did a soldierly about-turn, went into the shelter and sat down on a bench. What did Hitler want here in this autumn of 1943, when he had been unable to take Moscow, Leningrad and Stalingrad, when his U-boats were being blown out of the water, when the Reich lay roofless, open to the bombers? I pictured him going down into the crypt and lingering before the statues, a mere man faced with the omnipotence of the dead. This city had never meant much to him. Granted, he had delivered some propaganda speeches here, in the Crystal Palace even, before he came to power. But he had never given the Trade Fair a second thought, far less the Brühl and its Jewish furriers, while the National Library had left him completely cold. He could derive much more aggressive satisfaction from Nordic dreams of victory at the Tannenberg Memorial or at bunkers on the Siegfried Line or at the launch of a warship. What was he doing here, where homage was also paid to the memory of Russians, when Russia was at his very throat?

After a quarter of an hour or so, I poked my nose out of the entrance. The sentries on the Preussen Strasse stood motionless, a traffic jam had built up by the cemetery gates; lorries, with their wood-alcohol generators belching clouds, horse-drawn carts, curious onlookers, trams. I was stuck inside the cordon and would dearly have liked to slip through it. I wanted to go for lunch, to go on shift, just to go, for it was always possible that something might happen, it didn't have to be an assassination attempt. Maybe the Führer would be taken ill, have a gall-bladder attack, then he might be brought into my shelter and we'd be off again with 'What are you doing here, man?' I could have given the Führer some succour from our bunker first-aid kit . . . don't talk daft, I told myself, you've no business here, so, out! But up above my tunnel the Führer was shuffling down the slope, slipping into each downward stride, and I prayed, please don't let him stumble! That was all I needed, to be there watching as he slipped, before one of his entourage could catch him, and landed on his arse and slid down as if on one of our 'runners' – suddenly a terrifying thought hit me: if you're a witness to that, you'll be whipped off into a concentration camp, never to be seen again! So I ducked back into the shelter, sat on the bench: who, me? – just having a break, take five. No idea, Hauptsturmführer, sir, haven't been outside in the last hour, not me; must've been another bloke, I dunno nothin', Obersturmführer, sir!

Only when I heard trams stopping and pulling away did I venture out. Two armoured scout-cars were speeding off away from the city, and from that I concluded that Hitler had already made off in that direction, giving the Reich's Trade Fairs City a wide berth; perhaps he was rushing away to a special train waiting in a siding in Liebertwolkwitz, but it certainly wasn't an occasion for riding in his open Mercedes, standing up, hand angled back in salute, through a tumult of cheering. I had seen that picture so often in the newsreels that I couldn't imagine Hitler any other way. Now, though, I had experienced the sight of him plodding about like any park-stroller.

Over lunch, I told my Marianne all about what I had seen, and her eyes went wide as saucers. I warned her: not a word to anyone! I didn't so much as mention it to the children, and during my shift at work I kept my mouth shut. What the eye doesn't see . . .

The following day was spent clearing away unexploded incendiary bombs in Wolfen; we blew up the duds in a sand-pit. The travelling and the waiting put in the time, the work itself barely took more than an hour. After the last detonation we sat on the slope, chatted a bit, watched Russian prisoners of war loading the scrap-metal remains onto a lorry, back-breaking work for these scrawny blokes.

I couldn't get Hitler's visit out of my head. I tried to work out why I was so convinced that this house-call had to be kept secret, even though it hadn't the slightest significance, neither strategic nor in terms of the war effort. Every year, he paid tribute to the dead outside the Feldherrnhalle in Munich, but I had never heard of him pacing across, say, the war graves at the Somme or in Champagne, he had never been sighted at Verdun, where lay the bones of Viktor Machul, nor at the Lingekopf. Hitler doing the rounds of the dead at the Battle of the Nations?

Next day, up at the Monument: bright-looking types bustling around, some of them in the uniform of the Todt Organisation, civilians in white lab-coats pointed upwards and exchanged conjectures in loud voices, they asked for blueprints, but the Monument attendants simply shrugged: nothing of that sort here, maybe you could try the city archives? 'Orders from the Führer,' I heard, 'The Führer's instructions!' But even a command from God doesn't automatically make documents materialise, so I helped them from memory: height, breadth, weight, the number of supporting buttresses and of the horsemen in the dome, the proportions used in mixing the concrete, due honour was paid to Felix Linden, as to Voiciech Machulski and to Clemens Thieme. To be sure, I didn't have at that time as I have today the feeling that Carl Friedrich Lindner and Voiciech Machulski, for example, live on within me. I had not yet come across Carl Friedrich's tombstone in Otterwisch, while Voiciech, well, my father had of course told me about him and I had instinctively sensed some of his feelings of guilt towards him, but I had thought very little about the relationship between the two of them. I had not yet set foot in, never mind demolished, Fürchtegott's little palace – in other words, I was then standing only at the threshold of the formulation of my present view of things past. But I knew the Monument well enough to be able to tell the architects more about it than all the caretakers and the guides put together. The gentlemen made notes, measurements and estimates, balanced drawing-pads on their knees, and what emerged from their scribblings were Monument-like sketches, domes set in limitless landscapes under fleeting clouds. These weren't the small patchwork fields of Mölkau and Engelsdorf, but rather the Steppes

100

beyond the Don and the Dnieper. From there had come the Huns, and now were coming the T34s, as one of the artists whispered in answer to my question, that was where the Castles of the Dead were to be erected and under them the divisions that Hitler had despatched into these vast expanses were to have their last resting place. Führer's orders.

After a few days, it became the regular practice for the architects to come in and sit with me in the underground shelter during their morning break. They had been billeted, they told me, in a hotel on the Rossplatz, where they were able to live a relatively merry existence: there were cinemas in the vicinity where they could have a good laugh at films starring those great ladies, Leander and Rökk, and Messrs Lingen and Platte; there the war could be forgotten for an hour and a half. 'Buy me a pretty coloured balloon' – song hits were as much a part of these times as the wailing of the air-raid sirens. Round the corner was the Panorama, a circular, steel-and-glass building; didn't it have a revolving dance-floor, lit from beneath? If you were that way minded, you could cross the Tauchnitz Bridge and pay a visit to the Gewandhaus to listen to its famous orchestra. I could reel off to you the names of all the cafés and restaurants and dives all the way down to the Bavarian Station. Who was to know at that time that that quarter had only a few more weeks to live?

Führer's orders, muttered the architects, Castles of the Dead, Theoderich's tomb in Ravenna. I heard talk of death as the culmination, the crowning point of life, they quoted from the Edda: eternal is the glory of the deeds of the dead. They repeated it, savouring its rhythm: the gloryofthedeedsofthedead!, as if burning with the desire to charge, in the firing-line, perched on tanks, to surge, peering through the embrasures of their gun-turrets, ever eastwards, straight into the maw of their own mausoleum. Round-arched windows like those of the Battle of the Nations monolith dominated all their sketches, and I had the vision of skeletons, draped in tattered uniforms, their bony fists still gripping machine-guns with barrels fused by heat and rifles with shattered butts, marching in through these arches. I pictured Hitler among them, as sloppy in his movements as he had been a few days previously, Führer, command, we follow! They ran after him right up to the portals of the Castles, columns of them rattled past him into their crypts. Suddenly, it came to me, like a bolt of lightning it hit me: the war was lost, and Hitler knew it.

101

Having reached the halfway stage of their work, the architects held a celebration, and invited me along. The remainder of their time here, they confided, would be taken up with the testing of materials, the construction of models and fitting the whole thing into given dimensions. On a piece of open ground in the Southern Cemetery, not far from the stadium of the VfB, who at that time couldn't make any impression on the Sportclub from Dresden, they trowelled and raked out a mini-landscape complete with two river-banks, one steep and one shallow; they marked out marsh and scrubland, and brooded over whether or not they should build a little bridge on piers. To the east, the plain was open and barren, on the steep west bank the memorial was to rise. They then dropped the idea of the bridge after all, since what was wanted was not communication but isolation; for those who had made the journey to this place, there was no way back. The question was how many dead were to find their resting place here, ten thousand, fifteen thousand, even eighty thousand – grown men played with little building blocks representing little houses, and toy tanks with cannons inclined; flanking the approaches to the burial mound, they set up tiny poplar trees they had had sent from their children's toy-boxes. They positioned their plaster of Paris monument prominently on a ledge jutting from the steep slope and then lay on their bellies on the flat east bank to squint at the visual effect. They could have been lying prone in very different circumstances, of course; they might have been pressing their faces into the muck of some barrack-square, or in a foxhole out in the real Russian vastness, and they knew only too well that an abrupt translation to that particular environment would be their reward if they came up with anything less than the desired first-class product.

Two of them had got their wives to come to the party, we drank French red wine, ate cake that one of the ladies had baked, with real fat, in peaceful Pomerania, while the other had brought sausages from the Bavarian Forest. One architect had in his case some Slivovitz, spoils of war from the mountains of Bosnia, another had lean bacon from the Dutch coast. We passed round cigarettes and pouch tobacco from Greece. With my explosive expert's dexterity, I showed them the trick of laying the tobacco on the paper, packing it and rolling the cigarette ready for the finishing lick of the tongue – all with *one* hand. One of them ordered meat-balls all round and paid for them with his precious traveller's ration coupons: no bother, he assured us, his brother owned a butcher's shop in Neukölln in

Berlin. And so we feasted – a feast it was, if the standard of living at the time was your criterion – and drank to the success of the Castles of the Dead project, and nobody spared a thought for the poor sods for whom they were designated. As for me, could I be sure I would always be exempted? Cheers, friends! We raised our glasses, the two wives hung fondly on the necks of their husbands while the others eyed them with mingled envy and lust, for their wives and sweethearts were far, far away and they hadn't yet managed to get to grips with any of Leipzig's girls or widows. I was getting pretty merry and was completely in agreement when one of them, who even on this occasion wanted to talk shop about crypts and ossuaries, was put firmly in his place. And, as the clock-hand approached ten, the architects gathered round the Blaupunkt radio set and twiddled and listened until they were sure they had found the Belgrade station on the dial, and then that song to end all songs lilted out into the silence: 'Underneath the lantern, by the barrack-gate,' Lale Andersen's every word glowed in the innermost corners of every heart, 'Darling, I remember the way you used to wait,' awakened yearnings and fulfilled them, that song spread its warmth from the Steppes of the Ukraine to the Siegfried Line in the west, and over us; at that moment, in the south of Italy, perhaps British and German artillery were pausing in their mutual bombardment to listen for a while before resuming their barrage, ''twas there that you whispered tenderly, that you loved me, you'd always be . . .' was heard by German soldiers' wives and French partisans alike, 'I'd hold you tight, we'd kiss goodnight,' that grabbed at your soul, and melted it, and I make no claim to being an exception to that, we drew silently on our cigarettes, 'Even though we're parted,' even if I'm incinerated, drowned, shot up, shot down, 'you'll wait where that lantern softly gleams,' life goes on, mate, pal, comrade, even if yours doesn't, volunteers, one pace forwards, open fire! We all stared straight ahead, not daring to look each other in the eye, and, as the last strains died away, tadumdadadumdadadumdada, the last post, the man next to me laid his head on the table.

'Come on, we'll get a breath of fresh air,' I suggested and pulled him to his feet. His face was waxen, and I was afraid he'd puke all over the place. A sentry stood in the hotel foyer, giving us a suspicious look, I led my unsteady friend past him and said, all matter-of-fact, 'He'll be OK.' Once outside, sure enough, he did vomit his guts up.

Before us lay the darkened street, the pitch-dark street; not even when a door was opened did light penetrate. A perfect wartime nocturnal street-scene, with the sounds of footsteps and distant voices, into which the man said: 'Did you know, the Führer was at the Monument?'

I was immediately on my guard. 'Why shouldn't he be?'

'Have you ever yearned after death? Up there?'

'Rubbish!'

'It crushes everything that lives,' he was talking more to himself than to me, 'anybody that wants monuments like that has lost all faith in victory.'

'Listening to that schmaltzy song just now has been too much for you,' I said soothingly, 'and don't let anyone else hear you talking like that about victory.'

'I'm only telling you.'

'You're just a bit maudlin. Now not another word about it.'

'Ten thousand dead, sixty thousand – why not a million? What's the population of Leipzig?'

'Seven hundred thousand before the war, the Jews and the soldiers have gone, but in their place we've prisoners of war and foreign workers – can't be many less than that.'

'A memorial to them all, all dead in one single bunker, and the Führer . . .'

At that, I put my hand over his mouth. 'Anybody can see you're blind drunk,' I said to him, clearly and firmly, 'and if you don't keep your trap shut, I'm going to stand you on your head.' He gurgled a bit, but didn't struggle. Warily, I tried taking my hand away from his mouth, and he sniffled. Then I said, 'Go on, get yourself back inside. And you can tell the others I didn't feel too good and I've gone home. And thanks again for the meat-balls.'

For some days after that, I saw nothing of the architects. Everyone's afraid of dying, I reflected, perhaps it comes easier when thousands go to their death together? Maybe it wasn't so terrible for Voiciech after all? It's a lonelier death in bed at home or in a hospital ward than with a 'Hurrah!' on your lips. Carl Friedrich Lindner never shook off the fear of death and had tried to fight it, his teeth had chattered. But then look at Fürchtegott, capable only of tired words out in these fields of silence – would he not have preferred to ride, he who was barely able to sit a horse – alongside thousands of others into the Valley of Death? Thou, sword at my left side, what the hell bodes thy gleam so bloody bright? On now, the time is nigh, my steed, so be it, for we ride against . . . I no longer considered my architect in his cups quite so crazy; it was simply a combination of red wine and Lili Marlene making him spew out a few thoughts. And I wondered: because everyone's afraid of death, maybe they make a bee-line for it when it can be had at a bargain price? Even though we're parted . . .

So far, Leipzig had been barely grazed by the bombers as they paid their nocturnal visits to the petrol refineries in the surrounding area. On those occasions a stick of high explosives would maybe rain down here and there, or a clutch of incendiaries. Then half a house would have disappeared, a roof would go up in smoke, children would collect bits of shrapnel and swop them for cigarette cards.

I did my fire-warden's duty at the post in the Schenkendorf Strasse. To get there, I'd take the number 22, past the Monument, across the level crossing at the Bavarian Station and on down to the abattoir. From the bridge I could see across the city centre with all its towers, roofs, the gasworks, the domes on the roof of the covered market, the biggest of their style in Germany or indeed in the world. With sirens wailing and blue light flashing, we'd race out to Leuna or to Bitterfeld, where we would use both water and foam to extinguish fires, and I'd crouch over bombs and mines and go to work with my forceps; we chalked up our defusings like fighter pilots registering their kills. Now and again we had lectures from colleagues from the Rhineland, in which they explained the methods, practised by the British and Americans, of mixing explosives and incendiaries together, or incendiaries first and then, in a second wave an hour later, the high-explosives, so as to hit the fire-fighters, and then finally dropping blockbusters into the heart of the fires. A terrifying word went the rounds: fire-storm. If individual fires joined up and spread into an inferno right across the city, then it was beyond all salvation.

On one further occasion, I watched the architects, face down in the cemetery, squinting up at three miniature burial mounds. The first dome was built out on a mini-bend of their mini-river, the others stood further back, flanking it. The architects chatted on about charnel-houses and ossuaries in just the same tone as other folk would have talked about larders and nurseries. The next evening, so they told me, they were going to have a farewell party, and I was most cordially invited. Sorry, I lied, but I had to be on duty. With that, they stretched out again in their imaginary expanses and peered through winter-grey grass, pretending it was maize; they conjured up for themselves fields of sunflowers, rutted tracks, little houses with interwoven fences, little wells, tiny cows and oxen and the little peasant on his pony and trap, only they didn't think in terms of 'pony and trap,' but, in Wehrmacht gobbledegook, of 'indigenous unit of transport'. Nor in terms of 'peasant', but 'Russkie'.

That night was my night off; I went to bed early. I woke from a dream, bathed in sweat: an old man had been walking beside a horse and cart through Leipzig's southern suburbs, down Kantstrasse and Steinstrasse, emptying waste-bins, for there was a campaign on to cheat the Squander-Bug, whose menacing, wide-mouthed image glowered down from posters everywhere, and every last kohlrabi leaf was to be refined by pigs' digestive systems. But it wasn't potato peelings and carrot stalks he was tipping into his cart, but human skulls, some of them bleached, others charred and blackened, many of them with staring eyes still in their sockets. Apart from the skull-collector, the streets had been deserted, the clattering of the horse's hooves the only sound. I could still hear it once I was wide awake and fully aware that I was lying in my own bedroom, with Marianne breathing beside me. There was no prospect of an early return to sleep, so I went into the kitchen and drank a few mouthfuls of water. I pulled up the creaking roller-shutter that was our black-out and opened the window; dark was the night, and soundless. I switched on the radio, twiddled the tuning knob and listened in to the wire-messages on the short wave; once again it was all action high above the Reich, Freya transmitters were trying to get a fix on bomber-fleets, in an attempt to distinguish between where the raiding formations were headed and where diversionary Mosquitos were simulating attacks; night-fighters over Quedlinburg; it was a safe bet that everywhere it would be raining strips of silver foil in a game of hide-and-seek, with snowstorms shimmering on radar screens. My thoughts turned back to the skull-collector and I tried to banish them, but they kept sneaking back in between the radio reports. Pyramids of skulls, a man driving his carriage over Leipzig's boneyards – now the reports from the present-day Reich of the living and the dead were again gaining the upper hand in my attention: combat formations had been located between Magdeburg and Berlin, diversionary raids in the Dessau area, heavy bombers over Thuringia, heading north-east, all the indications were that the capital was in for a bitter night of it. I still can't explain today what made me get dressed; I rolled the shutter down again and wrote a

106

note, which I left on the kitchen table: 'Gone up to the Monument.' When I put my cap on, it was ten minutes to three.

I hadn't got all the way up the Schönbach when the early warning was sounded. From the north-west came the rumble of flak, the city was being given a preview of the instruments of its torture. The time-lag between the early warning and the defensive barrage seemed unusually short, I thought, when suddenly the sirens howled out their full-scale alert, presumably the British, in a surprise manoeuvre behind a curtain of tin-foil, had veered abruptly off their course to Berlin and were rushing towards Leipzig. I broke into a run – I knew every inch of the path leading down between the fences and the plane-trees – and, just as the last wails of the sirens died away and I had almost reached the embankment, the horizon was filled with that droning, which I shall never forget until my dying day, that thundering that rushed down from the skies and propagated itself in vibrations through the ground, the battle-roar in the night sky of four hundred and fifty four-engined assailants, that set the heavens and the earth quaking. At the entrance to the bunker, the thump of running feet and the Babel of voices drowned out the rumbling from the sky. I heard one of my civil defence colleagues shouting to the people to move on quickly, and went up the stairway in front of the Monument. It was impossible to make out the city under the cloud-layer, all lights were covered, every sound had died away, the trams and the trains had all stopped. The city played dead before its enemy. The roar pushed closer, like an approaching storm-front, a glowing orb fell like a comet, and in that instant I knew: the raid had begun. In their nimble Mosquitos, the Markers, specialists in advance target-spotting, sped in first – they operated under a terrible trade name: Master-Bombers. These masters of their profession radioed their instructions back to the first Pathfinder group, who released flares that floated down on parachutes and provided light to guide the second wave of Pathfinders in the accurate placement of their heavier flares. Behind them marched the cohorts of Bomber Command, battle-hardened over so many a German city. I spread my hands on the stone wall and propped myself on them, a shiver of fear ran through me as I was struck by a thought: what if Marianne and the children were still in the flat? I was too paralysed by fear and curiosity to run down and creep behind the ramparts, and so I was able to watch sheaves of light waft brilliantly down onto the city; these flares – Christmas-Tree, they were called – were the final signal. Then bombs fell with that spattering sound that is quite unique. Fire-bombs struck the city centre and threw up splashes of flame, squirting out over roof-tops, there were detonations here and there amongst it all which my demolition expert's ear identified as aerial mines. And again that spurting of fire towards the south, it was all surging forward at the quick-march tempo of the British up there, yet in the midst of all my terror there was room for the realisation that, at least on this approach, the bombers would spare Marianne and my children and the house that I called home. The banging and crashing was above me, in me, reached down into the crypt, the stone sentries trembled in the din of the engines, the horsemen in the dome rode homewards through the pandemonium of the raid, and in front of me, death galloped across the city, now it was in the Braustrasse, at Trades Union House, and that was another land-mine, roofs were blazing in Connewitz now. Then I ran down the steps, along the embankment, skirted the lake and the cemetery. At the plinth topped by Napoleon's Hat, commemorating the spot where he had admitted defeat, I swung off left, and here began, for Regular Fireman Alfred Linden, the duty-turn to end all duty-turns. From the bridge, out over the railway lines leading to the Bavarian Station, I could see a wall of flame towering above the roofs all the way to the domes of the covered market; the city, still the fourth biggest in Germany, was a raging inferno. I ran on into the darkness, unable to make out where I set foot, and heard the receding roar of the bombers, who were now threading their way back home to base through night-fighters and ack-ack, their crews perhaps lighting up cigarettes, assuming of course that smoking was permitted on board a bomber, for the hardest part of their shift was now behind them. They would fight their way home to a breakfast of tea and bacon and egg, while I ran to join my comrades in the fire brigade. Now even the last spare engine would be pressed into service, the replacement hoses would seek glowing targets, the last sand-bucket and the shabbiest fire-beater would be called upon, and the demolition expert was now first and foremost a fireman. I was thirty-one years old, in peak condition, and engaged in a profession that demanded agility, and I trotted to the Schenkendorfstrasse in ten minutes. I had loosened my scarf and had my cap in my hand, I ran down the middle of the street, the sky over the houses grew brighter and brighter, reds and yellows mingling, I ran towards the city centre, thinking, my God, every single house is on fire there.

Our chief was standing at the gate, yelling orders in all directions. Still pulling on my overalls, I leapt onto a tender standing ready with its engine running. When I had buckled my belt and pulled on my helmet, it set off for action with orders to head for the Augustusplatz. Houses were ablaze in the Kohlenstrasse, in every side street, the householders there would have to fight the flames on their own. At the Bavarian Station, in the Windmühlenstrasse and at the Rossplatz we could have found any amount of work, flames were leaping out of the upper storeys, incendiary bombs hissed on the roadway and gnawed their way into the asphalt. People tried to block our passage, we should save *their* homes and not somebody else's; our driver drove straight at them until they jumped aside. The Augustusplatz! The flames raged out through every window on the square; in the hotel where the memorial architects lodged and where I had been invited to the previous evening's festivities, flames were roaring out of the front entrance. We sped across torn-down tramway cables towards the Opera House, which was blazing fiercely, as was the General Post Office, we coupled our hoses to a hydrant and ran out our ladders. The water bulged along the hose, the jet ran along the roof edge leaving a dark trace, well, at least it reduced one little bonfire to smoking embers. In normal circumstances, there would have been three, five, perhaps eight fire appliances drawn up here, surrounding the rambling building on all sides, but now we fought alone along the façade, with no idea of what was going on in the inner courtyards. Maybe there wasn't a soul in the place, no one knocking incendiaries off piles of parcels for the troops and carrying them outside on a shovel to douse them in a bucket of water, no one hauling sacks of letters to and from the front lines out of the danger zone, no one rescuing sheets of stamps bearing a hundred copies of the Führer's portrait, just us, directing our column of water in through a window, drenching indiscriminately greetings cards and news of the birth of a second war-baby, the letter from a company commander bearing the tidings that your courageous brother, son, husband, brother-in-law had, in the front line of battle, laid down his life for Germany, convinced of ultimate victory. The Museum was beyond all hope, as was the Opera, the Café Felsche was burning only fitfully, the University Church next to it not at all, three tenders were at work at the façade of the University itself. The thought crossed my mind: a second raid with high explosives now, that would send us running for cover and force everyone down off the roofs, and the city would be a goner.

A couple of hours on, and we were reinforced by soldiers from the barracks in Gohlis. Together we broke our way into a courtyard, dragging a hose behind us, so that we were able to prevent the fire spreading over to an undamaged wing – it's still standing today. We gave up the front section of the building for lost and, from the Grimmaischer Steinweg, deluged a stretch of roof, the soldiers threw parcels on to a trolley and manhandled it out into the open. Commands were bawled and obeyed, and, when we had isolated a second wing, we propped ourselves against our tender or flopped on to piles of mailbags, the soldiers unscrewed the tops of their canteens and passed mugs round, we poured water from the hydrants down our throats, and then somebody remarked that we had been in action for nine hours. On that 4 December 1943 daylight never came to Leipzig.

The soldiers had thrown parcels and packets, some of them singed, some soaked, out of the windows and into the yard, where they now lay, burst open, gloves and socks, packets of cigarettes and cakes lay in confusion, and looting carried the death penalty. I told my brigade chief I'd have to report back to our station now, because it was time for my shift at work, so that soon I wouldn't be a reserve fireman any more but a duty foreman explosives expert. But I didn't rush directly to Schenkendorfstrasse, instead, I hurried past the burning St John's Church, along Hospitalstrasse. Book Trade House was ablaze, as was the old folks' home on the Ostplatz. This was where the fringes of the carpet of bombs had fallen, for then I emerged from the heat and smoke into an area where I could breathe again; at a baker's, diagonally across the Ostplatz, only some fifty metres from the crackling window-frames of the burning old folks' home, people were queuing for bread. I turned off into the Stötteritzer Strasse, walked, broke into a run again, in our street all the windows shone like mirrors, in the hallway of our block a woman cried, 'Herr Linden, what a terrible mess you are!' Nothing had happened here, she said, the children were playing in the copse and my wife had just gone out, probably shopping. I felt like someone who has just been released from Hell and realises that the world isn't one great hell, there are little flecks of Paradise in it. I left word that I, too, was safe and sound and that I was now going to work, I'd be home some time but had no idea when, my wife was just to go ahead and not wait for me.

Up Schönbach again, past the Monument and across the bridge, and I could see fires burning from Connewitz Station across to the city centre and on towards the east, but Stötteritz behind me was still in one piece. Many houses had been completely destroyed, their

110

interiors had collapsed and lay in smoking heaps, I saw women carrying bundles and pushing piled-up handcarts; the homeless were leaving the smouldering city. All this went on enveloped in an oppressive silence; it was as if people could no longer bring themselves to say any more than was absolutely necessary. In one fell swoop, children became adults, eight- and ten-year-olds were suddenly mother and father to their younger brothers and sisters. Everyone did the needful and the essential without complaint, amazed at still being alive; relief at still being able to breathe inspired these efforts, the tears would flow later. Soldiers shovelled their way through rubble towards the entrance to a cellar, boys of the *Jungvolk* marched past, singing 'The Blue Dragoons are riding . . .' Singing wasn't forbidden just because people lay dead under the ruins, and anyway, the Royal Saxon Blue Dragoons had been dead for a long time.

I started my shift right on schedule. Reports of unexploded bombs were pouring in, the police had evacuated houses and cordoned off streets. When my two assistants and I pushed our way through the onlookers, we were met with looks of mingled fear and trembling admiration, in the eyes of these people we were heroes who risked life and limb for the sake of furniture, clothing, books, photo albums and hoards of food, and also for their sons' Field Post numbers.

A mine lay in a courtyard among fallen rafters and broken bricks and tiles, a prize specimen that could have wiped out a whole block of flats; all it had done here was to smash a wash-house to smithereens. I was familiar with these Royal British landmines from my theory studies, this one was 'medium capacity', the model with reinforced casing for increased penetration, weighing four thousand pounds. I snooped around it and established that special relationship with it, without which no explosives expert can hope to survive: it's you or me, and how do you feel about me? Everybody has seen it all in the cinema, surgeons scrubbing up before an operation and whistling to give themselves courage, then gradually falling silent, their expressions becoming serious, and nurses and assistants attentively fussing round them. In the same way, I gathered my concentration, my assistants laid out the tools and warily we sniffed and probed around. The detonator was accessible although unfortunately it had been dented a bit. It wouldn't be an altogether smooth ride. I sent my helpers back to take cover round the corner of the neighbouring block of houses, and then I put my pincers in place, concentrated one hundred per cent, shut my eyes and was barely aware of an

111

ambulance siren wailing in the distance – someone being rushed to hospital – when I felt the pressure, the resistance put up by a jammed British screw-thread, and I wished I could have beside me the joker from Liverpool or Coventry who had cut that thread and been such a sloppy worker. All the same, he would have quite rightly reckoned that it was destined for use only on a one-way journey – there was no provision for customers sending back faulty goods. Nevertheless, his shoddy workmanship could cost me my life. I felt it yield just slightly, my hands, my arms picked up this first movement, geared down the pressure, in synchromesh, you might say, every sinew, every muscle, every nerve responded, and I thought, after that frantic night-shift at the General Post Office, it could have been a lot worse.

Once the detonator had been laid on a rag, I called my assistants over and passed on the details of the job, not without pride and an air of composure. We took away the detonator, auxiliaries would busy themselves with the now harmless monster; maybe it would be tarted up and returned to sender by German pilots? Not our problem, though. We rumbled over to the railway yards at the Central Station, past one burning house after another, at least on the Dittrich Ring there were still a few standing. The Schauspielhaus theatre had been destroyed, like the Opera, soot, flames and smoke drifted out from the Blücherstrasse. Viktor's lions had padded down here – gone, forgotten; at the spot where they had broken loose, a thousand-pounder lay among the track ballast; this one I recognised from my training course at Zeithain, it would give me no trouble, provided the thread-tapper on the enemy islands had earned his money honestly this time. I let one of my assistants finish off the job, just as a surgeon leaves one of his juniors to put in the last stitches after an operation. We trudged across the railway tracks and saw the glassless skeleton of the Central Station canopy and some burning goods sheds and finally the ruins of the Crystal Palace with its famous Albert Hall; never again would wrestlers parade in to the strains of the 'Entry of the Gladiators', the seats for fifteen thousand spectators were no more. Leipzig had buckled at the knees that night, it was groaning and writhing, twitching and bleeding, it had gone through the most terrible day in its history. In the Täubchenweg I drew the life from one more bomb, an M64 all-purpose high-explosive, and then I was at the end of my tether, muttering that I had to get to bed now, or else the next sample would go off around our ears. We rolled the dead bomb to the kerbside, a woman embraced us in gratitude, stammered something and finally kissed my hand.

I was so exhausted that I knew I wouldn't be able to get to sleep. I went home the long way round. I wanted to see what had become of the Post Office, whether there had been any point in all our frantic efforts. In front of the Opera, where after the war a pavilion would be erected and then torn down again because it wasn't to Ulbricht's liking, a field-kitchen had drawn up on the corner and survivors were standing around it, holding out bowls, plates or pots for a helping of noodles and meat. Bombed out of their homes, they moved on in silence, not even breaking it to exchange details of what they had lost, their grandfather, perhaps, or their only child, every stick of furniture or their plumber's workshop. There would be plenty of that later on, but for the moment they were being given, without coupons, a helping of stew with enough meat in it for half a week's ration. An SA-man was ladling out the food: Felix Linden. He had pushed his cap back off his forehead and unbuttoned his coat, his belt hung on a hook intended for fork and ladle. My father held the ladle with both hands and each time performed a circular, swinging, dipping movement before he raised it up over the edge of the cauldron, waited till the noodles and gravy and bits of meat stopped dripping off it, and then carefully brought it over the plate or bowl or mess-tin, tilted it with a movement of his arms, not just his hands, and let the stew with all its exquisite ingredients slide off it so that not a single drop was wasted. What he was doing seemed to me then a sublime human activity, like the work of a midwife or one of those women who lay out a corpse for burial, or of a peasant in those old pictures, cutting the corn. The people moved on, as if it had been settled beforehand that each would receive only the one helping, whatever the size of his dish or the intensity of his hunger. Nobody claimed to be fetching umpteen portions, maybe for his sick or injured family; my father doled out even proportions of meat and gravy, irrespective of who the customer was, for this first warm meal after the conflagration. There were children there, and soldiers, Hitler Youth and old women, and I hoped I might recognise among them one of the architects who had, not far from this spot, in this night of raging fire, been celebrating the completion of their task.

When his cauldron was empty, my father handed his ladle to a Hitler Youth, who scraped out any left-overs. Storm Trooper Linden lit up a cigarette. 'Hello, Father,' I said.

'Freddie lad!' We shook hands and I took one of his cigarettes.

'Stötteritz wasn't touched,' we both said almost simultaneously. I had never seen my father looking so old, and he said, 'Freddie, you

113

look dead beat.' He was waiting for his field kitchen to be towed away by a lorry and refilled at a central canteen; three times already he had dished out stew in bomb-ravaged parts of the city. We gazed at the horror around us, the smoking ruins, the blackened façades. All that was left of one of the most beautiful squares in Europe were St Paul's Church and a part of the University. St Nicholas' was undamaged, according to my father, and crammed full of bombed-out families. I had heard that in Lübeck, during a second raid, the crowded churches had been smashed flat.

'Freddie,' said my father, 'our beautiful city.'

I wanted to say, 'But the Monument's still there.' It would have cost too much effort.

'You could've had a helping of stew.'

'Too done-in to eat.' I shook Father by the hand, he said, 'Love to the kids and Marianne.'

'And say hello to Mum for me.' I dragged myself along the Grimmaischer Steinweg and thought, how long will it be before the trams are running here again? Two women behind me were talking about how unfair it was that *everyone* in Leipzig was to get a special ration of coffee beans. In some parts of the city, they said, not a single bomb had fallen, they'd be having a good smirk to themselves there all right. It would suit them fine if the city centre had a raid a week.

An hour later I was home. Marianne helped me to wash. Six hours after that, I reported for duty again at my warden's post.

No lorry did come to fetch SA-man Felix Linden's field kitchen, and so he was still standing a couple of hours later on the Augustusplatz watching flames licking out of the northern end of the Augusteum. There was still something combustible there that hadn't been consumed, out of the glowing ashes flames climbed up a beam. With that, my father buckled on his belt and set off in the direction of St Paul's. The door stood wide, shouts rang out from inside, a mixture of warnings and cries of fear. He pushed his way in through the fleeing crowd and saw two men armed with buckets and fire-beaters rattling at a door till they forced it open; behind it a stair led upwards. Together, the three of them stood at the top, in the maze of beams above the arched ceiling, listening, sniffing, no, there was nothing burning here, and Felix Linden asked, 'Are you connected with the church?' They weren't, they said, they had been bombed out of the Ritterstrasse, they were a caretaker and a bookseller. 'Do you know your way around in here?' Again, no, they didn't. My father recalled an occasion when he had seen flames shooting out of a church, the synagogue it had been, only five years ago, and here, high up in the roof-truss of St Paul's, he could not shake off the notion that these flames had now returned to wreak vengeance. Perhaps, in one of the bombers, there had sat a man who had been driven out of Leipzig in those bygone days: a son of the furrier, Katzenstein, baptised by his father in the name Horst-Heinrich, but who, conscious of his racial origins, had changed it to Samuel, known to his fellow-airmen as Sammy. 'Nothing doing here,' reckoned the bookseller, relieved, and my father said, 'I'm not so sure, I've got a funny feeling. I'll stay on for a bit.'

It was gloomy up in that network of beams and rafters; the smell was of dust, not smoke. Felix looked out of a skylight down onto the square, his field kitchen was just being towed away. He knew nothing of the history of this church, the foundation walls of which had supported a monastery in the Middle Ages, nothing about the remains of a cloister under its stellar vault, nothing of its carved altar, the statue of the Margrave Dietzmann, the seated figure of St Thomas Aquinas, the tomb of Principal Caspar Borner, nothing about the organ, the façade dating from the most recent restoration and forming a unity with the Albertinum, the work of Arwed Rossbach. My father was a proletarian, not an art connoisseur, but he had seen a church burning once before. Now perhaps young Katzenstein had flown overhead, bent on revenge. When that thought occurred to my father, he was assailed by doubts as to whether it was right to try to stay his hand. If the church was destined to burn down, then he should not try to change the course of fate – or shouldn't he?

'We're off, then,' said the caretaker, who no longer had premises to take care of; he and the bookseller, whose books were floating as ashes over the city, took their leave. Felix Linden groped his way to the staircase that led up to a small turret, less a stair than a ladder in the criss-cross of the beams. His thoughts went to the stone steps inside the Monument to the Battle of the Nations, he had climbed up with his lad through the leg of the guardian, and at the top Freddie had yelled, 'I can see the whole world!' Steps up the Lingekopf, steps down into the Douaumont fortress – steps led down here, at the West Gable, in amongst the arches, but where to? That's where Felix Linden stepped on a plank, and from under it flames spat and sparked upwards, as if they had lain in wait there, hiding, mocking, fed by ancient timber and dust, perhaps bedded in woodworm-mull.

115

Under his boot they burst forth, which they might otherwise not have done for another day or so, and in an instant they had set a section of the floor alight. Felix Linden flailed at the flames with his beater, throwing up a shower of sparks, he ran back to the stone stairs and called down, 'Up here, everybody up here!' When he heard footsteps, when he caught sight of the cap and shoulders of a man at the bend in the stairs, he ran back to the seat of the fire, beat at it again, sparingly used the little water left in his bucket to soak a cloth, smothered infant flames under a beam, bawling, 'Bring water with you! And beaters!' He could feel it getting hot under the soles of his boots, so he had, in the nick of time, come upon a nest of fire, a vipers' nest, he took one step to the side, his foot went through, he heard a crack, sparks swirled up, he spread his arms to support himself, to gain a hand-hold, but there was nothing to hold but hot, crumbling timber, he cried out, it was more a gurgle than a cry, and then the bookseller and the caretaker saw him disappear in the fountain of sparks. He fell only some twenty metres, onto the wonderful, so precious stellar vault, and vanished in dust and decayed timber, which now flared up in the turbulence. The bookseller and the caretaker shouted to him and stretched out the handles of their fire-beaters, down towards him, but no hands reached out to grasp them. Felix Linden was asphyxiated, even before his SA greatcoat turned to tinder and his belt crumbled.

An hour later, firemen who had doused the seat of the fire pulled up the body of Storm Trooper Felix Linden. His face was still recognisable. Above the eyebrows the head had been badly burned. In one of the Trade Fair's exhibition halls, which had been turned into a mortuary, I confirmed that, yes, that was my father, there was no possible doubt. Around me, tarpaulins were being lifted from faces that were faces no more, I heard sobbing, no loud cries. At that time, people cried out into themselves.

The funeral service for those who died in December 1943 was held at the foot of the Monument to the Battle of the Nations, in the sight of the Archangel Michael and the Furies of War. The Lord Mayor made a speech; eighteen months later he shot himself in his parlour at City Hall. Marianne and I supported Klara Magdalena Linden. In my imagination, I thought, any moment now Hitler is going to creep up to the Monument from behind and peer over the wall, his hat down over his eyes. There was no more appropriate spot in Leipzig for such a funeral service, and I

116

hated the Monument for that. Was it the famous choristers of St Thomas' who sang, or was it just any old Hitler Youth choir who intoned a minor key?

> In the stars our oath is written.
> He who guides the stars will hear us.
> Ere the alien may usurp your crown,
> Germany, we shall die, shoulder to shoulder.

There it was again: not alone in bed, not too late, like most of them, as Nietzsche saw it, but at the appointed time, shoulder to shoulder, the dying was to be done. Then the burying, too, could be cheek by jowl, and a layer of lime on top. Mass graves demand simultaneous mass demise. Murat's cavalry charge, machine-gun fire at the Lingekopf, bombs on Leipzig, it was always the same. Felix Linden had quarried the stones and, with Voiciech, had slid the last slab into place on the top. He had piled up his own monument. While everyone else bowed their heads, I lifted my gaze. 1,100 tons of bombs had killed 1,182 citizens of Leipzig. One ton of bombs per person seemed to be considered a worthwhile investment, the going rate. The embankment paths were black with mourners, black the pylons up on St Michael's balcony, and on top of them flames leapt up into the winter sky out of the large flat dishes. The Lord Mayor, SS-Gruppenführer Freyberg, declaimed: 'The blow aimed at our city was dealt precisely at a time when the German people were preparing themselves for the most profoundly emotional and the most ancient of all German festivals, the Christmas Festival, during which the victory of light over the forces of darkness is celebrated.' Christmas as a German festival without Christ.

The dead were interred at the spot where the monumental experts had lain in the withered autumn grass peering into imaginary eastern expanses. Some of these architects are lying there now, too, shrivelled corpses retrieved from the hotel on the Rossplatz. The *Leipziger Neueste Nachrichten* carried the following report: 'Profound solemnity shrouds the faces of the people. But this is no mourning that abandons itself spinelessly to the pain of the suffering that has been sustained. No, what is shining in every countenance is that defiant determination that draws new strength out of grief, and on the lips pressed together in bitterness lies an unspoken "Now on, with a vengeance!" '

117

The graves were covered with stone slabs; they had been cut from blocks which, having been struck from all the plans for the Richard Wagner memorial, had lain redundant by the Elster lock. The elements have since obliterated the names on them. I haven't been there for a long time now. Fürchtegott, the skull specialist, could supply information as to whether we can still talk in terms of 'shoulder to shoulder'.

CHAPTER 8

You rescued the Monument?

I've talked little of the wives of my ancestors. Carl Friedrich Lindner died a bachelor, Fürchtegott's wife, repeatedly impregnated by him, has not once been mentioned up to now. Erna Machul has been given her due place. My mother and Marianne were courageous proletarian wives, self-sacrificing at the side of their men, impeccable mothers; they never sought the limelight. Let's put it this way: the Monument to the Battle of the Nations is men's business. Wouldn't you agree?

After the service for the air-raid victims, Klärchen and Marianne Linden made their way arm in arm towards town along the Preussen Strasse and down Schönbach. Erna Machul had brought her little ration packet of fresh coffee along to the funeral tea. Hildrun's telegram of condolence from East Prussia lay among the cups. The wooden figures that Father Felix had carved were set up on display, and Joachim was allowed to run his hands over them. 'It was Viktor

119

that got the wood for them,' Erna made her customary reference. She was all set to rehash the story about the lions, but we managed to stop her. The coffee was praised, *real* ground coffee it was, when did we last have a cup of that? It seemed to everyone as if real coffee had been part and parcel of our daily consumption before the war. The cake was heavy and tacky from the Masurian lard in it. Christmas was just round the corner – would there be a special ration allowance, and how generous could it be? Flour and sugar for baking Stollen, for sure, but what about fat? Meat? And would the next year see the end of the war? A second raid on Leipzig would have little point. What was there worth bombing in Lindenau and Plagwitz, Gohlis and Stötteritz? 'Oh, my Felix,' Mother blew her nose and wiped her eyes.

'He saved the church,' I said, trying to preserve dignity, 'I'll keep an eye on the Monument.'

Between then and Christmas, I defused thirteen high-explosive bombs; nobody kept a count of the half-burned or even intact incendiaries we disposed of. Everyone in our fire-station slaved a fifteen-hour day. A week after the raid itself, we were still digging survivors out – eight altogether, two children among them. The city still smouldered on; if flames shot out of the ruins, nobody bothered about them, so long as they didn't endanger undamaged houses. It was only a matter of a few days before we set about demolishing gutted buildings that threatened to collapse onto the streets. Scorched façades, teetering chimneys, gables leaning crazily. Modest charges were sufficient for the job. Drilling, sealing off, packing, detonating – a rumble and a crash, and another wall tilted and toppled into what had once been the interior of the building. Another piece of Leipzig had gone, a block of homes, a pub, a cinema. On the Brühl, we brought down the big block in which Katzenstein had traded in fox and ermine. A heavy layer of cloud pressed down on the city, as if the ruins were not worthy of sunshine. The snow that would have drawn a veil over so much was taking its time about coming. All over the place, people moved about, pulling handcarts, shifting what they had salvaged of their property, or taking empty window-frames to the glazier. When the wheels of the first trams squealed again outside the Central Station, that was an event that was talked about the length and breadth of the city.

On Christmas Eve, Mother, Marianne and I went to St Paul's. We looked up into the arched roof; a damp-stain showed darkly in the plaster. Above it, Felix Linden had laid bare a cancer whose metastases could have devoured the whole church. I hadn't been at a church service for years, and didn't know any of the hymns, and I was surprised by the smoothness of the interplay between preacher and congregation in the antiphony of preces and response. The talk was of the Infant Christ, who was supposed to have brought redemption upon the world, of God's protecting hand which preserved His house in the midst of the flaming inferno. Tears glistened in the eyes of my mother and my wife. For my part, I drew a comparison between the deaths of Voiciech Machulski and Felix Linden; no question who came out of it better. I surveyed the memorials down both sides and imagined a plaque being consecrated to Felix, the saviour. God gave men and women the strength, I heard the priest say, to protect this church. Did he perhaps feel that he would be doing God out of His full share of the glory if he mentioned my father by name, as God's tool? The organ wailed. A stain in the plaster – a caretaker and a bookseller, and after them the fire-brigade, had worked to put out the fire, both before and after they had extracted the body of Storm Trooper Linden from the embers. I made the wish that, if ever the church was renovated, that stain would be reproduced, just like Luther's ink-stain in the Wartburg, and, in centuries to come, tourist guides would point upwards: there, a man gave his life, guiding the church's deliverers. The priest prayed for all Leipzig's dead, especially for those of his parish. Naturally he included in his prayer none of those British airmen who had lost their lives in the course of that raid, not even air-gunner Samuel, alias Horst-Heinrich, Katzenstein, who grew up in a villa on the Johanna Park and who, in the rear turret of his Liberator bomber on its flight back to base, had been unable to fend off the attack by a German night-fighter over Lüneburg. In that night of horror, too, Gestapo files had perished in the flames, and with them details of plans for the deportation of those related by marriage to Jews: there was more than one side to that raid. For the first time since confir-mation, I joined in the praying, Our Father, which art in heaven. Now Felix Linden was in heaven, too, if there was such a thing as a heaven and if members of the SA were allowed admittance. The minister prayed: and grant us Thy peace. Not for the triumph of German weapons did he plead, nor for the life and well-being of the Führer, Adolf Hitler; those beseechings went out from many pulpits in Germany at that time. But not that night, and not in that church.

Back home, we put three candles into a candelabra, we talked of other Christmas-times; this one was the blackest so far. Should we get the children out of Leipzig, perhaps to Hildrun, in peaceful East Prussia? And should Marianne stay there with them? But would that be allowed, for who would cut out butter-coupons then, or measure out the bluish skimmed milk, exact to the last droplet? There was still left in us a little of that strength that the preacher had tried to arouse, a trace of faith in providence, that it couldn't be totally merciless.

In January 1944, we brought our underground air-raid shelter up to the very highest standards. Now, all the tunnels interconnected, the fresh-air vents were ready, an emergency generator made us immune from electricity failures, and the first-aid cupboards were stocked up. Night after night, people moved in, looking for refuge, even when the sirens remained silent. They secured the best places for themselves and settled down to sleep; if the sirens did go, the howling barely reached their ears. For many a one, the bunker became a second home.

And, once again, the Monument played host to visitors. This time, we had advance warning and I was to be their guide. Some high-up expert in the war economy, the boss of some armaments factory, was accompanied by other civilians and some Luftwaffe officers. This man didn't stalk the Monument secretly, taking it from the rear, as Hitler had done; instead, he drove up with his entourage to the open area next to the mass graves. He shook me by the hand and introduced himself by name: Freitag. 'Right then, show us the lot!' He was a director of the Henschel concern, one of the top organisers in air armament. I led him through all the tunnels, showed him the various rooms in the shelter, the anti-gas air-locks, the toilets, reeled off statistics about the thickness of the roofs. The height of the dome was of no interest to him whatsoever, he never so much as glanced up at the horsemen. He went down into the crypt, rapped on the pillars and inquired about the proportions used in mixing the concrete. The members of his entourage nodded their appreciation. 'Unfortunately, not enough room for machine-tools,' complained one of them. 'And think of the transport problem!' At that, the gentlemen shrugged their shoulders. 'Pity,' they agreed regretfully. 'Otherwise, ideal.' Director Freitag gave the order for all the rooms and passageways to be measured. 'We could accommodate fifty per cent of the engine production here, no trouble at all.' Production – did that mean that these people were going to draw the bombers towards the Monument and Stötteritz? My blood ran cold.

The gentlemen disappeared, to be succeeded by white-coats with folders and note-pads, just like the architects of the Castles of the

Dead in earlier days, and once again I was to be the one to satisfy their thirst for information. I reduced the proportions of cement to sand in the concrete and, when questions followed, claimed that I had unfortunately made a mistake during the first visit. Sorry. I described the rock roof of the underground chambers as crumbly, with an ash content from the tipping in the earliest days, leading to repeated subsidence during construction work, and I put on a show of irascibility: 'Go on, please yourselves, dig away, it's all the same to me. It'll all cave in on you. But go ahead, carry on!' At that, they all jotted down, with furrowed brows, more modest figures, hurried away, came back again the next day with, in their midst, a man of about sixty, in a shabby donkey-jacket, a foreman in the aircraft factory at Thekla on the north side of the city; he inspected the tunnels and snorted, and when we were alone he said, 'All right, so you don't want to lose your shelter. I can understand that. But you're on a loser here.' Since there was a danger of raids on all aircraft factories, Göring had given the order to disperse the centres of production; so the factory at Thekla was to be decentralised, too. A Fighter HQ with highest authority had been established, he said, and Freitag was reckoned to be one of the top men. 'Take my advice, chum, and don't make trouble.'

'Who, me?' I tried to look as dumb as I could.

In the days that followed, whenever I was asked for further details, I acted very cagily. I didn't exactly tell lies, just played everything down, so that my replies couldn't be interpreted as sabotage. I passed the bad news on, on the quiet, always in the hope that those who used our shelter might be stirred to protest. Faces turned earnest, eyes fixed, but other than that, nothing.

The foreman's name was Hallermann. He was stocky, with almost no neck, and bald; he had a quiet voice and small, grey eyes. He came back again and said, quite placidly, 'Just don't do anything stupid, mate!' He was armed with tape-measure and note-pad, he measured and noted, whistling tunelessly the while, and now and then muttering that there would be room for three lathes here, for two drills there; our little shed, on which we had nailed the 'Shelter Management' sign, he requisitioned as his office. 'All on Göring's orders, nothing you can do about it, mate.' That's the way it was all over the Reich, he said. Hitler's orders were for narrow mountain valleys, in Saxon Switzerland for example, to be roofed or covered over and for production to go on underneath. 'Bombproof,' murmured Hallermann, as he went on measuring, 'all bombproof.'

123

And then Göring appeared on the scene. In he strutted, through the galleries leading in from the Preussen Strasse, wearing a white uniform and all his medals, and he raised his Marshal's baton as I reported in due military fashion 'Volunteer Civil Defence Monument Shelter Warden Linden!' and stiffly presented arms with the shaft of my fire-beater. Göring stood with legs apart, his breeches arse-packed. His voice sounded forced, breathy. A cap? Of course he was wearing a cap. One of those steep-peaked ones. He took it off once to wipe the sweat off his bald patch. At the back of his head he had a small round bald patch – look, you're confusing me with your questions. I remember meeting Göring in the bunker, not outside, or not only outside. I suppose you're just waiting for me to claim that Göring had his Leipzig lion with him, on a leash, and other lions, revolutionary lions, you might say, unleashed by Tadeusz, leapt down from the shoulders of the giant statues and there was a yellow flurry, a bloodbath – forget it; nothing of the sort. There was no duel to the death, Simba *v*. Caesar, although I can see it would be very appropriate. Göring taking to his heels – no, nothing so cheap! Hallermann summarily dismissed the objections raised by the engineers: with three hundred men the whole place could be rejigged in a week and production could start. Göring never so much as spared a glance for the sentries up under the top-stone or the horsemen of the dome, and no one asked my opinion, of course. This is supposed to be a memorial to the dead, I should have said, not exclusively a monument to peace, I'll grant you that, but certainly not one to the glory of war – would that not have been reason enough to preserve the peace and quiet, which was after all only fitting and proper for a graveyard, from the roar of engines? A sin, to produce weapons here, of all places. I should maybe have made reference to the Furies of War in stone out at the front, and to the reliefs of horses rearing in mortal combat, but nobody gave me the chance. I talked about it at home in the evening. Marianne, in an attempt to ease my burden, assured me there was absolutely nothing I could have done. That's not what my father quarried the stone for, I said, Katzenstein didn't sit on the committee for that, and that's not why the dying Viktor Machul hallucinated that he had come home to the Monument. Marianne shot me a suspicious glance: 'And where did you get that bit about Viktor?' I just knew it, and that was that.

Dawn brought a clattering and shuffling, prisoners in striped jackets and trousers, clogs and pattens on their feet, made their way up the Reitzenhainer and bunched in a crowd at the entrances to the

124

bunker. Then Hallermann's voice, anything but quiet now; brandishing a spanner, he doled out shovels and instructions on how the digging was to be done and where the excavated earth was to be piled up, so that lorries could drive right up to the bunker doors. I found myself staring into faces where the skin was drawn tight over the cheekbones and the eyes were unnaturally large, I saw yellow stars on the jackets and heard Hallermann yelling. They were Jews, from Serbia, he told me later, and they reacted as if they understood not a word of German. Maybe, but how to work was something he aimed to teach them!

That's when I considered blowing up the bunker. I figured out how I might lay explosives with a time fuse at an entrance to the bunker during an air-raid and then put up a warning: 'Danger. Unexploded bomb!' When everyone had been evacuated from the danger zone, the charge would go off. No easy task; the explosives would have to be acquired and hidden, I'd have to manage without an accomplice. In my fire-station I purloined a flak detonator and examined it thoroughly to see that it was in good working order. A flak detonator is a precision instrument, and I could well understand someone putting one in their display cabinet as an ornament; heartbreaking to think that, in the proper performance of its function, each detonator has to be blown to pieces. I hauled a defused British four-hundred-pounder, hidden under potato sacks in a handcart, halfway across town and deposited it in the shed in our yard. Then I waited for an air-raid, or at least for an occasion when enemy bombers flew over the city.

Meanwhile, Hallermann and his German workers drove the Jews on. Guards stood by with shotguns, men of the local Landsturm militia, all of them yelling and laying about them the way people now say only the SS went on. One day I saw Felix Linden standing up there, on the embankment. I waved up to him; no reaction. He was looking down towards where a dozen or so feeble figures struggled to drag beams off a horse-drawn cart, poor, half-starved Jews, in constant fear of a beating. Along the Preussen Strasse came an old-fashioned carriage drawn by two white horses. It stopped, its occupant stepped down and threw the reins to a boy who happened to be hanging about, startled, he caught them and stood, wondering what to do with them; nothing like this had ever happened to him before. Fürchtegott von Lindenau had driven across the battlefield and now, for the very first time, he saw the Monument, and it was far more immense than he had ever dreamt. Then, all of a sudden, up on the embankment, the earth burst open and two figures emerged, the one with his skull smashed, the other one-legged, on a crutch, the one in Saxon uniform from the days of the Battle of the Nations, the other in the field-grey of the men of Verdun: Carl Friedrich Lindner and Voiciech Machulski leapt up and, side by side with Felix Linden and Fürchtegott von Lindenau, bore down on the tormentors. My father was wearing the threadbare suit in which, for many a long year, he had travelled to his work in Beucha, not the Storm Trooper's uniform of his dying day. He helped Voiciech over a pile of planks; that was no easy matter for the man with one leg. Voiciech swung a sapper's shovel and bawled, 'You swine, swine!' Carl Friedrich was first to reach the guards, he grabbed one and threw him down the embankment slope. Hallermann emerged from the tunnel, opened his mouth as if to shout something, but not a sound came out; Carl Friedrich stood four-square in front of him – with his gaping frontal bone and bloodied face, he must have presented a gruesome sight. Hallermann took to his heels, he tried to head across to the Preussen Strasse, but there, whip in hand, stood that mildest of men, Fürchtegott von Lindenau. In Voiciech, all the rage, all the shame engendered by the failures and defeats suffered by his party and his class, suddenly boiled over. The guardians high up on the Monument still stood with swords between their feet and not spades. And now they stood and watched as, beneath them, torturers went about their work and once again war and death were to issue forth from the Monument – with that, Voiciech swung at Hallermann with his shovel. Felix Linden, the one-time 'German Oak', roared himself empty of rage, laying about him with his quarryman-goalkeeper's fists; within three, two minutes they had mopped up, or perhaps it was only one minute, or mere seconds . . .

Can I have a glass of water, please? I haven't said a word for fully a quarter of an hour, and you haven't once urged me to go on. You could have interrupted me, should have done, when . . . when something came over me that puzzles me now; I hope that hasn't often happened before – or at all for that matter. Maybe you thought at first that I had just got confused in the timing of the sequence of events, that Felix Linden had died trying to save a church after, and not before, the attempt to desecrate the Monument. The resurrection of my ancestors to preserve the Monument from dishonour – that's something that had never occurred to me before. And yet it's a beautiful idea, sublime even. The more I think about it, the less it shocks me that, for a few minutes, I accepted it as a reality.

126

And now you ask what, of all I've just related, can be proved. Did I really mention Göring? He never came to the Monument. The bunkers were indeed intended to be used as a factory, that's for sure, there was talk of it. And did I cart a British bomb through the town? Well, certainly not for that purpose. I did know a foreman called Hallermann, it was common knowledge that he beat foreign workers and prisoners of war. Serbian Jews were employed in the aircraft works at Thekla, I saw their corpses after the air-raid. Of course, now you leap at the opportunity to mention the men in yellow overalls. They are no mere figments of my imagination – Doctor, why don't you order a visit to the scene of the crime? Why can't we go down into the crypt together? No, no, I'm more or less all right again. Still a slight feeling of pressure behind the forehead, but headaches like that are nothing unusual. Well, then, couldn't we shorten these proceedings a bit by visiting the Monument? Your answer is a familiar one – it was regularly employed with some relish by the gentlemen in that other institution on the Dittrich Ring that prefers to remain anonymous: we have plenty of time. I'm a pensioner, and, in addition, I find myself in this peculiar situation, which you refuse to call by its proper name: under arrest. Why shouldn't I have all the time in the world?

Thanks, the break did me good. A cup of coffee, now that I have after all swallowed the pills you had the nurse bring. To stabilise my circulation and heart-rate, according to you. Irrespective of whether we go on talking of my vision or not, it's going to remain with me for a long time.

Shortly after that, Leipzig suffered its first daylight raid. American bombers laid waste the Thekla fighter works, all the buildings and machinery, engines, wings, armaments, half- and three-quarter-finished planes, foreman Hallermann, Soviet prisoners, German workers and Serbian Jews, the lot. It was a pin-point attack, out of a cold sky. The Central Station took a hit or two, almost as an afterthought, and, as it turned for home, a Flying Fortress dropped a couple of high-explosives into the ornamental lake in front of the Monument. I was on watch at the bunker entrance at the time, and I heard them whistling, I ran inside and pressed myself flat against the wall and heard them hit the ground. Everyone in the shelter sat silent, motionless, hardly daring to breathe. My Joachim had pressed his lips together in a most un-childlike way, reacted like a man; he had only just turned seven. He had put both arms round his little sister. If I were a sculptor, I'd do a statue of a group like that. I'm surprised it's never been tried. Or maybe it has, and I just haven't come across it.

The bombs had torn open the clay lining of the basin, and a day later all the water had seeped away. Once more we set out to defuse duds, and we helped to carry away the dead or to clear a shelter where the roof had been smashed in. That was the same kind of hell as after Murat's charge on the first day of the Battle of the Nations, or at Verdun, bodies lying crushed and shredded, a mangled mess of guts and brains, scraps of blood-soaked clothing. We laid the remains in wooden boxes and sprinkled them with lime: when we had done our job, we slunk away; some vomited. Carl Friedrich Lindner couldn't have felt worse during that raging night before the great battle, Viktor Machulski couldn't have suffered more acute agonies between Douaumont and Fleury. My father in the gas attack on the Somme – I went through all these experiences then. When the prisoner Carl Friedrich Lindner was herded past the naked corpses of the French, on whose breasts their Christian looters had laid little mounds of earth, he was at the end of his tether, just as I was after that job in Thekla.

Once again, hearses drove out to the Southern Cemetery; this time there was no Lord Mayor to deliver an address – it was too much to expect him to do it after every raid. A few aircraft were salvaged, one or two undamaged engines were taken to other factories, but production never got going again here. There was no longer any call for machinery to be transferred to the bunker under the Monument to the Battle of the Nations. The petroleum plants all around us were ablaze, a daylight raid laid waste the marshalling yards at Waren; from the ramparts in front of the Monument, I watched the flashes of the explosions. The saddest job I had to carry out in those weeks was in the ruins of the Crystal Palace. My search for a 'VM' scratched into the plaster was a vain one; this was where I had joined in the applause when the wrestlers made their triumphal entry. The Albert Hall was a burnt-out shell, and we brought down the scorched skeleton of the dome. No routine job, this, with just a few kilograms of Donarite; we had to lay about twenty-five charges and detonate them simultaneously. There was a rending of steel, a bursting of pillars, and all that was left of Germany's greatest pleasure-palace was a mere heap of rubble.

In a letter from East Prussia, Hildrun told us her husband was having to help dig anti-tank ditches. Her parcels of flour and fat had stopped coming. No question now of sending our children off to peaceful Masuria; on the contrary, my mother worried about how, if the worst came to the worst, we'd manage to accommodate Hildrun and her children. Auntie Erna offered help. But that day, we hoped, was still a long way off; the Russians were sure to be thrown back at the frontiers of the Reich. Hildrun wrote to say she wanted to get out, but it wasn't allowed, for anyone who left their homes at this stage obviously had no faith in ultimate victory. We wrote back that there was room at Auntie Erna's, admittedly not a lot, and the western suburbs, so sorely decimated last December, were surely no longer worth further attention from the bombers.

That was the last we ever heard from Hildrun, her husband and her children. Wherever my mother wrote after the war, there was no information to be had, neither from local villagers nor from the missing-persons authorities. Missing, incinerated, or frozen to death.

The war was all but over, that was common knowledge, and, no two ways about it, it was lost. In those March days, women and children lay on the lawns around the Monument and along the ramparts, basking in the sun even before noon – it was the earliest, brightest spring I can remember. When the early warning sounded, they all fled underground like moles. By the time the full alert came, every place in the shelter was taken. Latecomers had to duck down behind gravestones in the cemetery.

We dug over our gardens and sowed radishes and planted potatoes and went out on the hunt for every last dollop of horse-droppings. The dairy, where Marianne worked, was now open only three hours each day. And two and a half of those were a waste of her time.

We hoped the war, our war, would come to a quiet end. However, one early morning, there was a swarming of grey-black characters around the Monument: Waffen SS. They arrived at a time of day when Leipzig folk were asleep in bed, five in the morning when there was no fear of an air-raid, the British airmen's night-shift was over, the Americans' day-shift hadn't yet begun. When, about eight o'clock, I went out to check that everything was in order, lorries were roaring up the approach-road, double sentries with sub-machine guns had been posted on all the paths. I showed my identity card, 'Voluntary Civil Defence, Monument to the Battle of the Nations', but it made little impression. 'Combat area,' barked one of them, and I replied, 'Nobody knows this place as well as I do.' At that, he went off to fetch his superior officer.

Eventually, I found myself talking to a wearer of the Knight's Cross. 'I'm the boss around here,' I said.

'Marvellous,' he shook hands. 'Then you can show me round the whole works. And, incidentally, *I*'m the boss now.'

Once again, I did my guided tour. In my commentary on the relative proportions in the concrete mix, I made it so thin that anyone with the faintest idea of the building trade would have been at a loss to understand how the Monument didn't disintegrate from one moment to the next. I pointed up to the round-arched windows: 'They'll not keep anything out.'

'Fine,' said the Knight's Cross, 'I'm appointing you our liaison man with the civilian population. Explain the new situation to them. Air-raid sheltering days here are over. The Yanks'll find us a tough nut to crack here.'

A headquarters was set up in our cabin. Telephone lines were strung up like spaghetti, I heard a voice reporting down from the top platform; the air-raid look-out confirmed that he had a clear line of sight over the whole city. I put on my arm-band, in the hope that it might lend me a little authority. When I stepped out into the open, I saw little knots of people on the Reitzenhainer Strasse, but they soon dispersed, realising off their own bat that the situation had changed and that they'd best go off and find some other bolt-hole. Knight's Cross and I walked along the ramparts and I outlined our network of ventilation shafts to him. On the flat space that had once been the lake, an army camp had been erected. SS-men, some sleeping, others putting up tents, smoke rising from campfires. More SS were dragging bundles of wooden fencing over from the cemetery, and I remarked, 'Just like before the Battle of the Nations. Only then the weather was lousy.' Knight's Cross laughed. 'A fantastic position,' he reckoned. 'Like an old fort. All we have to do is block up the entrance over there at the front.' I hadn't ever considered the ramparts in that light. 'Just like Douaumont,' I conceded, hesitantly.

On the square, where the buses park now, there stood two 88mm guns manned by ack-ack gunners and Hitler Youth. Shells were being carried into the burial chambers. 'Wouldn't be a bad thing,' said Knight's Cross, à propos of nothing, 'if you were to volunteer for the SS. Then I could put you in command of all the surrounding streets. Eh? What d'you say?' He seemed highly delighted by his own bright idea. 'I'm a fireman,' I said. 'Sorry, but I just can't up and leave like that.'

'We can fix that,' he said brightly. 'When the time comes, I'll promote you to Untersturmführer. For the moment, dismiss. Report back at two. Understood?'

'Everything OK, chief,' I said. At that, his face suddenly took on a grim expression; he seemed to be trying to make up his mind whether I was taking the mickey.

Marianne had made soup from crushed rye-grain, given a flavour with browned onions. Naturally, the SS was the sole topic of our conversation. 'I'm never going back up there again,' I said. Then it occurred to me that, after the death of my father, I had sworn to protect the Monument. 'Well, anyhow, you'll have to find yourself another air-raid shelter.'

'Maybe we could dig a hole for ourselves out in the fields?'

'No need for panic, but don't put it off till it's too late, either.'

When I tried to get back to the post to report in, I was told that Knight's Cross had gone off on a reconnaissance of the western outskirts of the city. I watched as more and more supplies were loaded into the Monument and the bunkers. There were foxholes and machine-gun nests peppering the ramparts. Down below, the camp had been tidied up, tents stood in rows, the corners were marked out by four-barrelled AA guns. Goulasch with macaroni was being dished out at a field-kitchen, an SS man offered me a mess-tin and a spoon, and as I wolfed down the unrationed food I thought back to the noodle stew my father had ladled out. Things had to come to a pretty pass in Germany before the ordinary man got the chance to fill his belly.

The skies remained empty of the enemy, Knight's Cross got back without being chased by fighter-bombers. Next to him sat a civilian – I realised with astonishment that I had thought of him immediately in terms of 'civilian', not, say, 'elderly gentleman' or 'typical bald-headed civil servant'. Knight's Cross looked at me as if he had to rack his brains before remembering who I was. 'My building expert,' he said finally with a wave of introduction. 'And my historical adviser, Herr Bemmann, school-teacher.' We shook hands with a slight bow, murmuring, 'Pleased to meet you.' An odd picture, right enough. Nearby, two SS-men dropped a cardboard box, tinned food rolled down the slope. Knight's Cross eyed a vapour trail with suspicion, no doubt a Mosquito on high-level reconnaissance. 'Maybe that's the first aerial photographs of Fort Battle of the Nations being taken up there,' he said, with an air of self-importance. 'You should consider yourselves honoured to be in the picture.'

Officers and NCOs flung out an arm in salute and reported on progress in various areas of work going on. Apparently there were ample supplies of ammunition and stores available, although two tanks that were supposed to have joined the combat group had, for some unknown reason, failed to show up. 'If we get a hold of these jokers,' announced Knight's Cross, 'we'll string them up from the trees out there. Eighteen hundred hours, in the crypt: all section leaders will report for an evening of political instruction! Volksgenosse Bemmann will be giving a talk. He and Volksgenosse Linden are to be taken on our rations complement. Dismiss!'

I 'drew' half a loaf, a tin of blood-sausage and one of liver-sausage, ten cigarettes, two rolls of fruit drops and a packet of Scho-Ka-Kola. When I muttered something about having four children, I got six extra rolls of fruit drops. Back home, Marianne laid the table as in peacetime. She kept most of the drops for sweetening our tea. We polished off the bread and the liverwurst, so that Joachim almost felt sick as a result of this over-indulgence. When he grew up, he assured us, he was going to join the Waffen SS.

To open the instruction class, the section leaders sang 'When all have proved unfaithful, our loyalty will remain,' a song with a difficult rhythm. They had brought blankets and tarpaulins and squatted down at the feet of the giants. Paraffin lamps sputtered dimly, Knight's Cross gave permission to smoke. Up till that moment, no one had ever dared light up in that place.

What I heard next was one long hymn of praise to the death's-head and crossbones. The Lützowers as the forerunners of the SS, Theodor Körner a precursor of Horst Wessel, the Monument as a defiant symbol of the hero's death for the ethic of the Reich and the Volk – the acoustics forced Bemmann to form his phrases slow and stately, and so he slipped into the intonation of a sermon. 'The Füüührer,' he chanted, 'in the bunker at the Reeeichs Channncelloryyy, looks to his warriooors, gaaathered heeere for the laaast greaaat connnfliiict.' An Untersturmführer tossed me a packet of cigarettes and I helped myself without further ado. 'From Valhalla, our aaancestooors gaaaze dowwwn on us, as we defeeend the blood and soooil of our Faaatherlannnd.' Napoleon had come from the west and been dispatched back there in short order, and the Americans would meet the same fate. I could see from the face above the Knight's Cross that this interpretation was exactly to his taste. I tried to imagine what the proletarian Machulski would have made of all this; then I caught sight of him next to the statue symbolising Bravery; he was leaning against its left calf, one trouser-leg tucked up

132

with safety pins, his crutches propped up beside him. Since he had burst up out of the earth and descended upon the tormentors of the Jews, he had apparently tidied up his uniform and had a good wash. I raised my cigarette and gave him a half-guilty look, but he dismissed it with a wave of the hand, that was all in the past, now. While the teacher unreeled all his patter about the blood-line down through the centuries since Arminius and the Teutoburg Forest, I had time to take a good look at the SS officers. Apart from Knight's Cross himself, not one of them was over twenty-five, they had all twisted and reshaped their hats to create some devil-may-care effect, and each set his at a different angle to suit his own particular idea of *chic*. They were all clean-shaven, neat, well set-up, fine lads. Not one of them without an Iron Cross, two with the German Cross in gold, most of them with campaign decorations, close-combat bars – their grandfathers had ridden into battle at Mars la Tour, their fathers hadn't won at Fleury, their great-great-grandfathers had deserted at Stünz or had either stormed or defended the Grimma Gate. Now they were getting all geared up to be heroes.

Knight's Cross was brief and to the point in his closing address: 'At the fortress "Monument to the Battle of the Nations", the enemies of the Reich, whether they may come from the east or from the west, are going to get a hell of a lot more than they bargained for. Long live the Führer!' Every man leapt to his feet, cupping his glowing cigarette in the hollow of his hand, and they sang, 'What is that gleam in the forest, in the suhunshine, Hark how its roar draws nigh!' This song is a bit tricky, too, but the SS choir carried it off in masterly fashion. Knight's Cross yelled, so that his voice echoed high up to the horsemen in the reliefs above, 'Comrades, we'll die together!' I thought, shoulder to shoulder.

We stepped out into a mild evening, to the sound of the blackbirds in the cemetery trees. The sun was setting behind wisps of cloud, and the air was clear as it will never again be over Leipzig. Not a factory chimney belched smoke, there was hardly a car on the streets, and all the factories from Kulkwitz to Leuna had doused their boilers. The city was waiting for the enemy, the liberator.

I looked up to the guardians of the dead, they were wreathed in a reddish glow; now there was to be another new generation added to the dead. Blood sacrifice, an old expression. Shoulder to shoulder.

'Come with me,' said Knight's Cross. We went to the cemetery. Alongside the path, trenches had been dug in a zig-zag pattern, while on a bend a machine-gun nest had been shored up with beams and stone slabs. Not by any means as artistic a construction as Voiciech had devised at the Lingekopf; from the embrasure, a marksman could sweep the tops of the trees and pin down an adversary among the crosses on the headstones. 'You've thought of everything,' I broke the silence. The expression 'deathly silence' occurred to me, and it bothered me.

'We need a tunnel connecting with the cemetery. If we were to be encircled, a scout or a contact man could get out.'

'No problem, chief.'

'As of now, the expression is, Yes sir, Sturmbannführer.'

'Yes sir, Sturmbannführer.'

'And what's the best way of going about it?'

I thought it over and started, cautiously, 'We'd have to start by getting out through the foundations. Up till now, we've always avoided that, for reasons of stability. But if it's only a narrow passage, then there'd be no harm done.'

'How many men do you need? And how long will it take?'

'Four from one end, four from the other – a week, maybe?'

'You've got two days.'

There were any number of gaps in the fence, the SS campfires had devoured planks and spars, just as the sentries' fires at the Battle of the Nations had consumed every post and every board for miles around. Just in front of the tomb of the von Pussenkomm family, whose names I could no longer make out in the gathering darkness – and anyway, there was no reason to – I pointed to the ground. 'Do you want the tunnel to come out here?' My chief nodded.

A quarter of an hour later, two SS-men began burrowing there, with two others standing by, ready to take over when one of them needed a breather. The light, provided by a couple of paraffin lamps, was pretty meagre, the wind rustled in the trees, the Monument loomed black above us. The soil was tipped into barrows and carted away, and in the morning the first shoring props were set in place. A miner from the Saar, now an Oberscharführer, was promoted to site manager, and from then on I had nothing more to do with the progress of the passageway from that end.

Between two supporting buttresses, away down below, deeper than any visitor has ever been allowed, I had to come to a decision on a matter of conscience. Was I to show Knight's Cross a spot where the concrete wall is no more than two metres thick, or insist that it was ten metres thick all round and couldn't be penetrated in less than a week, even with a pneumatic drill? I decided on the former course.

You don't make things difficult for a fleeing hero. On a secondary pillar I discovered a VM in the concrete. If Voiciech had given me the nod at this point, everything would have been easier. 'Here,' I said. With his dagger, Knight's Cross scratched a rectangle a metre high and half a metre across into the surface of the wall. 'If you're buggering me about,' he promised, without so much as raising his voice but letting just the trace of a smile cross his face, 'if it's more than two metres through to the soil on the other side, I'll put you up against a wall.' Half an hour later a pneumatic drill began rattling away at the spot.

I finally got home at midnight. Next morning, I went to see Mother and took her half a loaf and a tin of smoked sausage. Everybody in Stötteritz, I heard, was terrified: if there was to be a battle at the Monument, their houses would catch it, too. Anyone that could had already got out of the place, some were camping out in holes in the open fields. It was early days for that, I said. 'Just leave it to me,' although I was only too well aware how little weight there was behind my words.

At lunchtime I went back up to the Monument. Wehrmacht reports on the radio told of fighting in the Naumburg area, in the Thuringian Forest and south of the Harz Mountains. The SS-men expertly worked out how long the leading tank units would take before they turned up at the gates of Leipzig; I had the feeling that it wouldn't have bothered them in the least if the battle had been due within the hour. I read their cuff-titles: 'Prince Eugen', 'The Reich', 'Viking', in vain I searched for names reminiscent of the Battle of the Nations; but of course there was no 'Lützow' division. The garrison had grown in strength, stragglers from all manner of army units and some Volkssturm home guard were digging trenches or lining up at the field-kitchens, even a troop of sailors, shouldering bazookas, trotted through the park to the north end of the cemetery. There, so I heard, a defensive ring was to be drawn. The fortress was developing. Ten men were engaged round the clock on the tunnel, bringing out and carting away the soil. The miner from the Saar yelled out that if he didn't get beams for shoring up the walls in the next hour, he wouldn't be able to go any farther. Not far away, trenches were being pushed out into the cemetery, zig-zagging across the lawns and along the paths, avoiding the graves themselves. Above them, the trees were dressed in radiant green, titmice twittered, twenty metres ahead of the shovelling soldiers two old women cleared the dead leaves of last autumn off the graves of their

135

loved ones. A florist's shop at the North Gate was open for business, selling birch twigs, potted pansies and garden peat. In front of it was parked a Tiger tank under a camouflage net, hard against the trees. The tank crew sat in the little room behind the shop, warming up army-issue tinned soup on the little stove.

I drew my daily rations – a tin of pork and a jar of blueberries among other things. Along the Preussen Strasse strolled the teacher, Bemmann, and Fürchtegott von Lindenau, deep in animated conversation; no doubt historical parallels were being drawn. Fürchtegott was wearing an infantryman's greatcoat with no insignia and no belt, although with a Volkssturm armband; from the way he had slung an Italian carbine over his shoulder, I noticed his lack of experience in such matters. Then the sirens howled out a full-scale alert, flak rumbled to the south, soldiers ran to their gun-posts. For safety's sake, I went down into the crypt. The foundation wall had been pierced, and here too, earth was being removed, and with it builder's rubble and fragments of brick from the days of the Monument's construction. Knight's Cross greeted me cheerfully: 'Everything's hunky-dory. Lucky for you, mind!'

'It'll be a marvellous fortress,' I nodded. His men toiled on, pouring with sweat. 'We're using everything we can find for shoring up,' said Knight's Cross, 'paving slabs, even carbines. Grant me just two days, and you will not recognise this tunnel,' he parodied his Führer. The anti-aircraft guns were cutting loose, and the tremors worked their way right down to us. I said, 'You won't really be needing me here any more, will you? Only, they'll be starting to worry down at my fire-station.'

'You're my indispensable expert. And anyway, surely you've made up your mind at last to volunteer for the Waffen SS?'

'On the Führer's birthday. Promise.' That was in five days' time. At that, Knight's Cross gave me a look that suggested he would happily have shot me on the spot.

Then the sirens wailed the continuous alert. We had read in the papers what that meant: attacks were to be expected imminently, the warning time had become too short – we were now front-line. This signal included a warning of tank-attacks.

From that moment on, quiet reigned over the Monument, no more lorries bringing in supplies of crisp-bread and Scho-Ka-Kola, schnapps and tinned food. The soldiers dug deeper, spoke in whispers, smoked more intently, the skin drawing tight at the corners of their mouths. I went down Schönbach once more and brought my family two-thirds of my rations. Mother had come over to our house, she felt it was best for the family to be together at such a time. Involuntarily, that damned phrase of Knight's Cross flitted across my mind: 'We'll die together.' Shoulder to shoulder, the flag is mightier than . . . I shook off these thoughts. 'It'll be all over in a couple of days.' One way or another.

That day was sunny, too, windless, the skies blue, the grass green. The birches wore a golden shimmer, the season of daphne, pussy-willows and the first bees was upon us. The evening was velvet-soft, an evening for falling in love. From the west a rumbling approached; bombs or heavy artillery – not even battle-hardened SS-ears could distinguish with any certainty. Tinned food was issued all round, I filled my knapsack with green peas, traded some back in order to stock up on haricot beans, and finally did another swop when corned beef came on offer. Tin upon tin was spooned out in silent application, one cigarette was lit from another, the bottles of corn schnapps and kümmel went the rounds. I caught scraps of conversation: so where could we fall back to? Russkies or Yanks, either way we'll be hacked down.

I slept a few hours on a cot in the shelter, then I went down into the crypt, just in time to hear a yelling and bellowing inside the gallery: the two tunnels had met. 'Lucky for you,' Knight's Cross repeated, as if I had been a hostage to the success of the enterprise. As dawn approached, the look-out on the top-stone reported muzzle-flashes on the western outskirts, where the battle for the anti-tank defences was on. But then all the shooting stopped, scouts telephoned in from public call-boxes in the suburbs that white sheets were hanging from all the windows, women were dragging their Volkssturm husbands off home, handbills put out by some Committee for Free Germany had started turning up; in a word, the city was capitulating.

Towards noon, Sherman tanks probed forward from the direction of Connewitz. All the time, reconnaissance aircraft hung in the air above us. The noise of battle from the south: probably a flak battery being taken apart. When that was all over, everything went quiet again over the city, a quiet broken now and then by the rumble of tanks. At the tomb of the von Pussenkomm family, the mouth of the tunnel was carefully camouflaged. I crouched beside Knight's Cross in a trench on the embankment overlooking it, and he said, 'Linden, you stay here till I send for you, right?'

I laid the back of my neck against the rim of my foxhole and turned my face to the sun, tanning myself and thinking of the rain and the storm before the Battle of the Nations and the misty winter sky after the conflagration in December 1943. The SS-men near me had stuck grass and twigs under the camouflage nets on their helmets, and I thought, well, why not a posy of violets in your button-hole, too?

It was the rattle of tanks coming up from the VfB stadium that told us we were surrounded by a wide ring. In Stötteritz, too, now, white sheets hung from the windows, prompting an enraged Unterscharführer to let off a volley of shots in that general direction. I presumed that round about the Weisseplatz, too, the war must be on its last legs, with people creeping out of their cellars and smiling up into the sun. No more bombs, no more fighter-bombers, at last the war had been lost. I would dearly have loved to chat with Fürchtegott about the feelings of the defeated Saxons of 1813, and to inquire about the degree to which happiness dominated the frame of mind of the losers, but neither Fürchtegott nor the teacher was to be seen. An explosion just under the top-stone, fragments thundering down, best-quality granite from Beucha had suffered a direct hit from a tank-shell. The cigarettes in the corners of SS-mouths suddenly went out, all that was to be seen was a slit between helmet-rim and parapet, and through that centimetre they peered, as they had been taught and had practised a thousand times, making final adjustments to the sights on their machine guns and sub-machine guns, and reaching for their bazookas. But no attack materialised, Murat didn't drive his cavalry élite forward, there was no repetition of the battle for Probstheida till no stone was left standing on another. In Marienbrunn, the Americans were evicting the inhabitants from their homes and stretching out on their beds, laughing negroes were giving away chocolate and chewing-gum to awestruck German children, officers were supervising with the utmost punctiliousness the pouring away down the drain of a hundred litres of best-quality broth at which the GIs had turned up their noses. It was post-war time already in Schleussig, Holzhausen and Meusdorf, before, next morning, the tanks set tracks towards Naunhof, Grimma and Colditz – loyal and defiant, the Fortress of the Monument to the Battle of the Nations waited, unmolested since that first shot.

Knight's Cross came to fetch me at dusk. He raised his head over the ramparts and beckoned to me. I crawled out of my hole and rolled over the edge – I had never learned to do this, in fact, it just worked out that way. I followed him into the Monument and down into the crypt. Behind the statue of the Spirit of Self-sacrifice, he produced a satchel and said, 'Scouting party, the two of us. Understood?'

'Of course, Obersturmbannführer, sir!' We ducked into the gallery, where, by the light of his torch, I could make out the paving slabs, beams and carbines that had been used to shore it up. With our combined efforts we pushed aside the slab covering the mouth and cautiously poked our heads out; no sign of movement. 'Keep a look-out!' whispered Knight's Cross. I heard a rustling behind me, he was changing his clothes. 'Mechanic's overalls, just the thing,' he said, 'this way we'll get through. We'll slip down to your house. After that, we'll see.'

'And the sub-machine gun?'

'I'll hold on to that, just to be on the safe side.'

Here was one who wanted to survive at all costs, no different at all from Carl Friedrich Lindner a hundred and thirty-two years before; then, too, a man had tried to save his own skin, with no intention of dying, either together with others or on his own, and here a middle-ranking SS-officer saw things no differently from the Reichs-Big-Shot. But maybe I was going to die alongside him if we didn't make it the way he had planned – but I had no time to think that one through.

He clambered out of the hole. We closed the covering slab again and crept among the graves towards the crematorium. The night was fairly clear and very quiet, for the major part of the city it was the first night of peacetime. My head was buzzing with thoughts; I could leap to one side and scram amongst the gravestones, I could jump the bastard and disarm him – after all, an old wrestler never forgets the most important holds. How well would the streets down to Stötteritz be sealed off?

'You go first,' he whispered, as if he had read my mind.

Outside the crematorium, I veered off left and skirted the rhododendrons alongside the pond. My aim was to make an exit from the cemetery near the stadium, behind which there were private houses and gardens; it might be possible to strike out in an arc through Probstheida and then round to Stötteritz. Knight's Cross the SS-man in our house – a frightening thought, but, for the moment, the sub-machine gun in my back was of more immediate concern. 'No funny business!' He didn't have to say that twice.

Noiselessly we passed over short grass, on the paths gravel crunched under our feet. For a brief instant I was disorientated among the confusion of gravestones, then I hit the open space where the mausoleum architects had lain flat on their bellies, and in which the air-raid victims were buried. And then it all happened at once. Right in the corner of my field of vision, I caught a figure, I swung my head round, saw the flash from a muzzle, threw myself flat, jumped up again immediately and zig-zagged away, dived flat again, lay gasping and heard a voice, unmistakably the voice of my father – 'Freddie!'

I stood up, all fear gone. Half-staggering, I made my way back. There lay Knight's Cross, face down, his cap had fallen to one side and the back of his head was a bloodied mass. I looked over to where the figure had stood, nothing there but shadowy trees, bushes. Again I took off at a run, stumbling over headstones, got caught up in a tangle of ivy, staggered on and finally lay still, until my breath became more regular. Then I crept in under some bushes, drew my knees up under my chin as a shiver ran all down my back, and now I had no clear idea whether I really had heard my father's voice or whether it had all been some hallucination.

Two Americans flushed me out next morning. They hollered at me as if they were having to buck up their own courage. I stood with hands raised while they frisked me. Then I had to lower them a little, so that one of them could relieve me of my wristwatch; the other took my wedding-ring as compensation. 'Du SS?' I denied it with a vigorous shake of the head. They pushed me out of the cemetery. For me, the main thing was for us not to be visible from the top-stone of the Monument, all I needed just then was a burst of machine-gun fire from up there! My heart was light, I enjoyed the happiness of the defeated, the penitent, without weapons, without colours to rally to, all decision-making had been taken off my shoulders, I wouldn't be beaten up for the sake of a Thaler, I was a man full of fraternal feelings. I turned my head and looked joyfully at my captors, they were still soldiers, poor sods, and I was a harmless civilian who had never so much as raised a ripple, and they would soon send me back to my wife and children in the Weissestrasse, no two ways about it. From here on, things could only get better.

On a practice pitch next to the VfB stadium I came back to reality with a bump in a hastily thrown-together prison camp; soldiers of the Wehrmacht, Hitler Youth, Red Cross nurses, even railwaymen, were squatting on the ground, there was a steady stream of newcomers. SS-men were being driven out of the cemetery under a hail of blows – had they been part of the garrison in the Monument and slipped away just like their commanding officer? I sidled up to an

American I took for an officer. 'Ich Feuerwehrmann,' I said over and over and tried desperately to find the right gesture to convey fireman-like activities; I pretended to be holding a hose in my hands, even felt tempted to try to imitate the hissing of the water. 'From work,' I said, 'me, from work, just going home.'

Why had none of Katzenstein's sons emigrated to the USA and now come back as an officer, or at least as an interpreter?

'Jacket off, shirt off!' I had to raise my left arm, and, when no Waffen SS blood-group tattoo was to be found, I was allowed to dress again. 'Go home,' said the officer. And I replied with the utmost civility, 'Thank you very much! Thank you very, very much indeed!'

As I strolled along between the cemetery and the stadium, past jeeps and soldiers, lorries and tanks, I stole a glance up through gaps between the trees and the houses, to the Monument, the scar under the top platform was clearly visible. A heavy gun was in position behind a hothouse in a market-garden, its barrel trained on the Monument. Some Americans were kneeling beside it, and in their midst stooped a man on crutches; he had tucked up one trouser-leg and secured it with safety pins. On the glass top of a cold-frame lay a map, and the man with one leg pointed at it in explanation and then up to the Monument and back to the map again. There seemed to be no communication problems at all; maybe that really was one of Katzenstein's sons talking to Voiciech Machulski. The south side of the mammoth lay before them bathed in sunshine, the round-arched window grew larger through the lenses of the field-glasses that they occasionally trained on it.

Now just don't betray the slightest interest in military matters, not now! I was a civvy, harmless to the core, with not the faintest idea what a gun was. It would have suited me down to the ground if I could have shouldered a rake and wandered off through the streets as a peaceable gardener, humming a little tune, lifting my hat politely to the officers. Meanwhile it must have been about lunchtime, maybe I'd arrive just in time to find Marianne serving up her rich stew made out of wartime tinned foods. I was an altogether blissfully happy Saxon, totally defeated and neither able nor committed to change sides under, say, a General Thielmann, or to hunt anyone down, like perhaps the fleeing SS, as far as Torgau or Mittweida. The most peaceable Saxon is always a defeated Saxon.

As I crossed Naundorfer Strasse, a shot rang out behind me; a shell shattered a brace in the arched window in the south face and sent granite splintering and glass raining down into the crypt. A second shell sought and found the opening, a smoke grenade which at once started filling the vault with grey, stinking clouds. That was enough for the defenders, who after all, in order to be able to run faster, had long since thrown away their gas-masks in Normandy, at Remagen or in Thuringia. Now, with hands raised, they tumbled out into the open, coughing and spitting, in their midst Bemmann, the schoolteacher, who showed not the slightest sign of shame that the forefathers from Valhalla might now be watching him fleeing, too. These two shells delivered the *coup de grâce* to the Battle of the Nations Fortress. Up on the top platform a white rag was being waved, a shirt maybe. The news of the surrender swept through all the passageways, passed on with a sense of relief, and SS and Wehrmacht, Volkssturm and lesser National-Socialist bit-players streamed out into the open.

How do I know all this? Because that's the way it must have been. You don't have to have actually been everywhere in order to be able to picture the scene. The word 'fantasy' that you have just come out with strikes me as almost too high-flown for this simple process. Is memory, after all, anything other than the constant reproduction of imagination?

On the stroke of twelve, we sat down at table and ate up the stew I had anticipated. We talked quietly and happily throughout the meal. 'We'll soon have news from Hildrun, too,' said Mother. In the street below, an American tank clattered past, and Joachim rushed to the window. The SS fruit drops were forgotten. The first chewing-gum of his life was stuck under his chair.

CHAPTER 9

What was it like after the war?

I've gradually become used to life here. I've never had any complaints about the food, the nurses are friendly. Mind you, I did have to get it across to one of them that I do not appreciate being addressed as 'Grandad': 'To you I'm still Herr Linden!' Rather standing on my dignity, I admit. But it worked. When I put the light on during the night to go for a glass of water, I wait until the cockroaches have scuttled away under the wash-hand basin. Horrible, that crunching and crackling, when their little shells splinter under your slipper. No, I don't really want visitors. If Marianne were still alive, then perhaps. Joachim wouldn't really know what to say – and anyway, where is he? And it would be unfair to expect my daughter Erika to undertake the long journey. She gets the shakes every time at the border crossing, so what would she be like visiting a detention centre on top of that? I'll write to her now and then.

I'm glad we always begin our conversations in the forenoons; I find

143

concentration easiest then. Most of what I'm talking about happened only two or three kilometres from here. I can reach across in my mind. We ought to go for a walk again some time, so that I can catch a glimpse of the Monument, even from a distance. I have, after all, suggested a return to the scene of the crime often enough.

The SS had just crawled out of their last hidey-holes, whooping and cheering Americans had tossed down the machine-guns from the top platform, and the anti-aircraft guns had been towed away when I drove up with a fire-engine. I had got our brigade chief to type out a note establishing our *bona fides* as a bomb-disposal squad. An American sentry stood guard over a pile of rifles, sub-machine guns, hand-grenades and ammunition boxes, I threw him a sort of salute, pointed to my paper, the Monument and then myself. He shrugged and waved us through. We went along past the lake, empty of water now, but instead, full of the debris of war, tarpaulins, mess-tins, blankets – I had to hold my lads back from starting their salvage operations right there and then. From the front, I could see no change in my colossus. All the doors stood wide open. No Americans here either, nobody at all; through the breach in the south side, the sun warmed statues of heroes, rubble, empty tins and mounds of shit that the SS had laid in their panic. A limited shambles. We'd soon sort that out. We started rummaging, after all everything was of some value in those times, every rucksack, every tarpaulin. I uncovered a carton full of jars of jam and reminded the others, 'Don't be greedy, lads, it'll be fair shares for all!'

The entrance to the tunnel the SS had driven through the foundations had been tolerably well camouflaged. I glanced at it out of the corner of my eye; lumps of stone had been piled up in front of it, paving slabs leaned against them – anyone unfamiliar with the place would have suspected nothing at all. So I went on rummaging with the others and we found magazines for sub-machine guns, a bazooka minus its detonator, and added them to the large heap by the sentry outside. Then we tried on boots, had a high old time exchanging generous presents of padded trousers and fur-lined jackets, and I settled on a winter overcoat with runes and stars; Marianne would soon get rid of the black collar. Vests and socks, tins of Italian tomato purée – well loaded down, we made off. At the door, we met a woman rattling a bunch of keys; the first of the attendants had come back. 'Closing up, eh? Just as well,' I commended her. 'I'll be back. Got to check everything for explosives. Don't let *anybody* down there!'

144

'I'll keep an eye on things, Herr Linden. Leave it to me!' An anonymous 'activist of the first hour'.

In the afternoon I had my empire all to myself. I heaved the slabs to one side, pushed away blocks of stone and crept into the tunnel. On the pillar to the left: a 'VM' in the pressed concrete. In a niche, tinned food had been piled up, and hand-grenades and small-arms ammunition, cartons of cigarettes – it was a treasure-house, worth its weight in gold, and the black market hadn't even got going yet. Not many knew of the existence of this gallery; its initiator was dead, the others were perhaps at that very moment being bundled on to lorries and shipped off westwards by drivers drunk on victory. For the first time, I thought: *my* tunnel.

I covered over the entrance again, and on the following day I bricked it up, plastered it over and scratched my initials, FL. In front of that, I piled up flag-stones, applying the principles of leverage just as Voiciech had done in the western suburbs. Once learned, never forgotten. Then I told the attendant it was quite safe now to go into the crypt and she could make a start on the task of clearing up. The exit at the cemetery end was neatly closed up and camouflaged. I was sailing before the wind now, at worst only the cigarettes would be affected by dampness. But now it was time to clear off, so as not to raise any suspicions. My moment would come.

The Americans made no changes in the hierarchy of the police and the fire service: all the Nazis kept their jobs. Our first detail was to clear away a shot-up anti-aircraft battery near Böhlen. The scene that met us there was gruesome: artillery and strafing planes had, as the saying goes, 'knocked the living shit' out of the position. We pulled out bodies, soldiers and Hitler Youth, it was just like a year before, after the raid on the aircraft factory, only this time the corpses had been lying in the sun for days. We worked with damp cloths over our mouths and noses and without a ration of schnapps, we staggered away, took a deep breath, and went back to work till we were fit to drop. The Americans stood smoking at a comfortable distance. One day, the chief of our fire-station was taken away by military policemen. Of course, he had been a member of the NSDAP. Years later, I heard he had risen to be head of the fire service in a South German city. The Americans pulled out and the Soviet Army occupied our city, almost without anyone noticing. Fuel for our fire-tenders became scarce, and we got a new chief right away.

During that summer, we filled in the underground air-raid shelters, having first removed the wooden supports and the planking, which would come in handy for heating. I made certain that the rubble and earth were tamped down hard, so that there would be no risk of the embankments caving in later on. Progress was much quicker, hastier, than when we had dug them out a few years previously; it was as if we wanted to wipe out remembrance of the war with the bunkers.

Once more I acted as a guide to visitors, this time officers and men of the Soviet Army. A very few of them spoke some broken German; mostly there was an interpreter with them. I caught myself making more and more frequent references to the Russians at the Battle of the Nations rather than to the Austrians and French, the Prussians I mentioned only in passing, the Saxons not at all. The officers wore battle-dress blouses festooned with decorations, and boots with flat heels, and, once inside the Monument, they would take their caps off as if in a church. The Russians had delivered a crushing blow here to sundry other European nations; gradually I shortened my commentary to centre on this one theme.

In early June, one morning at four o'clock, when all was still, I clambered through the von Pussenkomm family vault into the tunnel. I had brought a bag and my briefcase, and I filled them with cigarettes, Scho-Ka-Kola and tins of meat. It wasn't just the cold that made me shiver. I was fumbling my way down into a bygone era; the fact that it stretched back no more than a month was neither here nor there. The rifles propping up the roof, the SS tarpaulins, a belt with a buckle, a knapsack – the beam of my torch flitted over them all. I was seized with greed, which struggled with the desire to get the hell out of there as fast as I could. I stuffed my bags full, listened – was that footsteps? Shuffling feet farther in towards the Monument? Don't be an idiot, I told myself, your fear is playing tricks on you, just as on the last night of the war you thought you had heard your father's voice. And Voiciech standing by the gun – phantoms thrown up by a fear-ridden imagination. Maybe rats, gnawing at one of the tins, or moisture dripping from the rifles. Just the same, I heaved a sigh of relief when I was back outside and had pushed the gravestone back into place. A careful peek all round – a squirrel, a blackbird. I scuttled off through a gap in the fence and down the Schönbach.

I wasn't what you would call a crafty or resourceful black-marketeer. Marianne, in her dairy, sold off the cigarettes under the counter or bartered them for bread. I had to support Mother and she in turn looked after Auntie Machul, who was suffering from ulcerated legs, for which there was no medicine to be had. As a fireman, I was

146

entitled to a heavy labourer's ration card, with its thirty grams of fats a day, and that more or less kept our heads above water. I went back to the underground passage and returned with tins of fatty meat, jam and pea-meal; we made a marvellous stew and Mother took a little pot of it to Auntie Machul. Also hidden in my bundle were scratchy, military-green underpants, and Marianne swapped them with a farmer for rye. Other families were suffering hardships like those after the Battle of the Nations, boiling up nettle soup and going on the hunt for cats and birds. Old people died of hypothermia in damp beds, many were finished off by a simple cold. But everybody knew that the hard times would pass and then an unimaginable boom just had to follow, the Monument would point up into everlasting peace – that thought was what kept us going as we sickled grass off the embankments for our rabbits.

One afternoon we were oiling locks, two women and I, and discussing the fact that the Reitzenhainer and the Preussen had been renamed the Leninstrasse. We had read in the paper that all war memorials were to be removed; the metal monstrosity at the Market commemorating Leipty/Leipty-one had apparently been melted down already. 'They'll not touch our big fella here,' was the opinion of one of the women as she climbed a ladder to wipe dirt off the doors.

Two men stumped up, wearing party badges and carrying brief-cases. Sent by the municipal department of culture, they said, to carry out a stock-taking inspection. One of the women joked, 'The stock? That's us!' The comrades smiled. The Monument had to be closed down, they said, until an ideological conception for the guided tour had been worked out. Who was supposed to do that, I asked, and they merely shrugged. They were about to leave when some Soviet officers arrived, and I gave them my little lecture as per usual. I reeled off the names of Russian generals and gestured towards the west: that was the way Napoleon had fled, with the Cossacks hot on his heels. The Corsican had fared no better than Hitler – at the end of each section, I looked one of the officers in the eye and underlined my explanations with a 'Du verstehn – understood?' This was met with nods and agreement; at the end I was rewarded with 'papyrossi'. When the officers had gone, the comrades from the cultural office asked who had developed and approved this philosophical approach. 'Good, upstanding, proletarian-progressive instinct for history,' murmured one of them. Then, out of the blue, he asked whether I perhaps – after all, such

147

coincidences happened – knew where Lenin, in 1905, had had a certain newspaper printed, the *Iskra*. In Probstheida, maybe, or in Stötteritz? I promised to ask around, but soon forgot the whole thing.

Of course, the Monument to the Battle of the Nations wasn't pulled down – who would have had to do the job anyway? A few men from the old Civil Defence, attendants and their wives, and myself, blocked up the shell-hole in the south face with beams and boards from the underground shelters. A sign hung on the door: 'Closed for technical reasons.'

The people of Leipzig never treated their trade mark more shabbily than at that time. They were ashamed of it – I might even say they wiped it from their consciousness. Many a one finding it in his field of vision seemed to manage to see nothing but fresh air. That's very much a Saxon way of coming to terms with awkward details of the past. There was rubble to be cleared, roofs to patch, windows to re-glaze, briquettes and a crust of bread to scrounge. Monument to the Battle of the Nations? Never heard of it! Not exactly showing great strength of character, that's for sure. It just occurs to me that the Leipzigers never did come up with a nickname for their mightiest edifice. No satirist ever tried to, and we had a few of them, like Hans Reimann or Helene Vogt; and nothing of the sort ever emanated from the pubs. Maybe the Monument doesn't matter as much to many Leipzigers as I imagine? I have to admit it, I am something of an exception.

On 11 November 1945 Clemens Thieme died; not so much as a word about it in any of the papers. The minister at his funeral spoke of epoch-making achievements, which, he hoped, would be given due honour in the near future, of the ups and downs of the passage of time, of the uncompromising spirit of him who lay before us on the bier. I should have got myself a wreath for the occasion, with a ribbon bearing the names of Felix Linden and Voiciech Machulski; one's best ideas always come too late. And the name of Katzenstein, too . . . I looked around, searching among the aged gentlemen for someone, perhaps, who had sat at Thieme's side on the committee of the League of Patriots. There had been pictures of them all in many contemporary publications, but more than thirty years had wrought changes in the faces. A man with one leg limped along on his crutches in the cortege; it wasn't Voiciech Machulski. At the graveside, an old greybeard made a speech, giving himself out to have been a friend and comrade-in-arms of the deceased. He spoke of the great common enterprise, without even mentioning the

Monument to the Battle of the Nations by name. No one glanced up through the bare branches to the crowning platform. I threw four little spadefuls of earth onto the coffin, one each for Father, Voiciech and Katzenstein. No choir sang, the traditional songs having become tainted with suspicion, like 'Lützow's wild and daring charge' and the tune about the good comrade, 'No better will ye find.'

By the time Christmas came round, I had cleared the tunnel of everything that was of any use; the last mess-tin, rusting already, and a few mouldering camouflage jackets, these I threw into the dustbin. Right at the back, close by the wall that I had plastered over on the other side, I came upon five anti-aircraft shells. They lay there, in a wooden case, among wood-wool and oil-paper, as shiny as the day they left the factory. The detonator on a flak-shell is a work of art, I've said that already. What prompted me to look after these particular ones was the love of an explosives expert for a *pièce de résistance* of his trade. I smeared them thick with engine-grease and packed them in extra protective layers. One last time, I pushed the gravestone back into place; almost thirty years were to pass before I returned.

The comrades from the office of culture turned up again, looking glum. We talked about the reopening; they were sorry, but no formula for the commentary to tourists had been worked out yet. Wouldn't I like to put in writing what I had narrated on that previous occasion? 'Forgotten it, long since,' I insisted. And had I looked around for a printer's, in which Lenin . . . ? 'There's a tiny old place in Probstheida,' I improvised furiously. 'Not far from here.' And could I perhaps take the comrades there?

We entered the primitive workshop in the Russenstrasse, neither the owner nor his employees had ever heard anything about any *Iskra*. Lenin, explained the comrades, had been in Leipzig in 1905, and now the military commandatura had ordered that the relevant printer's should be traced in time for the imminent birthday of the revolutionary genius and a place of pilgrimage be opened at the spot. One old comrade, the story was, had been Lenin's guide there, and, oh yes, Lenin had not yet adopted his famous beard. They had gone for a stroll through the Johanna Park, where Lenin fed the squirrels. But unfortunately, the comrade could recall nothing about a printer's shop.

'Naturally it all happened under a cloak of conspiracy,' I added and caught a glance of appreciation; obviously, my proletarian-progressive instinct for historical fact had just served me well. I became bolder: 'But who could actually *prove* that Lenin *didn't* in fact get his printing done here?' That was the answer – simplicity itself.

The owner of the workshop, a man of pensionable age, made the most of his chance. 'Somebody keen on buying out the business? Well, if they were really interested . . . And then, *Iskra, Iskra* – the more I think back, the more it seems to me my old man . . .'

'What's your price for the dump?'

'A lease would suit me better.' The man had obviously realised how little the Reichsmark was worth.

It was plain to see from the comrades' expression what a weight I had taken off their party membership books. Their comrade bosses had ordered them to find the old printing-works, come hell or high water, they hadn't a clue as to how they were to go about it, and now here was someone confronting them with the wisdom of unavailable evidence to the contrary. I pursued my hypothesis: 'Lenin might well have preferred this printer's on the edge of town.' The secret police would have been on the alert in the city centre, but out here nobody would have suspected anything illegal. What if a few old machines could be dug up from somewhere as well? And then, to top it all off, a stuffed squirrel with a sign saying that, during his visit to Leipzig, Lenin had fed squirrels?

'Man, that's great,' they heaved a unison sigh of relief. 'You could be in charge here – what d'you think?'

They came back again, having retrieved from the scrap-heap in a printer's in Lindenau an old, warped platen machine. I carted it and some filthy old letter-cases out to Probstheida in a vehicle belonging to the fire service. Five days later, I read in the *Volkszeitung* that a museum was soon to be opened where the first editions of the legendary *Iskra* had been printed, and that the name *Iskra* meant 'The Spark'. From that spark, the flame of revolution had sprung, and it was from here that Lenin had carried the blazing torch . . . You'll find the article in my archives.

At the official opening, I stood among the workers who, with a real heave-ho effort, had put in new windows, installed lighting, whitewashed walls and painted mottos on lengths of red cloth. 'Marxism is all-powerful, because it is truth,' I read. 'The Hitlers may come and go, but the German people, the German state, will remain.' Busts of Lenin and Stalin stood among the junk that was about to be consecrated. A Soviet major made a speech, followed by one of the comrades who owed this hour of glory to me. 'On this spot,' he orated, 'hand in hand with the working people who had gone through the school of Bebel and Liebknecht! On that machine there, with letters out of this case! Under the lash of the Tsar and the heel of the Kaiser! Within walls now to become a memorial!'

Never so much as a conspiratorial wink to suggest we knew better. There was more to us Germans than simply losers, just Nazis, last-ditch resisters in Fort Battle of the Nations, Fascist-brown to the core, a disgrace to humanity, the ultimate scum. Now, close to the Monument, in its very shadow, a progressive deed of the utmost significance had been accomplished. I looked round the company; a newspaper editor, a lean young man in baggy sailor's trousers and a leather jacket that had belonged to one of Hitler's tank drivers, was busy taking notes. As the nimble scribe was to formulate it next day, only in conjunction with Lenin's thought and side by side with the great Soviet Union could the German nation rise again out of its ideological and material deprivation. In my mind's eye I pictured a scene: that was Voiciech, wasn't it, on his way back down into town from the building site at the Monument, walking beside a brisk little man whose lively eyes darted all around him, at people, trams and squirrels, who, in unobserved moments, clenched his fist on his breast, for yet another flash of genius had just emanated from his brain. Perhaps Maria and Tadeusz, as Lenin's bodyguard, had taken parcels of explosive writings to the post office, declaring their contents as Sunlight Soft Soap. Lenin *must* have seen the Monument under construction, and it was a simple matter for me to work out to the nearest metre how high it had stood at that moment, and what layer of granite, cut by Felix, was being lifted by an electric crane made by the firm of Wolle. Lenin strode down the Preussen Strasse towards town, saw Voiciech Machulski, a mere dot away up there, and, naturally, thought: Workers of the world, unite, d'you hear! Greetings, Polish-German Comrade!

Most of the time, Doctor, I've found our conversations far from tiresome, sometimes they even afforded me an opportunity to reconsider some things that had slipped my memory. Now, though, to be honest, I'd like to be alone, I'd like to ponder possible meetings between Lenin, Viktor and Tadeusz. I'm none too sure, at that, whether I'll be able to tie up the loose ends of.fragile threads, to order, as it were. It's a delicate business, this dealing with your ancestors, take my word for it.

At the end of the ceremony, the workers were treated to a handshake from the principal speaker, who looked us all straight in the cyc with an expression that conveyed the full significance of the occasion. When he came to me, there was still no conspiratorial smile, no grin to suggest that we two were in the know: a new truth pervaded him. 'Don't forget the squirrel,' I whispered.

And so it is, nowadays, that the tour buses that park for half an hour at the Monument don't have far to go to the *Iskra* shrine; if it were out in Plagwitz, the tourists would have to go halfway across town. Men sweating in their sauna-like dark suits, ribbons and medals on their chests, women in knitted caps or headscarves, can have their thoughts switched from one great heroic Russian deed to the other without the intrusion of alien impressions, Schiller's cottage or, for that matter, shopping for perfume, hair-curlers and coffee sets. So, even today, my choice of venue has the double beneficial effect of reducing emotional stress and saving petrol. As for the stuffed squirrel, it was for years on end part of the fittings; at least there wasn't a notice under it claiming that Lenin had done the catering for that specific squirrel.

It must have been towards the end of the forties when I learned from the newspaper that a working party had been formed within the *Kulturbund*, the new League of Culture, with the aim of blowing the dust off the history of the city in search of its revolutionary past, and the Battle of the Nations and its Monument were to be the starting point. Naturally, I went along.

The introductory lecture was given by League-Member Bemmann, the former schoolteacher and ideologue of Fort Battle of the Nations. Dismissed from the education service, he had found here virgin territory for his activities. He had lost a fair deal of weight, his bony shoulders came nowhere near filling a baggy suit, his neck had shrunk three sizes away from his shirt collar. A basic conception had to be formulated, I heard him say, with the idea of peace as its focal point. Admittedly, chauvinistic conceit had, at the time the Monument was built, misled its creators, however, closer inspection of the building did reveal certain characteristics which justified its place in a new era. The yearning of the peoples for peeeace, now newly won at last, which would enable swords to be beaten into ploughshares! So that no mother shall ever again weep for her son, let those sowers of discord on the Rhine take note, the answer is a resounding 'No!' Bemmann's chin jutted, the loose skin at his throat wobbled like a turkey's wattle. 'Peeeeace,' he boomed, 'Karl Liebknecht and Rosa Luxembuuurg would be overjoyed if they could but seeeee how weeeee heeeere are defennding the achiiiievements of our

Faaatherlaaand. Hannd in hannnd with the peoples of the Soviet Uuunion . . .'

I sat there quietly, a simple worker, thinking: I bet this warms the hearts of the Culture League boys – a proletarian element, hitherto excluded under bourgeois tyranny from the realms of intellectual values, was drinking at the fountain that sparkled at last. I pictured to myself the blades of the stone sentries' swords even now flattening, broadening out into shovel-heads; Voiciech had had that idea, long ago. 'We shall throoow off the old, the corrupt, and carry all that is of value out of the ruuuins and out on to a sunnnlit meadow of peeeace.' – 'A beeeacon for Geeerman yeeearnings that shiiines as far as the Rhine, the Danube and Schleswig's strand' – I was reminded of words by Arndt. Concluding, Bemmann asked who, among his audience, would be prepared to join a committee which would draw up a fundamental philosophy as a basis for a commentary to visitors to the Monument; I put my hand up and a contented Bemmann registered me as a 'Member of the Federation of Trades Unions'.

A week later we held our constituent meeting, and, lo and behold, there was one of the comrades who had me to thank for the siting of the *Iskra* museum, presiding next to Bemmann at the top table. 'How's it going, then, comrade?' he asked brightly without waiting for a reply.

Peace, they all affirmed with due solemnity, peace! May the hand of any German wither, should it ever again reach for a weapon. I managed at last to catch the name of my co-fabricator of the *Iskra* shrine: Heinz Lohse. He was now Cultural Secretary in the Leipzig city executive of the Socialist Unity Party. Bemmann belonged, as was revealed in the course of the introductions, to the re-education party of repentant Nazis. 'Comrades and colleagues,' Lohse lowered his voice for effect, 'it is the wish of our Soviet friends that the Monument to the Battle of the Nations be reopened as soon as possible as a place dedicated to peace.'

'What about next month, on the eighteenth of October?'

Lohse raised his hands, a pained expression on his face. This interjection by the representative of the liberated working class made it all too plain to him, he said, just how much debris still had to be cleared out of hearts and minds. No offence to the friend of peace with the calloused hands, of course, and far be it from him to take his suggestion as a provocation, rather it was a slip of the tongue, but naturally it was an impossibility to hand the Monument over to our democratic public on the anniversary of the bloody battle. What was important was not some massacre or other, but peace!

'It should be renamed,' proposed the representative of the Democratic League of Women. 'No more the Monument to the *Battle of* the Nations, but the Monument to *Peace among* Nations!'

We were dumbfounded. I thought I caught a look on Lohse's face that showed he was kicking himself for not having thought of this first. As for the Women's Leaguer, she blushed redder and redder as the silence inspired by her words deepened. 'My thanks to our friend of peace' – Bemmann scanned his list – 'Lieselotte Schupkoweit, for her proposal, which I now throw open for discussion. On behalf of the National Democratic Party, which has adopted the banner of peace . . .'

'On behalf of the tenants' associations nine to thirteen of clectoral ward number Roman eleven . . .'

'The whole workforce of the People's Enterprise VfB Electrical Motor Works, Leipzig, Factory Three . . .'

'We tram-drivers have of course always . . .'

Monument to *Peace among* Nations – we developed ideas, concepts, each one more dazzling than the last. Naturally, now and then someone would let slip the old name and then, with a sheepish grin, eat their words, and all around would smirk their forgiveness. Monument to *Peace among* Nations – what a lot of implications had to be considered! The Archangel Michael held death-dealing steel clenched in his fist – shouldn't it perhaps be a spanner? Or an iron broom? I added my tuppence-worth: 'As we are all aware, Lenin strode towards the city down what is known today as Leninstrasse. I propose that, a third of the way up the Monument – this would of course have to be calculated to the exact metre, something which, thanks to documents in my possession, I would be in a position to do – we should paint a red stripe that would be visible from far off, with the inscription, ' "The Monument was this high when Lenin saw it!" '

Bemmann made notes. While, in the light of difficulties caused by the present shortages, there could naturally be no thought of extensive changes, it would nevertheless be a good thing to embed them firmly, right from the start, in the philosophical conception. 'The familiar memorial will become the Monument to *Peace among* Nations – we shall re-, re- . . .,' and then he got stuck. 'Re-name it' was suggested, but was rejected as too colourless. 'Reconstruct' –

154

several nods for this. 'Re-hew,' my wording, was the one to be preserved in the minutes.

A further meeting was necessary; Bemmann resurrected Berta von Suttner, and read from her book, *Lay Down Your Arms*, Friend of Peace Schupkoweit quoted a poem by Erich Kästner, 'If we had Won the War,' which ended with 'And luckily we didn't win.' I told the story of an unsung builder of the Monument, Voiciech Machulski by name, who, mortally wounded at Verdun, had lain in the casemate in Fort Douaumont, convinced he was in the crypt here in Leipzig. Heinz Lohse praised those patriots who, in the Eifel Mountains, had made the supreme sacrifice while cementing over bore-holes so treacherously drilled in German bridges by Yankee mercenaries, or had at least daubed 'Ami, go home!' on the pillars. A representative of the Free German Youth, a student of educational theory, brought to our attention the beauty of the song, 'Build, build, Free German Youth, now build!' and proposed that visitors to the Monument should sing it together prior to their sightseeing tour. 'What about the commentary?' Colleague Schupkoweit asked in a low voice. The central idea for it had still to be found.

The committee didn't meet again in such a hurry. In any case, my life was full enough without meetings; we were busy retrieving shells from woods and bazookas from ponds. Out in the fields near Böhlen, farmers had harvested defused bombs and buried them in craters, and now that open-cast mining was eating its way across the district, there were regular occurrences of excavator drivers leaping in terror from their cabs whenever their grabs came up with duds between their teeth. I was called out there alone thirty, maybe fifty, times.

Auntie Machul never got out of the house now, and hardly ever even out of bed. On her birthday, I carried her downstairs and into a taxi for a sightseeing tour of the city. We did the rounds of the places where she had lived and Viktor had been involved in the building, and she sniffed into her handkerchief. The Crystal Palace – gone. The Thüringer Hof hotel – only a shell. Naturally, we went to the Monument. 'Just once more,' sniffled Erna, 'I'd like to see Viktor's initials in the wall.'

'They're always deep in the inside.' After all, I couldn't very well drag Auntie into the tunnels, could I?

Not long after that, she died. My mother, Marianne and a few of Erna's neighbours followed the coffin. She had no close family.

155

Afterwards I went to the spot where I had last met Voiciech; he had been showing American gunners the best place from which to crack open Fort Battle of the Nations. Lettuce was being planted out there now. The south window was still temporarily covered over, the old wound on the capital still gaped. I thought of Voiciech, of Felix, and of the fact that never again would I hear from Auntie Erna's lips the famous story about the lions. I walked all the way round the colossus: that was where Felix and Voiciech had burst out of the ground, and over there Fürchtegott and Bemmann the schoolteacher had strolled together. Lenin and the squirrels – what stories!

At the next meeting of the *Kulturbund* working party, which now bore the title 'City History from the Progressive Standpoint', Heinz Lohse pithily informed us that the work of the committee was now superfluous. 'Well now, my friends, what has happened? We laid the results of our previous efforts before our Soviet friends. And what was the response from our Soviet friends? They responded to the effect that renaming the Monument would be an unhistorical move, one which leap-frogged over several stages of its development. The history of the Monument to the Battle of the Nations is a complex dialectical process. Our colleague in peace who brought up the idea – with the best of intentions, we grant her that ! – should consider carefully what inner motives she had for this radicalist proposal . . .'

My thoughts were wandering, and I paid no more attention than was necessary to note whether Lohse would at least once let slip the term 'Monument to *Peace among* Nations', but he avoided it scrupulously. 'That ill-considered idea, that would-be radical turn of phrase, top-heavy from its desire to leap over and ignore several historic epochs . . .' After all that, we sat speechless, only Friend of Peace Schupkoweit's sniffs wafted through the room. Did anyone wish to comment on his report? Not a hand was raised, even Bemmann was stumped for words. Next, Lohse outlined the basis for a lecture to be given by guides to tourist parties: Russian *friends*, with allies from *all* the German races, had punished the western aggressor, and that would be the fate that awaited anyone daring to infringe German unity. Today, the Soviet Union stood side by side with us to guard and defend the peace. Even then, Blücher had crossed the Rhine at Kaub, he declared. The days of the Yanks on sacred German soil were numbered. This was the way I had talked to the Soviet officers. Anyone wish to have his say?, asked Lohse and continued in the same breath to declare his proposal thereby adopted unanimously.

156

Three months later, with the minimum of fuss, the Monument was reopened. Or, put it this way: at nine o'clock one morning, the doors were opened, postcards were on sale at the kiosk, the sign giving details of the guided tours was back in its metal frame next to the main entrance. We had, of course, swept the place clean and cleared the stairs of dog-turds. We nodded to one another, smiling; our giant had proved more than a match for any of them. Three young women had learned Lohse's lecture off by heart. Through struggle, onwards to peace, they sang in our adaptable dialect, in those wonderful acoustics, across the Rhine at Kaub and away with Adenauer, Schumacher, Globke and their gang, these poisonous advocates of division, side by side with the socialist patriots in West Germany! Adenauers come and go.

Visitors gradually began to find their way to the city, and from there to, and into, the Monument, and Leipzig folk got used to their symbol once again. Granite from Beucha is more durable than any committee decision.

It was about that time that I demolished Fürchtegott von Lindenau's little country seat. I salvaged his papers and the skull, read the manuscripts, tuned in to their echoes. On Sundays, I'd cycle out there, sit on the foundation walls, walk through the park, following the curves of the paths along which he had driven in his coach. Sometimes I took Joachim along, but he soon lost the notion. 'You and your old stones'; by that he meant the memorial stones set at the focal points of the battle. I considered for a while whether I might set him some little educational task, whether there might be something he could investigate for himself, but I couldn't come up with anything. Who knows, if he had been able to grub up a skull or a cannon-ball with his own hands, then maybe his life might have taken a different turn? But even at ten, Joachim was determined to stand in no one's shadow, least of all his father's. Hardly your typical Saxon, that.

I read a lot in those days; it was a time when Leipzig's second-hand bookshops were still well-stocked. I got to know one of the most obsessive of the booksellers, who, in deep vaults near the Market, hoarded his treasures rather than offering them for sale. He's long dead now, the building has either fallen down or been knocked down. In Otterwisch, I discovered Carl Friedrich Lindner's gravestone – I've stood for hours, staring at the weathered inscription. It was a long, hot summer that, for weeks on end, refused to make way for autumn; people were still able to bathe in the open

157

right up till early October. The leaves on the cemetery trees lent a golden glow to the light and swathed the colossus in their shimmer.

That summer also brought tensions between Marianne and me. My head was too full of all these old things, she groused, I was forever bringing more and more junk back, Sundays I was seldom at home. I invited her to accompany me now and again on my cycling trips, which she did – once: she stood at the gravestone in Otterwisch, shaking her head. Death and date of birth – coincidence; similarity between two names – coincidence. So what did I think was so special? I just couldn't bring myself to talk to her about my intuitions.

You're interrupting my narrative with a lot of questions today, Doctor. You may well be right in suggesting that in those years my turning to things past was accelerating, that there must have been some noticeable sudden change. No, I don't regard your questioning in any way as an intrusion, as trespassing on my inner self, nevertheless I beg leave to doubt that that way my salvation lies. If it is the case that, as you suspect, certain crusts have formed within me, then I would ask you just one favour: just consider for a moment whether I might not in fact need them as a reason for going on living.

I was approaching the end of my thirties, I was at an age when most fathers can understand and fire the imagination of their children. That was unfortunately not so in my case. I had tried in vain to kindle in Joachim an interest in the Monument and its history. As to whether I took him up onto the top-stone on his tenth birthday, that I can't recall at this moment.

At that particular time, I was happiest at my mother's. Whenever I brought her something, she showed her delight. 'Freddie, you're my good lad.' We'd sit quietly together and she'd talk of how, that 20 October 1913, she had been taken by surprise by the labour pains, of Father the gymnast, of Father quarrelling with Viktor. Although she was already drawing her pension, Mother worked part-time in a printer's, because, she said, she'd get bored sitting at home all the time. Sometimes she would bring home a sample of what had passed through her hands during the day. Most of it was of no interest to me. She talked of the Leipzig of her childhood days and how she moved into this house. The old sofa with the broken springs had stood over there. Mother had filled in the dent with a cushion, later with two cushions. Father's place. I said, 'He never talked much, did my Dad.'

'But he thought a lot.'

'Maybe always about the same thing, going round in circles? Tell me, what did he say, that day he joined the SA?' I was surprised at how insensitive I had been in those days to everything that didn't immediately concern me, especially politics.

'D'you remember how the two of us used to go to the Big Roller?'

I recalled the enormous cabinet, driven back and forth by a motor and pressing down on the cylinders. And the noise of the protective grille springing up, the calender block coming to a halt and then, screeching and rumbling, starting up once again. These monsters, also known as 'mangles', creaked and grated in backyards all over the place. I had helped pull the handcart, had sat quietly on a chair watching Mother heaving the rollers about, sprinkling water on the laundry, taking it out, folding it up neatly. 'I'd never give my laundry to anyone to do,' she said. Then silence would reign for a while. It felt good to sit like that, not waiting for the other to think of something else to talk about. Even in those days, I wasn't all that desperately keen on new topics of conversation.

The *Kulturbund* group limped on. Bemmann disappeared from the scene as soon as it became evident to him that there was no prospect of ideological flights of fancy materialising there. One day, his successor was to be elected, and all eyes turned to me. When all was said and done, it seemed only natural that I should be chosen, for who, after all, knew as much about the Monument as I did? Marianne just shrugged, Mother teased: 'And if one of the sentries up there on the top should ever buckle at the knees, I suppose you'll take his place?'

When Erika, my daughter, was still little, I sat her in a basket on my handlebars and cycled out into the countryside with her. I prattled on about all sorts of things, none of which she could understand. But it always did my heart good to have her with me. Later on, she too couldn't be bothered coming. It never entered my head to reward her on a birthday by taking her up to the top platform. I felt pretty lonely, I must say.

Joachim's confirmation came and went, and his leaving school; he got on much better with Marianne than with me. Many a decision they took together without consulting me. I'd have been happy to see him go into the building trade, in Voiciech's footsteps, you might say; after all, in the age of concrete, quarries were no longer as important as they once had been. But he wanted to be a motor mechanic, and at least he was taken on as an engine fitter. I heard about that only after the event.

Did I have a friend? No, never, I suppose, and certainly not then. A lone wolf. Not a very flattering description, but it fits.

Aren't we stopping a bit earlier than usual today? Aha, you have to go and see if you can get an exhaust for your Trabant, have you? Well, in that case, I wish you lots of luck, Doctor!

CHAPTER 10

Today, we ought to talk about your children.

I was standing right at the top; to right and left of me, two young men had taken station. Chain-smokers, both of them. They ordered me to lock all doors behind us and to open them again only on their express instruction. When their hands weren't busy with cigarettes and matches, they were plunged deep into the cavernous pockets of their calf-length overcoats. They had taken me along with them because the locks had become rusted and jammed to such an extent that only someone with real know-how could outwit them. I inserted the key, applied pressure, a slow turn to the left and two sharp ones to the right, and then came the muted crunch as the worn bolt ground through the notched obstacles to its path. Well-crafted junk!

The pair scanned the sky suspiciously, it was a cheesy yellow, and they obviously expected to find in its depths Anglo-American pirates, who this time wouldn't drop Colorado beetles as was usually claimed, but poisoned sweets and, maychance – you remember the

161

word – agents on parachutes, in an attempt to scupper, under our very noses, the festival we were in the throes of preparing. The period of unbridled peace was over.

My fortieth birthday was just round the corner, but of course that wasn't what the celebrations were to be about, but rather the hundred and fortieth anniversary of the Battle. In my capacity as convener of the aforementioned Culture League group, I had led the two comrades from that organisation that so much prefers anonymity up to the top, where they now stood, pistols in shoulder holsters, eyes sweeping the heavens. Far below, among the cemetery trees, I saw some newly dug graves, while my mind's eye pictured the two of them floating down on outspread coat-tails, with bullet holes in their chests, straight into the open graves. I wanted to chat about the Monument, but my efforts at conversation inspired little reciproca-tion. Still, I did get out of them that one had been born in Saxony; the other one's speech was hard, grating – a Silesian. Little wonder, then, that I ranked the former, on a trial basis, among that battalion that had trudged across the plain on the banks of the Parthe, a hundred and forty years before, a remnant of the loyal Saxons. He had a miserable, pinched face with pale eyes that might conceivably have been described as kind, if only he hadn't continually been at pains to endow them with a defiant, aggressive expression. The other I consigned to the Silesian train that supplied Blücher's regiments with schnapps and oats: might not one of his forefathers have put his shoulder to a wagon wheel next to Carl Friedrich? All together, heeeave!

We had gone aloft in the afternoon, while below, the final preparations were being carried out, squads of the People's Police testing spotlights and hoisting flags, and tightly packed youth groups practising their chorused chants and cheers. It couldn't be all that easy, answering the solo shout of 'Long live Comrade Walter Ulbricht!' with a unison three cheers. I looked down on the tents marked with the Red Cross, where stretchers and smelling-salts stood at the ready for those who wilted. The exit to the rear was blocked by stalls selling frankfurters and cigarettes, and containing the stockpiles of food-packs of salami, sweets and biscuits, part of the so-called 'material basis'. From the direction of Stötteritz, columns of brass bands and drummers were marching up, blaring the good old march of Lützow's wild and daring charge, with their trumpets slanting brashly upwards and outwards. Among the drummer-boys was my Joachim. All these endeavours sounded fairly

162

primitive to a connoisseur who had heard the song sung by choirs so adept at whispering the echo *pianissimo* that you wondered, were they still in fact singing, or was it just your imagination? I hummed along with them, 'Hark, the rohoar comes nearer and neaherer!' Ah, my poor, simple Körner, as you lay over yonder in a fever! I turned my gaze to the west; there, the rubble from the city's ruins had been piled up in one great tip, countless tipper-trucks had been hauled up there by a narrow-gauge locomotive, till now a mountain towered above the rooftops. It really was a mountain and not the sort of thing that's raising its humps all round Leipzig in recent times – yes, I understood your remark and detected the note of ridicule in it. It wasn't simply ashes and domestic garbage that that tip contained, but the ruins of the Brühl and the Augustusplatz, the General Post Office, and the Crystal Palace, and the hotel in which the mausoleum specialists were incinerated.

Down below, the drums boomed. The lads wheeled in six abreast, at their head, one of them twirled his staff, and from up top it looked like the twitching of some insect. Joachim was seventeen – a dangerous age for drumming. It was all completely different now, so he had tried to enlighten me, *his* drumming would scare off the war-mongers. I had seen him on one or two marches and watched the concentration on his face. That was exactly the way Prussian infantrymen in their squares tightened their lips when Napoleon's most fearless cavalry had borne down on them. Or vice versa.

By now his column was stamping up the broad approach from the south, up the way the lorries of the SS had come, the boys drummed and fanfared as they climbed; march number four, their leader raised four fingers accordingly – I couldn't make that out from up here, I just knew it. Just short of the stairways, the column fanned out, their drum-skins were white spots to me, they swung onto the parapet, and now there were drummers and trumpeters standing on every stairway and platform, sending their noise down over the city. Black clouds of crows rose from the cemetery and made off out over the fields. Drums are like cannon and bugles like death-cries.

The Silesian rasped to me to open up, their watch was over. On the upper observation promenade, two of their colleagues were leaning over the parapet, there were two more in a niche on the stairs. The drumming and blaring surged up into the dome and down into the crypt. Outside, it was bright sunlight, and through the loud-speakers came the order to practise the chorus of welcome once again, because it had sounded pretty damn lame first time round.

Right, then! 'Long live Comrade Walter Ulbricht!' Once more the young drummers and buglers and the blue-shirted rank and file of the Free German Youth responded without noticeable zest.

Back home, and at the kitchen table sat a young man in the blue shirt. He got up and introduced himself as Ralf Bleckschild. As a member of a Young Writers' study group he had been sent to me by Comrade Lohse – I was an acknowledged expert. He wanted, so he told me, to write a story about the role of the popular masses in the wars of liberation in Mölkau and Holzhausen and wondered if I knew anything about it. What he had in mind was principally the sabotage activities behind French lines, perhaps patriotic farmers and peasants had conspired to damage vehicles and burn down bridges, or maybe turned road signposts the wrong way round, so as to lure Frenchmen into the marshes.

I muttered something to the effect that I had no knowledge of any such disruptive goings-on. Joachim came home from his drummering and sat down with us; at once, the two of them were agreed that something of this nature *must* have taken place, and then out came the word 'typical' – at any rate such activities had been *typical* of those times.

In the meantime, potatoes were cooking on the stove, Marianne prepared them with caraway seeds. Joachim unpacked his ceremonial rations, hard sausage, oranges, a knob of butter and fruit drops, and issued an invitation to the budding poet; so there were four of us to dinner. The two of them talked about the forthcoming celebrations: completely new angle, opined Bleckschild, revolutionary reappraisal of the national inheritance, and first, foremost and all down the line, the tradition of German-Russian comradeship-in-arms. He produced a brochure, in which an FDJ functionary had written that the important thing was to retrieve the fire from history and not the ashes, and the fire element was, firstly, the alliance of Russians and Germans in the face of foreign domination threatening from the west, and, secondly, the revolt of the popular masses, the social component, if you like. That, Bleckschild assured us as he sucked fruit drops, was his theme.

I adopted a more amenable tack: 'The wounded Körner was given medical treatment and was kept hidden – you could be put to death for that sort of thing.'

'What about road-signs turned the wrong way?' Bleckschild was insistent.

'Not to my knowledge.'

164

But that had been typical, my son maintained. 'Did Lützow's men have drums?'

'Probably not,' I was being cautious. 'They rode as partisans behind enemy lines – what would they have wanted to drag drums around with them for?'

'But it would have been . . .' Joachim choked back the next words.

No doubt during your house-search you found – and probably confiscated – my photo albums. You can take another look at them, just to form a picture of my son in those days: not much left in him of the 'German Oak', his grandfather. In our family the women have made all sorts of contributions to our genetic make-up – Klärchen, my mother, for example, saved me from burliness, and a great deal of Marianne's nimbleness had rubbed off on Joachim. He was slim, medium height, quick in his movements; he used to infuriate me, the way he'd bolt his meals in three minutes flat, get up from the table still chewing, leave everything lying and be off down the stairs – his mother would then clear his plate away.

'You see, it's a competition,' said Bleckschild, 'for the best short story. Road-signs turned round the wrong way in Holzhausen, a French patrol loses its bearings and rides into an ambush by Prussian territorials? What d'you think, eh?'

'How would it be,' I ventured, 'if Saxons sent out scouts to offer their desertion, but the East Prussian territorials were in such a rage that they . . .'

'Saxons?' demanded Joachim and Bleckschild with one voice. 'And East Prussians?' added Bleckschild reproachfully.

So there it was again. Russians, Prussians and French all got a mention in the booklet, but not a word about us Saxons. 'And *East* Prussians,' Bleckschild admonished me, 'it would be better not to refer to them at all. Could be interpreted as revanchism, you understand?' He made it sound so condescending – this was the voice of youth, talking to someone who hadn't quite been able to take in all the latest, crucial, developments. All of a sudden, he brightened: 'It's time for Freedom Station 904!' he cried. 'Can I turn it on?'

Joachim switched the radio on; at nine on the dot, a voice ringing with fighting spirit announced that it was addressing the patriots in the western zones of occupation. Bleckschild did his best to enlighten me: for some little time now this station had been putting out an exciting two-hour programme every evening, swingy music – frowned upon in the GDR, actually – interspersed with news items inciting people to rise up in struggle against the Yankee occupying forces. There were also supposed to be secret messages directed at underground resistance groups: 'Mayfly three calling Sugar Loaf! Open grand is bid. Gerlinde having coffee with Hannibal.'

Marianne didn't say a word until Bleckschild had gone; Joachim had gone downstairs to see him out. 'Don't like him.'

'Me neither.'

'A right know-all. Doesn't listen to a word anyone's saying.'

It was half an hour before Joachim came back up. 'He wanted to get me to join the Police Stationed in Barracks,' he said. 'Our future Red Army.'

'And?'

'I'll think it over.'

I withdrew and read a few more pages from the works of Ernst Moritz Arndt, trying as I did so to make my inner voice sound like the announcer on Station 904; to my amazement, and to my horror, it worked.

The *Volkszeitung* next day carried a special feature page. The familiar engraving of the storming of the Grimma Gate by the *East* Prussian troops was accompanied by a caption stating that they were Prussian territorials. A kind of bacillus in me made me read everything through in search of tendentious distortions. 'German-Russian brotherhood in arms,' I read, although only Prussians and Russians had fought side by side, while all the others, first and foremost the Saxons and Württembergers, had stuck by the Corsican. Infuriated, I put the paper down.

In fact we had been due to bring down a disused factory chimney that day, but we were given new orders at short notice: which of us was trained in the use of mine-detectors? All of us older ones were. Drop everything else, and wait for orders to go into action! Our first reaction was, has anybody got a pack of cards? Suddenly, it was just like in wartime again, a touch of devil-may-care eased the tension, everybody was curious, but nobody would admit to it. The more abrupt the orders, the more your defence mechanisms go into compensatory action: all right, don't wet yourselves! And then it's as if you are swaggering about, cap shoved back, a cigarette hanging from the corner of your mouth. Real B-movie stuff.

A lorry drove up, and sitting next to the driver was my grumpy Saxon, with whom I had stood up on the top-stone the day before. We clambered onto the back of the lorry, and there, sure enough, lay mine detectors. We sped out to the Monument, through barriers and cordons, past piles of spruce branches and under flags and banners, and parked in front of the ornamental lake, where we jumped down, yes indeed, *jumped* down, and it irritated me when I realised that I had allowed myself to be infected by the atmosphere of self-importance and secretiveness. 'Right, listen. It's like this,' said Grumpy. 'The path from here, along the left side of the lake, and the area around the stands has to be combed. Comrade Ulbricht will be walking up this way tomorrow.'

We put on our earphones. I hadn't had this kind of instrument in my hand since my training days in Zeithain, and I had to remind myself how to handle it. You slide the flat disc across the ground, and it reacts to metal with a bleep. From the sound alone, an expert can tell pretty accurately the size of any object and how deep it's buried. We walked slowly in a line down the path, attentively swinging our detectors. I felt like a sower in the old pictures, but we were harvesting: we dug a magazine for a German sub-machine gun from under the grass verge. I thought of my ack-ack shells and hoped we wouldn't get too close to them, or that the concrete and earth would be too thick for the beams. We got a fix on a tin helmet and the lid of a mess-tin, then we took a break, spinning a yarn to our monosyllabic Comrade, something about our instruments having to be switched off after an hour's work so as not to overload the condensers. We squatted on some steps and had a smoke, feeling like schoolboys who have put one over on their teacher.

On the spot where Clemens Thieme had delivered his inaugural speech, a stand had been erected from which Ulbricht was to give his address. Over there had stood the box into which one of the Kaiser's adjutants had placed the batons carried in the great marathon rally. That was only forty years ago, and, a year after it, war had broken out. And what will happen a year from now?, I thought. Behind the ramparts, there was a rumble yet again. Joachim and his fellow drummers had been given the next few days off work. We continued our search under the stands without finding anything else. Greenery was nailed into place and red cloth spread out. I said, 'And all this just because I'm turning forty.' My mates grinned patiently. The Furies of War were half obscured by flags and the stands, but at least I could still make out something of their flowing hair.

That evening, Joachim mumbled that he needed my signature. He pushed a sheet of paper across the table – there was something odd going on, I could see it in his face and hear it in his voice. He spread his elbows on the table and then immediately removed them again,

167

he slumped in his chair and then straightened and leaned back, all that in the minute it took me to read the form: Joachim had passed me an application form for acceptance to serve with the *Kasernierte Volkspolizei*, the Police Stationed in Barracks. Marianne was the first to speak: 'You're not serious, are you?'

At this, Joachim deluged us with stuff about anyone joining now having the best chances, when the KVP was being established promotion would be much quicker than later on, in a year he could be a sergeant or even an officer. 'It's all different nowadays. It's in the cause of peace!'

'You're off your head, lad!'

Joachim hadn't yet come of age, so he needed our consent. 'You're not getting it.' To mark the occasion of the hundred and fortieth anniversary of the Battle of the Nations, he countered defiantly, there had been a recruiting drive at his works, and half of his FDJ group had volunteered. There were times when it was right to go to war to preserve peace. And especially now that . . .

'That's enough!' I broke in. 'You can talk till you're blue in the face. And don't go thinking your mother will sign.'

To which Joachim, his eyes lowered, answered – and I have to be fair to him on this, without the slightest trace of impudence in his voice – 'I'll be conscripted in six months anyway, when I'm eighteen. You don't have to sign.'

That was when Marianne and I realised that Joachim was no longer a child – it's something that comes sooner or later to all parents, and mostly comes with a jolt. 'Your grandfather . . .' but I didn't finish the sentence. Your Uncle Voiciech, I thought, but I wasn't going to start on that. Sometimes all your experience isn't worth a damn, along comes youth and knows it all better than you, so I just pushed the form back across to him and went to my room and looked over to the skull on top of the cupboard. I read something just recently about some woman writer and her vision of cobblestones: the dead are standing upright in their graves and we tramp back and forth on the tops of their skulls.

Next day, Joachim and his trumpeters marched this way and that all over the place and were fed from packed meals and field kitchens; he beat his drum and he knew no fear.

We heard Ulbricht's speech on the radio in the evening. Russians and Germans had driven Napoleon off westwards, and now Soviet citizens and German patriots stood firm against the Yanks and their henchmen, the old and the new Fascists, the warmongers from the

Rhine. Under my breath, I added: across the Rhine at Kaub! I could see the glow of torches and searchlights, the sky flushed red, as if Probstheida was on fire, like that other occasion long ago. I had a vision of my city blazing from Connewitz right into the centre, flames bursting out of the General Post Office. I stood next to Marianne at the open window, march music reverberated across to us, and then, from behind the trees in the park, the fireworks blasted off, that substitute for war, and I closed the window, sat down at the table and buried my head in my hands.

It's a funny thing about round-number birthdays, those milestones marking the end of a decade in your life. You reflect on your achievements, you are seized by fear of having neglected this, failed in that. Of course, I stood a round of drinks at work, of course my mother came to supper, Marianne gave me some present or other, there were flowers on the table, a half-bottle of advocaat, courtesy of Joachim. Best of all, I thought, would have been if I had been able to go out on my bicycle, and take in a few surrounding villages and fields, all by myself, in mild autumn weather. But there was a wind blowing, the clouds hung low, and anyway I hadn't the time.

The bands blared on until midnight. In my dream, Private Lindner was fleeing across sodden fields, he had thrown away his rifle and was trying to pick up someone else's; like a wall, Russian cavalry stood in his way, their lances dipped. This time, tanks would push forward, T34s and Joseph Stalins, and at Kaub they'd ford the Rhine, hot on the Yankees' heels. There, in one tank, would be sitting my Joachim, the justified warrior, it would drive over a mine, he'd leap out and run off panting across Hessian fields, on the heights at far-off Sedan Private Joachim Linden would stand watch with his comrades and be mortally struck down by the enemy's bullet. Or perhaps he would be part of the wedge driving through the southern sector, crossing the Rhine near the entrenchment at Strasbourg and then, Sapper Linden, gasping his way up to the Lingekopf – it's folk with limited imaginations that are the lucky ones.

In the morning, I opened the paper and came upon a short story by the budding author, Ralf Bleckschild: 'The Signpost'. It told the tale of how, between Zwenkau and Störmtal, a farm boy, Wilhelm by name, angry because the Lützowers had rejected him on account of his youth – 'Laughing, they called down from the saddle: You'll have to grow a bit yet, laddie, come back next year!' – had turned a signpost round and, instead of riding on Beucha, the Frenchies had blundered into the marshland near Otterwisch, and there, once their horses had got stuck up to their bellies in mud, they were finished off by peasants with scythes and flails. Their leader had been the blacksmith from Dölitz, whom Bleckschild had endowed with the outrageous name of Jörg Wackerbarth – Doughtybeard.

An artist had illustrated the story: Jörg Wackerbarth looked like Andreas Hofer, the Tyrolean popular hero. 'Just look at that bloody rubbish!' I said to Joachim when, around eleven, he had at last managed to drag himself out of bed.

'Now just don't start that up again,' said Marianne as she served up roasted sausages with sauerkraut.

I didn't ask whether Joachim had volunteered, and Marianne reproached me for this omission as we went out that afternoon with the handcart to lay in more potatoes. I was every bit as stubborn as Joachim, she said, I should try to understand him and his youthful defiance: 'It's always the same, when things get serious, you hold back and I'm the one that has to carry the can!'

Neither of us said a word as we loaded the sack onto the cart and rattled off home. Only once we were back in the cellar picking over the potatoes did I venture a reply: 'Every generation has to make its own mistakes.' In her rage, Marianne hurled a mouldering spud at the wall, where it disintegrated with spectacular effect.

A few weeks later, at supper, Joachim mumbled, just sort of by the way, that he had been called for his medical at ten the next morning. Marianne took a deep breath, while all I could find to say was, 'In the old days, budding recruits used to go and get blind drunk afterwards.' Joachim enlightened me with the information that such mindless petty-bourgeois rubbish was a thing of the past, they would be visiting the *Iskra* memorial and after that a meeting with Soviet friends had been arranged.

Next morning, Marianne and I went off to work as usual. I was lying under a vehicle, inspecting something or other, when I was called to the telephone. A woman's voice asked circumspectly if I was the father of a certain Joachim Linden. 'This is the surgery in Liebigstrasse. Please, don't be alarmed, your son is here, a traffic accident. He's in the operating theatre now. Please, don't alarm yourself.'

My blood ran cold. I went into our rest-room. Please, please, don't let the fire-bell ring now, not now, up a ladder, down into a crater to an unexploded bomb – not now. Must tell Marianne – well, that could wait till evening.

At the waiting-room door at the clinic, three figures in dressing-gowns were hanging about, one of them with his arm in a frame, the others with plaster-of-Paris collars. Not a porter to be seen, not a nurse; the three seemed eager to help. 'Your boy? An accident? There's one in the bed over there, by the window on the left, mate, I'll have a look.' And he came back and said, it wasn't as bad as all that, fractured shinbone and maybe something else to do with his ankle. The trio informed me they couldn't let anyone in, visiting hours were Sundays and Wednesdays, the food was lousy and, sure, they'd pass on the things I had brought along. 'An' if you've any problems, just let us know!' They had promoted themselves to this position of responsibility, regarded themselves as orderlies, the Professor's right-hand men. Then one of them shuffled off again and returned with the news that my boy had been knocked down *before* his medical, hit by a motor-cyclist. I passed round cigarettes.

Sunday afternoon, we stood at Joachim's bedside; Marianne immediately bent down next to him and smoothed and straightened the bedclothes, his leg was strung up in the air, bandaged and plastered. 'Won't hurt so bad now, eh? What's it like at night? Can you get some sleep, or does it hurt at night, too?' One of the ones with the plaster collars ambled past. 'Everything OK so far?' Joachim nodded. One expert to another.

Then we got the story. Joachim had been heading from the square in front of the Opera House towards the Franz Mehring bookshop when a man on crutches – he had lost a leg – had come lurching towards him. 'Really daft, it was,' said Joachim, 'I go one way, so does he, I go to the other side, so does he, I just couldn't get round him! And that's when the motor-bike caught me from behind.' A crowd had gathered, a tail-back of trams had built up, he had been lifted onto the pavement, police, an ambulance . . . I asked: 'And what about the bloke with one leg?'

'He just beat it.'

I could feel Marianne's sidelong look. How long would he have to stay here, I asked, and Joachim gave a snort. Four weeks at least, maybe six, he certainly wouldn't be out of plaster before that. Then after-care – that would probably take a good two months. And I thought, two months and no medical.

Joachim came out of hospital a changed man. Marianne and I carefully avoided any mention of the Police in Barracks. One day, Joachim told us how at work recruiting officers had come round looking for bright, hard-working, committed young men and

171

women, and they had begged him too, wouldn't he like to study? Mechanical engineering, medicine, law, Art history – take your pick, help yourself. 'I said I'd think it over.'

Marianne was sceptical. He'd get less money, and as a boy he hadn't exactly impressed either his teachers or his parents with his industriousness. I said, 'Well, nobody's ever yet got stupider from studying.' That was simple, harmless enough. I wondered what I might have done if, at eighteen, I had been offered a chance to study. If the subject had been explosives, I'd have jumped at it, I wouldn't have fancied anything else. No, not even history. Not then.

That next autumn, Joachim was back in the classroom. He swotted up mathematics and physics – I could understand bits here and there, but only in his first year. Most of the time I saw him in the blue shirt of the FDJ; over the desk where he did his studying, he had hung a picture of Stalin. He helped his sister Erika with her homework, something he had never done before; no doubt he was proud to be able to show her how much he knew. Of course he bullied her about in the process, but that did nothing to diminish Erika's love for him.

I watched Erika growing up, heard her talking, laughing, but her world was not my world. She was a normal schoolgirl, never ambitious, and never in danger of having to repeat a year. She had an uninhibited way of drawing: birds, flowers, half-timbered houses, leafless trees against a winter sky, and, hanging from every branch, trumpets. Once – she was perhaps twelve at the time – she showed me a drawing of a man with deep, hollow eyes and no mouth. 'Because you haven't talked to me for a week. That's you, you see?'

I said, 'What'll we talk about, then?' At this, her shoulders stiffened, she hurriedly drew in a mouth, no more than a single line. 'Didn't mean to do it that way,' she said, annoyed at herself, and it sounded as if I wasn't meant to take any offence either.

Joachim was always somewhere about the middle of his class. Sometimes our conversation came round to my favourite topic. Joachim had nothing but scorn for the Monument: feudal-bourgeois relic, anyone with an interest in history might at least try to apply it positively and constructively. I was within an inch of letting slip the secret behind the *Iskra* shrine.

Six months later it came to my ears that his history teacher's name was Bemmann. I considered whether I should tell Joachim of my encounters with him: I had, for example, seen Bemmann in conversation with Fürchtegott up on the ramparts. But then I thought, there are some things that are better kept from young ears – too complicated they are, and therefore too likely to be drowned in derision and lack of understanding. I asked what aspects Bemmann lectured on; the Spartakist Revolt, the International Brigades at Madrid and Walter Ulbricht in the trenches at Stalingrad. No room there for us poor Saxons, always with the Prussians breathing down our necks. There was great talk of us Saxons being the fifth occupying power in Berlin, of red Saxons stamping their mark on the GDR. You, Doctor, you're a Prussian, too, and it certainly would be a difficult job to get you to understand what actually happened. The Saxons, with Ulbricht at their head, who had moved to Berlin, had changed once they were there, and now they ruled as Prussians. Blücher and Fort Battle of the Nations, the invention of the *Iskra* shrine – all Prussian ideas. No one has ever investigated what might have happened if Germany's recovery had been governed by the Saxon spirit. Oh yes, well may you slander and abuse us, and the very way you pronounce the word 'fowksiness' just oozes malice. But remember this, 'folksy' has to do with *people*, and that can't be all bad.

Then came Erika's *Jugendweihe*, where she was confirmed in dedication to the cause of Socialism. Comrade Bemmann – he had switched party-allegiance in the meantime – delivered the address at the ceremony: every young person had to be prepared to defend the Socialist Fatherland against Imperialism. Shoulder to shoulder. After that, Erika studied draughtsmanship. 'When you've finished your studies and if you'd like to do me a favour,' I said to her, 'you could maybe do me a cross-section plan of the Monument, to scale, for my bedroom wall.' 'I'll do that for you, Dad.' But, when the time came, she forgot.

Her boss manufactured hydraulic ramps and fork-lift trucks for an important factory on the northern side of the city. Her boss was a whiz-kid and was even sent to England to negotiate contracts and boost the export trade. Maybe, I reckoned, he could design a special platform for the interior of the Monument, one that could be raised when the inside of the dome had to be cleaned and painted. I wrote him a letter and gave it to Erika to deliver; the man expressed an interest in the idea and we arranged to meet one Sunday morning. The Monument Choir was singing; 'Lützow's wild and daring charge' was now part of the standard repertoire again. In the programme note, I read: 'The Choir of the Monument to the Battle of the Nations endeavours to cultivate the inheritance of Socialist and patriotic songs handed down by progressive forces throughout

German history.' The hydraulic ramp manufacturer looked up with interest at the horsemen and measured the height with a sceptical eye. Once the famous acoustics were no longer required to serve the cause of patriotic tones, he said, 'Basically, we can build anything. The question is one of cost.'

We both stood with heads thrown back, and I waited for the familiar giddiness to take me, when the horsemen would seem to start riding in a circle. 'We must look for some lofty connection for the project,' I said, trying to use the jargon. 'Bring Ulbricht's name into the story somewhere. He's done a lot for his native city.'

The man asked for precise figures – I could send him them via Erika – he wanted to think the thing over carefully. We parted, and never saw each other again.

For fate decreed that the production of fork-lift trucks was reallocated by the planners away from the GDR altogether; it was to be the Bulgarians' responsibility in future. The upshot was a shambles; fork-lift truck deliveries from the Balkans fell well short of requirements, and as far as spare parts were concerned, that was an absolute dead loss. And the whiz-kid himself, instead of heading down the Danube to pass on his technical know-how, the tricks of the trade, to former tomato-growers and sheep-shearers, he vanished, to resurface in Heidelberg. From there, he sent his former colleagues coloured postcards, extolling the beauties of the Neckar Valley and extending a warm invitation to anyone who'd like to build real fork-lift trucks to join him in a modern factory overlooked by vineyards.

I've a bit of a headache; let's stop for today, Doctor. Well, all right, I'll answer your question about the Saxons' most outstanding characteristic. It's not easy to find one expression that will cover such an awkward, unmanageable bundle of contradictions. I'll give it a try, though: We Saxons just don't want to win.

174

CHAPTER 11

About that picture in your room . . . ?

Which one is that? Ah, that one, I might have known. I knew the artist well. That's why I hung the print there. And also because it's a view from the Monument . . . that's plausible enough, isn't it? Yes, I have altered a few details in the picture. If you weren't familiar with the original, you'd never have noticed, well, obviously.

The painter – I'd prefer to stick to that term, for that's what I called him in my thoughts before I found out his name. One day he just appeared, laid his sketch-pad on the parapet above the Archangel and began sketching, the city sky-line, domes, chimneys, churches. I followed him down the steps, eyeing his shoulders, his bald patch, and stealing a glance at his pad. That was early in the sixties, eight years after Ulbricht's performance and my son's accident. By then, the scars on the top-stone had been smoothed over by amateur mountaineers who volunteered for the job, the craters in the lake had been filled in, water rippled once more and was visited by ducks and seagulls. My daughter Erika had cleared off to the West with her boy-friend. In the terminology of official Western documents, a refugee. That smacks of danger to life and limb. Erika had simply beat it, with stealth, agility and two suitcases, out through West Berlin. Now she, too, was working in the fork-lift factory, and her sweetheart was earning his daily bread in the vicinity. There had been a deal of whispering beforehand; my mother, Marianne and Erika had had long discussions about the pros and cons, wiping many a tear from the corner of their eye. I had been excluded from all this – but you were asking about the picture, which was to become famous and be reproduced many times in calendars and postcards. I had a print of it framed, barely half the size of the original.

You can't just stand there and watch an artist at work – he has to concentrate and can't be bothered answering questions, and he certainly has no time for idle chatter. Painting is like bomb-disposal that way. Once he had been standing there sketching for the third time, working now on the ornamental lake tapering away in accord with the rules of perspective, I suggested, 'You could have another look at the view, from higher up. I could take you up.'

Strange, I brooded, the colossus has been photographed and painted thousands of times, but this is the first time anyone has drawn the view of the city *from* it. I tried to find out why nobody had hit on the idea before, but the artist just went on scribbling; maybe he wasn't even listening. 'On the other hand,' I said, 'you've got it right: every visitor has had that view, twice, once on the way up and once on the way down.'

He came again, and wrote in letters and numbers on the drawing; these, he said, were his scale of colour and light values; vertical format, with lots of sky over the city.

'A dirty sky,' I assumed.

'Blue sky.'

'Like at the end of the war?'

He looked at me quizzically, and that started me off. I told him how the factories had shut down, there wasn't a single locomotive belching smoke, and all the copies of *Mein Kampf* and all the Hitler Youth leaders' braid, already reduced to ashes, were past polluting the air. 'You weren't here at that time, I suppose?'

'Prisoner of war.'

'I was here the whole time.' A comforting phrase; I knew what I was talking about. I sneaked a sidelong look at him: dark hair, cut

176

short, going a bit grey at the temples, a bald patch on the top of his skull. He was clean-shaven, wore a pullover and a woolly shirt, open-necked, and corduroy trousers. He wasn't done up like an artist at all. Spectacles, yes, but very plain, not those thick-rimmed efforts with half a pound of black plastic round them or anything like that.

What I'm talking about now took place at the start of the sixties, a quiet time in my neck of the woods. The wall around our cosy little country was complete, nobody wanted to cross the Rhine at Kaub now, concrete stood guard at the Brandenburg Gate and at Eisenach, there would be no advance by latter-day Napoleons. The guardians up on the Monument stood at ease, in close ranks; the way members of workers' combat groups were being photographed in Berlin, with sub-machine guns held at the port.

I went about my trade between Altenburg and Delitzsch, Schkeuditz and Wurzen, and was recognised as the most experienced explosives expert in the district. The period between my fortieth and fiftieth birthdays was the best of my life. My position as chairman of the Leipzig South and South-East group of the *Kulturbund*, Friends of the Homeland Section, was unchallenged. Marianne had risen to be manageress of a cooperative food shop, so we had gammon and better-quality beer on the table, and tomatoes and cauliflower even outside the seasonal gluts. We bought new furniture, a wall unit and a swivel armchair. Marianne kept on at me to treat myself to a writing-desk; no doubt she would have found that a more bearable location for my historical messing about, as she described my collecting and sifting. Television and spiced steak tartare, cardigan and middle-age spread – it was the most normal period I can remember. Once – we had just switched off the TV and were about to go to bed – Marianne said, 'Freddie, something I've always meant to ask, you've long since stopped imagining you saw your father, haven't you? Or Viktor?'

Presumably Marianne had been nursing this question for weeks, chewing it over and waiting for exactly the right moment to unburden herself of it. I stared into the blank TV, Marianne didn't move a muscle, and I even considered pretending not to have heard and going into the kitchen to brush my teeth. I hadn't been surprised by the appearance of Felix and Voiciech, but neither had I reckoned that the phenomenon would necessarily repeat itself. 'That was at the end of the war,' I said, 'when everything was topsy-turvy. And always at the Monument.'

'What about when Achim broke his leg?'

'Certainly not then.' I knew well that was barely half the truth.

'You can't kid me, you know, Freddie.'

I laid my hand on her arm and turned to look at her.

'And that's what you thought at the time?'

'I thought that was what you were thinking.'

'Have you sometimes worried: Freddie's tuppence off the shilling?'

'Everybody's got their own screw a bit loose.'

'They haven't come back, and I didn't expect them to, either. Times are quiet now. Life just goes on.'

'That's true, yes.'

We sat on in silence for a while, I left my hand resting on her arm. Maybe we never understood each other better than in those moments. 'We're doing all right, eh?'

'Sure, we're doing fine.'

One day there was a cloudburst and I rushed with the painter to take shelter in the little stand-up bar in one of the temples to the dead at the far end of the lake. We in the *Kulturbund* had fought this tooth and nail – a desecration of the Monument! But an economist had pointed out to us what it would cost to put up a wooden booth, and wouldn't that, of all things, look absolutely dreadful cheek-by-jowl with the Monument? And *our people* had a right to their frankfurters and beer. One of the joys of life in those days was the frankfurter, soon to be supplemented by the jumbo frankfurter. Our people had the highest consumption of frankfurters in the world, so why shouldn't that also round off their experience here?

So, under a metre-thick layer of granite from Beucha, safe from lightning and bombs, each with a beer and a short, we leaned on the bar; quite imperceptibly, we had slipped into the familiar form of address. I asked, 'Are you going to stick to the clear skies idea?'

'I'll maybe put in one white summer cloud. A round one, like a pillow.' And he told me of how, in Siberia, he had done a picture of a woman comically balancing on an oil pipeline, with a summer cloud up above. Another beer, another schnapps, and then he said, 'You must come and visit me some time. I'll show you round. By the way, I've started on the painting of the view from the parapet.'

Then I performed my famous trick with the beer-mats, fourteen of them perched one on top of the other with only three touching the table. I told him what I was as to trade. 'Sorry I can't return the

178

invitation, for you to watch me at work.' We both had quite a laugh at that.

He lived in high-ceilinged rooms on the Johanna Park, crammed with pictures and unusual furniture and art-books. Somehow, in these surroundings, the familiar '*du*' didn't come so naturally to me as it had in the pub, and it seemed to be the same with him. The painting stood on a tall easel, the ornamental lake gleaming in a rich blue. The outline of the city against the horizon was indistinct, the sky above it comfortingly empty, and I thought, seagulls and crows in there, or not? The Monument as a border, right at the bottom of the foreground, and if it were to disappear – it was a thought that almost made me dizzy – then the viewer would be floating in mid-air. So I said it was just as well it had been done from the parapet and not from the top-stone. The feeling of soaring, of being completely detached, stuck in my mind. It was impossible to imagine the city without its colossus, it held Leipzig together, the whole city directed its gaze up to it, and now the gaze was being returned. And yet, the Archangel hadn't thrust his sword skywards when the bombers came. Then I thought, hold on, you're letting your imagination run away with you; for the painter, it's a matter of perspective, no more than that.

Somehow the conversation came round to New Year's Eve. 'I'm happiest when I'm out in the open air,' he said, 'in the mountains or in the woods. In Leipzig, I like to go up the rubble-mountain in Connewitz.' I knew the mountain from the vantage point of the Monument, and had watched it grow above the rooftops, and many a time I had thought, there lies the old Leipzig.

'You really must experience it for yourself,' he exclaimed. 'If the weather's not too bad, maybe we could meet up there? I've already done a picture of that hill.' He rummaged among pictures standing against the wall and held one up; I could make out the slope, the rubble overgrown by shrubs and goldenrod, a track leading through tough undergrowth, along which a boy has run to the top and, arms aloft, is shouting, 'Wow! I can see the whole world!' I knew that anyone who lifted himself so high out of Leipzig's flat streets was bound to be overcome by giddiness, for he realises the world isn't two-dimensional after all, as he had always assumed it to be. An ant, scuttling around on a globe of the world, has no idea of what is up and what is down; that's exactly the lot of an inhabitant of the Fairs City. And then, suddenly, there he is, standing fifty metres high! In one corner of the picture, boys have raked together a pile of junk and made a little bonfire; an idyll in miniature, a commonplace pleasure,

179

but that boy up there is on the way to the stars. 'You can believe it if you like,' I said, 'but once I shouted "I can see the whole world," too. I was the same age as these boys then, and my father had stood me up on the edge at the very top. I was convinced I could have flown. Maybe we could go up to the top of your mountain together? Let's not wait till New Year's Eve, when the place is swarming with lads.'

Behind broken-down fences and a dilapidated gate was the start of a cart-track, and here stood a little stone house, minus doors and windows, and just behind it lay a confused heap of concrete posts. The painter said, 'I've talked myself blue in the face to people in authority, trying to convince them that this place should be cleaned up to give nature a chance, all this profusion of wild plants, acacias and beeches and oaks, and that marvellous parasite, spurge – you wouldn't believe the frothy, feathery cotton-wool it decorates the branches with in autumn.'

We went round the foot of the hill, skirted by a ditch full of a stinking black sludge reeking of phenol from the chemical works above the town, with blue cushions of foam floating on it. The sides of the stream were plastered together with heavy, solid deposits of filth, and I thought, even if, one fine day, clear water should flow here again, it would keep on being polluted from out of these banks. How could you remove such poisonous masses? You'd need some special kind of digger, and then where could you dump the stuff? The acrid smell was always there. My question sounded almost mischievous: 'And how do you portray a stink like this in a picture?'

There was the narrow path, trampled down by the feet of children, and up on top stood, at a drunken angle, a mast. Hollows had been dug into the undergrowth, shored up with boards that had collapsed again. He said, 'I've seen rabbits and hares and partridge here, pheasant, too, and once even a deer. That great lump of debris there, maybe a young artist could do it up a bit, not paint it over, but just intensify the expression in it. Look at the reinforcement rods sticking out of the concrete, isn't it marvellous, the way they twist and twine? Like a piece of modern sculpture. The mountain as a work of art and a work of nature at one and the same time, see what I mean? Those idiots I've told about it never understood a single word I was saying. They nodded and muttered a yesyes, and probably they were thinking, that nutcase, what's he on about now?' Gradually, I began to see it through his eyes: a hollow over there that should be left exactly as it is. A cascade of broken bricks that mustn't be allowed to become overgrown. Of course, the paper lying over there, and those

180

rusting metal drums, that would have to be cleared away. 'But on no account a kiosk on the top,' said the painter. 'Folk can drink their coffee and eat their frankfurters somewhere else.'

When we were at the top, naturally my eyes went first to my colossus. It was bathed in afternoon sun, a tiny window up near the top blinked at us. Below us lay the city, serried ranks of rooftops either side of the Karl Liebknecht Strasse, beyond them the cupolas of the covered market, the spire of the Russian Church. To the south and west, the green life of tightly packed treetops. 'The open-cast workings are pushing across from over there,' I said, 'they'll swallow up half the trees eventually. And then all that sulphur in the air.' All at once it struck me, 'Goldenrod probably thrives on sulphur!'

'See you on New Year's Eve, then.'

Our Erika soon sent her first picture postcard from the Black Forest. For Joachim, things had changed somewhat: he now had a close blood-relative in the West and so was now relegated to second grade in the trustworthiness stakes, not acceptable for either the police or the army – no sword by *his* left side! Before he sat his final exams, the discussion ranged back and forth: dentistry or chemistry, civil engineering or something in the export trade, or what?

At that time, so he told me, the 'Cultural Scientist' had been invented, someone who was well versed in literature, painting, music and the theatre could run a cinema or, equally well, a youth centre, could become a Municipal Arts Director or for that matter the manager of a theatre. Since Joachim had hitherto shown no particular interest in any of these areas, he seemed ideally suited for tackling the lot of them. He went off to take up his studies in Greifswald, and we saw him only during vacations. Even then, he was often away under canvas, once on a work project in the Ukraine, where they wielded their shovels in the construction of an industrial plant and sat round the campfire singing songs and practising *druzhba*, 'Friendship', with students from Bulgaria, Poland and Czechoslovakia, and there he fell in love with a girl studying internal trade, Claudia, from Schkeuditz. After the campfire session, they went off into some Ukrainian bushes or maize plantation, far from home, each heart beat fast for its compatriot, maybe to the wafting sounds of the balalaika or the *garmoshka*, the harmonica – they bent half-dried stalks over till they had a bed.

When the harvest effort was over and the conscripted students were on their way home, they sat in the train, looking at each other,

181

sad and bewildered, forcing a smile, and in Leipzig, on the Central Station, as the group dispersed, Claudia said, in a tired voice, 'You'll write, won't you?' But he didn't write, or perhaps he just hadn't written yet, and then a letter came from her. So he half-suspected, and what he heard, sitting with her on a bench between the Central Station and the Opera, confirmed his fears: Claudia was expecting a child. He asked shamefacedly if she was sure that it was his, was she absolutely certain? And she nodded. And Joachim plucked up all his courage to choke out the hardest question he had ever asked: 'So do you feel I ought to marry you now?' And she asked, 'Do you want to?' And he looked at her, miserable with embarrassment. And she said, 'No, in fact I don't want to marry you, either.'

Claudia moped about with downcast eyes, she was pale, and when term started again, she got one bad mark after another. Joachim had made off again, back to his Greifswald refuge, and if Claudia had scant news of him, we had even less. It wasn't until just before Christmas that Marianne first got wind of the whole mess. Churned up inside by the conflicting emotions roused by the shock – the worry and the eye-moistening thought, 'I'm going to be a grandmother!' – she made the journey out to Schkeuditz. Claudia, her mother and Marianne sat together over coffee and the seasonal Stollen. As well, they drank Hemus, a sticky-sweet wine much favoured by Saxon women. Yes, well now, and did they have enough room here for the child? What about Claudia's studies? And what, Marianne inquired, could they do to perhaps stir his lordship, the father, to the view that he, the student, might make some contribution towards the welfare of his offspring?

How often does it happen, I wonder, that a male member of the family – to wit, me – doesn't get to hear about this sort of thing until much later? 'Oh, by the way,' Marianne opened the conversation one evening, and then I was simply informed, not asked for my opinion or, for that matter, my advice; the fact of the matter was that I just didn't have a part to play in what had to be done now. Even if they had only come to me for money. Claudia's father was a lathe operator on shift-work in an engineering works in Schkeuditz, her mother a cook in the canteen of a nearby mill. They lived in a little house built with the support of the Nazis post-1933 as part of an SA housing estate, for this family too had a veteran in its ranks. 'It'll be fine for the little lad, out there in the countryside,' I said.

'Or the little lass.'

It was a girl, and Claudia and the two delighted grandmothers called her Julia. Joachim didn't get to see his child, that was the way Claudia wanted it. He took his exams undisturbed by infant cries and got a job in a Film Archives office in Berlin – which surprised me, even though experience had by now taught me to expect the unexpected where he was concerned. I had never really seen him as an enthusiastic cinema-goer.

On the evening of New Year's Eve I met the painter on the rubble mountain. There was snow on the ground as Marianne and I trudged up the slope, the night was clear and I heard him, up on the plateau, calling while we were still some way off. We shook hands, he produced a half-bottle of whisky, I reciprocated with corn schnapps. 'Didn't I get the moon just right!' he rejoiced and pointed to where it hung, just like in a painting by Caspar David Friedrich, shining down on the city and its Monument. Some men were setting up rockets at the edges of the plateau, boys had accumulated a hoard of tinder in a hollow and already flames were beginning to flicker; it was all just like the painting, 'Wow! I can see the whole world!' Cheeriness and high spirits all round, and shouts of how much nicer it was to bring in the New Year in company, with the city at your feet, than on your own at home.

I had never seen Leipzig like this, it glistened, sparkled, it wasn't early closing day, or shut for stock-taking or restocking, or because of the black-out or the end of the war, the oldest housing estates were just as brightly illuminated as the new blocks of flats, no pond or stream, nor even the sky, could be dulled by Leipzig's filth, light flooded from every window and every crack, and in that night my Leipzig warmed the cockles of even my heart. Five to twelve, and here and there a rocket, unable to contain itself, whooshed into life. Hip-flasks were raised once more, and the painter bayed his joy at the moon. The circle of light had almost closed right round us, only to the south were the woods and fields dark, but even beyond that blackness a refinery beacon flared. Ah, my city, I thought, how my heart aches for you, and how often have you given me a pain in the arse, but now, now you're quite simply wonderful! All the best and hugs and kisses! and, above all, good health! Here's to magnificent pictures, I wished the painter, and he reciprocated, may your fuses always be dry. At that moment, Leipzig exploded at our feet.

Up spurted a shimmering carpet, woven out of arcing silver threads, leaping and hopping, its pile twice the height of the houses. Out of a white glare, flares soared, blue and red and green signals, here we are, we're alive, we're celebrating, greeting the heavens and

183

the New Year that's going to be better than the old, and how could it fail to be! I raised my flask in greeting in the direction of the lowering Monument. Here, there and all over the place this magical fire poured itself upwards into the sky. As if each and every Leipziger himself was trying to leap heavenwards! And now sparks, like stars, were hissing up from the edges of our mountain, and I became aware that for some time now I had been holding Marianne's hand. Unlike other fireworks displays, my thoughts at this one hadn't turned to air-raids, to master-bombers and the avenging Samuel, alias Horst-Heinrich Katzenstein, nor to canisters of fire-bombs and so-called Medium Capacity land-mines, block-busters as big as boilers, and then I heard the painter's shout, 'I'm going to paint this!' 'You'll never manage it, nobody could, you have to *see* it, and tomorrow, in an hour's time even, we'll not so much as be able to recreate it in our imagination.'

A quarter of an hour later, the first threads of the carpet of lights began to go out, the glowing stars became fewer and farther between, one last sparkling cascade, one shower of lights like a Christmas tree, the Leipzigers had sent a fortune up in smoke, had overspent in more than one sense of the word, and now they were returning to their brick and concrete shells to plug themselves in and dance to swing and bebop or whatever the current craze was, with whoops and hollers and kissing and cuddling and bowls of punch and now and then a quick schnapps in between times. The moonlight came into its own again. There was still light shining from ten thousand windows as the mountain climbers stoppered their half-empty bottles, threw the dead ones down in the snow and set off for home. I thanked the painter for his tip, and he assured me he would come and see me at the Monument in a day or two, adding that tonight he'd had a new idea.

He returned with his sketch-pad, trying to decide how the sky over the lake should look in his picture. He asked, 'Do you remember telling me the Monument was in honour of the dead of only one side? There ought to be a new monument, over on the mountain of rubble.' When the new approach road from the south was finished, it would lead directly to the mountain, which would tower up over it. From all other sides you had to approach it through narrow, crumbling suburbs. A memorial to *all* the dead of this century, he went on, to the war-dead of *both* sides, to the victims of concentration camps, of the bombing, and I wondered whether he was going to include the dead SS-men, like the commander of Fort Battle of the

Nations for instance. 'A fist,' he said, 'a gigantic fist, and the words, "In spite of everything!"'

A few weeks later, an art exhibition was opened at the Market, and in the *Volkszeitung* I read that the painter had works on show in it, his drawing entitled 'In spite of everything' got a mention. I stood in front of it for ages. A fist, with all kinds of human figures festooning the arm, falling and clinging on, struggling and tumbling, rearing up, and flames, too, barbed wire, spearheads, twisted reinforcement rods, and still more and more bodies. I fought down simple judgements like, I like it, or, I don't like it. I was waiting for different emotions: pride or apprehension or awe. A lady was explaining the exhibits to a group of visitors, and they formed their semi-circle in front of 'In spite of everything', too.

It was, she was saying, a reminder of the words of Karl Liebknecht, and she referred to the repeated revolt of the working class, proletarians had fallen in the Spanish Civil War, had perished in the concentration camps, and our thoughts might turn also to the brave people of Vietnam. And Thälmann had said that five fingers made a fist. The graphic language of the artist, perhaps unfamiliar to many of them – that, too, was Socialist Realism. The fist was an admonition to vigilance, for warmongers would continue to pose a real threat, and they must be vigorously opposed and repulsed . . . The artist had given expression to the idea that the ultimate victory of Communism, despite all sacrifice . . . I thought to myself: I suppose the painter will know best when it's time to speak up for himself.

On one or two occasions I had work to do in connection with the building of the southern approach road; we were blowing up the foundations of a disused railway bridge. I looked up to the rubble mountain behind the trees and pictured to myself the towering fist on the top, in the different seasons of the year and in the changing light. From the twisting path I looked out over the tops of the oaks and beeches and marvelled at the extent of the forest that stretched along the arms of the river through Leipzig. My colossus stood illuminated by the bright evening light from the west. What, I wondered, would the visitors to the monument on this hill one day think as they looked across there? There was no hint of jealousy in the thought.

By this time, Joachim was sporting the Socialist Unity Party badge in his lapel. Now, as he approached thirty, his hair was thinning at the temples, not something that ran in the family. Erika had sent a parcel, but, when he paid us one of his rare visits, we put neither the

Westphalian cottage-smoked sausage nor the Emmentaler cheese on the table – we didn't want to offend our Comrade Guest. He talked about his work in Berlin, where he was no longer employed in the film archives but had instead been assigned to some particular committee, 'with connections in high places' and 'directly responsible'. 'And who to?' I asked, to be answered with a look of astonishment. One didn't ask such things. 'And how do you get on with Berlin folk?'

Joachim gave a slow shake of the head. The whole of Berlin was being poisoned by the propaganda from RIAS in the Western sectors. The high-ups in other regions were casting jaundiced eyes on Leipzig, because Comrade Walter held a protecting hand over his birthplace, there were mutterings that he was channelling hefty sums of money its way – the sports academy, the stadium, the opera house. Comrade Walter would have to be on his guard against intrigue and conspiracy; even the committee in which he, Joachim, worked was riven with tensions.

As he spoke, Joachim cut up his food neatly on his plate and put a piece in his mouth; as he chewed, he was cutting again already, and I thought, that's the way people ate when they snatched a bite in the canteen, no way to eat when you have your feet under your parents' table, though. He had been a father for a few years now, but still I couldn't imagine him being at all at ease dealing with a small child. I had, in the meantime, got to know Claudia, and Julia too, a dark-eyed little thing with a pony-tail, and the latest was that Claudia wanted to marry a man in internal trade, a divorcee and father of two children who were to remain in their mother's custody. All these affairs were part and parcel of Marianne's world, but didn't really touch mine.

Marianne asked whether there was a girl-friend, after all, it was high time he thought about getting married, wasn't it? Joachim swallowed hastily. Oh, he was unbelievably busy, just simply didn't have the opportunity, and a girl in the party . . . and then, to carry on debates at home the same as at work – it was better the way it was.

Joachim stayed for three days, stuck in meetings dealing with difficulties in long-term planning. A few people wanted to deviate from the party line – there were revisionists everywhere. I said, 'Maybe somebody's putting up misleading road-signs and luring you all into the marshes?' Joachim looked at me as if I had grown horns. A name cropped up that I could latch on to: Comrade Lohse was now the culture boss for the region. 'There's supposed to be some

186

mountain made of rubble out Connewitz way,' Joachim asked. 'Know it?'

''Course I do.'

'There's a lunatic who wants to plant some conciliatory monument on it, some woolly-headed piece of pan-humanism. I'm sure you know the old saying, "I love my Leipzig, because Leipzig belongs to me!"'

'It comes from one Paul Fröhlich, our regional lord and master. He's praising Leipzig because it belongs to him – have I got it right?'

'I'd really like to know whether you're capable of learning anything new at all!' Joachim glanced at the clock. Another consultation, he said.

Two days later, I went to see the painter. I was reminded of my father; he had run through a night of fire to Katzenstein's house. To be sure, my reasons for calling didn't have the same life-or-death urgency, but I couldn't help thinking, an artist will surely cling to his creation as he will to life itself.

The painter was dressed in smock and bonnet. He apologised for not shaking hands, but he was in the middle of varnishing a frame. He had to do everything for himself, he said, the heating in his studio was on the blink, he went on complaining – more to himself than to me – as he painted.

Later on, as we sat at the table, I spilled the beans. 'Conciliatory,' I said, 'woolly-headed pan-humanist nonsense, that's just a selection.'

We went into another room, and there stood a metre-high plaster fist on a pedestal. Wire twined round it, bodies writhed and plunged. The painter pulled some sacking aside to reveal more, the whole thing, and I said, 'You really can't tell from the figures what side they fought on.'

Well, it wouldn't be right at all, he explained, to depict the figures in their respective uniforms, the function of art was to symbolise; just by portraying them all as having died, he would be putting a great deal of significance into it.

'You should have a text running round the base,' I suggested: 'In the course of this century, X-thousand Leipzigers died on the front lines, so many perished in concentration camps, so many were killed by bombs and so many were banished.' Come to think of it, Hildrun and her three children should be among them.

'I've a pretty shrewd idea where this salvo has come from. From Berlin. And the ones in Halle will be behind it too. Just and unjust wars – I've heard it all before.'

'You've got a Saxon standpoint, and they've a Prussian one.'

'But Ulbricht . . .' the painter went no further.

A wholly new Saxon consciousness, who had tried to put that about? Ulbricht and a thousand Saxons had tried to infiltrate Berlin, ah well, that was all water under the bridge now. 'What you need is a few strong arguments in your favour,' I ventured. 'You must use cunning.' The painter had fallen almost completely silent now. 'The sacred mountain of our city,' I went on, 'the idea came to me just recently. It's yours if you want it, with pleasure; you can make more of it than I can.'

'With that sort of language, I'd be cutting my own throat.'

Mountain of Destiny was the next one we tried, and then we fiddled about with words like noble and eternal, Hill of Remembrance – all completely unusable.

During those weeks we were busy blasting a way through the forest and up towards the hill. Boulders and tree-stumps had to be cleared out, run-of-the-mill work. Goldenrod shot up out of the grey remnants of winter, and down in the low-lying pastures the cowslips were in bloom alongside that plant that stinks of garlic. Phenol and garlic: the aromas of Leipzig. Up on the hill I sometimes saw the painter. He'd be standing at the spot where he wanted to erect his memorial, staring into the distance, way over my head, of course. I had done all the talking with him I could.

One forenoon, as I was just unwrapping my sandwiches, a little knot of people trooped up the mountain-side, and to my astonishment I recognised Joachim at their head. Comrade Lohse was there, too. Joachim was pointing upwards and downwards, he was obviously the one doing all the talking. I got up and, still chewing, went along another path, lost sight of the group and didn't get a view of them again until I saw them in mid-palaver at the very spot which, if the painter had had his way, would have been the site of his monument. More pointing into the distance. The group made its way off via the northern side, and I went back to my tree-stumps. I was curious as to whether Joachim would show up at home that evening, but he must have gone straight back to Berlin, I suppose.

Three days later, two bulldozers clattered up, and on the top they were signalled into position; the man waving his arms about up there was Comrade Lohse. A whole week long, these juggernauts carved out a hollow just where the memorial was to have stood, and the diggings were carted away. On one occasion I went up to inquire what was going on, and was told that the rubble was needed for a road embankment that was being thrown up somewhere. I said, 'And you have to take it from here and nowhere else?' Shrugs. On my way down, I got snagged on some reinforcing rods, tearing the seam of my trousers. Nothing unusual, in my job. I bent down, and next to the rods there were grooves in the concrete. A weather-worn VM?

Some weeks after that I was out on one of my cycle runs when I spotted the painter near a little rounded hilltop they call the Kolm, to the east of Liebertwolkwitz. If that other wing of the hospital weren't in the way, you could see the hump from the window here. The Kolm had always had an attraction for me. Standing up there, I've often visualised the regiments passing across the plains during the Battle. On the top, there's an obelisk in memory of two generals and a large number of victorious dead. There are plants growing there that you won't find anywhere else in our region, flora normally native to the desert and the Steppes.

After the war, somebody erected a wooden tower up there, and from it, tests were carried out using radar beams, then it was hung with directional antennae for jamming transmitters, sending out whistles and whines into the ears of RIAS listeners. Now all that's left of the tower is a virtual ruin, yet nobody will pull it down. Fences all round it, all trampled down. Then, later, garages were built for lorries, but they're derelict now, their doors torn off. Everywhere, debris and garbage, and in amongst it these rare plants, tough and tenacious. In the autumn, a machine for steaming potatoes burbles away up there and there's a stench for miles around and all that's left at the end of the day are piles of muck. The Kolm's just being worn down, eroded away. But why should it get off more lightly than the city itself?

Anyway, near there I met the painter. He was in an allotment, swinging a pickaxe, he had taken his shirt off, and the sweat was running down his back. 'I've bought myself a bit of land here.' He waved a hand over grass and rubbish and thistles; there would be no lack of work to do on this. 'Nearly a thousand metres of land, none better to be had for miles around.' The ground sloped gently away towards the city, with an uninterrupted view, and of course my colossus rose in all its majesty against the horizon. I had the feeling, though, that the painter was not all that delighted to see me; maybe I was keeping him back from his work. I was still by his side when he took up his pick again. 'If you ever need a hand.'

'I haven't got a building permit yet,' he said. 'It's to be a multi-purpose shed.'

The term wasn't new to me. In those days – there was an economy drive on building materials – you couldn't build a garage, not without a special permit, and only party functionaries, writers and sportsmen got them. Everybody else made do with permission to build a multi-purpose shed, that's to say, they built a garage with a veranda on it or with a tiny water closet and a lean-to for the watering-can. 'Sure thing,' I said, 'if I can give a hand, you know where to find me.' He was already hacking away again at a tangle of roots.

A few weeks later, I cycled along that way again, and there had been all sorts of changes. The painter was in the middle of giving some men instructions as to where he wanted lumps of granite they were unloading from a flat truck. 'That's going to be some foundations,' I said. 'Or are you intending to throw a massive wall all round your plot?' He looked exhausted, both nervously and physically. 'Granite from Beucha,' I said, knowledgeably.

On Joachim's next visit, I asked what had become of the idea for a monument. 'The man's obstinate,' Joachim smiled, 'but so are we.' He helped himself to more soup. 'We offered him a marvellous trip, Egypt, Spain, India, wherever he wants. That's the quickest way of making him forget his crackpot idea. We've altogether different things on our minds.' It seemed that plans for the inner city were being discussed at the highest levels, focusing principally on the perspective of the Karl Marx Platz. A church on a square bearing the name of the greatest revolutionary of all time? The very idea!

'Your grandfather saved it from destruction.'

Joachim had some difficulty in going on. 'There are even people who are of the opinion that if the church had gone up in smoke with the rest, we'd have one problem fewer today.' In the Soviet Union they had sliced historic buildings off their foundations at ground level, turned them on their axis and moved them dozens of metres, and that's what they wanted to try here. I couldn't take my eyes off my boy, trying to picture him as he had been as a little lad, during the war. Now here he was, blowing in from another city and dictating the fate of my city. The painter was a Leipziger, I was one, Ulbricht had once been one. 'I think,' I said, 'our city is doomed. It's going to go under, just like Vineta in the legend, long ago. We're standing on brown coal, and very likely one day that will be more important than the Old City Hall and the Central Station and even the Monument to the Battle of the Nations.' Joachim laughed. The way conquerors laugh.

The next time I pulled up at the painter's plot at the Kolm, I froze

190

in amazement. Granite was piled metres high, there was a wall enclosing one corner, six metres long down one flank, three on the other, and more than two metres high. Behind that, earth had been banked up; you wouldn't expect to find that kind of boundary wall round even the most grandiose property. Half a dozen men were at work. I propped my bike against an old plum tree, and right away one of them rushed up to tell me they could get along fine without snoopers here.

'Just hold your horses,' I said, 'what I'm standing on is a public right of way, and you've no say there, mate!' I stared him straight in the eye, so he turned on his heel and went back to his pals. After some whispering, they got back to work. Down in the plain a cloud of dust rose, a carriage drawn by two horses dashed up, and in it sat the painter. He pulled to a halt in front of me and I almost expected him to toss me the reins. At least, I wouldn't have been at all surprised if he had.

'Coming on, isn't it?' he called.

'Some multi-purpose shed!'

'*Faits* have to be *accomplis*!'

'You're right there,' I said, 'Thieme did exactly the same.'

The painter took the bits from the horses' mouths to let them crop. Their coats were wet under the harness; his movements suggested he was accustomed to handling horses. 'It's a good vantage-point,' I said, 'maybe even better than on the mountain of rubble. Here you can look out from one monument over to the other. And maybe the people in high places will tidy up the Kolm as well; they can steam potatoes just as well somewhere else. When you were excavating, did you come across any bones? Or skulls?'

'It's a bit late for that now, a hundred and fifty years on.'

'Fürchtegott had it easier that way.'

The painter didn't look up at the mention of that name, and didn't ask who he had been. 'The plinth's to be five metres high,' he said, 'and then the fist on top of that, another ten.'

'If you run out of cash, you can have whatever's in my bank account, the lot.' At that time, Marianne and I had saved nearly twenty thousand Marks.

The painter went over to his tradesmen and had a chat with them. He walked round behind the pedestal, hidden from my sight now. I waited a while, then got on my bike and pedalled off towards Liebertwolkwitz and back into the city. Some character, I thought, he just won't give in. Multi-purpose shed! I had a laugh to myself.

I went back once more, it was a misty summer evening and a light rain was falling, blurring all the contours. Some fifty men were working on the monument, passing blocks of stone to each other without a word. Some wore long, shapeless coats, even though it was quite muggy. Everything was going on in a strange silence, with unnatural haste. The painter was nowhere to be seen. No doubt he had found volunteers to help, maybe young colleagues he had infected with his plan. I didn't go any nearer, not just because I didn't want to disturb them, but I was overcome by an unaccustomed timidity. So he hadn't gone to India or Egypt, but was grafting away here at his great project. There are sagas, in which men rise from the grave and carry out a task which a later generation is neglecting. One thing was plain: Joachim, or, for that matter, Comrade Lohse, must not get wind of what was going on here.

Between my fortieth and my fiftieth year was the best time of my life. The state celebrated its fifteenth anniversary with a feeling of 'We've achieved something, we're no mere starving wretches!' Right down to shop-floor level there was feasting and drinking, at home we had eel and tongue and trout on our plates, wines from the Unstrut and from Bulgaria, corn schnapps from Nordhausen, all the beer we could drink. A few weeks later, I turned fifty. I invited friends and workmates out to a beer-garden, I broached the barrel of beer myself, and on the barbecue there were sausages and marinaded spare-ribs. I was a normal, well-fed citizen, I cuddled Marianne, had a drink with everybody. Some thought they were being very witty and wished me all the best for the *second half* of my life. I clinked glasses with Joachim and said, 'If you only knew!' And Joachim replied, 'Father, all I can say is: if *you* only knew!' He drank a lot, and quickly, like somebody who can't wait to get drunk and still can't manage it.

A week later, I said to Marianne, 'You're coming with me today. I want to show you something.' We took out our bikes and pedalled through Holzhausen and Zuckelhain, right round the Kolm, and as we went we gathered up apples and pears from the roadside ditches or picked them off the trees bordering the dilapidated roads. We pushed our bicycles up a muddy track, churned up by tractors – very likely, in amongst all the rare plants, potatoes were being steamed for pig-food once again. I wanted to approach the memorial from above, maybe the fist was by now towering from its plinth, maybe part of the inscription had already been carved. A length of fencing had fallen right across the path and we had to make a detour round it, through the undergrowth, and then, when we emerged on the other side and had a clear view, I looked down, and there was absolutely nothing there.

'Well, what did you want to show me, Freddie?'

Beneath us, a few twisted old plum trees. There was no boundary wall, no plinth, not even a pile of stones, granite from Beucha. Maybe the painter had given up, or Comrade Lohse had exercised his authority; who knows what Joachim had meant by his sinister words on my birthday. My heart began to ache.

It was a long time before I saw the painter again. Six months later, his painting showing the view of the city from my Monument hung in an exhibition. The sky was criss-crossed with vapour trails which were mirrored in the lake. This was intended to be serene, optimistic, or at least that's what all the papers said; the painter had no comment to make. Something had happened inside him, no doubt about it. The Berlin boys had outsmarted him. Was he now exacting his revenge by depicting the new menace over the city? I didn't find the vapour-trails the least bit amusing, on the contrary it seemed to me as if the planes were practising for the real thing. In that December night, they had laid waste half the city, and now they were coming back in broad daylight, just a practice run, but they had come all the same.

I am not going to pass judgement on what artists can get away with nowadays and what they can't, or where, in their case, strength of character starts or finishes, or how circumstances have changed since Thieme's day. Thieme was able to build his monument, whereas my painter could not.

Six months after that I bought myself a print and painted out the vapour-trails in the sky and in the lake. And that's the way the picture looked when I hung it in my room. No, I didn't imagine for a moment that by doing this I could protect the Monument and the city from disaster. Not *that* way.

CHAPTER 12

You've been in prison before?

The circle is beginning to close. Or you could say that, as in a spiral, one always returns to a certain point. Sometimes a little higher up, sometimes lower down. But who's to say what's higher and what's lower? A terrible year, a dreadful Merry Month of May. What year? What May? 1968.

One morning, during our break, I opened the *Volkszeitung* and read that the elected representatives of the city had met to discuss plans for the new layout of the Karl Marx Platz, the meeting had also been attended by guests, at their head Paul Fröhlich, the regional party boss, of whom it was said he got on with Ulbricht like a house on fire and was certain to succeed him.

The Vice-Chancellor of the University had been there; and his predecessor, Georg Mayer, had been trawled out of one of his favourite pubs for the occasion. I have to name names today that will mean nothing to most people, but that keep sticking in my memory.

These are the names of ravagers of my city, and they should be preserved as such.

My slice of bread and butter lay beside me, the last bite remained unchewed in my mouth, and for the first time in my long career I wasn't back at work promptly at the end of the allotted quarter hour but was still sitting reading and re-reading my way through flowery and biting and woolly verbiage towards the real meaning of what was about to happen, and there could be no possible doubt about it, Leipzig's so-called city fathers had decreed the removal of the University and the church that belonged to it.

A new square, symbol of the new Socialist rebirth, more beautiful than ever and true to the fresh new spirit, so ran the arguments of some woman in the education world, Comrade Sorgenfrei – Carefree! Her colleague, Eisengräber, warned all would-be opponents: 'If representatives of Christian circles attempt to stir up opinion against the city's highest representative body, then we shall close ranks behind the view expressed by the Lord Mayor that these forces should be opposed with all legal means at our disposal! The intellectual rabble-rousers in this conspiracy are to be found in the Faculty of Theology and in the College of Theology!' Eisengräber moved the setting up of a committee to investigate these occurrences; the proposal was carried unanimously. Oberbürgermeister Kresse, I read, had vigorously condemned the attempts by some churchmen deliberately to misrepresent expert decisions as political decisions and to foment opposition to organs of state and their resolutions. The Lord Mayor referred darkly to machinations and intrigues. In the course of the debates, even a member of the Christian Party, Dr Paul Ullmann, had endorsed the demolition of the oldest church in the city. Dr Paul Ullmann, I repeat that loathsome name. The writer, Trude Richter, took the same line in the name of the *Kulturbund*. At least Professor Albert Kapr, the Principal of the College of Art, expressed regret that the church 'had to make way for the new', but he had previously voted, in a committee, in favour of tearing it down: architects from Rostock had, it was said, come up with a solution whereby the church would be preserved, but the proposal had been deemed *unsatisfactory*. I'm convinced that the most despicable executioners of all are precisely those who, just before the beheading, say to the victim, I really am most terribly sorry, sir! 'What's up, boss?' An apprentice was standing in the doorway. 'You not feeling well?'

'Carry on by yourselves, I'll be there in a minute.' But I read on:

the deputy principal of the University Library, Dr Fritz Schaaf, had voted in favour of the demolition, Hans-Dieter Richter of the Liberals had conceded that it was understandable that many a Leipziger had a soft spot for this particular building; then he, too, had given it the thumbs down. Only one solitary one, Pastor Rausch, had summoned up the courage to speak out against this proposal; even on Red Square in Moscow there stood a basilica, so surely Leipzig's Karl Marx Square could manage to get along with a House of God. Rausch had spoken of the age of St Paul's Church, of the remains of a monastery, erected as far back as before 1240, of the cloister, the statue of the Margrave Dietzmann, the carved altar; I would have given a lot to know whether his voice had rung firm and clear, like Martin Luther's once upon a time over in Pleissenburg Castle, or like Dimitroff's at his trial after the Reichstag Fire – oh yes, there have been real men in Leipzig. Pastor Rausch was the last of our heroes.

And now, the star guest had stumped up to the rostrum, Paul Fröhlich. Because the Marx Platz had been virtually one hundred per cent destroyed, they had to come up with a new solution. So the church my father had saved amounted, in Fröhlich's eyes, to no more than a few percentage points. And then he, too, put the knife in: 'There are, however, still some people who want to divert this objectively necessary town-planning decision into the realms of ideological dispute, and, worse still, to attempt to put pressure on the city's elected representatives and its council. Let everyone be fully aware that the city councillors will not tolerate anyone playing around with their decisions.'

Who was applying more pressure than Fröhlich? Nevertheless, one man did vote against the demolition of the church and the university – the aforementioned Pastor Rausch. All the rest meekly raised their hands. What would have happened if they had voted to throw out the proposal? Would they have disappeared into prison or forfeited their sinecures? The former would have been very unlikely, the latter a virtual certainty. Nowadays folk like to say in Leipzig, ah, these were turbulent times, it was Ulbricht and Fröhlich who had the church demolished. But every man jack of the city councillors of 1968 is guilty, with the sole exception of Pastor Rausch. Maybe one day he'll be made a freeman of the city? After all, the Protestant church doesn't have saints.

Lunchtime came and I was still sitting in our hut, the paper beside me. A lorry drove up. In it sat the Silesian who, years previously, had

196

stood by my side on the roof of the Monument, staring into the yellow sky. 'You can pack it in here,' he said, identifying himself as head of operations of a special task-force, 'gather everything together, tomorrow morning you're moving on elsewhere.'

I didn't go home, but instead took the tram into the city centre. The university and the church had been cordoned off, ropes put up, with a policeman hanging about every few metres. The façade of the university stood there, with its classical pillars, its frieze, its windows empty-eyed, behind them the well of the glass-roofed court, minus roof. Schinkel had designed the portal. Some wings of the university building were habitable and afforded shelter for a few departments with their libraries, offices and lecture-rooms; in the quadrangle stood a statue of Leibniz. There were a lot of photographs being taken that bright evening, people's faces wore a closed-up, shuttered expression, they talked less, and more quietly, than usual.

Look, Doctor, if you have something you want to read, I wouldn't say no to a break. Today's topic is one of the most depressing I have ever experienced, and it would suit me just fine if we could leave it out. I beg your pardon? A witness's statement? Aha!

So, the painter never attempted to build, on his own property and with his own private means, a monument, and he swears to that, you say – that's good enough for me, if you read it out to me – I don't have to read it for myself . . . well, all right, if procedure requires it. I'm not going to argue; after all, even Marianne, if she were alive today, would testify against me. So the painter never owned a plot of land in Liebertwolkwitz, and you can prove that from the entries in the land register, he never had granite delivered from Beucha – Doctor, wouldn't you share my happiness if he had done? Taking on such a grandiose idea, only to baulk at the ultimate risk? Never realising that, given his example, the church might still be standing today? Because he would have given the city councillors courage? Strong language maybe doesn't sit well with an old man like me, but in this case there's no avoiding it: that gathering of councillors was, with the exception of Pastor Rausch, a bunch of out-and-out shits.

Right, where were we? When we drove up the next day, the university had been transformed into a fortress. The cordon had been reinforced, young blokes in the uniform of the riot police had been drafted in, from Mecklenburg and from the Oder. In an office, which a sign on the door proclaimed to be the Department of Germanic Studies, and where pictures of the German poets adorned the walls, sat police officers; the atmosphere here was heavy

197

with tension, as if with every utterance decisions were being taken, focs repulsed, as if the slightest lapse in vigilance could invite danger. 'You're going to be issued with special papers,' said an officer when we had come in, snap-boxes under our arms. 'You'll get your photo taken over there, and you'll come under the category of special staff. Right then, the first one, over there.' My lads looked at me, I was the foreman, and if there were any questions to be asked, then it was up to me to ask them, but I went over to the photographer. 'Cap off!' I crammed it under my arm, sat down, stared into the camera and obediently raised my chin and then there was a click and I had taken a first fateful step – most things begin quite insignificantly, don't they? My men followed me, the photographer informed us, 'You can pick up your identity papers this afternoon.' And finally, 'Go with the Comrade there.' In another room, the door of which assured us that we were in the Department of English Studies, lay blueprints of the university and the church. They had been prepared with the utmost care; here, experts had been busy working out how these walls could be dealt with. The demolition plans were a very neat bit of work indeed. 'We'll begin,' said the major, 'with the church. You'll be the second shift.' I looked down at the plans, I had long ago learnt what each symbol represented. I had been tested on this in my apprentice's and craftsman's examinations, now I was hearing a lecture from the major. I listened carefully to the accent, the intonation. The man was from Leipzig. I would have given anything to be able to identify him as coming from somewhere else. From Prussia, naturally. But he wasn't even from Dresden or Karl-Marx-Stadt or Zwickau. The major concluded, 'It's a job that'll require all your energies. Now get your gear off the lorry. I expect you to make a start in half an hour! The Comrade here will go along with you.'

I reacted like some marionette. Somebody just had to pull a string, and I moved a leg, an arm, my jaw dropped. Next to our lorry, brushwood had been dumped, along with some three-metre-long spruce trees; they hadn't been felled for decorative purposes, like at the opening ceremony for the Monument to the Battle of the Nations or at some gymnastics festival, they were to contain the side-effects of detonations, absorb shock-waves, ensnare flying lumps of masonry. The sun burned down on the church roof, the little spire stood out sharp-pointed against the empty sky. I thought, for one more week. My arms were hoisted as if by wires and they reached out for a pneumatic drill, and I waited, expecting something, someone or other, to cut these wires. I shouldn't have sat on the police photographer's chair, shouldn't have come out here, I could feel the weight of the drill, familiar with every last gram of it, my arms still obeyed, I was no better than these traitors to the city, bound as they were by all manner of things, party discipline and party policy, salary and privileges, and open to accusations from spouses and offspring hoping for educational advancement that they could be putting so much at risk, whole careers, and would it all have been worthwhile, was it worthwhile, and anyway you were certain to be outvoted – at that, my arms let the drill fall, and it crashed on the floor of the lorry.

I could feel my lads looking at me and avoided their eyes. There are some things you can't drag others into, you can't just lead the charge and 'Follow me, you rabble!' I went across the quadrangle and up the stairs into the university. Piles of books were being carried out. 'Lecture Room 40' stood above a door, it was wide open, inside, all the lights were on, the benches empty. Along one corridor, the sun streamed in – photos of the old university have been preserved; you should have a look at a book of these some time and compare it with the cheap-jack jerry-built stuff thrown up in its place since. I stepped into the famous Great Hall, designed by Albert Geutebrück it was, and Klinger adorned it with a mural. Arwed Rossbach renovated it – how do these names sound to your ears? This hall, the Aula, had been gutted, but its walls were still standing, the roof could have been rebuilt, should have been, long before. Birch saplings were growing from the ledges. May sun, and May greenery, and down below the drills were chattering. I measured the room with my eyes – you should take a look at the hovel that has been foisted on the professors of today's university for a conference room, they can hardly push their way past behind each other's chairs. As for a Great Hall, there's no such thing, and no *auditorium maximum*, and yet, with so many students crammed in together, you'd think they might come up with something.

The noise of the pneumatic hammers rattled across from the church. I went back down; at the main door I was stopped by a plain-clothes man, he wanted to see my special pass. It was just being made out, I told him, but in any case my workmates were in the church – or were they? I ran them to earth in the vaults of the wine bar under the wing of the university, the one hard against the foundations of the church. They told me everybody had been ordering them about, all wanting something different, and the ones who were drilling up there were pioneers belonging to a special unit.

In the late afternoon we got our special identification papers, just before knocking-off time; my lads were unanimous, there was no point in starting anything off today. For a whole day, we hadn't done a hand's turn. I took the tram home, ate little and exchanged few words with Marianne. I wondered whether I should report sick, even reckoned I might really become ill in such circumstances, maybe some organ not functioning properly, my stomach, or my heart.

Shortly before nine, the doorbell rang; Joachim was at the door. 'Father, I've got to have a word with you.' That sounded so very urgent, of such great import, never had Joachim opened a visit in this manner. We sat down at the living-room table, and he started talking right away: 'I've heard you've been assigned to duties at the Karl Marx Platz.' It seemed various people were determined to salvage all sorts of things from the church and the university; they wanted to dismantle the organ and the seating. 'Listen, Father. Fröhlich and his people are absolutely determined. They'll not give these folk a moment. And I thought, maybe you . . .'

'Well, I'm just glad at least you two aren't arguing,' grunted Marianne. Would Joachim like something to eat or drink? She practically ran to get him a beer and pour it out.

'There's nothing anyone can do about it,' insisted Joachim. 'The first of them have been arrested this evening already. They had sat down on the ground in front of the barriers. Father, you won't do anything stupid, will you?'

I would have liked best just to have gone off to my room. 'For the moment, I'm dog-tired,' I said, evasively.

Marianne grumbled again. 'I'm just glad you're not arguing! And it was nice of you to come, Joachim.'

I would dearly have loved to be sitting at my mother's, thinking, together with her, of the church. Then Joachim said, 'Listen, Pappy, I'm forever having problems because Erika's over there in the West. Don't make any more trouble for me, will you?'

'I've told you already, I'm dog-tired.'

Joachim finished his beer and I went to the front door with him. After I had opened it, he said, 'Oh, Father!' For an instant I had the urge to draw him to me. I hadn't done that for twenty years.

Next morning, on the tram, I read in the paper that the city council hadn't just decided on the revamping of the Karl Marx Platz – rebuilding was now really to get going all over Leipzig. Modern, radiant colours had been decreed for the houses in the street named after 18 October, a design competition for the Bayerischer Platz had been announced, interesting construction engineering projects were

200

planned for the Johannis Platz and St Matthew's Churchyard. And in the next column, readers' letters: all Leipzig was apparently intoxicated with the prospect of all that was to come about. And not a word about the church. The architects for the new university were named: Hermann Henselmann and Horst Siegel. I thought, fine names for people who trample over corpses. The houses in the October blocks, that concrete desert, never did get their bright colours, on the Bayerischer Platz nothing has changed, other than that in the meantime one house has been pulled down because it was in danger of falling down. Nothing new on the Johannis Platz, either. Only in one respect were the city fathers proved right: on St Matthew's Churchyard there now stands yet another State Security Service monolith.

This time I got through the cordon without any difficulty and even got into the church. The thundering of the pneumatic drills made the very walls vibrate, masonry dust hung in the air. I asked where my mates were, and the machine we had off-loaded from the lorry the day before; nobody knew anything about it. I looked up to the ceiling, and there was the damp-stain that had survived the death of the church-saviour Felix Linden.

On my way out I showed my pass again. Some way in front of the church, ropes had been put up, with signs hanging from them: 'Construction site. Keep out!' The pavement in front of the flower-shop (Leipzigers still call it Hanisch's) was the nearest people could get to the site, and there stood a policeman armed with a walkie-talkie. He, too, was jumpy. The people walked past slowly, tight-lipped, looking up at the church, but saying nothing. What, I wonder, would have happened if a thousand people, or maybe three thousand, had pressed forward here, torn down the ropes, shoved the guards aside and smashed the pneumatic drills to bits? No, that could never have happened. Not in Saxony.

'Move along,' said a young man, and as he said it he looked past me, but it was obvious it was me he meant. To think of all the things that had graced this square in the past, for example the Café Felsche, alias Français; it hadn't been torn down in 1914, nothing so drastic, they just renamed it instead. Certainly, Bemmann the teacher would have found some blazing patriotic justification for the obliteration of this café of shame if he had been instructed to do so. But now, I thought, Katzenstein Junior ought to be making his approach in his Liberator bomber for a low-level roaring swoop that would drive the demolition-crazed fanatics away. But jolly vapour-trails in the

201

Leipzig sky were there to testify that he wouldn't have an easy job, peace in the skies was a peace armed to the teeth. Blücher's East Prussian territorials had advanced along this narrow street, wounded men had died on straw in the church. Now the church had to give way to a few flagpoles, a sculptor was already working on a design for some pipes and tubes that would have water bubbling out of them – away with the old, in with the new and just let anyone try to stop us! The Swedes, the Imperial ones, had been quartered here, they had rededicated other people's churches, but at least they had left them standing. And now, along came Paul Fröhlich from Bautzen, the town famous for its penitentiary.

'Right! Let's be having your papers!' So in fact I hadn't moved along. I thrust my special pass under his nose and said, 'This is where the detonators will be set off from. Then it'll be *you* that has to move along!'

He gaped, taken aback. 'Well, be quick about it, otherwise others will think . . .' Carl Friedrich Lindner had been as young and as stupid as that, the scabies had tormented him and then finally he had been beaten to death. Desertion at the eleventh hour was wrong; treason always was a question of getting the timing right. Masonry dust had always been part and parcel of my trade. 'It'll send up a huge cloud,' I said to the upstart. 'Just you make sure you're not standing here when it does.'

'No talking to sentries!'

I went round the corner into the Nikolai Strasse, went into the Blue Pike, sat down and ordered Gose. Opposite me sat a man in old-fashioned clothes, with a wickerwork suitcase beside him, a kind of travelling-bag with a curved handle. 'Are you in the building trade?' He pointed to my jacket. 'And are you also one of the ones that are protesting?' He tapped the *Volkszeitung* lying in front of him. 'It's in here: "Outraged building workers rounded on idlers and layabouts loafing about the city centre as if they didn't know where their place of employment was. They should be taught a lesson on what work really means. Foreman Fritz Timper said, "I've a good mind to shove a spade in these layabouts' hands." Nice, isn't it? You're not by any chance this Foreman Timper in person?'

'Not by any chance, no.'

'I'm in town on a visit, in from my little estate near Borna.'

My Gose was brought, and I . . .

What's that? I said myself that Gose had fallen victim to

202

rationalisation? True. Then it must have been Sternberg Silver Pilsener. What's the odds?

The old man at my table talked about how he and others had worn oak-twigs in their hat-bands as they marched through the inner city, gymnasts, up and into the fray! I'm a demolition expert, I wanted to say, but couldn't get the words past my lips. I've let myself be photographed for a special pass, it always starts with something insignificant, and now I don't even know if Voiciech Machulski and Felix Linden had photos in their pay-books when they were on manoeuvres on the Bienitz. A musty smell emanated from the old gentleman, as if he hadn't been in contact with fresh air for a long time. On the wall hung an advert for Döllnitz Manor Gose, and it all seemed to me as if it had been long ages since I had last sat here, yet I was able to remember every detail. There was a loud bang outside, I didn't even flinch, after all, I knew it would be a while yet. A car backfiring, or something like that. 'I saw your coach recently,' I said, 'at least, I thought I had seen it. You often used to drive out over the battlefield, didn't you?' He obviously hadn't heard me. 'You must come back up to the Monument some time,' I said.

'If time permits.' He seemed to reflect on this, and giggled. A smell wafted over me just like the last time I was in the SS escape tunnel, among the rotting tarpaulins and camouflage jackets. I ordered another Pilsener. All this in working hours. I sat thinking of my instructor out in Beucha, of Father, when I set off my first charge, and the beer after it – now, something in my life was coming to an end. 'I've demolished your estate,' I went on, 'but it didn't matter. It wasn't worth much any more, and anyway we had salvaged every chair and every window-frame beforehand. I kept one of your skulls.' I wasn't sure whether he had understood.

I paid up and went out into the street. The sun stood bright over the roof of St Nicholas', a vehicle went past, piled high with skins, but then of course if you went on down the road you came to the furriers' shops on the Brühl. Something drew me back into the church and the university, the thought of my lads, maybe, for years now there had always been somebody taking instructions from me, do this, watch out for that, pass me this, get rid of that. My voice had had to have the ring of level-headedness itself; a master craftsman that yelled at his men? There's no such thing in the explosives business. I went round St Nicholas', came back out on to the Grimmaische Strasse, the King's house had stood on this corner – flattened by bombs. Behind it loomed the west gable of St Paul's, the droning of the pneumatic drills rose in a crescendo, and then the thought hit me that surely my lads must have long since been assigned to another foreman, and that I myself, even if I were now in or around the church, would have no more say in matters than the merest apprentice. A major was running things now, and it was he who made the decisions on which charge was to be laid where. From the rim of a flat-roofed building, two men watched the street below. So there were look-outs overhead, too, and I imagined a hot-line leading out to the earnest Fröhlich, listening in to reports in the local party headquarters: the organ is ready for blasting, the figure of St Thomas Aquinas will fly from its cross, despite all the nails, and there will be room for a bronze relief complete with the Marx-head, the Marx-beard. For flagpoles and bubbling spouts. And if the crowds of layabouts and rubbernecks doubled in size, if they multiplied like voles and rats, then old Paulie would just have to get tough. I love my Leipzig, for Leipzig belongs to me! Away with the ruins, and a church was opium for the people. I could just visualise the man of power, sitting in his office, his legs stretched out wide before him, waiting for his adjutants' reports like Napoleon at the snuff-factory as the Battle turned. The Napoleons and the Fröhlichs, they come and go. Maybe a painter was at that very moment doing his portrait, with a view to including him in a painting about the building of the new university, so that the Party Secretary might go down in history as a patron of learning rather than the man who lit the fuse. For years, he had been working towards demolition day, and even yet, at the eleventh hour, somebody might throw a spanner in the works – not a bishop; Fröhlich had nothing but contempt for church leaders. They had all been provided with beautiful, purring limousines, almost as powerful and every bit as shiny black as those of the Politbüro men: that kept their mouths shut. Somebody might set fire to himself in front of the church, thought Fröhlich suddenly with a shudder, a village vicar, a fanatic. Then there would be an outcry world-wide. The most emphatic way of writing history was with dynamite, just as the best sentence was the death sentence. Could Fröhlich already feel death creeping through his own veins, I wonder? Because not long after he did in fact die in hellish pain, his blood simply decomposed, and no doctor could come up with an antidote. He never did get round to pronouncing a death sentence. At best, he had blazed away at hares and deer and wild boar in the fields around Torgau and in the woods around Annaburg, like most men of power he was heartily trigger-happy, and he had had a hunting lodge built there, with the scalps hanging on the walls. When it came to those creatures that walked upright on two legs, the farthest he got was to be able to say to his State Security Chief, get that character out of my sight! Then the poor sod would be despatched to Bautzen penitentiary for five, seven or maybe ten years. Or maybe the dodgy customers in question would have had Fröhlich's boys tramping on their toes for so long that they finally chose the easy way out and scrammed into the West; and then it was a clear-cut case: traitors, lackeys of the class enemy. By such means he had purged the University of Ernst Bloch and Hans Mayer, cleansed the cabarets of Reinhold and Zwerenz and sluiced Pastor Schmutzler out of the students' Christian society. Unfortunately, some would return from their term in Bautzen and Waldheim, loony liberals, jazz nuts, scribblers, but here's hoping that while inside they'd have been properly taught to keep their traps shut. But nobody had invented a magic powder that could make a church, blown into its component smithereens, fly together again into its former configuration, or resurrect stones from dust.

Uproar! Somebody had sat down in the roadway and was being carried or dragged away. I let myself be borne along by the crowd towards the Market, from where it wasn't far down to the spot where the synagogue had blazed. It was quiet there. Katzenstein Jr and his fellow bombers had exacted their revenge in full measure here. Not far away, Voiciech had laid paving slabs and swung himself up scaffolding – everything was twisted and crumbling now, the empire of goldenrod and acacia in that year of 1968, and even more so today. I gazed at the plaque commemorating the synagogue and the Jewish citizens of Leipzig murdered by the Nazi citizens of Leipzig. Across that yard there, through that garden, Felix Linden had made his desperate dash. I walked through the park, saw the City Hall tower behind the trees. All around me, ducks, swans, children and grandmothers – I had sought refuge among them like someone shutting eyes, ears and mouth, locking up his heart, someone who would like to forget his father, who didn't deserve to have had a father. So I went back to the university and showed my pass to try and get in, and a police officer informed me that all the workers had long since knocked off for the day, and all I could think of in reply was that I wanted to look around for my men. 'But I'm telling you they've all gone, two hours ago! Come back tomorrow morning.' Then he pushed off to check a lorry, jumped onto the tailboard and began lifting and laying sacks and tarpaulins; maybe he was afraid somebody was trying to smuggle out an organ pipe.

I was up punctually next morning. It was a glorious May day. Leipzig history has never reached a peak in May. In October and November yes, plenty had happened in those months, wars broke out in high or late summer, the Yanks had come in April, although then the sun had shone like in May. I tried to pick up snatches of conversation, but the tram was rattling too loudly. With the number 4, I rode from Weisse Platz through winding streets, away across the Riebeck Bridge, from the rise I glanced down at St Nicholas' and the tower of the City Hall, but I couldn't get a sight of the university between the blocks of houses. I got off at the Marx Platz. Cordon-ropes all over the place. I went round the other side, past the Schinkel portal, there was a gap back there. A rubber stamp was pressed to my pass, yet another to go along with the rest, I was sent up to join detachment III, I'd see the notice on the door in that corridor to the left. Two of my men couldn't disguise their excitement on catching sight of me, and one of them gasped, 'Hey! There you are!' The other called to the officer behind the blueprints, 'Our foreman!'

'Right, then, you can get started. You've to concentrate on this point here.' I can't have been listening properly – or, let me put it this way, I wasn't capable of listening properly. When the officer asked, 'Is that clear, then?' it wasn't I who replied, but one of my lads. He took me by the elbow and gave me a gentle shove and I went along; on the stairs, he said, 'What's up with you, boss?'

I asked, 'Have you drilled the boreholes?'

'Of course we have. Under the university, in the wine bar, in the wall through to the church . . .'

'In the cloisters, you mean.'

'That's one hell of a wall!'

'There's something I have to see to,' I said.

'What, again?' That was a good, decent colleague asking that, one I had known for years, and there was anxiety in both his voice and his eyes. There was something eating me, he could see that. Was I ill? Running a temperature? A cold?

'Don't you bother your head about me,' I said.

I managed to get into the church, despite the special checks by the special unit, went up the spiral staircase as my father and the two men from the neighbourhood had done. Masonry dust here, too, the rumble of the drills in all the walls and beams, sounding clearer than the roar of the bombers had done then. All the sensations merged and swam, the smell of burning and the smell of stone, the rumbling and the roaring, the howling of the sirens and the shimmering of vapour-trails and their reflection in the lake. Under the roof beams it was stifling, dim, hot. I groped my way over to the place where Felix Linden had tried to put out the fire and had fallen through. You couldn't tell from looking at the boards that they were hardly more than twenty years old, as against the others that had been there for several centuries. They hauled me down from there the next afternoon, by which time I no longer possessed a pass; why, I've no idea. Some of my mates had seen me again that evening, so they testified later, and Marianne had been prepared to swear that I had been at home that night, but her testimony received scant attention, ruled out on the grounds of conjugal interest. Later, my lads became uncertain, maybe they could have been wrong about the exact day.

Next day, I was bundled down the stairway by two young men, one going in front, the other behind me. In a corner just behind the main entrance they ordered me to put my hands behind my back and stand with my face to the wall, and warned me that if I tried to escape they would be obliged to resort to the use of their firearms. For an hour I stood there, somehow not all that surprised at this unknown, undreamt-of situation, which neither Carl Friedrich nor Fürchte-gott, Voiciech nor Felix had ever stumbled into. Once I heard the voice of one of my colleagues: 'Yes, that's him.' And the whisper that followed, 'Oh hell, Freddie!'

In the quadrangle stood a closed-in delivery vehicle, like a baker's van. In a cubicle inside it, I had just enough room to sit down; a light-bulb glowed behind a barred hatch. I tried to make a mental picture of the bends in the road, left, right, left again, two minutes at the most, and the van came to a halt, I climbed out as I was ordered, looked up into a narrow courtyard and saw row upon row of barred windows – I was, as I later found out, in the prison belonging to that institution which looked after me recently, before I was brought here to this hospital. A kind of cell-door was opened and inside was a desk, with a chair behind and a stool in front of it, and on the chair sat a man in uniform, who immediately asked, 'Why did you cut the hoses? And why did you cement up the bore-holes? You could make things easier for yourself by confessing.' They had taken finger-prints, he said, and now all they were waiting for was for me to own up. Who had I given my identity papers to, and why? Who was behind it all? What else did I get up to during the night under the roof? Did I have an aerial on my own roof for receiving broadcasts from the West? A young sentry belonging to the special unit gave evidence to the effect that, when I had passed him, I had been wearing a grey, calf-length overcoat, a kind of soldier's greatcoat like the ones you see in a museum, then he became less sure of himself: he remembered me as having been taller, broader, and he couldn't be absolutely sure of the exact time. I was sent outside, the two of them must, I suppose, have had some sort of discussion, and when I was led in again they had agreed on a new variation on the theme: according to this, I was supposed to have given my pass to this aforementioned big man in the shabby greatcoat. My answers were minimal, often I remained completely silent, reflecting on how on earth this had all come about, and gradually a strange calmness percolated right through me: it was a piece of nonsense that I should be sitting behind bars; this whole thing paled into insignificance when compared to the deaths of Carl Friedrich, of Voiciech, of Felix. I asked, 'Has the church been blown up yet?'

According to an old saying, there are three kinds of people, those doing time, those who have done time, and those who will do time. So I regard everyday life in the nick, with its mindless routine, its fears and hopes, as something familiar to most people. I surrendered to apathy, indifference, even lethargy. In interrogation sessions, I missed quite a few questions. It was the same thing over and over again: who had the man in the greatcoat been, had I given him my papers, did I myself own such a coat, where had I got the mortar for filling up the holes, who had put me up to it? Imperialist secret services? Shady characters from the Faculty of Theology? 'How long have you known Pastor Rausch?' I sank deeper and deeper into my own thoughts.

There was always plenty of activity in the building, hustle and bustle, doors slamming, and bawling and shouting, too. The van that had brought me in seemed to be kept perpetually busy, every now and again I could hear its engine droning in, doors slamming, shouts of 'Move yourself!' of 'Face to the wall!' or 'No talking here!' And so it went on, day and night. Maybe somebody had dragged a cross up to the church, as Jesus once did up to Golgotha. During those days, I regretted not being able to pray. An essential part of prayer is the ability to visualise the god you are turning to.

On the very first day I was asked who should be informed of my arrest. I had given Marianne's name. I imagined the Silesian who had stood on top of the Monument staring at the clouds, and who had later transported our drilling equipment to the church, standing at our front door saying, 'Frau Linden? I have to inform you . . .' And then, of course, house-search. The skull on top of the cupboard. I asked whether I'd be allowed to write a letter to my wife – that would not be possible until inquiries had reached a certain stage, and that was, of course, up to me, depending on when I wanted to make a full confession. I composed that letter during my many empty hours: Dear Marianne, don't worry, I'll soon be . . . In vain, I tried to remember when I had last written to Marianne. We had always been together, after all. During the war, perhaps, when I was training in Zeithain? I had sometimes added my signature, 'Your father,' at the foot of Marianne's letters to Erika. Now, in my mind, I wrote, Dear Marianne, I'm so sorry to be causing you this worry, but . . . Some very strange circumstances have combined lately, but everything will sort itself out and soon, before we realise . . .

One morning the interrogator had a folder in front of him, he was leafing through it, reading here and there; I craned my neck in vain. 'Your son's making great efforts on your behalf,' he said after a while. 'Hm, yes, you've got quite a few connections with these old walls down there. And somebody once told you how to block up the Yanks' boreholes, and he reckons you might have remembered something of that. And your son warned you not to do anything stupid, didn't he? Why didn't you listen to him?'

I said, 'Maybe my son's efforts are intended a bit on his own behalf, too.'

One morning, everything started off so very much more quietly than usual, nobody was allowed down into the stone cage that was the exercise yard, there were no howling vehicles, no doors being slammed. From a nearby church I heard each quarter-hour striking. There were no trams humming up the Peterssteinweg, normally I could hear their motors each time as they revved up the hill. My view was blocked on all sides, but my hearing had sharpened. An explosives expert has to have not only sensitive fingers, but a sharp ear, too. If rust starts to crackle in a detonator, then death is winking at you.

I sat down on the cot. It was just so high that no one's feet could quite touch the floor – a Soviet invention. You're not allowed to lean back, otherwise a guard thumps on the door and bawls, 'Get away from that wall!' It's a tiring balancing act. Since everything had gone so eerily quiet, I was afraid even of the barely audible shuffle my shapeless, worn-out, athlete's-foot-polluted camel-hair slippers would have made as I walked the triangle. Nine o'clock, quarter past, half past, quarter to ten – I didn't hear ten striking. It was 30 May 1968, a sunny day. Early that morning – so I was told later – a safety cordon was drawn in a three-hundred-metre radius round the church. Nobody was allowed inside this circle, since there were alleged to be bombs from the Second World War still under the ruins, and they might be set off by the blast. The city bosses wanted to keep all Leipzigers well away from the church. Only from the Johannis Platz could its roof be seen, and, I was told later, there were thousands of people crowded there. And, for all that, somebody managed to take pictures from the multi-storey block diagonally opposite – but I'm running ahead of myself here.

I felt the tremor before I heard the bang. From the church to my cell was some seven hundred metres, the quake ran through the ground and up the walls into my cot. In one of the floors above me, a man began to sing 'Ein' feste Burg ist unser Gott,' a safe stronghold is our God, and he kept on singing, right through all the verses, without once faltering either in the tune or in the words, and no guard ran to his cell to crash his boot against the door. Two hours later, when life gradually began to return to the building, when vehicles were driving in and out of the yard again, I was still sitting there, motionless on my cot, my legs dangling, my slippers long since fallen from my feet. Through the gaps between the rows of glass bricks, masonry dust drifted in.

CHAPTER 13

Once again – What happened with the shells?

Mondays, thin potato soup, Tuesdays, thin semolina soup, Wednesdays, peas or haricot beans, of which I could stomach only a few spoonfuls, otherwise I would have been tortured by heartburn. Thursdays, herring with potatoes boiled in their jackets, and cucumber and onion as well, Fridays, cabbage or carrots, leeks, kohl-rabi or a mess of all these together, Saturdays, insipid barley broth, and on Sundays, boiled potatoes, red cabbage, some gravy and a slice of roast pork on top. The ship's bell to sound reveille and lights out, the so-called recreation hour, that lasted ten minutes, sometimes even only eight, toothbrush and towel and soap put into your cell in the mornings, but not evenings, every Saturday under the shower, but so briefly that you only had time to soap either your head or your belly or your feet, then, at the double, back upstairs. Oh yes, and the interrogations.

Three men had a go at grilling me, first a tubby one who hadn't a clue about anything, neither explosives work nor the church nor my city. He had a one-track mind – I was his enemy, it was enemy this, enemy that, enemy all down the line. His head was full of what they call 'Feindbild' – 'image of the enemy' – and he pursued his duty to unmask an enemy with total dedication. Whenever I watched him beavering away with furrowed brow, putting a trick question together, I could see him, a farm-lad from the depths of the Uckermark, in amongst the Prussian dragoons frog-marching a trembling Saxon youth to Otterwisch – and so sometimes I didn't hear his question and he'd shout at me; no point in that, for a start. When had I gone into the church, to whom had I given my identity papers, my hatred against Socialism – most of the time I simply answered, 'My father saved the church.' Disjointed talk, no conversation in the sense of there being a thread leading from question to answer to counter-question. Just a simple young lad being driven like a head of cattle that gets caught up between fences but has to go on; and again and again the fences buckle and the animal stumbles on, unable to turn back.

The second interrogator was a chain-smoker, yellow-faced, with deep lines running down from the corners of his mouth, obviously a martyr to stomach trouble. He took over the second week, his predecessor no doubt having realised he was getting nowhere. 'It's an open and shut case,' he began, 'so let's have no messin' about, innit?' With him, this 'innit?' ended every second sentence, typical Saxon, that; it was an abbreviated version of 'isn't it?', or 'doesn't it?' or anything else he chose, intended as a sign of agreement, even mateyness. 'You're coverin' up for somebody, innit? No point in that, no point at all! Mebbe we already got the other fella as well an' we're just tryin' to find out if you're tellin' the truth. There was a bloke in a long coat – see 'im, did you, know 'im, do you? He showed your pass. Where'd 'e gettit? That's got you, innit?' I tried to picture this interrogator as a foreman given the job of setting up a workshop under the Monument to the Battle of the Nations, where he had to be ready for all sorts of obstacles and complications. OK, we'll soon knock things into shape, innit? He wasn't short-necked like that foreman from the past, but I could well imagine him bawling and shouting the odds like him if he felt it would get results.

'Right then, who was the bloke in the long coat?' I shrugged, at which my interrogator took a deep breath, but it re-emerged from his lungs with a noise that was almost a groan. Then he resorted to another cigarette. 'Come on, start talking!' I pictured him standing behind the desk in a builder's office, questioning the Polish mason, Machulski, on where he had worked previously, being shown references: 'Mhm, right. Hard work and no nonsense! Let me catch you pinching anything, and you're out!'

'How do you see your future?'

'I've had it for work with explosives.'

'You can bet your life on that! We're not goin' to let the likes of you get your grubby paws on anythin' that goes bang! An' what you thinkin' of doin' till you get your pension? You know, once you get out!' As he said this, he looked expectantly at me, obviously desperate for me to ask timidly, please sir, how long do you think I'll get? They won't be too tough on me, will they?

The third interrogator tried to unsettle me with volleys of random questions, but I conjured up my picture of him as one of the defenders of Fort Battle of the Nations, hard as nails and always shooting his mouth off, even when Sherman tanks were already rumbling across the bridges in Leutzsch: Where the German soldier stands, let none other dare set foot! 'We're not going to have our programme buggered about by the likes of you! We're building the new Leipzig! And the Western press can foam at the mouth as much as it likes – you want to be a martyr, that it? How long have you known Pastor Rausch?'

I'd never seen him, I answered, and had come across his name for the first time in the paper.

'When he cut loose with his tirades of hate, eh? Right?'

'Is that what they were?' I had to be careful. That much became increasingly obvious in the ensuing days, as this man worked at building a bridge for me to stumble across: this pastor's speech during the debate had incited me to chop up hoses, entrust my pass to complete strangers, I was a sacrificial victim, a simple worker, unsuspecting, led astray, but now the scales had fallen from my eyes – Pastor Rausch had led me off the straight and narrow and down the path to destruction.

Suddenly I had the feeling that these gentlemen had played their last trump-card. I pictured the interrogator stumping along the ramparts in front of the Monument, peering down into fox-holes and asking, 'Field of fire wide enough? You've been told often enough: field of fire comes before cover!' I imagined him saying, 'I'm the boss here now!' A fine phrase from those times: 'Air-raid-sheltering days here are over.' Then I stopped listening and had before me only the vision of Mother and Marianne and their amazement as they stared at the tins of meat I had scrounged out of old Knight's Cross and his lot.

'Now think back carefully. When you read what Rausch had said, you felt something snap inside, didn't you? From then on, you acted as if under duress, isn't that right?'

I sat on my stool, just too far away from the wall to be able to lean back, with my hands on the knees of my striped dungarees. I rubbed my fingertips lightly over the cloth I had known since my apprenticeship days. I'd never wear working overalls again, never taste stone-dust again. The fuse of a British 250-pounder – all in the past. In my guts, the stodgy State Security bread was fermenting. For a while, will-power triumphed, and then, as the Saxon soldiers on the Lingekopf and at Douaumont used to say, I opened the nozzle, and quietly, gently, broke wind, one little puff after another. Carl Friedrich Lindner had shit in square formation, in the trenches on the Lingekopf the sappers' shovel-blades had served as an underlay and then the pile was swung up and hurled into the barbed-wire entanglements, where the dead Frenchmen hung. The SS in the Monument to the Battle of the Nations – ah yes, an extensive subject indeed! My interrogator sat some distance away, had opened the window, but sometimes, when my wind came from the right quarter, his face twisted.

'You scratch our back, and we'll scratch yours.'

I pictured to myself the horsemen high in the dome; they were riding for home, their shields slung, their swords sheathed. Another chapter closed. How about this, then: me as a gateman at the Monument, just tearing tickets, no talks on Russo-German comradeship-in-arms, or Yanks go home and across the Rhine at Kaub and 'A Nation Rises up' and 'May the hands wither, that . . .' and 'Swords into Ploughshares'.

'You can't help Rausch, and you can't do him any harm. And you want to get out of here, don't you?'

The memorial experts had lain on their bellies and played at scouting across Bug and Dniester. 'All a matter of perspective.' The interrogator's face began to twitch.

Three days later, and he was at his wits' end. 'You'll soon see what good it'll do you!' he thundered in desperation. 'You surely don't want to spend the rest of your days as a gateman! You'll see, our arm is long!'

There's one word I have never been able to stand – to smirk.

214

Never in my life did I want to smirk, except at that moment.
'We'll soon wipe that grin off your face!'

Then it was Thursday; the herring came meticulously cleaned, not a vestige of skin left in the abdominal cavity, every last tiny bone plucked out, and I reckoned this was the work of women, prisoners like myself, employed in the kitchens. Free of distraction by husband or bawling children or correspondence-course studies, they had devoted all their tender ministrations to the herrings. Could Friday perhaps be a discharge-day, or was it the one when guards would want just to get away promptly and home to the wife and the car and the allotment?

Monday came before I was led to the property room, where I swapped convict's overalls for those of a master demolition expert and was deposited outside the prison gates, to stand blinking into the light and unaware of what I was supposed to feel. None of my forefathers had been inside, a relatively rare record in Germany. What the hell, what did a few weeks matter! I wonder what the average per head for time done inside by Germans works out at over the last fifty years.

I ambled up the Peterssteinweg to the Leuschner Platz and lent an expert ear to the revving of the tram motors. From my cell I had been able to distinguish clearly whether a tram was heading up the hill or down. I could smell masonry dust, hear lorries roaring and the thumping of lumps of university falling from the jaws of mechanical diggers onto the metal of the trucks' loading platforms. The knocking down and carting away was in full swing, there wasn't a moment to lose; I love my Leipzig, for Leipzig belongs to us! I pictured Paul the Churchbreaker, sat in receipt of his daily statistics on how many tons of Gothic or of Classical had been demolished, followed now by the pews and roof beams; the stain in the plaster had long since been reduced to powder. People were walking past, some of them quickly, some unhurriedly, one woman was carrying milk bottles in a shopping-net. On the Leuschner Platz, the trams halted as usual, heading for Gohlis or for Connewitz, passengers boarding, passengers alighting, ding-ding. Out in his district headquarters, no doubt Fröhlich was sitting at that moment, watching as a painter laid out sketches before him: a mural for the new university, historical figures and scenes to mingle with contemporary ones, Chancellor Emeritus Mayer right in the middle, watching a dancing student, her skirts flying, and the painter would be saying, with due heartiness, 'And you, Comrade Fröhlich, I'd like to place here, in among the construction workers!' And the Comrade, with a modest laugh, 'Well, if you absolutely insist!'

I went to the Marx Platz, which was half cordoned off by railings. Lawns had been trampled, foliage smothered in dust. In my hand I held my battered briefcase, in which I had carried my snack to work thousands of times. The façade of the university was still standing. Behind it, the tower of St Nicholas' stood in an open space, the Mende fountain fenced in – construction site, keep out! Away with the old and in with the new!

I got on the No. 4; between there and the Johannis Platz, three lorries piled high with church rubble hurtled past me, out along the Leninstrasse. When I got off, it was half past eleven, I had never got home from work at this time of day. I went into Marianne's grocery store; she was sitting at the check-out. Nearby, customers were unpacking their baskets, macaroni, sugar, Silver Pils lager. I went and stood where Marianne was bound to see me when she looked up. I looked at her grey hair, the veins on the backs of her hands. So many years together, I thought, good years, all things considered, although mind you she hadn't had an easy time of it with me. A customer stared at me, leaned over to Marianne and whispered in her ear, and from the movements of her lips I could read what she was saying: 'Your husband!' At that, Marianne gave a start, as if she had been hit. Nobody in the shop moved a muscle now, all eyes were on me and I said – well, what else was I supposed to say? – 'I'm back, then.'

One of her colleagues dealt quickly with the customers, and Marianne hung a sign on the door: 'Temporarily closed for delivery of stock.' In the passageway leading to the little back-shop, she took me in her arms and kissed me and ran her fingers through my hair – it was just like when we were first courting. Was I hungry, was I well? And I assured her everything was fine, although I certainly wasn't short of an appetite. At that, her colleague bent down by the fridge, and from its lowest compartment she brought out some cooked ham, reserved for staff and special customers only, and then she put on the coffee pot; now Marianne was at last laughing, albeit through tears. She opened a tin of sardines, there was white bread, salami, cheese – I chewed and mumbled through a full mouth, 'They'll be having potato soup inside just now.' It sounded like the oldest of old lags talking. I had to laugh, myself. Just at that moment, Marianne began to sob.

Hand in hand, the way we hadn't done for years, we walked home.

216

I was just about to close the door of my room behind me when Marianne said, 'Did they tell you Mama had died?'

My hand lay as if frozen to the door-handle; now it was up to me to ask, when? But I didn't move, just waited for Marianne to go on. Mama dead – I was surprised I hadn't even asked how she had taken the news of my arrest, Klärchen Linden, Klara Magdalena.

'Two weeks ago.' Marianne took my hand from the door-knob and led me to the table and sat me down on a chair. 'She had been laid up for only three days.'

'And did she know?'

'Yes, I told her all about it. She just shook her head and kept saying, "Freddie, Freddie."'

'No, I mean, did she know she was dying?'

'Probably. Her heart, see? At the end, she was afraid of every breath she drew.'

We talked in short, simple sentences about the simple death of an old woman. 'I didn't put anything in the paper,' said Marianne. 'Who for, anyway?' She tried to force a smile as she added, 'They wouldn't have let you see it inside in any case.' Who had been at the funeral, even what Marianne had worn – I thought: the last of a generation. Now I was next.

'Joachim sent a telegram: "Sorry, can't get away."'

Where was she buried, I asked, and Marianne described the spot.

That same afternoon, I went up the Schönbach, and I hadn't been walking a minute when the first lorry loaded with rubble raced past me. I continued in that direction, past the Monument, along the embankment into which we had driven our air-raid tunnels. Another lorry, splintered beams, broken bricks, and, on the top, a twisted iron girder. Behind the Monument, the tipper lorries turned off, that's where we played in the sandpits as children. Now a bing had been heaped up, with a bulldozer creeping up and down it. A notice: 'Keep out!' And next to it, a policeman. At the side of the road, a traffic-police patrol car, uniforms all over the place. A load of rubble was being tipped out, then it was immediately spread flat by the blade of the bulldozer for its caterpillar tracks to grind it to dust. No doubt they had long since crushed and pressed down whatever had remained of, say, the rose-window in the nave, salvaging mementoes hadn't been permitted and now I was too late anyway. I followed a path tramped out by children, round the back of the tip, and there, too, a policeman was hanging about. A guard was being mounted on the grave of the university and its church, as if stones could rise again. I had intended gathering up a handful of debris, pretending that it had come from the stain that had been left by Felix Linden's death; I wanted to let it run through my fingers over Mother's grave. But I hadn't been out of prison long enough to have risked anything like that.

Once I had found the grave, I couldn't think beyond the strange question of what feelings one was supposed to have there – mourning is such an imprecise term, isn't it? Over there, Mother had felt the onset of labour-pains, fifty-five years ago, as she gathered brushwood. She had brought bean soup or potato broth to the building site, and taken firewood home – no, that had been Auntie Machul. She had taken me with her into the fine houses over there in the Naunhof Strasse when she went to do the laundry, and watched as I sledged down the embankments on my 'runner'. My mother, Klärchen Linden. I cleared withered flowers off the mound and straightened the wreath: 'From fond neighbours.'

Three days later, I went to my firm, to hand in my notice. The papers were lying ready, as if my decision had been anticipated. The personnel officer spoke a few understanding words, he said he regretted the step I was taking, but made not the slightest effort to talk me out of it. Of course, he'd send on impeccable references. Ah well! So what now, then?

Marianne took some leave and we went off for a couple of weeks into the mountains down south in Saxon Switzerland, where we went for long walks. It had been an eternity since I had last been out in the fresh air. There was a gentleness in our relationship – yes, I was tender towards Marianne too, believe it or not. During this period I came to realise how difficult, how obstinate, I could be. Once, she said, 'Do you know, there were times when you hardly spoke a dozen sentences to me all day?'

I asked in return, 'Was it really as bad as that?'

'It was that, Freddie.'

When we were back home, I got myself taken on at the Monument as a gateman; again it seemed to me as if the authorities had anticipated my arrival. I was given a uniform, jacket, trousers and cap, the black shoes I had to provide myself. The explanation of what the job involved took no more than five minutes, by which time I knew when I was to be on duty, tearing tickets at the entrance or as a guard up in the gallery, at the door to the stairs leading to the upper storeys, or in the kiosk. I went down into the crypt and gazed up at the four giants, and my thoughts were with my father, with Voiciech

Machulski, Katzenstein and Thieme. I pictured the lions, leaping onto the shoulders of the statues. Over there was the wall behind which the SS tunnel began, and in there lay my five shells. Standing on the crowning platform, I looked over to the hill where the painter hadn't been allowed to erect his memorial. One thing was missing from the familiar silhouette – the little pointed spire of the university church.

My life as an attendant at the Monument was far from monotonous; it seems to me now that I went willingly to work every day, whatever the weather, whether my colossus was lit by the sun or swathed in mist or whether the warning lights were shining brightly down through the gloom. From the Schönbach every morning I'd get my first glimpse of the great block between the houses and through the trees, my eyes would flick over in its direction, almost automatically: yes, still there! When I was on patrol in the hall of fame, there were times when I didn't have to utter a single word from the beginning of the shift to its end. Visitors would come in, fall silent, stare up into the dome. I would have got annoyed if children had run about the place. I kept the staircase clean, sweeping up leaves and cigarette ends. At lunch-times I warmed up my little pot of soup in the attendants' hut. I was fifty-five – that seems perhaps an early age to be satisfied with such a humdrum occupation. Some forenoons, especially if the weather was bad, or in winter, not a soul appeared for hours on end. I had time to do some reading. I browsed at random, novels and short stories. Anyway, there wasn't all that much about the Monument and my city coming on the market. At home, I didn't have much to say; sometimes I had the feeling I didn't need anyone at all.

From up on the parapet, I watched as a multi-storey building rose up on the Karl Marx Platz. Autumn came and went, winter, spring, now and again a bus full of Soviet visitors would pull up in front of the burial chambers; after it had moved on to the *Iskra* shrine, the reek of perfume still hung for a while in the main hall. Sometimes I was on duty up on the top-stone; in fine weather there could be a hundred people up there, pointing in all directions, then I'd be on my own again. Once a horde of young sportsmen had thundered up there, their trainer had given the command, 'At the double, right to the top!' Panting, they staggered onto the platform, their faces red and streaming with sweat. They clung on to the parapet and their trainer, who strolled up, all calm and composed, some time later, praised them: now that had been *real* fitness training! I would dearly

219

have liked to report the fool to his sports college, but then, would they have actually given him a ticking-off?

Round about this time, Ulbricht was deposed; Honecker had been Ulbricht's protégé, and now he kicked his political godfather up the backside. Once, when Joachim, after a long absence, was sitting in our house, he described to us how, in Berlin, everyone was at great pains to forget the old man, his name had already disappeared from all the newspapers and now it was to be expunged from school textbooks, too. I said, 'Wouldn't it be a good idea if they just bulldozed his native city out of existence while they're at it?' And Joachim told us of how persistent the rumour was that there was a clandestine Ulbricht clique in Leipzig who grudged Honecker his youthful glory and would have loved to resurrect Old Goatee from his limbo. 'Now other cities are getting the cash. Leipzig's had its day.' And I said, 'Serves this city damn well right.'

Every city has to die sooner or later. In many cases, ruins remain for tourists to wander through: the Parthenon in Athens is just such an attraction, and Venice will soon be a city of ruins. In the case of some capital cities, only the name survives – Carthage, Sparta. Memleben, on the Unstrut river, once was the hub of the German Reich. If history had run a different course, Berlin would not have become the German capital; it would still have been Memleben. I read of ghost cities near Samarkand, swept by the wind, of Estergom, the seat of a power which ruled the whole area between the mouth of the Danube and the ridges of the Erzgebirge on the Czech border. A pity about Leipzig, that had enjoyed only such a brief heyday.

One day, an easel was set up once again and the Monument was being sketched. I peered over the shoulder of a young woman and was surprised at her stark, angular style. She designed porcelain, she said, and I had no objection to her making some sketches here, had I? Her firm would get in touch later with the city authorities regarding the legal side of things. Although I was indeed wearing a kind of uniform, I replied pleasantly, that didn't mean my word carried much weight. And what kind of a firm was that? The porcelain manufacturers in Meissen, I was informed. 'I've no idea yet what it's to be,' she said, 'a plate or a statuette. All depends on how my sketch turns out.'

'Consider me your first customer.' And she laughed.

She came back another three or four times, and asked if I could tell her the precise measurements of her subject; of course I could reel them off the top of my head. 'It could be done in Böttger porcelain,' she said on one occasion. 'You know it, don't you? Reddish brown.'

'Certainly not radiant white,' I agreed. 'That would produce a weird and wonderful effect: all it would need would be a border of onion-pattern or garlands of pretty flowers.' Again she laughed, and I rather took a liking to her.

Were the domes already mushrooming up around Leipzig at that time? Well, certainly, I hadn't made the significant connection yet. From time to time, I'd go for a walk in the city and the surrounding countryside. The spot where St Paul's had stood I avoided completely. Nevertheless, I sometimes had to pass it on the tram. They were building with concrete slabs, which, with their horizontal seams, reminded me of sloppily hung laundry. Later on, coal dust was to gather in these grooves, which the rain then washed out and smeared over all the flat surfaces. I really can't advise you strongly enough to compare photos of the old university with today's shabbiness.

The new Head of State didn't manage to get out our way. Twice every year he would be in the vicinity, on a visit to the Trade Fair. Then, exhibition halls would be closed off, the place would be swarming with secret police, and the Chairman would stride through in his light-coloured suit and, for the Autumn Fair, a little straw hat; he came from a neck of the woods that the Prussians had once purloined. For a century, the Saarlanders had fought against becoming spiritual Prussians, and it was ironic that a slater from there of all places was to become the highest neo-Prussian in the land and hold sway over us Saxons – history throws up some curious quirks, right enough. Had the order perhaps come from Berlin, I wondered, for the Monument to the Battle of the Nations to be done in Böttger porcelain? After all, all ideas for Saxony emanate from Berlin these days.

Three years later – I had long since forgotten the woman from Meissen – I discovered a reddish-brown reproduction on the shelves of the Intershop. It stood some fifteen centimetres high and cost a hundred and fourteen Marks – Westmarks, that is. Between me and it stood a sales counter, one and a half metres of open space, two salesgirls and a shortfall of ninety-four West German Marks. Erika, during one of her visits, had left some West-lolly, twenty Marks, which Marianne and I had set aside for the purchase of a

221

pound of coffee and some soap, maybe even a few spices. 'Take a look at that,' I said in amazement, and Marianne replied, 'I've just noticed it.'

'I wonder if they're to be had in the ordinary shops here?'

Next morning, Marianne was on her shop phone, calling round half of the Republic until finally she had someone in Berlin on the other end of the line who assured her that all the reddish-brown little items went either directly for export or, as we had seen, into the Intershops. That evening, Marianne said, 'Even if it had cost a thousand East-emms, I wouldn't have minded. I'd have given you it for Christmas.' We didn't know anyone who would have changed our Eastmarks for West.

I went back to the shop and hung about in front of the replicas. They weren't much bigger than my fist, and yet the artist had managed to bring out all the important details, the front staircase with the parapet, the Archangel and the sentries up towards the top-stone. There were three of them in the Intershop at the Trade Fair exhibition grounds, and four each in the city-centre hotels. Once I asked to be shown one of them and weighed it in my hand, and I had to fight the temptation to take to my heels and try to run for cover somewhere with my booty. But then I was already coming on for sixty; I wouldn't have got very far, that's for sure. 'Marvellous workmanship,' I acknowledged. The salesgirl replied straight from the sales textbook: 'A very popular line with the customers.' I handed the miniature Monument back, we exchanged smiles, and in our eyes lay an unspoken 'Ah well, it's just not for the likes of us, it's for the others, isn't it?'

About that time I often heard a deal of talk to the effect that people should have nothing to do with the Intershops and the extortionists in the 'Exquisit' luxury stores – what kind of a workers' and peasants' state was that supposed to be! The gossip was that, somewhere at the back of beyond, where it was difficult to prove one way or the other how much truth there was in the story, stones had been pitched through shop windows, in Sangerhausen or Rudolfstadt, Güstrow or Gransee.

And it was during that time that I sometimes caught myself eyeing the Intershops and trying to work out whether and how one might plant a small explosive charge in them. Casualties had to be avoided at all costs. The Astoria and Stadt Leipzig hotels were immediately ruled out, because they had guest rooms above the shops and bars and dining-rooms close by. The shopping area in the Hotel on the

222

Ring seemed more isolated, but the street outside was a busy one, even at night. By contrast, the Intershop at the exhibition grounds seemed ideal: a one-storey building, closed at night, the whole surrounding area dead and empty.

On the one hand, the destruction of three or four replicas as an objective, and on the other the danger to life and limb for other people as well as myself – no, the discrepancy was immediately obvious to me. At the start, I just amused myself by running the plan through – maybe I could get a job as a watchman in that Intershop? But then that would have drawn suspicion straight to myself, a former explosives expert who had been working there only for a short time. Or what if Marianne were to try to get a transfer to the Intershop, then I could sound her out on the layout – but I soon dropped that one.

A time fuse, how about that? I looked around, to see where a charge could be set just before closing-time. In the entrance there were usually piles of empty boxes, and it would have to be a pretty big bomb there if the blast was to get through the door and into the sales area and then blow the statuettes off their shelves. That was when I hit upon my flak-shells. I saw myself retrieving a shell from its hiding-place, transporting it home in a handcart, covered with brushwood, through the park and across the bridge; and then checking the fuse in our shed. When Marianne was out at work, I brought the fuse into the kitchen because I needed a good light to work in, and there I cleaned the old grease off all the parts and oiled them afresh. I considered the possibility of building a launching ramp, the way terrorists do, but then a shell isn't a rocket. Now, if only I had hidden away a few bazookas as well . . .

It was all a pure figment of my imagination, playing games. One day, when I had thought it all through, I would have my moment of triumph: I'd show you all! Of course, after the attack, like any self-respecting underground fighter, I'd have to make a great fuss of claiming responsibility, I'd call the *Volkszeitung* with a ringing declaration to that effect from the 'Revenge for Leipzig' Action Group. When this idea hit me, I had to laugh.

The Trade Fair came round again, and again the Head of State visited my city. From the roadside I watched the black Swedish limousines swinging into the car-parks previously cleared by the police, the little Saar-Prussian getting out and jerkily waving a hand in the air, just in case there might have been someone cheering him from far off. There were a few folk standing about, most of them annoyed at not being allowed into the exhibition halls; they were wasting a few hours' precious time. I could imagine him scuttling from stand to stand, shaking hands and exchanging cheery words. 'What d'you say,' he was maybe suggesting, 'I could put a thousand mini-Monuments to the Battle of the Nations your way?'

There were hills growing up all around the city – was he perhaps hawking them around too? There was some talk of an enormous power station to the north of Leipzig that would saturate the air with sulphur, drain away all the ground-water and kill off the forests, and all that so as to be able to sell the electricity to West Berlin. Honecker was selling off umpteen square kilometres of Saxony, so why not a whole city?

Occasionally, Joachim sat at home with us, taciturn and fatigued. He talked of the complicated situation and how, if we hadn't had our lignite deposits, the much-maligned and scornfully written-off brown coal, we'd have been done for long ago. These deposits afforded a breathing-space of some twenty years, by which time atomic power stations would have to be built, and the thought occurred to me, if we're already selling electricity made from brown coal, then why not from uranium? And what possible significance could Leipzig have for a man from a residential paradise with its thorn-hedges all around, a man who only sees Leipzig twice a year through the curtains in his car? It was the old, old story: the dragoon from the Uckermark, the Prussian Governor in Dresden, poor Saxons at Verdun, who wanted to be more Prussian than the Prussians themselves, Ulbricht, who had become a Prussian. And now, the little guy in the straw hat.

Marianne retired on reaching sixty, and about this time she made her first trip to the West, to see Erika. She came home with the usual tales: the shops over there had absolutely *everything*. I asked about reddish-brown mini-Monuments to the Battle of the Nations, but no, she hadn't come across those anywhere. I had a laugh at this, reckoning I had found an argument to refute her 'everything'.

Marianne died, only sixty-four years old, and it was all over within a month. Something to do with her glands, the doctor said. After being ill for a week, she was taken into the gynaecological hospital, and I went to see her every afternoon. We used to sit on a balcony looking out on the roof of the Russian Church. I said once, 'Do you remember, Maria and Tadeusz, over there?' Marianne smiled, 'Oh, Freddie, you and your old tales.' Sometimes I asked whether I could get her something to drink, or if she'd like her pillows rearranged and if she was warm enough. We could feel the inevitable creeping up on us, but were unwilling to admit it. 'Well, Frau Linden, and how are we today?' the nurses would ask in their bright and cheery way. Marianne would reply, 'A lot better, thanks.' And we'd all smile.

Once Marianne asked, 'Will you manage all right?'

'Don't talk like that.'

'You'll have to get your teeth seen to. You should really get all the top ones out. They don't look nice at all.'

'Has that bothered you?'

'And throw out that old grey suit right away. I always meant to, but I could never pluck up the courage.'

And then she was no longer able to get up, ate little and drank only a couple of sips at the most whenever I held the cup to her lips. I had a talk in the corridor with the doctor, who said something about us both being grown men after all.

Marianne died about two in the afternoon, so everything could be dealt with by the nurses during normal working hours, the transfer to the mortuary, all the paper-work, re-making the bed. When I came in shortly after six, the room had already been aired and I was able to take her few belongings away with me. Toilet things, cutlery, a vase.

It's only a matter of a few hundred yards from the gynaecological hospital to my flat; it took me three hours to get home. Time and again, I stopped in my tracks, staring ahead into space or at the tram-rails, and once, a woman asked me if I was feeling unwell and could she be of any help.

Marianne was buried in the south-west corner of the cemetery, the next three holes had already been dug out, while on the other side were mounds covered in fresh or wilting wreaths. A few folk from our block and some former colleagues of Marianne's followed the hearse. I threw a handful of earth onto the coffin and thought of Marianne and the poor vanquished of the Battle of the Nations, lying naked in the mud, three little piles of earth on their chest. We retraced our steps through the place where the mausoleum architects had built their scale models and where they now lay under stone slabs, granite from Beucha. On the left, my colossus towered up behind the trees. It was through this part of the cemetery I had run for dear life at the end of the war.

After that, a few years slipped past, one very much like the other. A close observer, listener, might have noticed the gradual sliding, grinding; a glacier moves only millimetre by millimetre, before it calves. Out in Probstheida they were still playing football, not a VfB team – that had long since become Lokomotive. There, my father had stretched out his great quarrier's paws towards the ball – but who remembered that now? In those days it was men who went along to spectate, the boys had leaned on the rail round the pitch, no more than a metre away from their heroes. Now there were high fences there, with sharp points on the top. From the Monument I'd look down on parading gangs of mere kids, the locals in black-and-yellow, the others in red or blue-and-white battle array, bawling their heads off. I could see police cars getting into their stand-by positions, it was always something of a minor military operation. A squad of a hundred riot police in lorries, traffic police jeeps nipping along, escorting every tram, pausing at all the stops, pulling away again, stopping again. I could also see vehicles with fierce Alsatian dogs in cages. On one occasion, the police established a communications centre on the open space to the south of the Monument, and reports from all points were collated there. At the stadium itself, the youths had to open their jackets and be frisked. I would have loved to go to a match, but if anybody had said to me, 'Come on, Grandad, open your coat, then' – no, no. Finally, every single kiosk and pub along the way from the Central Station to the stadium had to close on match-days, a corridor was dried out right through the city, so that these gangs of delinquent kids couldn't get drunk. On all the shutters hung signs saying, 'Closed for technical reasons'. I would have loved to show my father all this and then to ask him, 'Would you ever have dreamt, Felix, that it could come to this in your city, my city?'

Then the Monument was no longer floodlit every evening, in a campaign to save electricity; only when the Trade Fairs were on, so that visitors should get the impression we were well off for it. Once, at Whitsun, swarms of young people streamed up the embankments, and on that day the floodlights were on, and there was even a fireworks display put on in the evening. Nothing had changed since 1813, in that the message put across was that one had a duty to bear arms; the adversary shouldn't be allowed any, or, at the most, should have fewer than before, whereas we ourselves needed just as many weapons, and better ones. Little badges bearing the old legend, 'Swords into ploughshares', were cut out of sleeves – Thou sword at my left side, what the hell bodes thy gleam so bloody bright? I looked over towards the western edge of the city, where the wounded Körner had been treated, the silly little fool. If, once again, the earth had burst open, if the one-legged Voiciech had clambered out, if Fürchtegott had proffered his skulls, if the bomber pilot Katzenstein . . . The Monument was built to honour the dead of only the one side, and that will remain Thieme's mistake.

One morning, the trams raced as usual down the Leninstrasse, towards the city, but none were coming in the other direction. Then cars were tearing northwards, most of them Trabants, those noisy, whining two-stroke Saxon plastic boxes on wheels, with which no other race on earth would allow itself to be fobbed off, which are a source of universal derision, and without which so many Saxons would now find life intolerable. The Trabbi is as much a part of us as our dialect.

It was October. Once again, the city was encircled by enemies, the bulldozers were eating their way forward. From the south I heard the daily thud of explosions, like when a layer of stone is blasted loose, our last bastion. The smog, the stink of the power stations enveloped us, but my master demolition-expert's nose detected in addition the biting tang of cordite. I pictured the last Saxon battalions gathering in the plains on the banks of the Parthe, the terrified Carl Friedrich Lindner in their midst, hauling themselves out of the mud and onto their feet, fixing bayonets and marching against the bulldozers, I could see the last nineteen Saxon cannon spewing fire and scoring direct hits on the electric locomotives on their tracks at the open-cast mines, riddling the dumper-trucks, so that the good old Saxon soil should no more be scarred and disfigured by excavation. In the quarry to the south, each mechanical digger would break its teeth on my Beucha granite. By the Parthe, Saxons in square ranks stood waiting on the soggy banks, and to the north lay the motorway as a protective bulwark. None of our people doubted for a moment: the Prussian bulldozers would never venture across the Autobahn.

I went out by tram. Leipzig was turning out *en masse*, as if a gymnastics festival was to be celebrated, or the Monument to be officially opened. Many of them were carrying spades and shovels, as if they were ready to throw up barriers, as they had done once before in Leutzsch, when the Sherman tanks had clattered towards them.

227

To the motorway! the word went round, if we don't hold the Autobahn, we're finished. Then Gohlis will fall, Möckern will fall. Breitenfeld is already in ruins, haven't you heard? The Prussians are coming, but they won't get past the Autobahn.

The wind was coming from the north, with rain and tatters of mist in it. On the open country over towards the slab-works, camp-fires were burning, men in padded jerkins and grey overcoats and lads in jeans and hooded anoraks were fetching wood from the housing estates. The wind tossed the bare crowns of the fruit-trees. Trabbis all over the place. Barricades had been wedged into the underpasses cut through the motorway embankment, I heard, nobody would get through there. The critical sector was ten kilometres long, and it had to be held. Maybe I was looked upon as some old man whose home lay in the danger zone and who was still trying to salvage something, a photograph album or a few books or the family birth-certificates. What they should do now, I reckoned, was to blast out the roadside trees well short of the motorway, so that they fell in a criss-cross pattern, explosive fuse, wound round seven times, or cartridges in bore-holes or small parcels of explosives taped on and all detonated in one fell swoop, and that would spoil the bulldozers' fun!

Then I caught sight of the painter; he was dragging his easel along a path tramped out by the young lads, up onto the motorway embankment. All over the place rockets were going up. This time, though, the Leipzigers weren't firing their stars of joy into the heavens but were instead sending up a clear signal: we've put up with enough, and now it's got to stop! Thus far and no farther! There were also some people there arguing, dissuading, no doubt *agents provocateurs* deployed by Fröhlich's successor, another of those nurtured under Ulbricht's wing who now no longer recognised his name. They were going on at great length about order of priorities, higher necessity, about insight, one day our great-grandchildren would enjoy on this spot a wonderful vista of lakes and hills, white sails, tents, happy cries filling the air! 'Don't let them lure you into the marshes!' somebody called out. I knew who that was.

The Trabbis were patrolling the motorway, driving slowly with headlights blazing on this foggy day. On the grass verge stood the painter, and at one moment the wind snatched a corner of his sheet of paper loose. He was sketching the figure of a man, marching along, taking huge strides. One leg he coloured in black with his

228

charcoal, the other remained white. One hand was clenched into a fist and, with the legs, his arms formed a cross. Black, one arm, white, the other, and blood was running down one leg. Or was it the red seam-stripes of a general, a general winning the battle against my city but, at the same time, losing his own life? Small, the head was, seemingly scorched black, with no room for brain or eyes or even a smile. The man was running, soaring, far beneath him ran a line which pointed his path, from which he was unable to deviate. Were those medals on his chest, or bullet-holes? I stood behind the painter; once, he turned his head. How dreadfully long it had been since he had painted the blue sky over the city.

Ten kilometres of motorway, a rampart, overgrown with hawthorn and beech and German oak. But never a Leipzig linden. Concrete, bridges, metre-thick layers of road-metal. At one point, where the motorway runs no higher than the surrounding land, Prussian dragoons rode up at last. Thielmann's cannon had failed to get through, and now the cavalry hacked at the roofs of the Trabbis with their sabres. Plastic splintered like skulls. The drivers took flight behind their steering wheels and attackers and fugitives became fused as if in the painter's picture, melding the clenched fist and the black-scorched fending hand, the sound, fit leg and the booted one with the streak of blood. Behind the cavalry rattled the bulldozers.

The painter and I carried his picture as we fled, surrounded by fear-drenched, rage-swollen faces behind Trabbi-windows. The trees in the gardens were bare, the garden fences trampled underfoot. Once, the painter turned towards me and pointed to the west, where the sun was drowning in the blackness. We lost each other on the edge of a sandpit. I slid down the face, but he didn't follow me. At the bottom, I took off my shoes and shook the sand out of them. Nearby, people stood with bowed heads. Trabbis had ground to a halt, spades were being thrown away, as weapons once had been – they wouldn't be needed any more. I walked for almost a day, an old man, and looked over to the hospital, to which Voiciech had carted his loads of stone. That was where the airship hangar had stood, where two soldiers had been dragged up into the air – being Prussian means doing a thing for its own sake.

Another year on, and then another – in Stötteritz, grass sprouted up out of the roof gutters, chimney-heads tilted, plaster crumbled off walls (spring cleaning, scoffed a woman who worked beside me), and goldenrod had long since taken over all the railway embankments. At the beginning of my century, the streets of Stötteritz had been lined with hawthorn, now the bushes were dying off, and nobody so much as hit on the idea of planting new ones to plug the gaps. So, what good to me was my philosophy of the transitoriness of each and every city?

Day in, day out, I went up the Schönbach to work, looked out over the city from the parapet, or out beyond its edges from up on the top platform, and that was how I became aware of the domes growing up, the ones we are repeatedly being told are no more than plain ordinary rubbish tips. But, you know, I was there when the big bosses from the Rhine and from the Saar closed the secret deal that goes far beyond the trade in porcelain statuettes and yet, in principle, is just the same thing. Now you might raise the objection that I couldn't possibly have been a witness to any such conversation, but the fact that I can imagine it is good enough for me. Who made the original proposal is of no consequence; two sets of interests were mutually accommodating. The bosses of the Western Republic had to reckon with getting into scuffles with protesting demonstrators wherever an atomic reactor was being built in their country, police batons were being swung in leafy villages – everybody has seen that in the TV news. And then, in a flash of inspiration, these clever-dicks had come up with the bright idea of exporting their reactors. Or maybe my little Saar-Prussian had invited them to do so – for a price. What came first, the chicken or the egg? So what if the waters of the Elster and the Pleisse were to be heated up to eighty degrees – where there aren't any fish anyway, that won't bother the fish. So what, if the hawthorns in Stötteritz and the coppices in the Southern Cemetery were decimated by acid rain or some stray atomic ray, what difference did it make? We Leipzigers would live a risk-laden life, but, against that, good, hard Western currency would flow into the country so that we could buy modern kilns for Meissen porcelain, and onion-pattern and garlands of pretty flowers would flow back out – an ideal cyclical model. Our decrepit rulers could then acquire white Swedish ambulances to go with their black Swedish limousines and to follow them everywhere; if one of them had a sudden heart-attack or his liver conked out, then the necessary high-speed technology would be right there, on the spot and ready for action. I could just see our little boss raising his glass of Saar wine in a toast to a good, fat business in atomic piles, twelve nuclear furnaces in a ring round Leipzig, now that was really something! The city was encircled, just as it had been by cannon-maws a hundred and seventy years ago, it was on the road to kicking the bucket anyway, okay, so maybe just a bit sooner now. It might well be that the Elster would suddenly and rapidly boil up and all the deposits of phenol lumped on its banks might dissolve in a thick, lilac-coloured mist that rolled down towards Wandlitz, but then our man from the Saarland would take off in a white helicopter to his refuge on a tiny, white, sandy island in the Baltic that, lo and behold, since only recently is no longer marked on any map. There he'd bide his time and return when his spies told him the air, so to speak, had cleared.

My city, it finally came home to me, was no longer worthy of its symbol. I gathered together blueprints out of my various drawers, took measurements and made calculations, resurrected old tables of figures from my master demolitionist days and worked out a spot at which two main buttresses came close together; the solid stone floor would prevent the pressure dissipating downwards, so I'd only have to seal off its upward escape. If two pillars were buckled outwards by the force of the blast, the dome would collapse in on itself, the front face would swamp the Archangel, and the falling chunks of stone would tumble right down into the ornamental lake. There would even be rubble reaching the Leninstrasse, the von Pussenkomm family tomb would be smashed in and nobody would be able to find the SS escape tunnel to reconstruct the route of access to the Monument an avenger had taken.

The Monument had been closed 'for technical reasons'. We attendants had been told that the inside of the dome was due for repainting and the figures of the horsemen were to be cleaned; the work would take a good six months. A few of us were redeployed to the museums in the city centre; I took some leave and after that I worked at the cash-desk in the zoo. Now and again, naturally, I still took a walk up the Schönbach.

One morning, I came upon tyre tracks, lorries must have been up there, the way the SS had brought in their supplies. The doors of the Monument were locked, there wasn't a sound from inside. Next day I found fresh grooves, deeper this time, presumably made by more heavily laden trucks. The stairs up to the parapet were blocked off by iron railings, taller than a man and lashed to the banisters with chains and padlocks. A woman I met now and again on my walks remarked that it was all very strange, she lived just over in the nearby Gletscherstein Strasse, and night after night there were vehicles rolling up – she had seen headlights and heard the noise of engines, she said. We sat on a bench and looked out over the lake, the wind had driven all manner of rubbish and paper into one corner of it, and reeds were taking a hold in it. It really ought to be cleaned out, I thought, and then: but that's where the lumps of top-stone would land.

Yes, I wanted to blow up the Monument, and I make no plea of extenuating circumstances; on no account did I back out of my resolve of my own free will, as legalistic jargon might have it. One night, I pushed aside the gravestone over the von Pussenkomm vault and climbed down inside. The SS escape tunnel had subsided in quite a few places, so that I had to proceed on all fours. I pushed my torch ahead of me – an attempt to hold it between my decaying teeth proved a failure. There lay the five shells, and at last the passage was high enough for me to be able to stand upright. A steady droning or humming was coming from the crypt. I took a few steps in that direction and saw the VM in the concrete; that had to be where the wall was that I put up at the war's end – but instead I came up against an iron door with two bolts and a trap in it, it was so new I could still smell the paint. And behind it, the humming.

I felt no fear as I slid the bolts, rather a feeling of bewilderment. I pulled the door open and an even, pleasantly yellowish light flooded out. I stepped into it and it was as if the light itself hummed or as if this hum gave off the light. I assumed I was standing opposite the memorial statues symbolising self-sacrifice and bravery, each of them weighing four hundred tons, but they were gone, and in their place stood consoles with switch panels and pressure gauges, TV screens and rows of winking lights; I had seen things like this in pictures of space stations on the television. Another few steps forward, I was holding one of the shells in front of me with both hands, an anti-aircraft shell, one of the legendary 88mm . . .

The men who rushed me were wearing yellow overalls, as I've said already. They ran forward on rubber soles, well anyway, without making a sound, one was wearing spectacles, another had a beard. They were scared out of their wits, one held back, another grabbed me by the arm, yelling, 'Don't drop it, d'you hear? Just don't drop it!' Then he grabbed at the shell and now we both had our arms wrapped round it. A third had made a leap for a telephone. He tore the receiver from its rest and put it to his ear without taking his eyes off me for a second. 'Terrorist attack!' he was making a distinct effort to articulate clearly. 'Control, this is Gorleben Two! Terrorist attack! Come to Gorleben Two immediately!'

232

The men wrestled the shell from my grasp; I didn't offer any resistance. They frisked me and searched my pockets, then they led me upstairs. In the hall under the dome, I had to wait, so I stood with my head thrown back, looking up, and after a while it seemed to me that the horsemen up there were riding home, round and round, round and round.